VALE[NTINE]

"Erosino and Venu[...] [...]ra suggested. "Maybe t[...] [wit]h love hearts, which the[...] collect and exchange for currency."

Lyle shook his head. "Smooching," he said with mild annoyance.

"And what's wrong with that?" Sefra asked. "Tactile is good, isn't it?"

"I don't want anything that's productively sleazy."

"It's plenty of kisses," she said. "The gamers will love it. I know we did."

THE PRICE OF KISSING

"Gordon! You're in love!"

Ashley smiled and threw her arms around him. "I'm so happy for you!"

He sat down on the couch. She sat down next to him. Too close. He wanted to wrap her in his scoundrel arms and kiss her dizzy. But Ashley deserved the things that went along with a serious kiss, like love and commitment. He was sure about the love part. He could give her that. But could he love her enough to stick around?

THE PERFECT DATE

Justin fought to restrain himself as Sierra's body bumped and bounced against his. He'd fashioned himself a man full of self-control, but at this precise moment he was losing the battle of keeping his hands off her body. She had unbuttoned her jacket two songs ago, and the thin camisole did little to hide the supple curves of her body. The perspiration glistening across her face and chest had him imagining how she would look after a passionate night of lovemaking.

**BOOK YOUR PLACE ON OUR WEBSITE
AND MAKE THE ARABESQUE
ROMANCE CONNECTION!**

We've created a customized website just for our very special
Arabesque readers, where you can get the inside scoop on
everything that's going on with Arabesque romance novels.

When you come online, you'll have the exciting opportunity
to:

- View covers of upcoming books

- Learn about our future publishing schedule (listed by
  publication month and author)

- Find out when your favorite authors will be visiting a
  city near you

- Search for and order backlist books

- Check out author bios and background information

- Send e-mail to your favorite authors

- Join us in weekly chats with authors, readers and other
  guests

- Get writing guidelines

- AND MUCH MORE!

Visit our website at
http://www.arabesquebooks.com

A Thousand Kisses

Sonia Icilyn
Kim Louise
Doreen Rainey

ARABESQUE
★BET
BOOKS™

BET Publications, LLC
http://www.bet.com
http://www.arabesquebooks.com

CONTENTS

CONTENTS

Valentine's Bliss

SONIA ICILYN

To my daughter, Parissa, who wrote for me the poem
"If I Were a Flower"
when she was six. Thank you, sweetheart.

Prologue

The personal computer game story so far . . .

Emperor Claudius the Cruel has outlawed love. He has condemned to death Saint Valentine, the patron saint of marriage, and imprisoned Cupid and his bow in the temple dungeons.

Two lovers—Erosino and Venusina—hide out in the nearby enchanted island where they plot against the wicked emperor. They decide to seek help to get rid of Claudius once and for all.

They are protected by the goddess Aphrodite, who helps them collect the six talismans required to open the magic portal that will lead them into the temple in the hope that they can free Cupid and his bow.

Only Cupid's arrow can stop Emperor Claudius and his dastardly plan to outlaw love forever, allowing the two lovers to live happily ever after.

Disc loading . . .

One

"God Almighty!" the bespectacled, clean-shaven, slim young man gasped as he sucked in a ragged breath. His mobile phone was wedged between his shoulder and chin while he stared across the hotel restaurant at the door facing his table. "If I hadn't given up the whiskey and dry, I'd swear I was hallucinating."

"What is it?" Sefra Grayson asked, thumbing through a foreign edition of the morning newspaper on the breakfast table while Zara, her secretary, poured her a hot cup of tea.

"Lyle's here," Clive announced on a high note.

Sefra instantly raised her head, ignoring the latest headline that spoke of war in the Middle East. The only battle she knew of was between man and woman, and that had been fought five months ago to the day, leaving her licking her wounds. The last thing she wanted to be reminded of on a bright, sunny morning in February was the name of the man who had broken her heart.

"Don't be silly," she admonished, dismissing the handsome face that flashed through her troubled mind. "He's in Los Angeles. Remember?"

"Not anymore," Clive protested, certain he had seen

the tall, distinctive frame of his sister Sefra's estranged husband. "He's here."

"Did you see him?" Sefra demanded of her brother, knowing he often made mistakes.

"Yes," Clive insisted, pointing in the direction of the men's room. "He just went in there."

"The john?" Sefra said. The men's room was down a short hall behind the bar, not far from their table in the dining room.

"Who's Lyle?" her secretary asked. The young, attractive woman was eavesdropping on a conversation that had gone horribly wrong. As secretary to one of the best computer game designers in London, she still had a lot to learn about the nuances of her boss's life.

"Lyle's the guy who dumped my sister," Clive said, shutting off his mobile phone to reach for his own cup of tea.

"We had a mutual parting of ways," Sefra said, correcting her brother.

Elegantly dressed in a designer yellow silk shirt and a tangerine-colored skirt and white jacket that seemed to ooze self-confidence, Sefra seemed surprisingly insecure. She nervously clutched her gold pen, aptly inscribed with the words *cheetah lady*, between her manicured fingers. Her Palm Pilot with her itinerary for the day was in easy reach, as was the bowl of strawberries and muesli to kick-start her day. But now, she was unsure whether she should leave her table at the hotel.

"He dumped you!" Zara could hardly believe her ears.

"No." Her boss shrugged in irritation. "But the moment you put a man out of your mind and get on with your life, there he is right back in your face," Sefra continued. She turned to her brother. "Did he see you?"

"I don't think so," Clive said, slipping his phone into the jacket pocket of his Savile Row tailored suit. "What are you afraid of anyway?"

"The ghost of Valentine's Day past," Sefra recalled, closing her eyes briefly in the vain hope that she would forget. That was hardly possible considering that her urgent meeting in Japan had fallen on that Valentine holiday weekend.

"I wonder what he's doing here," Clive said absently.

"Knowing my luck," Sefra began forlornly, "he'll be spending his time with his new hussy." She pulled her breakfast bowl toward her, exchanging her pen for a spoon. "Assuming it *was* Lyle," she added. "Did you see him with anyone?"

"No, he was alone," Clive replied.

"Maybe he *is* alone," her secretary encouraged, noting the sadness behind Sefra's dusky brown eyes.

"Not Lyle." Her boss chuckled, adding milk to her muesli. "Take it from me. He likes company."

"So when was the last time you guys saw each other?" Zara asked, her curiosity piqued.

"Five months, fourteen days, and eight hours," Sefra replied. They had been together for much longer than that, four years by her last reckoning.

"And still counting," Clive chided. "When are you going to quit?"

A deep baritone voice suddenly intruded. "Did I hear you say quit?"

Sefra was immediately taken aback seeing the object of her conversation standing less than a foot from her table.

Lyle Fairthorne had not changed a bit. He was impeccably dressed in a slate-blue designer suit, with a white Hilditch & Key shirt opened at the collar and an Italian-made Officine Panerai watch strapped to his wrist. His Afro was cut close to his head, yet styled in such a way as to lend him some street cred. A glint of fire still burned in his arrogant stare, revealing ruthless determination and an ancient African warrior spirit. Sefra was not afraid of his hard edges and cut him a look that was brimming with confidence.

"You look familiar," she said, coyly.

"Wesley Snipes?"

"No. He's better looking."

"And you look like someone I once knew," Lyle retorted.

"Jada Pinkett-Smith?"

"No. She's much cuter."

"You've grown a mustache."

"And you've cut your hair," Lyle observed.

Sefra flinched. She was loath to admit it, but she enjoyed the way Lyle faithfully charted every change in her face. "Is there something you want?"

"Yes," Lyle said. "But I let go of that a long time ago."

"Five months, fourteen days, and eight hours, to be precise," Clive interjected.

"Excuse me?" Lyle asked, somewhat bemused.

"Why are you here?" Sefra demanded, shooting a sharp look toward her brother. She hoped that Lyle had not brought a companion with him to Sapporo.

"Ah," Lyle mused, rubbing his chin. "I'm here in Japan to negotiate a license for *Temple of Love* to the same game manufacturers I assume you're here to see."

Sefra's jaw dropped. "Lyle . . . I . . ."

"Nice to know my darling wife is prepared to stab me in the back," Lyle continued.

"Wife?" Zara gasped, glancing back and forth between the two and annoyed at Clive for not having had the common sense to clue her in. "*You* must be Lyle Fairthorne," she enthused. "I thought Ms. Grayson—"

"Zara," Sefra cautioned.

"So you're back to using your maiden name?" Lyle asked, burying his hands in his trouser pockets.

"I'm getting accustomed to the sound of it," Sefra said,

trying hard to forget how she had been so thrilled at becoming Mrs. Grayson-Fairthorne.

Lyle was quick to detect that the young secretary had not been properly informed. "Keeping you in the dark, is she?" he said, slyly. "Well, that's just like my estranged wife. Mrs. Sefra Grayson-Fairthorne is very good at manipulation. You do realize that's why my game became such a hit. I was always having to stay one step ahead of whatever scheme she was planning next."

"*Temple of Love* is *my* game," Sefra insisted. "If it hadn't have been for my genius input, you'd still be struggling to write the damn program."

"Now listen," Lyle began, straightening his broad shoulders. "I own the rights."

"Those rights are mine," Sefra said angrily. His standing over her table looking down at her did not help matters much.

"Hey, hey," Clive interrupted, concerned that the heated exchange would offend the other hotel guests seated nearby. "What is this? Erosino and Venusina falling out?"

"Shut up," Sefra and Lyle snapped. They both glared at each other, the battle ready to commence for a second round.

"I'm seeing an Asahi DVD executive this morning to discuss my new version of the game," Sefra offered.

"Over my dead body," Lyle said adamantly.

"Believe me, that can be arranged," Sefra shot back, her face suddenly turning sad as she remembered the last time she had seen Lyle Fairthorne.

After a marvelous evening at their favorite restaurant, they had returned to their luxury seven-bedroom house in London's fashionable Belgravia and were having a nightcap in bed. At the restaurant earlier, celebrating with their creative team after receiving yet another award nomination for *Temple of Love*, Sefra had been thinking about what she was going to do with Lyle once they got home. That night, for the first time, she was going to tell him how much she was prepared for them to start a family, to have a child of their own.

During their four years of marriage, Lyle had shown her a hundred times and in a thousand ways how much he loved her. There was no need for them to delay having a baby. She knew how unhappy Lyle had become at her excuses, and now that their game was doing well in the marketplace, she knew the time was right to tell him. But just when she was about to take the initiative, Lyle said something that changed all that.

"Sefra," he began, "I think Tiya and I should do the sequel. We've been discussing it for months now and I really love working with her. I want to give her a chance."

Plagued by her own insecurities, she immediately assumed there was something between her husband and Tiya, a young animator in the creative department.

Sefra and Lyle had then argued. And eventually Sefra rolled over in their bed but slept uneasily. Before the week was over, she had packed her bags and moved out. She decided not to tell Lyle where she was staying, refused to go into the office, and screened her mobile when he called.

That was five months ago. Since then, she had not allowed herself the bittersweet luxury of thinking about him, not even for the briefest moment. Until arriving in Sapporo yesterday morning, she had believed she could go on without him, until the sound of Lyle's deep voice made her whole body quake as she remembered what they had once shared. Now after so many months, the conflict had started again.

"I control the intellectual property rights for *Temple of Love*," Lyle insisted. "And I'm looking to get movie rights before any more deals are made."

"The game needs more levels before the sequel to *Temple of Love* can hit the big screen," Sefra said. "You're running away with yourself if you think that's gonna work."

"The only person who did the running away was you," Lyle accused.

"And who pushed me?" Sefra tossed back.

"Wasn't me," Lyle said, flinging both arms in the air.

"Excuse me," Zara interrupted. "I was thinking—"

"You're not paid to think," Sefra fired back, her mouth twitching as she felt tears forming behind her eyelids. "This man is trying to ruin me."

"Ruin you?" Lyle laughed loudly, receiving a few glares from around the restaurant. "You did that all by yourself the moment you tried to turn my own creative team against me. The Fairthorne Interactive Corporation is *my* company."

"And I invested money in it," Sefra reminded him, getting up to reveal a towering five-foot-ten frame. Though she was tall, Lyle still dwarfed her at six feet three. "I invested my entire life savings and I'm executive producer for *Temple of Love.*"

"But I own the most shares and I'm also the managing director," Lyle countered.

"A technicality that was quickly resolved when I filed for a directorship at Company House and made my brother the corporation's secretary," Sefra crowed in triumph.

Lyle stepped back from the table as though he had been struck. "When did you do that?"

"Last month, when I set up my own company."

"Your own what?" Lyle stammered, the news knocking him for a loop.

"Grayson's Media Games Limited is sure to be a contender in the marketplace the moment I license, for a fat fee of course, the rights to *Temple of Love* to be manufactured for Asahi DVD," Sefra said in her most businesslike tone. "So if you want to play dirty, you're in for a fight."

"You little—"

"Now, now," Clive interrupted. "You're both causing a scene here. I'm sure guests at the Sheraton Sapporo would rather you both took this argument someplace else."

"He started it," Sefra protested, childlike.

"And I'm gonna finish it once and for all," Lyle promised. "In divorce court."

It was Sefra's turn to be struck dumb. "What are you talking about?"

"I mean I'm gonna let a judge decide who owns what," he continued, ignoring the shock he saw in Sefra's eyes. It mirrored his own. "The only way to do that is to divorce you. Sever all ties. Make a clean break and move on."

Sefra felt her mouth go dry. "I . . . we need . . ."

"To talk," Clive suggested smoothly, a measure of panic evident in his own eyes. "Let's not be too hasty here."

"The only person who's been hasty is your stubborn, stiff-necked, selfish sister," Lyle told the younger man whom he had always liked as a brother-in-law. Clive was not one for arguments, preferring to keep things on an even keel, with everyone happy and content. "*She* was the one who accused me of having an affair last year."

"*You* were spending far too much time with Tiya," Sefra accused.

"Tiya is our lead animator," Lyle explained, his heavy-set brows furrowed. "What would you expect me to do? I work with her."

"You didn't have to work so closely with her," Sefra chided. "Every time I walked into the room—"

"Complaining why the game wasn't finished," Lyle added.

"You'd both go quiet," said Sefra.

"Because you kept adding one thing after another," he said.

"As a programmer," Sefra argued furiously, "I was

within my rights. For God's sake, the *Temple of Love* is our baby, not yours and hers."

"And we couldn't have done it without Tiya," Lyle said.

"Oh, please," Sefra scoffed, now aware that onlookers were beginning to watch what was going on. "All she cared about was how quickly she could get you into her bed, only you couldn't see it. I suppose she's succeeded?"

"There you go again," Lyle said, pointing a frustrated finger directly into Sefra's face. "Always making something out of nothing. I've *never* slept with Tiya."

"But you wanted to," Sefra said, feeling suddenly shaken.

"I don't have to listen to this," Lyle warned, his tone firm and controlled. "Just expect to hear from my lawyer."

"Fine," Sefra spat out, wishing the hotel restaurant was not so public. What she wanted was Lyle's gentle, tender persuasion to calm her down. She wanted to feel his kiss on her lips once again. But she was not a woman to beg. If he wanted to walk away, she was bullheaded enough to let him.

As Lyle turned to leave, Clive took hold of his arm. "Wait," he said, shooting a stern look to his sister, warning with his eyes that their meeting should not end like this. "What can Sefra do to make this better?"

Lyle gave a sideward glance toward Sefra's oval face. Deep down in his heart, he admitted to himself that he still enjoyed looking at her. Though she had brawn and brains, Sefra was still quite beautiful in his eyes. With her long, shapely mahogany-brown legs, her slim figure, and slender fingers—though he had to think twice about the new hairstyle—he could not imagine anyone else in his life if Sefra walked away for good. Even during their five-month separation, he had not so much as looked at another woman, but had kept himself trained on his work, hoping they would be able to sort out their differences.

But Sefra's endless jealousy had caused him nothing but frustration and he was now at the end of his rope. If a judge wouldn't sort out their problems, he rather hoped Clive could.

"She can stop competing and just listen," he said at last.

Sefra sighed dismissively. "And he can . . . he can . . ."

"What?" Clive prompted.

"Nothing," Sefra said, shaking her head.

"Cat got your tongue?" Lyle asked, annoyed.

Sefra was still so shaken by Lyle's threat of divorce that she could hardly bring herself to think. "All I want is to bring the game's sequel to a level that's suitable to my standard," she said finally.

"And haven't we been doing that?" Lyle's brow narrowed in confusion.

"No. I know we won the Best Original Game at the E3 Awards in Los Angeles last year and that *Temple of Love* sold three million units, which was brilliant, but Tiya's suggestions for our sequel is—"

"So this is about Tiya?" Lyle's face grew hard. "When are you going to get it?"

"All I get is that you put her ideas over mine," Sefra said. "Like when Erosino and Venusina finds Cupid and his bow, I think we should develop several more new levels for the lovers to overcome before they find the arrow, but you're not listening."

"What are you talking about?"

"My new version of the game," Sefra said. "That's why I set up Grayson's Media Games Limited. I've found a new animator and scriptwriter and am going to program this game properly, the way I want it to be, with a new graphic face-lift and cinematic subtleties. I've already done a demo for the people I'm seeing today and—"

"As I've told you before," Lyle interrupted. "I own the

rights to *Temple of Love*. If you're going to persist with this, then I'll see you in court."

"Then it'll be a cold day in hell if you think you can win this," Sefra shouted back. "I've already discussed the potential of a lawsuit with my lawyer."

"What?" Lyle paused a moment. "And what did he advise you?"

"He didn't suggest divorce, which is what you're implying," Sefra spat out.

"And what would you expect a red-blooded man to do?" Lyle asked.

Sefra stood back on her heels as though hit with a sledgehammer. "What?"

"I have a wife and you have a husband," Lyle reminded her. "I don't need to quote the minister for you to understand what that means."

"Lyle," Clive interjected, holding his brother-in-law's arm as he noted someone complaining to a nearby Japanese waiter.

"Let go, bro," Lyle said, shaking Clive away. "A woman should always have the last word in any argument."

"And anything a man says after that is the beginning of a new one," Sefra said, evidently hurt at Lyle's suggestion about their lack of intimacy over the last few months. She, of course, had moved out and was holed up in her brother's apartment, sharing the tiny two-bedroom space with his current girlfriend—Sefra's secretary. Though Clive and Zara had not complained, she knew her being there was indeed an intrusion on their budding two-month relationship. But she certainly did not want to concede that she had in fact missed her husband. "So, what else do you have to add?"

"Can I say something?" Zara dared to interject for a second time.

Stunned beyond belief that the younger woman even

had the guts to interrupt, Sefra widened the berth. "What is it?" she snapped.

Zara rose from her seat and walked around her chair until she was facing both of them. She was a small girl, slim but curvy with the type of smile that was both warm and inviting to even the most hardened of hearts.

"I just want to know if I've got this straight," she began with a cordial tone. "Lyle Fairthorne, *the* Lyle Fairthorne, is your husband, right?" she asked her boss, throwing Clive a *we'll talk later* look.

"Get to the point," Sefra said, her hands now on her hips in utter annoyance.

"And you both designed the *Temple of Love*, which became a blockbuster computer game worldwide?"

"Yes." Lyle nodded, tapping his left foot in exasperation.

"And you both are designing a sequel to the game?"

"We were until she went AWOL," Lyle said.

"Then why don't you both use today to try and settle your differences over the game?" Zara suggested. "You never know what you might resolve."

"She's right," Clive agreed immediately, waving a re-assuring hand at the head waiter, who was looking across the room at them. "Let's try to sort this out."

"How?" Lyle demanded.

"Look," Clive said, attempting to close the gap between them, "Valentine's Day officially began about eight hours ago. It was two years ago, on this very day, that you both launched *Temple of Love*. Surely that must mean something?"

"Clive . . . I—" Sefra began.

"She's opposed to the idea," Lyle spat out.

"Now you've both never seen Sapporo and you ought to, together," Clive said. He turned toward his sister, his eyes imploring her as he struggled to put his arms around both her and Lyle. Walking with them toward the exit, he continued to prod the couple into agreement. "Sefra, I can reschedule your appointment today. I'll just tell 'em you caught a chill or something. In fact, you both need to change clothes. We're not in a board meeting here. And let's face it, sis, you walked out on Lyle and took the game concept with you."

"I had every right to," Sefra responded quickly.

"That's debatable," Lyle shot back.

Sefra stared at her husband. "Are you going to agree to this?" she said, furious that Zara and her own brother could suggest such a thing. When Lyle simply shrugged, unsure whether to accept the proposal himself, Sefra turned to her brother. "What are you saying?"

"You owe your husband twenty-four hours."

"I don't owe him a damned thing," she protested, forcing back tears. "This is all too much."

Lyle's heart softened at seeing how dejected Sefra seemed. He was not used to this side of her. She was always cool, strong, dependable in a crisis. In meeting the deadlines for designing the first version of *Temple of Love*, she had performed under incredible stress, keeping pace with his hectic schedule until they had finished the program. Not once had he seen her cry. Seeing the tears behind those dusky brown eyes he adored made him instantly back down.

"One day," he agreed, though Lyle hoped it would not be a day he would soon regret. "That's all they're asking and it's all you deserve."

Sefra quickly regained her composure. She was not going to give in without a fight. The last time they had fought was in September, and Lyle had offered her no choice but to walk out. Did he chase her? No. It had been a cruel awakening to find herself dealing with such a torrent of emotions by herself, when it would have been better to share them with the man she loved. If he thought for one moment she was going to give him any leeway to resolve their differences, then Lyle would be in for a long day. She was the winner here, Sefra told herself, and if one day was all she deserved, as Lyle put it, then so be it.

"I'll meet you in the lobby in an hour," she said, tilting her chin in bait.

Lyle removed his hands from his pockets. "Done," he said, tossing Zara a nod of approval. "Smart kid. What's your name?"

"Zara. Zara Middleton."

"Are you a gaming girl?" he asked.

"Sometimes." She smiled.

"What are the odds?"

Zara shifted her gaze between Sefra and Lyle, seeing the glimmer of hope dancing in both their eyes. "I'd say fifteen to one."

"I like your odds," he said. Throwing Sefra one final glance, he hoped she would be up for the test. It was a challenge he was looking forward to.

TWO

"Why here, why now, on Valentine's Day?" Sefra wanted to know as she left the hotel lobby and stepped out into a cold February in Japan, having just changed clothes.

The chill was more like Alaska than Tokyo, and though their hotel was situated close to the Chitose Kuko Airport, some twenty-five minutes outside the city, Sefra was reminded that Sapporo was North Tokyo—a vast metropolis situated in the mountains of central Hokkaido—renowned for its short summers and long winters. For being in a place that saw icebergs off its northern coast, she had taken her brother's advice and changed into something more casual yet suited for the elements. A pair of faded Ralph Lauren Polo jeans, a cream-colored angora sweater, and a denim padded overcoat lined in sheepskin was more than ample for the Japanese weather.

Lyle was staring up at the overcast sky, having changed into an azure woolen jersey, Calvin Klein jeans, sturdy black leather boots, and a fur-trimmed olive aviator-style Prada jacket. "I could easily ask you the same question."

"Timing," Sefra told him, as they stood on the sidewalk and looked around the uncrowded streets. She had to admit the black woolly hat crowning Lyle's head gave him a certain sex appeal and made her ears feel unusually bare. "If I'm going to clinch this deal, I want it to be . . . special. Memorable."

"As do I when I meet the executives at Matsushita," Lyle responded.

"Matsushita?" Sefra gasped. "But I thought . . . you told me you were meeting the same people as I was."

"I assumed," Lyle said, "until you mentioned Asahi."

"You were going to see them without me?" she asked, feeling hurt by the extent of his betrayal.

"Excuse me!" With a cold breeze tugging at the folds of his jacket, Lyle approached Sefra. "And what were you doing?"

"Protecting our interests," she breathed harshly.

"*Your* interests," Lyle amended. "You forgot about me the moment you walked out."

"And you didn't give one . . . yen to find me," Sefra responded. "I don't recall you searching for my whereabouts."

"Considering you were holed up at your brother's apartment. Hardly a puzzle worth working out."

"Yeah, you're good at puzzles, aren't you? That's why you put more of your efforts into designing games than you do in me."

Lyle blinked, then stared at her. He could see that the misery of their breakfast confrontation had worn her down, as it had him. He did not want them to fight. Given that they had agreed to spend the day together, he wondered how he could inject a little humor and break the ice. "You should know by now that developing a game is based on a complex formula involving copious amounts of brandy, an abacus, compass, protractor, ruler, a few wrestling matches, and a game of strip poker," he joked. When he saw a brief smile cross her face, he added for gusto, "I rather thought you enjoyed the strip poker."

Sefra's smile widened, her soft lips curving into a seductive slant that made her eyes glow. This was Lyle's way of touching her. She had forgotten how his sense of humor could always cheer her up when she was feeling low. Perhaps today would not be so bad after all, she told herself. They had fifteen hours left. She wondered what they could do in that time.

"What do you know about Sapporo?" she asked, walking out into the road that would take them to the nearest train. The city was just one station away and she couldn't wait to see it.

"Nothing, except the 1972 Winter Games," Lyle replied as they emerged on the opposite sidewalk.

"There's the 2007 FIS Nordic Ski World Championships in three years." Sefra volunteered the information as only a tourist could.

"Oh, and earthquakes," Lyle added.

"What?" Sefra swallowed. "How active is this place?"

"Four to six tremors a day, most unnoticeable. In fact, for centuries, the Japanese believed earthquakes were caused by a giant catfish called Namazu, which lived in a cave deep underground. When this giant catfish shook his tail, the earth would move, or so the story goes."

"Anything else I need to know?" Sefra asked, feeling a little unsettled knowing about the earthquakes.

Lyle shrugged and followed her lead. "We could go and ask the tourist board," he ventured. "In fact, why don't we pick up a tour guide and work this city from A to Z, stop for lunch, dinner, maybe a moonlight dance, and then a bit of supper?" Sefra couldn't resist chuckling, and Lyle loved the sound of it. "What d'ya say?"

"I guess it's what couples do on Valentine's Day."

His heart dropped. "I can't cross this distance between us by myself."

"Okay," she relented clumsily. "I hear you." She turned

in the direction of the station. "If we're going to do this, let's make a plan."

"Anything you say."

"Then let's go."

The ride was short. Out on the platform Sefra looked around, absorbing the hundreds of Japanese faces that passed by with the unusual mix of reactions to tourists. When she followed Lyle through the exit point and into the expanse of the city itself, Sefra quickly realized that it lacked the dead ends that made Tokyo into a maddening labyrinth.

Sapporo was constructed after the Meiji Restoration of 1868 under the guidance of famed American architect Frank Lloyd Wright. It evoked images of the U.S. Stars and Stripes rather than the Far East. There were shimmering glass buildings, wide roads, teenage game centers, and the unusual contrast of a Russian clock tucked behind a selection of more modern structures. As Hokkaido's capital, it was also a city distinctly lacking in any pre-Meiji historic sights.

From a distance, it was not impossible to see the Sapporo dome. It was a huge gray and round building and looked almost futuristic. Sefra imagined it could pass for a flying saucer, but in fact it was a sports stadium, making it possible to shift from baseball to soccer and back to baseball.

"Look at that," she said in awe, admiring the structure, though from where they were standing, they could not fully appreciate the high-tech architecture. "We should go there."

"Not in those." Lyle pointed to her feet.

"What's wrong with my boots?"

"They've got heels and you know you can't do long distances wearing heels," Lyle reminded her as he looked at the brown leather three-inch Manolo Blahniks on his wife's feet.

"I'll be fine," Sefra said.

"It's your call." Lyle shrugged, watching as she swung a brown alligator field bag over her shoulder and began walking. "Don't say I didn't warn you. What's with the new hairstyle anyway?"

"I fancied a change." Sefra shrugged, absently reaching to stroke a fine strand of hair into place. "Don't you like it?"

"It'll grow on me," Lyle drawled, leading the way.

"Like the mustache?" Sefra added, realizing it made him appear a little older than his twenty-seven years.

"Don't you like it?" he asked, raising his hand to smooth the coarse hair above his lip. "Makes me look twice the man I was."

"I'd settle for half," Sefra chortled, loath to admit that he did look more handsome with it.

Lyle was more wounded than annoyed. "Can't a man at least try to look distinguished?"

"Depends for whose benefit he's making the effort," Sefra said without a shred of self-consciousness.

Lyle's brows furrowed. "If this is about Tiya again—"

Sefra's eyes lifted at the mere mention of the other woman's name. It was easy for anyone to see why women were attracted to Lyle. Sefra was aware of the raw sensuality that emanated from his tall, athletic physique. A shudder ran through the length of her body as his dark eyes moved leisurely across her face. Sefra was too distracted by the intensity of his sensual stare to answer. What could she say to such a handsome man who, even now, she still could not believe was her husband.

"Damn it, woman," he said, bristling. "You're not an easy person to be married to. Has anyone every told you that?"

"I've heard it said once or twice by my husband, who weighs himself at least twenty-five times a day," Sefra responded.

"Nothing wrong in a man keeping an eye on his weight."

"Depends on *who* he's doing it for."

"Myself," Lyle snapped. "At least I'm not always shopping for shoes and gloves."

"That's you all over, isn't it?" she countered, knowing Lyle was often annoyed and impatient whenever he accompanied her to Sloane Street, browsing around the London shops. "Too fidgety. Too restless to watch movies, can't listen to an entire CD track, and you always have to have the remote control so you can flick between channels."

"I'm fire-gazing," Lyle explained in combat tone.

Sefra was bemused. "What?"

"Cavemen used to stare at the fire to recharge their energies," Lyle explained, "and modern men like to flick between channels. It's our nature."

"C'mon," Sefra said. "You mean you have no patience at all."

"A man would have to be a saint to handle you," Lyle retorted, stopping dead in his tracks, feeling like a plank of wood with nails being hammered into him by someone who wanted to see just how far they could pound before he snapped. "What does a man have to do to spend one peaceful day with his wife?"

Sefra knew her husband had reached his boiling point. As she came to a halt, every instinct she possessed told her that if she was not careful, she could lose Lyle Fairthorne for good, and that was a fate she did not want to even contemplate. Overwrought and tired from jet lag, and fueled by jealousy and loneliness, Sefra found it hard to enjoy Sapporo with Lyle. Why had he not tried to resolve things with her sooner? Why had he put Tiya before her? Why did she feel so abandoned? These were things she needed to know without having to cope with the amorous feelings Lyle was stirring in her.

Sefra thought about how she should react. Inside, she just wanted to scream. But her keen mind and gut instincts told her that would not be the right approach. Maybe if they took things slowly, toured the city, had something to eat, and then talked, she could enjoy the day more easily. Gritting her teeth, she forced a smile as she glanced at Lyle. He seemed dejected and hurt. Sefra knew they could not go on like this, though the battle between them was far from over.

"I'll keep my mouth shut for one hour," she told him. "After that, I can't make any promises."

Lyle's eyes suddenly sparkled with amusement as he resumed walking, talking to himself. "If one hour is all the lady's got, then one hour it is."

Sefra swallowed as she stared after him, then slowly walked on behind.

1:12 P.M.

"What did you say you'd done with Claudius?" Lyle asked suddenly, as they left Odori Park, having spent a good part of the morning there.

They had gone to see the sights and sounds of the Sapporo Snow Festival, a weeklong event that happened every February. The fifty-fifth annual festival drew nearly 2.3 million visitors from all over Japan and abroad, with hundreds of snow and ice sculptures displayed at three sites in the city. Sefra and Lyle walked the route where most of the snow statues were located along the twelve blocks of Odori Park, stretching east and west through downtown Sapporo. Fifty-foot-high structures of ice castles, animals, and other snow monuments dazzled the couple. It was certainly a sight to behold and now as they left through the main entrance, it being the last day of the show, their minds were on something other than their feud.

"He's amassed an army," Sefra began with enthusiasm as they walked along slowly. "One thousand soldiers to find Erosino and Venusina. That means more points for the game player."

"Why an army?" Lyle asked, confused, holding the A-Z map of Sapporo, which they had picked up at the tourist center.

"If the men are not getting married, then what are they doing?" Sefra asked, having kept quiet for most of the morning. Seeing an intricately carved ice statue of the Taj Mahal at the snow festival served as a reminder of their love temple, which brought them to the subject of their game for another round of debate. "We can't just leave them dancing around at the pagan feast of Lupercalia, or exploring the temple without penalty. We might have gotten away with it in Game One, but in the sequel there have to be multiple ways to play."

"So you want gamers to search for combat?"

"Why not?" She shrugged. "It would make the game more accessible for multiple platforms like video and handheld games, not just the PC. And let's not forget the global revenue that wireless and on-line gaming has to offer."

"You've been busy," Lyle noted, eyeing her suspiciously.

"I've also been researching the Christian martyrs. I found some guy called Saint Marius, Valentine's sidekick," Sefra explained. "He helped perform some of the marriages, and we could use him."

"Is this all true?" Lyle wavered, his eyes widening.

"Authentic history," Sefra said adamantly. "And I've done away with all that raw graphic horsepower," she continued, hardly aware of the shock on Lyle's face. "I now know what makes a PC adventure game great and it's all in its being cinematic. The demo's DVD visual design really has to be seen in motion to be appreciated."

"You've done a demo?" Lyle gasped, stopping dead in his tracks.

"I told you I had. It was for the Asahi meeting."

"And I assume gamers will have to rebuild their PCs to play the game due to its high-end hardware demands," Lyle added.

"But the investment would be money well spent," Sefra returned, continuing to move ahead. "The way I'm visualizing this, even as a video version, it will support any media on-line."

"You have been thinking," Lyle teased, picking up his step.

"Which is more than I can say for you," Sefra countered.

"What's that supposed to mean?"

"I've been paying attention to what the editors of the top gaming magazines wrote about the game before they cast their votes at the E3 Awards last year," Sefra said. "A lot of what they said, I actually took on."

"Critics are allowed to make mistakes."

"Yes," Sefra agreed. "But we have two brand-name characters and we need to do a lot more with them."

"Like what?" Now Lyle was confused.

"Erosino and Venusina should kiss more often," Sefra suggested. "Maybe the gamer could be rewarded with love hearts, which they could collect and exchange for currency."

"Currency?"

"To buy passage to move around the temple of course."

Lyle shook his head. "Smooching," he said with mild annoyance.

"And what's wrong with that?" Sefra asked. "Tactile is good, isn't it?"

"I don't want anything that's sleazy."

"My intention is not to degrade the game," Sefra said, wounded. "I want to increase its popularity."

"By having the two characters kiss more often?"

"It's a Valentine's game," Sefra reminded him. "It's not as if we're taking the level of intimacy any further."

"Well, that's reassuring."

"What's gotten into you?" Sefra said harshly, her pace slowing abruptly. "You weren't like this on our honeymoon."

"That was different," Lyle admitted, coming to a standstill on the cold sidewalk. He gave Sefra a hazy look that made it clear he still remembered the wonderful time they had spent together in Wales.

It was ten days in Portmeirion, a quiet little village designed by an architect to fulfill his boyhood dream. His fairy-tale hamlet was built around some of the most beautiful natural, romantic coastline in Wales, where Gwylt woodlands with rare and exotic plants, sandy beaches, and wonderful scenery provided the backdrop to consummate their marriage. Lyle had been blessed with the perfect fairy-tale princess. She was everything to him then. Now, he was not so sure.

"In what way?" he heard Sefra say, as he turned to gaze into her face.

"We were in love."

"And aren't Erosino and Venusina?" Sefra asked, imagining what it would be like if Lyle kissed her at that very moment. With the image of his muscular physique, smooth skin, and the heady scent of his Geo. F. Trumper cologne, she remembered how much they had enjoyed making love.

"Yes."

Lyle's voice seemed to bounce against her as Sefra suddenly became aware of how much her body yearned to be in her husband's presence, and of the feelings stirring inside her.

"But—" he started again.

"It's plenty of kisses," she said. "The gamers will love it. I know we did."

"Did we?" Lyle's tone deepened as a glimmer of hope sparkled in his eyes.

Sefra swallowed. "Didn't you?" she replied, uncertainly.

Lyle's lips curved into a rueful smile. "Is this one of your trick questions to get me to try and kiss you, just to be sure that we did?" he asked dryly.

Sefra laughed nervously as she shook her head in denial, though her body said otherwise. "I didn't mean . . ." she began, through parched lips, words failing to cohere in her head when her eyes became fixed on her husband's gaze.

Regarding her with amusement, Lyle took one step closer. "Tell me," he teased, smiling down into her soulful brown eyes. "What did you mean?"

Sefra stared at him. For five months, she had deprived herself of being in her husband's arms, sharing his bed, making love, or simply being pressed against each other's body in the warmth of an embrace or a reassuring hug. She had also denied herself the power of Lyle Fairthorne's kisses. Could she refuse herself on their fleeting Valentine's encounter to know such a kiss again?

"I meant . . ." Her voice trailed off as Lyle's heavy gaze had dropped to eye the fullness of her lips. "That by making the kisses a component of fun—"

"Like this?" Lyle interrupted, pulling Sefra into his arms and taking her mouth into his own. It was what he wanted, to feel this woman weak and trembling in his arms, as he knew she would. Lyle reveled in the knowledge that he still possessed the power that had utterly devastated Sefra Grayson and left her whimpering in helplessness.

Theirs was a kiss that was fiercely sweet. It felt as though five months had never passed. Whatever Sefra expected, it wasn't this. Waves of liquid heat danced through her veins, her heart raced as if it were competing with time, and every fiber in her body reacted with an intensity that seemed to surpass the tenderness of their honeymoon. The separation of these past five months had left its mark. Sefra was aware that something more had been triggered, something quite frightening that left her body quaking and her lips quivering with Lyle's insistent nature.

His lips moved ceaselessly around hers and Sefra melted into the moment. Unaccustomed to the mustache that rubbed against her face, she delighted in the sensation it left on her lips. She was in love all over again. They had not lost the feeling, but rather gained new ones in abundance. Lyle kissed her as if it were the first time, remembering the end of their magical inaugural date when he had seen her to her front door, and beneath the moonlight had taken her lips. Their lips entwined, and it was the sealing of a friendship that deepened into love.

"I've missed you," he groaned, his mouth retaking hers for a second onslaught of passion that sent tidal waves of desire coursing through Sefra's body. She relished the endless plunder of his tongue between her lips, the familiarity of his manhood pressing hotly against her, and moaned in feverish delight at how much she too had missed her husband.

But the throbbing desire, Sefra knew, would be short-lived. There was the mountain ahead waiting to be climbed.

"Lyle." Her voice was weak and nervous. "I'm not sure we should be doing this."

He eyed her warily. "Doing what?" His voice had changed. "You're my wife."

"I know, but—" Sefra began.

"Kissing makes all the difference after all, doesn't it?" Lyle teased. "Not the innocent piece of fun that can gain points or . . . love hearts, as you say?"

"Lyle—"

He shrugged. "I guess you'll have to invent a default clause so players are aware of the consequences of having . . . just kisses."

Sefra felt the blood drain from her face as she watched Lyle resume walking. Immediately, she took chase, her mind churning over what she should say. Of course, he was right. She had not thought their one kiss would erupt into a volcano of lust. There could be no escaping Lyle now that he had taken her into his arms. In the bigger scheme of things, Sefra indeed wondered whether adding more kisses could in fact affect the game after all.

"Lyle, wait," she called out, taking larger strides that did not seem to match his steps. "I need to . . ." Suddenly, Sefra felt her ankle bend. "Ouch!" Without quite realizing how she had gotten there, she found herself on the ground. The panic in her tone had Lyle turning his head in an instant.

"Sefra?" The picture facing him of her on her knees, with two strangers rushing to her rescue, had him by her side within seconds. "What happened?"

"My ankle," Sefra whimpered.

Lyle glanced at her feet and located the broken heel from her boot. "I told you not to wear those," he scolded, picking up the heel and shaking it in her face. "You could've damned well hurt yourself."

"Stop yelling at me," Sefra cried, rubbing her right ankle sympathetically.

"Is missy all right?" the Japanese man and his wife inquired.

"She'll be just fine," Lyle said. "Nothing a spot of lunch

can't fix." He eyed Sefra with dark, brooding eyes. "C'mon." Helping her to her feet, he linked her arm through his own. "Lean on me and take the weight off your right foot," he ordered with enough authority to command obedience. "It's time we ate something anyway; then we need to find something sensible to put on your feet."

Sefra didn't argue. She liked the plurality of his suggestion. She simply nodded her head and allowed Lyle to take the lead, her one thought being that neither her reasoning nor seduction had won the battle. That, she was sure, was to come.

Three

2:01 P.M.

"How's your ankle?" Lyle asked, his thoughts unreadable as he surveyed his wife from across the table.

"Feeling a little better," Sefra said, disgruntled. As she gazed at Lyle in all his glory, heated fantasies came creeping back, only adding to her sexual frustration. "Not that I suppose you care."

Lyle tried to ignore her. "So, what would you like to eat?"

They were seated in Koriya, a restaurant downtown in the J-Box Building, which specialized in Korean food and inexpensive buffet lunches. Lyle was reading the simple menu, absorbing with fascination the variety of seafood dishes, when Sefra interrupted.

"You choose what we eat," she said. "After all, you're in control of everything."

Lyle tossed the lunch menu on to the table. "What is it now?" he said, annoyed.

"Tiya," Sefra tossed back. She had been unable to forget the woman.

Her lead animator was like a ghostly presence hovering in the forefront of her mind, tormenting her from the moment her husband had kissed her. She felt overwhelmed by feelings that were saddling her to the past, wearing her down again, and making her realize how much she missed the fire that only Lyle could stoke.

He shook his head in disappointment. "Not again."

"Why didn't you tell me you knew her before we were married?" Sefra pleaded, her eyes narrowing to take in the baffled expression on Lyle's face.

"I didn't think it was important," he told her finally.

"You didn't think . . ." Sefra could feel her blood boiling. "How did you think I felt when I found out?"

"Is there any need for this?" he asked calmly.

"Yes, actually, there is," Sefra said firmly. "Were you two in a relationship?"

"No!" Lyle protested. "Okay, I thought about it once, *before* I met you," he added. "She's a funny, confident, levelheaded person. But she liked her life in Japan and she wasn't looking for an escape. I was looking for someone to rescue. Someone to sweep up and carry away. Someone to save."

"Like me," Sefra finished, her temperature rising. "So you're saying I'm weak and she's strong—that's why you married me?"

"I didn't say that. You're reading too much into this."

"Am I really?" Sefra chided. "So why has she been in our lives for the last two years? Clive told me only a few days ago that you both went to the same university. He thought I knew. Then you hired her from Japan. You introduced her into our company, had her work on *our* game, and now you want her to do the sequel, not me."

"Is this about us or the game?" Lyle asked, confused.

"You're impossible," Sefra wailed. "I'm talking about us . . . and the game."

"Make up your mind," Lyle snapped.

"Both!" Sefra yelled, swallowing her pain.

She dipped her head and Lyle exhaled a deep sigh from his chest. Sefra loathed anything that remotely suggested self-pity and tried to compose herself. It was very hard. Theirs was a marriage that had been based on trust, a deep respect for each other, and shared values. Who was this woman—Tiya—to think that she could derail what they had? As she stared at the man who seemed to be allowing the situation to happen, Sefra felt more despair.

"Look," Lyle began, seeing that very despair. "Less than ten minutes ago, we were kissing. You *made* me kiss you. Now you're tripping on Tiya again. You can drive me insane with this kind of behavior."

"And you know how to raise this innocent act to an art form," Sefra tossed back. "I know the drill. Man settles down. Gets married. Takes wife for granted, then has an affair. I've seen too many friends go through it."

"What are you saying?" Lyle asked, alarmed. "That we're going to be a statistic?"

"You're the one talking about divorce," Sefra shot back, "not me."

"Only because you're making the chains of marriage feel so heavy I'm beginning to think the two of us can't carry them."

"But three can?"

"Tiya's a *good friend*," Lyle said slowly and carefully, wiping his brow with the back of his hand.

"A *good friend*," Sefra repeated, shrugging her shoulders. "Nice phrase for a little extramarital dalliance."

"Sefra," Lyle warned, his voice barely controlled, "don't test my patience. I happen to think marriage is like a cold pond. You just don't dive in. We didn't." He studied her more skeptically. "At least I didn't."

"I didn't either," Sefra confessed, sensing the same genuine tenderness she had seen in Lyle's eyes on their wedding day.

They were married shortly after her twentieth birthday in the picturesque Palma Cathedral on the Spanish island of Majorca with more than 250 guests. She had exercised the bride's prerogative by arriving in a vintage yellow Rolls-Royce exactly five minutes late for the two o'clock ceremony. The chauffeur, wearing an old-fashioned burgundy and black uniform and visored cap, had been standing at attention beside the Rolls and had helped her father with the ivory silk train of her dress.

She was so nervous, she accidentally pressed a button in the back of the driver's seat, which electronically activated a small rosewood writing desk that flipped open just above her knees. Her father, known for remaining calm and stoic, even in times of extreme stress, laughed so hard even Sefra couldn't help being amused by her own folly. They had never been in a Rolls-Royce before, and so the ride to the cathedral had been spent toying with the mechanical whir of the rosewood desk, watching it open and retract.

Sefra's eyes watered as she remembered walking down the aisle, dressed in a strapless silk ivory gown, embroidered in pale pink and green by French bridal designer Max Chaoul, with her cathedral-length train trailing behind and her father by her side. Around her were huge white lilies and cream-colored roses, which had filled the cathedral. At the altar, resplendent in a tuxedo, waiting for her was the man she loved. A young twenty-three-year-old, Lyle had hired and flown in a traditional gospel choir to enliven the ceremony and add spirituality to their hour-long service.

Afterward, their lavish reception had been held at the Grand Hotel Son Net—a luxury mountainside retreat favored by Hollywood stars that provided plenty of Spanish touches, including flamenco dancing as well as a fireworks display. The memory temporarily cooled her anger.

"Lyle, I . . ." Sefra paused, as the memory of herself on her wedding day, in a full-length ivory veil, her proud father by her side, popped into her head. "I just happen to believe faithfulness is a discipline."

"And jealousy is the gangrene of love," Lyle exclaimed. "So I'm only going to say this once: my heart has not been taken by anyone, except you."

He laid a warm hand atop hers on the table and Sefra looked at her husband in surprise. He was unlike any man she had ever known, but she didn't know if she was losing or regaining him, even after what he had just told her. In her eyes, he was extremely handsome. He turned her on like no one else ever could, but now everything seemed complicated. There was some sense of pride in being his wife, and he needed to see that. And if it meant that she would have to be the one to take control of the situation, then so be it.

"Let's take this one step at a time," she said, slowly pulling her hand away. She saw the disappointment in Lyle's eyes. "It's not that I don't want to enjoy today," she said rather hurriedly, "I just need a little distance to get through it."

Lyle nodded in understanding. "Okay." He attempted a smile and picked up the menu. "I suggest we try the sea bass with seasonal egg on rice. What d'ya say?"

"Sounds good to me. I'd like that with a glass of Canada Dry ginger ale."

Lyle summoned the waiter and broadened his smile.

"Did you know the only source of tension we used to have was you snoring and me stealing the duvet at night?" Lyle announced, as he munched into what little was left of his lunch.

"I didn't snore," Sefra protested, her brows raised as she placed her knife and fork in the center of her plate. They had begun their lunch in relative silence, which had given Sefra enough time for contemplation. She didn't want to bicker with Lyle, not really, and it felt like such a relief to her now that he was teasing her.

"You made a noise so loud once, it sounded like a warthog clearing his throat."

"Lyle!" Sefra chuckled.

"And the windows in the bedroom shook," Lyle continued, swallowing his last mouthful. "I swear you must've inhaled all the air in the room."

"And what did I do with it?" Sefra laughed.

"You spat it all out and that's why the windows shook."

"Lyle!"

They both laughed. Suddenly the chemistry was back, and with it came a rush of feelings. Any observers would assume they were looking at two lovesick teenagers. Lyle was not complaining. Finally, he had achieved what seemed to be the impossible. He had succeeded in putting a smile on his wife's face.

"That look, right there," he pointed out suddenly, impulsively moving a strand of hair from Sefra's forehead. "That's the one you had when you said 'I do.'"

Sefra felt a flurry of excitement, her cheeks flushing. "Remember when we used to have arguments about who loved the other the most?"

"And I was always insistent it was me," Lyle said.

Sefra reached for her ginger ale and took a nervous swallow before she spoke. "We never did resolve that one."

"I doubt we ever will." His eyes were lit up, the way they were when the couple were about to make love.

"Do you want to know what I was thinking of earlier?" she suddenly found herself confessing. "Our wedding day."

"You mean the day your bouquet nearly knocked your best friend out?" Lyle laughed.

Sefra giggled when she thought of the huge bundle of

white lilies and yellow tulips she had chosen for her bouquet. There had been a scuffle before her dearest friend landed the prize. "I chose a big bouquet, didn't I?"

"Are we still talking about the flowers?" Lyle joked, with a twinkle in his eye.

Sefra felt the rush of color in her cheeks. "Not unless you're referring to the size of your ego."

Lyle chuckled. This was how they used to be—joyful, playful, loving.

"Was there a reason why you should be thinking about our wedding today?" he asked, his eyes boring down on her.

Sefra instinctively twisted the two rings on her left hand. The first had been the engagement ring Lyle had given her six months before their marriage in Spain. The second was her wedding band, which Lyle designed himself before having it handcrafted by a local jeweler. His own was a much thicker version of the same design.

"Oh, no reason," she said. "It was just what you said earlier, about no one having taken your heart, except me."

"And I meant it," Lyle said in earnest.

Sefra nodded, then dipped her head. "This has been hard for me," she began, her tone softening as Lyle reached out and clasped both her hands into his. "We've been through so much together. I don't want to lose it, but . . ."

"But . . . ?" Lyle asked.

"When trust has been chipped away, even if it's just a little, it can create a crack that can take time to mend," she began slowly. "And for me, when you invited Tiya from Japan to work on our game, it really hurt. It did."

Lyle held Sefra's hands tightly. "Darling, I didn't mean to intentionally hurt you," he said quietly. "Like I said, I thought I was simply using her talents to create the best sequel to *Temple of Love.*"

"Well, if we're going to fix this crack between us," Sefra continued, "then I think it's time you let Tiya go."

Lyle instantly pulled his hands away. "Sefra," he cautioned, the tone in his voice now distinctly odd. "That's not an option."

Her eyes widened. "What?"

"I'm not going to fire one of the best workers we've got just because you can't handle my working with her," he said. "We're a married couple. We're stronger than this."

"I'm not," Sefra said.

Lyle shook his head. "What is this? Jealousy?"

"No," Sefra whimpered, feeling her world suddenly crashing around her once again. She could not understand Lyle's reaction. Why he should not understand that she wanted things back the way they were, when it was just the two of them, working on their baby—their game—to bring entertainment to the world. She didn't want a third party, an extra element complicating matters. What they had built together was theirs and theirs alone. She wanted nothing to interfere with that. "I want you back," she tried to explain.

"I'm right here," Lyle countered.

"Not like this." Sefra tried to think. "You've been so wrapped up in your work, in her . . . in the business . . . and I'm feeling . . . neglected." There, she had said it. She had finally admitted to the loneliness she had been suffering.

"Now wait a minute." Lyle's tone changed altogether. "We see each other every single day; at least we did until you went AWOL for five months. What about me?"

"You?" Sefra choked.

"I've been without a wife for five months," he reminded her again. "A very hard thing for a red-blooded man to handle, considering he has a wife."

"Don't you dare turn this around. So you've been without sex for five months. Big deal."

"Damn right it's a big deal," Lyle said hotly. "It's been torture. And if I was half the man I should be, I would've done something about it that would not have involved you."

"What about my marital rights?" Sefra shot back, incredulous that Lyle could actually have considered cheating on her. "Where were you when I had my needs?"

"I've always taken care of you. Even when you left. I discreetly asked your brother what you were doing for money."

Sefra's eyes widened. "We have a joint account," she recalled, narrowing her brow. "What did you think I would do for money?"

"You haven't been working for five months," Lyle said sternly, "which means effectively you haven't been earning a monthly salary."

A sickly feeling ran the length of Sefra's body. "Are you trying to tell me that the money I've been taking from our account was *your* money and not *ours* because I had decided to take five months off to reflect on our life?"

"I was simply trying to make you realize how much I cared, even though you made a decision without consulting me," Lyle continued. "It has nothing to do with money."

"Really!" Sefra chided. "Well, don't worry, I haven't broken the bank."

"You can spend as much or as little as you like," Lyle said, disturbed that she was troubled. "You've earned it."

"Damn straight I have," Sefra said angrily. "I worked hard for your company, Lyle. I gave it everything. My time, effort, and finances. All I wanted was for us to see it through, together. Now, I've been pushed aside and you're threatening divorce."

"You started your own company, Sefra. Let's not forget that."

"And didn't you ever wonder why? My creative ideas were being swallowed up and spat out by you and that Japanese . . ."

"Say it," Lyle dared her.

"Hussy." Sefra could not resist the final slander.

"That does it." Lyle rose from his chair.

"Where are you going?" Sefra asked, alarmed.

"Anywhere, away from you. There's no reasoning with you when you're like this."

"Like what?"

"Argumentative! We're talking about a woman who simply happens to be a close friend of mine."

"And you don't see the problem?" Sefra said, shaking her head.

"There isn't one," Lyle insisted. "It's all in your head."

"Right, then." Sefra rose from her chair also. "This day is over with. We can go back to the hotel."

An uncomfortable silence followed when Sefra walked around her chair and suddenly found herself hobbling on one heel. There was still the matter of her boots. She could hardly be expected to travel from Sapporo on the train back to the Sheraton Hotel in cold weather with a broken boot on one foot. There was still the small matter of finding a shoe shop.

Lyle's wife was being impossible. In his mind, he could not understand why such a beautiful woman, with mountains of intelligence, a body he could not stop dreaming about, and lips as sweet as cherries, could find such a plain, ordinary young woman—like Tiya—some sort of threat to their marriage.

During their four years, he had always felt he had done the very best to make his wife feel secure, loved, and cherished. Sefra was his rock. So what was he doing wrong? Just what was it he could not see? What was she not telling him? Her jealousy was wearing thin. But right now, all he could think about was finding some new boots for Sefra.

"We'll have to do something about that," he said, nodding at the broken heel on her sole as he watched her hopping toward the exit door.

"Don't worry," Sefra replied.

"I'm not the one who's going to catch a chill when the cold bites your pinkie," Lyle continued, following close behind. "So if I were you," and he tugged at her arm and deliberately laced it through his own the moment they hit the sidewalk, "I'd lean on my arm, behave like it's Valentine's Day, and let me help you get to a shop."

"Oh, so you're promising to buy me a present now?" Sefra said. She could still sense the hard muscles beneath his jacket, even though she had not physically touched them in a long time. Suddenly and inexplicably, Sefra found herself wondering why she had denied herself the perks of Valentine's Day. "Chocolates as usual, I suppose?"

"Which I would love to feed you through your lovely slender throat one by one," Lyle said.

Sefra fell silent. It was all beginning to feel unbearable. Being with Lyle again and arguing. She had told herself earlier that they could do this. One day. That's all her brother had asked. So why couldn't they? "I'd like you to surprise me this year," she suddenly found herself saying rather impulsively.

Lyle was thrown. "What?"

"No chocolates."

"What?" he repeated, his mouth agape.

"Total unpredictability," Sefra said.

"We're talking about a Valentine's present, right?" he asked, unsure.

"Unless you would rather forget you have a wife,"

Sefra cautioned. "In which case, that could swing both ways."

"I think potential husbands would run miles rather than deal with you," Lyle said, allowing a smile to play on his lips. "But if spontaneity is what you want, I'm prepared to go along with that. For one day."

"Good." Sefra nodded. "Now we can go and see about my boots."

"No rushing back to the hotel?" Lyle asked.

"And why not? Aren't you tired?"

"We have to see the brewery," Lyle told her excitedly, holding up the A-Z and pointing at the tourist attraction. "I don't want to leave this city without tasting the best beer in the world."

Four

Sefra contemplated the redbrick museum where the modern brewing technology of Hokkaido's most famous product was made. Snow sculptures and igloos festooned the site as was the custom in February. As Lyle dug into his pockets to pay the taxi that had brought them from downtown, she entered the cavernous, three-tier beer hall wearing new boots and feeling ready to experience Sapporo's famous beer garden.

The A-Z had said that Sapporo was considered one of the three great cities for beer in the world, so although she had wanted to return to the hotel after they had stopped off at the shoe shop and purchased new boots, she instead found herself looking forward to experiencing the grand tour and free beer-tasting.

"Good afternoon," the guide announced to the small group of some twenty people who were all waiting in anticipation at the entrance of the hall. "My name is Miko."

She was dressed in a trim red blazer and a stewardess-type hat and did not look any more than nineteen. Even so, there was nothing girlish about her. She had that same ruthlessly intelligent smile Sefra often saw in Tiya, and some instinct caused her to develop an immediate dislike for Miko. Sidling out of the tour guide's way, she positioned herself at the far side of the small group, just as Lyle arrived and came up beside her.

"Missed anything?" he asked, curiously.

"Just *her* making the introductions," Sefra said.

Lyle eyed her closely, detecting the tone in her voice. "You okay?"

Sefra nodded.

"Feet feeling all right?"

"The boots are fine," she assured him.

The shoe sales assistant had been most helpful. She was Australian, and had lived in Singapore for a time. She imported Italian boots and sold them in a small shop that was not too far from Koriya, where they had eaten earlier. Knowing how impatient Lyle could be when shopping, Sefra had taken little time in making her decision. She liked the dark blue polished leather, which Lyle had paid for. As her husband, he insisted on paying and she did not object. She had learned never to argue with him when he became insistent.

"Sure?" he said.

"I'm fine," Sefra blurted, annoyed that his further insistence should be upsetting her.

Lyle shrugged and turned his attention to the guide, who was beginning to talk about fermentation and using Japanese words for yeast, barley, and malt. Then the historic tour began. As he followed his wife, Lyle began to sense how hardened Sefra had become. He was not used to this behavior in his wife. She was usually more friendly, assertive, and outgoing, but after five months, he finally admitted to himself that she had changed.

Some of it was good. He liked her confidence and outward nature. He also liked the fact that she could stand up to him without making him feel small and ineffectual. He had still felt in control of the situation, even when she went to stay with her brother. Rather than give in to her emotional demands, he had continued to run the company and decided to allow her the space and time needed to resolve what was going on in her head.

But seeing his wife today, Lyle knew that the situation between them could not continue, at least not while he was physically attracted to her. What he could not understand and what frightened him was the strong attraction he felt toward Sefra. It felt stronger than ever. Was it because he sensed he could be losing her? He was not sure. But sometimes, when she spoke in that deep, forthright voice of hers, or looked at him with her dark, compelling eyes, Lyle felt like she was reaching out to him again and he to her.

Five months was a long time, he thought, a long time not to feel the touch of his wife. Had that ruined anything? he wondered. Then he remembered the kiss he had given her. The instant their lips had touched, his heart remembered everything about her. She was soft, tender, vulnerable even. And yet her hardened exterior practically denied the fact that she wanted and needed his kiss too.

He was confused. What exactly was going on with his wife? He decided at that precise moment that perhaps he should do something special for her. Make a grand Valentine's gesture that would open her up and maybe allow her to reveal what was really wrong.

He decided to send Sefra flowers. Not any old bunch either. Maybe . . . maybe the same type of bouquet she had carried on their wedding day. He would send it to her hotel room. No, Lyle thought, as he cast a swift glance at his wife. A bunch would not be enough. It would take more than a bunch. A cartload perhaps. Maybe he should go all out and fill the entire room. A broad smile spread across Lyle's face as he made his decision before scanning the A-Z for the nearest florist. The moment he could find some time alone away from Sefra, he would patch a call through on his mobile.

Sefra noted the grin and felt her legs weaken. Her heart surrendered to Lyle's smile. She felt the rush of blood into her cheeks and a pounding in her ears. For a brief moment, she closed her eyes and swallowed, feeling herself sway slightly. Only Lyle Fairthorne could have this effect on her. Only he could still wield this magic.

When she opened her eyes, she was embarrassed to find him standing next to her. As Miko spoke of copper vats and brewing techniques, Lyle reached out and took hold of Sefra's hand. Gently, he curled his fingers through hers. She accepted his warm hand willingly. The intimacy felt electrifying. Their eyes locked and suddenly a silent truce was declared.

The mood continued. As they walked along the long hallways of the historic redbrick building, they held hands, stroking each other's fingers sensuously and playfully. On occasion, their grip tightened when they felt their emotions stir within them. Sefra suspected this was why Lyle had disappeared into the men's room to calm down. Her own pulse was still racing out of control when he returned, so she was relieved somewhat when they were finally seated in a hall and given a selection of ales to sample.

Lyle was taking every opportunity to touch his wife. His hand gently brushed aside a strand of hair from Sefra's temple as she began to remove her jacket and drape it around the back of her chair. He saw her face blush at his touch beneath the mahogany brown of her complexion. It reminded him of how much he had wanted to make love to her that night in his hotel room.

"I've decided I like your hair," he said, drawing an unsteady breath. "It suits you."

"You don't look too bad yourself with that mustache," Sefra admitted quietly.

Lyle draped his jacket over his chair and faced his wife. "Looks like good beer," he said of the ale placed in front of them. "Hope it tastes good."

Sefra took a sip from her glass and nodded. "Not bad."

Lyle joined her. "I can go along with that."

Sefra smiled and for the first time began to feel truly relaxed. "I'm really glad you're not in Los Angeles," she said quietly.

"LA?" Lyle said, confused.

"Yes. I thought you'd have gone to that International Games Association Annual Dinner we both got invited to last year."

"I couldn't go without you."

"Me neither," Sefra breathed, feeling the deeper bond that was building between them.

"I can just imagine the industry magazine headline gossip about there being trouble at the Fairthorne Interactive Corporation headquarters," Lyle said.

"Close to treason." Sefra laughed, sipping more beer.

"They might even have suggested industrial espionage considering one-half of the successful team is now the full-fledged owner of Grayson's Media Games Ltd.," Lyle added in a casual tone.

Sefra cringed as she recalled how hurriedly she had gone about taking control of the situation. It had seemed a good idea at the time, when she had found herself spending Christmas at her parents' home with no husband. Refusing to take a taxi back to Clive's apartment, she had instead walked along the streets of London, making the sixty-block journey alone to clear her head.

Her life had felt uncertain. It was her darkest hour. Despite encouragement from her parents to call Lyle, she had stubbornly refused, insisting that he was the one who needed to make the first move. But he did not. She had learned through Clive that Lyle had driven up to

Norfolk to spend the festive season at his sister's house and was not planning to return until well after the new year. And that had been that. No present. No card. Just what appeared to her to be indifference.

And so on that long walk to Clive's apartment, she floated, anchored only by the two bags holding gifts from her family. While ambulances raced by, sirens hollered, and drunken loonies paved the sidewalk, she inhabited a private world where new ideas were emerging in her head. She had walked past the wine bars, past all-night dance halls, past garbage-lined streets, and homeless midnight muggers and junkies injecting their load. She ignored the streetwalkers and continued to pass dope dealers, party-goers, and male hustlers, and then finally past starry-eyed lovers who brought tears to her eyes as she thought of how much she wanted to be with Lyle.

After that, she made her decision to move on and set up shop on her own. At three o'clock in the morning, she had arrived back at Clive's apartment, having spent an enlightening journey that would forever shape her life. Grayson's Media Games Ltd. was born that very night as she lay beneath the covers of her bed in her brother's spare bedroom and turned out the lights. It is often said that to be able to read the future is a gift given to few mortals, but she had felt clairvoyant that night. Sefra had given herself power and it was something Lyle was not going to take from her easily.

"You left me with very little choice," she prodded gently, not wishing to break the ambience that had developed between them. "What else could I have done?"

Lyle trained his eyes on her carefully. In a flash, he saw what his wife had become. She was no longer a person he felt could easily be controlled by his persuasions. It was heart-wrenching and somewhat difficult for him to realize she had become a woman who no longer needed him in quite the same way. He was unsure of how to react. Should he even respond or was it easier to seek the answers?

"What have we been doing to each other?" he said at last, taking a large gulp of beer to bolster his nerves. He enjoyed the way the beautifully cultivated ale worked its way into his body.

Sefra was quick to answer. "If I was on the outside looking in," she reasoned, "I'd say we were playing games with each other and not inventing them."

"I haven't been playing at anything," Lyle told her truthfully.

He shot her a deep, meaningful look. Sefra felt her heart turn. The brief look Lyle sent her made it clear how much she still meant to him, but it did not sway her feelings.

"Then why are we still having problems?" she asked.

"Because you don't trust me," Lyle said, his voice quaking with emotion. The beer was certainly having its effect, but Lyle tried to steady himself by taking a second, third, and fourth gulp.

Sefra thought maybe her husband was drinking too much, not that it worried her. Lyle could always handle his ale, though it was often a couple of hours before the real effects of it usually kicked in. While he was focused, she decided it would be a good time to open up and tell him more of how she was feeling.

"Trust has to be earned," she began under the scrutiny of Lyle's piercing eyes, which had grown darker and more brooding. "You can't just expect me to hand it over."

"Not even after four years of marriage?" Lyle countered.

He watched his wife take a fortifying swallow of her own beer and realized his question had shaken her. Lyle found himself trembling, too. There had been nothing missing from his life. With Sefra, everything had seemed perfect. But the last five months had worn him to frustration. Impatient with his wife's discontent, he began to recount why she should be happy. She had a good job that paid well. He loved her dearly. He had taken her for his wife. What more did the woman want?

"Not with what we've been going through," Sefra said dryly.

Lyle took a heavy gulp of beer before snorting his disbelief. "You're a hard woman, Sefra Grayson," he snapped. "I don't know what's the matter with you."

"You're what's the matter," Sefra said calmly. "It's very hard for a woman to love a man who doesn't pay any attention to what she is saying."

Lyle's eyes widened. "I *do* listen."

"Only to what you want to hear," Sefra said lightly, not wanting to attract attention. More so, she did not want to hurt her husband's feelings.

She had enjoyed how he curled his fingers around hers. It was a clear sign that he was now taking what she had to say seriously. With them having strolled side by side down the corridors of the beer garden and focused more on touching each other, she felt it was Valentine's bliss to finally have a connection with Lyle again. It was also a connection she did not want to break.

"I've been feeling overwhelmed, Lyle," she continued, pausing briefly, "with loneliness."

"Okay, you said I've been neglecting you," Lyle conceded, the blow of her admission causing a numbness in his body that made him take another sip of beer. "Have I really?"

Sefra nodded silently.

Lyle took another huge swallow. In his childhood, he had often heard his mother accuse his father of taking her for granted. Was this what he had become, a man so wrapped up in his work, he could not see the forest for the trees? How was this possible? How could this have happened to him? He had never considered himself a selfish man, but perhaps he was and just did not know it. Something inside him did not feel good about where this was going.

Sefra could see she was getting through and that Lyle was not taking the news at all well. "I'm sorry," she whispered, taking hold of her husband's hand from across the table and curling her fingers around it. She sensed his warmth, bonding them for the moment, but there was still a lot to do. "I don't want to lose you," she added with honesty.

"You haven't," Lyle promised. "I'm still right here."

Miko, the tour guide, suddenly intruded. "How are you finding the beer?"

"It's very nice," Lyle slurred, chuckling as he realized he had hiccupped.

Sefra smiled. "I think we've sampled enough ale," she told Miko. Looking at Lyle, who seemed semisober, she added, "And I think it's time we got some fresh air."

"No problem," Miko agreed, in her carefully controlled Japanese accent. She indicated the nearest exit. "If you walk along that corridor over there, it should take you outside."

Sefra spent a panicky few minutes helping Lyle and herself into their jackets before walking with him along the corridor. When they emerged into the early afternoon of Sapporo, the sky had darkened slightly and the streetlights were lit. The sidewalk seemed a little more busy and there was a swirl of activity around them, the first signs of excitement on a Valentine's evening.

"We should go dancing," Lyle whispered in her left ear, as he worked his hand around Sefra's waistline.

Sefra's heart skipped a beat at the sudden closeness of

the man she loved. "Not on the sidewalk." She chuckled. "I think we should go back to the hotel now."

"And book dinner," Lyle enthused.

It was a good sign, Sefra mused. Over dinner and when Lyle had grown a little more sober, they could finish the discussion they had started earlier. "That would be very nice," she agreed.

Lyle's face lit up. At last he felt he was doing something right. "I'll arrange it when we get back," he declared. His free hand slipped around the other side of Sefra's waist. "I really would like to make this day special, if you'll let me."

Sefra felt her body melt. The last hour had, if anything, made Lyle more appealing. He was just as sexy as she remembered him. There was something about him and the way he was holding her on that cold, chilly sidewalk that invited touching. Was it the incredible pecs she knew were hidden beneath his jacket, or the strong column of his neck, or the incredible urge to kiss her reflected in his eyes?

It struck her anew how different he seemed and how much taller and more manly he had become. It was as though years of maturing had been learned in one brief talk. And Sefra loved it. For some reason, she could not take her eyes off his lips. Suddenly they came closer to her own. Fascinated, she stood riveted, watching as he dipped his head. His eyes sparkled expressively as he lingered for a moment, looking at her features, before she felt him take her lips.

Sefra swallowed convulsively, feeling as if her stomach had fallen to the floor only to bounce back as Lyle's mouth moved gently over her own. As he kissed her, his scent tickled her senses. It was a tantalizing mixture of cologne and ale, and she could taste the strong beer on his tongue the instant he delved into her mouth.

Sefra closed her eyes to inhale more, feeling herself

sink into the passion of the moment. Though it was cold, she could feel the heat from Lyle emanating from his cheeks as the chilly breeze washed over them both. But Lyle's lips were velvety smooth and soft, and sent a potent fire blazing through her body. Sefra was oblivious of the signs and moans that escaped her throat.

Lyle was not.

He held her close, deepening the kiss, skimming her teeth with his tongue until Sefra helplessly parted her lips and allowed him the access he needed. Lyle did not hesitate. He took the opportunity to reacquaint himself with his wife's kiss. She suckled his bottom lip, just as he remembered it. Then she ran the tip of her tongue along his own parted lips, inserting it ever so slightly into his mouth until he felt an overpowering urge for more.

Lyle crushed Sefra to his beating heart and repeated his torturous routine, sliding his moist tongue ever so slowly into her mouth and out again, nibbling her lips and playfully moving his mouth in tune with her own until Sefra began to feel her own body responding with a mixture of love and slow-burning desire. Lyle's deliberate, pulsating, and intoxicating slaughter of her lips was just the start.

In an instant, his lips were no longer on hers. Lyle's mouth made its way toward Sefra's neck. The unexpected touch of his lips on what little flesh he could reach beneath her padded denim overcoat sent a wave of passion right down to Sefra's groin. His teeth scraped a pulse point and Sefra felt a deep yearning to scream. Instead, a soft moan echoed into the Sapporo night, blending in with the ongoing traffic and the sounds of the city around them that felt surreal until Lyle finally released her.

Sefra was surprised by Lyle's reaction. She was just short of snuggling into Lyle's neck when he gently pushed her away. It was not abrupt, but it slowly dawned on her that there was a lot of ground to be covered before their day was over.

"I've forgotten how good it is to kiss you," Lyle drawled breathlessly.

"You shouldn't have waited so long," Sefra replied, almost in a whisper.

Lyle smiled at her, determined he would feel the flesh of his wife sleeping in his arms that night.

"I don't intend to wait much longer," he teased suggestively, his voice still slightly slurred from the beer.

Sefra made a mental note as she watched Lyle hail a taxi and decided that she would not commit to anything until they had talked further that night. Not even Cupid's bow could work right now, she told herself sternly. As far as she was concerned, that was imprisoned in the dungeons of her game and was not intended for mere mortals. Little did she know that she had just been masterfully lured into playing the love game after all. But the rules and the terms were being invented as they went along.

5:05 P.M.

They returned to the hotel worn and tired from touring the city. Sefra was amazed that Lyle parted with a hug before they returned to their separate rooms. He was staying on another floor and so went his way, and planned to call her room later in the evening to confirm their dinner date. As the elevator whisked him away, Sefra was left standing in the lobby, having spotted her brother at a telephone kiosk.

Clive returned the phone to its hook and was at her side within minutes of ending his call. From the look in his eyes, he seemed hopeful that his sister had smoothed things over with her husband, or at least had taken the opportunity to do so.

"And how is Venusina and Erosino?" he inquired, carefully charting her face. "Any blood spilled?"

"No." Sefra chuckled. "In fact, we seem to have ironed out a few problems."

"And?" Clive asked, seeing the twinkle in his sister's eyes.

"There's still a ways to go," she admitted.

"But?" Clive persisted.

"I'm hopeful we'll make it through," she finished.

"That's my sis," Clive said happily. "That's the best you can hope for at this stage and it's good news. Now here's the bad news," he added, frowning.

"What is it?" Sefra panicked. "Is it about Lyle and another woman?"

"No. It's nothing like that," Clive assured her. "It's Asahi. They refused to reschedule your appointment for another day."

"You mean they still want to see me today?" Sefra asked.

Clive nodded. "I've managed to cancel your original two o'clock slot with them, but they're adamant that—"

Sefra cast her eyes heavenward. "I can't."

"They want to see you at six instead," Clive concluded.

Sefra looked at her watch. That was in less than one hour. "What about Lyle?" She shuddered to think what he would make of the situation if he knew she was still planning to go ahead and show her demo to Asahi.

"What about him?" Clive asked, confused.

"If I keep this appointment, it could derail everything we have built up between us today," Sefra declared truthfully. "I don't want to lose him or my marriage."

"But he knows you have your own company now," Clive said, unsure why his sister should be so undecided. "That means you can make your own decisions."

"I know," Sefra agreed, thinking back to when she had made her new plans and had taken control of her future. "But Lyle threatened divorce, remember, and he's planning to contest my rights to ownership of *Temple of Love*."

"Well, it's your call. I don't know what to suggest. I love you both and this is something you both have to sort out together."

"Tell me about it." Sefra sighed. "I was hoping to do that over dinner tonight."

"You guys are having dinner?" Clive sounded surprised.

"Was," Sefra said forlornly. "I don't know how Lyle is going to feel about taking me out now if I keep this engagement."

"You're gonna tell him?" Clive asked, alarmed.

"What choice do I have?" Sefra countered, thinking it to be the most honest thing to do. "I've flown all the way from England to see Asahi. I've done my demo and put a lot of hard work into it, too. If I want to keep my marriage, I'm going to have to be honest with him."

"And hope he's the same with you," Clive interjected.

"What's that supposed to mean?" Sefra asked, quick to detect the change in her brother's tone.

"Nothing." Clive shrugged.

"C'mon," Sefra insisted, taking hold of her brother's arm and attempting to shake the truth out of him. "You're not known for throwing out innuendos."

"I just don't want to see you get hurt. I'm not saying don't trust your husband, but if it was him given this opportunity to see Asahi, do you think he would pass on it because of you and your feelings?"

"You're changing your mind on us, aren't you?" Sefra said, concerned that her brother's thoughts could change so easily. "I thought you wanted me to fix it between us."

"I do," Clive acknowledged, not wanting to sound too dismal about his sister's predicament. "I just feel that few opportunities come to any of us in life, and when they do we should take them. Six o'clock is the best they can offer and you can either accept that this is your break, which you deserve, or leave it. For what it's worth, I think you should go."

"I'll take that under advisement," Sefra answered, a touch unsure as she let go of her brother's arm.

"You do that. In the meantime, I'm doing a little romancing of my own tonight. I've just booked a table at some restaurant in the Susukino District for Zara and me. In fact, I should pass on the tip to Lyle. It's the place to be for the best nightlife in town."

"Lyle's gone to his room," Sefra revealed, her mind in a quandary of emotions.

"Then I'll pop by and see how he's doing," Clive said in a more friendly tone, "but don't forget what I told you. Life's too short to pass on the best deals when they come your way."

"I hear you." Sefra nodded. "So if I go, you'll have to tell Lyle that I've just popped out for some air."

"Buy him a present," Clive suggested. "It's still officially Valentine's Day."

"Yeah." Sefra sighed, bidding him farewell before taking the elevator.

She got off on the tenth floor and headed straight toward her room, her mind even more uncertain. If she were to go, that left her a good ten minutes to shower, another ten to get her act together—redo her hair and makeup, sort out her papers, and call a taxi—and less than half an hour to get there.

Outside her hotel door, Sefra resolved that maybe she should not tell Lyle after all. He should hear it from her of course, but he would stop her or insist on joining her, and she had not mentioned to the Japanese conglomerate that her estranged husband would be in tow. They were dealing with Grayson's Media Games Ltd., not the

Fairthorne Interactive Corporation. She could not risk any confusion when such high stakes were in play.

She reached into her handbag and took out her electronic plastic key card, passing it through the security lock to gain entry into her room. A green light flashed as she swiped the card and then she heard the lock release, giving her access. Sefra paused to rethink whether she had made the right decision before she pushed her door open. The dark met her immediately, leaving her feeling uneasy with her decision.

Closing the door behind her, Sefra turned on the light and was suddenly frozen on the spot. An abundance of flowers overwhelmed her senses. The sight of them, the scent of them, even the touch of them—as she reached out and pressed a shaky finger against a delicate petal nearby just to be certain it was real—overpowered her.

Every corner of her room was covered. Sefra felt the well of tears roll from her eyes and down her cheeks as she stared, in awe, looking around her room. White lilies, cream roses, and yellow tulips were everywhere. From the side of her bed, spilling all the way over to the floor, and trailing out toward the table and chair near the window. The table was covered in a blanket of more flowers that worked their way from the window back to the door where she stood in stunned amazement.

Uncertain whether she could take it all in, Sefra turned on her heels, thinking maybe she had opened the door to the wrong room. But as she turned, she saw on the floor a yellow envelope, which had been put under her door.

As Sefra picked it up, she realized the envelope was the same color as the tulips, the very ones she had chosen for her wedding bouquet to carry down the aisle of the church where she and Lyle had been married. She knew instantly that the card was from her husband, and in a flurry of more tears and trembling fingers, she ripped it open. She read the poem Lyle had penned in his own handwriting. Titled, "If I Were a Flower," it read:

If a flower could dream, it would dream of you.
If a flower could smile, it would smile happily at you.
If a flower could walk, it would walk to you and kiss you.
If a flower could dance, it would dance with you.
If a flower could speak, it would say "I love you."
    And I do.

Sefra choked back on more tears, knowing that the clock was still ticking. "Oh, Lyle," she cried. "What should I do?"

Only one thought troubled her. As much as she knew she still loved her husband, would he still love her in return if she accepted the opportunity Asahi was offering her?

Five

There was a time when couples followed simple rules that were expressed in marriage vows, but as Sefra sat in the taxi that arrived for her outside the Sheraton Sapporo and watched as it took her closer to her six o'clock appointment, she reminded herself that she was in a modern marriage where individuals made their own rules. She even tried to convince herself that everyone was doing it. Whether that meant it was shameful or acceptable that she keep her engagement with Asahi was another matter that left her feeling uneasy.

But her somber mood began to lift as she became aware of how much more alive the city seemed once she hit the sidewalk. In the distance, she could see the Sapporo dome, all lit up, competing with the amazing sunset that dominated the skyline. Sefra had not seen a sight like it anywhere. The mix of colors blended with the hazy mist of nightfall shadowing the sinking sun. The dark cloak was like Van Gogh's *Starry Night*, and for one brief moment she stared, in awe, before she turned and looked up at the skyscraper facing her.

She had read that the Asahi Building had been constructed with energy conservation in mind. The air-conditioning and lighting were divided into small units so that natural elements such as rainwater and solar energy were utilized. Somewhere inside were the two Japanese senior executives of Asahi with whom she was scheduled to discuss her global license for *Temple of Love.*

Sefra had changed her clothes to reflect the importance of the meeting, throwing on a dark blue pin-striped pantsuit, her jacket buttoned up over a white blouse that she now realized was not enough to protect her from the cold weather. She quickly girded herself for what lay ahead, putting a gracious smile on her face. She swept across the plaza filled with plants and fountains and through the revolving glass doors that took her into the building.

Her stiletto heels sensed the change from hard concrete to polished marble beneath her feet as she made her way to the reception desk, confident that as the only executive of Grayson's Media Games Ltd., she could clinch the deal that would change her life forever. The words *cheetah lady* flew to Sefra's mind as she recalled the nickname Lyle had given her two years ago when they had completed the first *Temple of Love.*

Sefra began to feel guilty. Why had she decided to conduct this meeting without Lyle? Why was she inside the building of one of the largest game manufacturers in the world without her husband? Sefra told herself she was doing the right thing, and kept her face fixed as she faced the pale Japanese attendant seated in front of the lobby's high-tech security console.

"Can I help you?" she asked, her heavy accent rich and lighthearted.

"I'm here to see Mr. Shinozota and party," Sefra announced, courteously. She nervously straightened her shoulders and subconsciously patted her hair into place, hoping the light breeze outside had not ruffled the short curls she wore.

"Ah, he is expecting you." The attendant smiled, briefly glancing at her watch and acknowledging Sefra's punctuality before she pushed a number of electronic buttons at her console. "I have alerted him that you are here," she added, rising from her chair to indicate the elevator. "Please go to the twenty-second floor. Mr. Chomei Shinozota will meet you there."

"Thank you." Sefra nodded, clutching her briefcase tightly before she crossed the expansive green marble floor.

As the elevator car closed behind her, Sefra swallowed hard and tried to convince herself that she was not doing anything wrong. Lyle had gone to a lot of expense to prove how much he loved her. There had hardly been room for her to move with all the flowers when she undressed, showered, and located her suitcase beneath a huge display of white lilies while she changed her clothes.

But Sefra simply refused to be shaken by Lyle's recent display of affection, resolving to see Mr. Shinozota and his marketing director. She needed to do this because . . . because she was no longer convinced she could rely on Lyle and she no longer felt she could trust him.

The elevator doors slid open and Sefra stepped out. Her high heels immediately dug deep into rich burgundy carpeting, and the air felt warm and comforting, the electronic thermostat obviously pitched to the right temperature. To her left, she could see a vast array of tempered glass windows with a spectacular evening view of the city itself. To her right, inside glass displays on the walls, was a showcase of cutting-edge-designed laptops and game consoles.

In front of her was a large boardroom table where two Japanese men were seated sipping tea from a porcelain decanter. They had been awaiting her arrival. As Sefra heard the elevator descend, they immediately arose from their chairs and came toward her. Towering a good six inches above the two, Sefra relaxed in an instant and extended her hand.

"Miss Sefra Grayson," the taller of the two said in a matter-of-fact tone before both men bowed to greet her.

In Japanese custom, she returned the bow. "How nice to meet you, Mr. Shinozuka," she said, raising her head, then feeling a rush of embarrassment. She had mispronounced his name, having instead referred to a Japanese war criminal who had carried out acts of brutality in China during the Second World War. "I'm sorry," she blurted, shaking her head the moment she saw his horror-stricken expression. "I mean . . ."

What could she say? She had come across the name in a recent newspaper article, which reported that the former soldier had recently been put on a plane back to Tokyo by U.S. immigration.

"Mr. Shinozota," she corrected, knowing she had made a bad start.

"I see you know our history," Mr. Shinozota declared with a tight smile, turning to his colleague. "May I introduce my comrade, Mr. Yoshimi Azuma?" he added with a gracious smile. "Not to be confused with Mr. Shiro Azuma, who confessed to killing thirty-seven women and children in Nanking."

Sefra saw his sense of humor and smiled, relieved he had taken her blunder with such ease. "I'm a little nervous," she admitted.

"With a commodity like *Temple of Love,* you have every right to be," Mr. Shinozota said. "Please take a seat." He beckoned her toward the head of the table where he had been seated with his colleague, then added, "Let's see if we can do business together."

"Tea?" Mr. Azuma asked.

Sefra nodded, then took her seat.

* * *

Considering she could be rock-solid in a crisis, juggle several projects at once, and meet pressing deadlines without breaking a sweat, Sefra had one main weakness: she needed emotional support when faced with business decisions, and that normally came in the shape of Lyle Fairthorne.

Facing Mr. Chomei Shinozota and Mr. Azuma, both of whom appeared excited about the latest version of *Temple of Love,* Sefra realized she could not make a decision or even commit to working with the Asahi Company without talking things over with her husband. Her uneasiness grew until Mr. Shinozota fired a question at her.

"We are interested in considering an option to license this," he told her, tapping the laptop in front of him in approval. "When do you expect we can have the completed game?"

Sefra realized she was stalling for time the moment she opened her briefcase and began to search for nothing in particular. Her mind had gone into a spin until she saw her gold pen with the words *cheetah lady.* Lyle had bought her that pen. He had given it to her on her twenty-second birthday. In a flash, Sefra was out of her seat and babbling nonsense.

"Actually," she began in a weepy voice, "I am waiting for another decision."

Mr. Azuma panicked. "Matsushita," he said, naming their rival. "We guarantee to improve on any offer they make."

"No." Sefra shook her head, extending her hand for the return of her DVD-ROM. She watched as Mr. Shinozota stared, refusing to move a muscle or return her demo. She continued. "You see . . . I need to make a . . . joint executive decision."

"Joint?" Mr. Azuma raised a brow.

"This is a . . . 'we' thing." Sefra swallowed, wondering if she was making any sense. "*Temple of Love* isn't just about me."

"We?" Mr. Shinozota repeated, confused.

"My husband and I," Sefra finished, her voice now sounding shakier than ever.

"But—" Mr. Azuma protested.

"Grayson's Media Games Ltd. is affiliated with the Fairthorne Interactive Corporation," Sefra lied, seeing a look of disapproval appear on Mr. Shinozota's face. "Unfortunately, Mr. Lyle Fairthorne could not be here so . . . I came."

"You are not the decision maker?" Mr. Shinozota said, pointing his finger accusingly.

Sefra instantly felt like a child admitting to a school yard prank. "Not entirely," she said feebly.

Mr. Shinozota tapped the eject button on his laptop and yanked out her DVD-ROM demo. In complete silence, he put the demo into the disc holder and tossed it across the table toward Sefra. "We do not deal with time wasters at Asahi," he said sternly. "This is a very serious company and we talk only to decision makers."

"Yes." Sefra nodded, retrieving her DVD. Placing it in her briefcase, she hardly knew how to react. "I'm sorry to have taken up any of—"

But the two men were already walking away from her. Without even a backward glance from them, Sefra watched as both went through a set of mahogany doors at the other end of the boardroom. In true Japanese style, she had been dismissed. Her mouth fell open for the better part of three seconds before she snapped her briefcase shut and turned toward the elevator. At that moment, Sefra felt like the most conflicted woman on earth.

7:28 P.M.

Whether it was guilt or out of love, Sefra found herself returning to the hotel with a Valentine's present for Lyle. Perhaps it was the sudden realization that she still needed Lyle, but when Sefra closed the door to her room and found herself faced once again with all those flowers, she felt one thing. Relief. Relief that she had not gone behind her husband's back and done something she may well have regretted later on.

Breathing a huge sigh of relief, she slipped out of her jacket, tossing it along with her briefcase on the bed, and placed Lyle's present beside it. No sooner had she taken a second breath than there was a knock at the door. She jumped at the sound before realizing someone was at her suite. She thought that it was probably Clive, curious as to how her meeting went, but as she opened the door, Sefra found herself staring at Lyle.

He was handsomely dressed in a charcoal-gray suit, with a pale lilac shirt. His imposing presence filled the entire doorway, instantly sparking every fiber in Sefra's body. She was filled with sexual tension as she gazed at the one man who could drive her to distraction.

For what seemed like an eternity, Sefra stood planted to the same spot in the doorway. Everything about Lyle registered. The sheen of his Afro, the smell of his cologne, the soft pink of his lips that she longed to kiss, even the arrogant arch of his eyebrows beguiled and aroused her.

"You're not ready?" he asked.

His voice sounded like music to her ears, snapping Sefra back to reality. "Ready?" she returned. "For what?"

"Now there's a question," Lyle teased. "Didn't Clive give you my message?"

"Message?"

"Dinner, at eight."

"Oh." Sefra hesitated. "I was—"

"You look great," Lyle interrupted, switching his gaze from her face to the length of her body, "but I thought you'd be in a dress."

"I was"—Sefra tried to think—"trying on a few things to wear when you knocked. It's cold out there."

"Your hair looks nice," Lyle noted, standing nervously in the doorway, his eyes on Sefra. "Are you going to invite me in?"

"Yes . . . of course." Sefra swallowed, moving herself to one side.

Lyle entered and heard her close the door behind him. His eyes immediately scanned the room, taking in the splendor of the flowers that filled it. This had been what he wanted, complete abundance. He wanted his wife to be overwhelmed in a romantic way. Only she did not look that way now. He had expected to find her dressed in a long evening gown, with pearls at her neck and wrists, looking like a package awaiting to be unwrapped. Instead, Sefra looked as though she had just finished a business meeting.

"Secret admirer?" he taunted, turning to face her with a wry grin.

"My only admirer," Sefra teased, approving of his floral delivery. "He seems to be very keen."

"Do you think he's going to get lucky?" Lyle pressed, taking a step toward her. His eyes had dropped to her finely sculpted mouth and refused to budge.

Sefra's heart melted. "I don't think his luck's run out just yet," she replied.

Lyle's eyes lit up. "In that case." He reached toward her, circling both arms around her waist. "I'll take my chances."

Sefra did not resist. When Lyle's lips met hers, she

happily accepted him. Her hands rose to his neck and cradled him. The tip of her tongue touched his and tasted him, and the covert dealings she had tried to conduct behind his back were quickly forgotten the moment he cradled her body to his and passion took over. Her heart opened and Lyle flooded it. Sefra was lost in his world.

They fell onto the bed and Sefra heard the hard crash of her briefcase as Lyle pushed it to the floor, his body pressed against hers. Instantly, she reached for the violet-covered box that was his present and placed it under a pillow before she kicked off her shoes, paying little attention as they rustled against the flowers that carpeted the room. Then came the soft thud as Lyle kicked off his own shoes and then silence as their kiss deepened.

Their legs entwined and he realized she tasted like Earl Gray tea, which confused his senses as it mingled with the scent of her perfume. But as his tongue claimed hers, Lyle was lost and knew it. He wanted Sefra now more than he had ever wanted her, and nothing short of her abandoning him could stop him from seizing the moment. When his arms slid around her waist and she tilted her head back beneath his, Lyle wanted more.

He laced his fingers through her short dark hair, aware how much more different it felt from when he had touched it last. The soft silky curls caressed his skin and aroused him until Lyle could not help pressing Sefra to his fast-beating heart. He stroked her face with his tongue, kissed her nose and eyelids, delved to nip the back of her earlobes, which he knew excited her, and when she finally made a soft sound in the back of her throat, telling him she had surrendered, Lyle lifted his head to look down at her.

The soft lighting in the room and the flowers that cascaded around her made her seem almost angelic. It was the perfect haven for such a beauty to be in his arms. Lyle savored the moment before lowering his head. Sefra kissed him again, her mouth soft, damp, and ready to consume his every affection.

Her hands almost shook as she took the lead and slid her fingers under Lyle's pale lilac shirt. It took her a moment to remember that she had not touched him in such a long while. She was nervous, fevered, and yet, feeling the soft curls of Lyle's hair on his chest aroused her more than she had ever known. With her eyes closed, she allowed her fingers to do all the seeing, each brush, caress, and stroke revealing to her mind how fit and remarkable Lyle's body was.

His body heat elevated through her hands. His nipples felt hard as rocks, and the softer hair on his back excited her beyond endurance. She felt him tremble, ecstatic at the power she still possessed to cause such a reaction. Sefra knew she wanted to know the force of her husband inside her again. She desperately wanted to feel the energy of his lovemaking, which always left her gasping for more.

Already, her free wrist was being pushed back against the bedpost by the strength of her husband's lust. Sefra loved the way he gently pulled her hand from beneath his shirt and was pinning her to the bed, her body squirming as his hips pressed down against hers. She felt his hardened member against her groin and loved the electric shock wave it sent through her. Lyle was raring to go and she was riding the wave with him.

He rocked his hips against her. "Feel good?" he asked. His voice was a mere whisper.

"Better than before," Sefra replied hoarsely. She felt blood rush to her cheeks. Lord, she was on fire. She tried to hold still beneath her husband to savor every moment, but it was hard to do so. Every part of her body was writhing, twisting, and wriggling beneath his touch.

"I'm not going to rush this," Lyle said into her ear, staring at the dark, sensual brown beauty beneath him. "Dinner can wait."

Sefra did not answer. She did not need to. Lyle always liked to take their lovemaking slow. The longer it took, the better. And tonight, she was not complaining. This was Valentine's night. Tonight was a test of how much love they could show one another, how much they still meant to each other. That knowledge made Sefra shiver in Lyle's arms. It was a tremor of pure pleasure, of what her dealings earlier that evening had nearly cost her. She would make it up to Lyle, she told herself the moment his lips retook hers and she cradled his head in her arms.

Lyle groaned deep in his throat, controlling his urgent need to thrust his manhood against his wife. Even though he wanted to bide his time, he was uncertain how long he could wait. His voice had sounded rough and desperate, and every fiber in his body felt intense and in need of release. The pressure was building and it was strong. For the first time in his life, he felt he was losing control with Sefra.

"Darling," he said and smiled, abandoning all reason, "I can't wait."

It was all the prompting Sefra needed. After all, she had denied herself for so long staying away from Lyle. She'd suffered sleepless nights, torture, and frustration, tossing and turning in sexual frustration, which could have been settled with one phone call. They had both been insensitive and headstrong. They had both contributed to this endless pain of wanting and needing to be together, yet each had refused to resolve the matter. How could two people who loved each other do this?

Even now, Sefra tried to figure out why, but her brain

and body were too aroused in the presence of Lyle. She could hardly believe he was with her, in bed, touching her with such joy and passion. She could see in his eyes how much he wanted her. He wanted everything to be as it once had been between them. And tonight promised a new future.

Lyle's lips pressed against her neck, warm, tender, and sliding down the column of her throat to her breast. He had let go of her wrists and was now slowly loosening the tiny buttons on her expensive white blouse, his mouth following where his hands had unbuttoned, tasting the sweet scent of her skin. Sefra closed her eyes and moaned. God, it was good to feel her husband's lips against her smooth, velvety flesh.

He had full control, pushing the blouse off of her, his eyes taking delight in the lacy scrap of a bra she was wearing. Lyle was quickly pulling off his jacket and taking off his shirt, sending both items of clothing soaring across the room. Sefra heard flowers falling and chuckled, knowing that each discarded piece of clothing would disturb the flowers arranged around the room. Finally, naked, their bodies were pressed against each other. They yearned for their hot, hard flesh to meld.

"I haven't forgotten what you like," Lyle said softly and seductively. He circled Sefra's navel with his tongue, delving inside so skillfully, arousing her, and then making a trail upward toward her breasts. He touched her slowly, taking the tip of each breast into his mouth and then rolling and biting her nipples gently between his teeth. Sefra's whole body arched in supplication, her hands reaching for Lyle's shoulders where she dug her nails in deep.

"Ouch," he murmured against her skin, enjoying the sweet pain that she gave him. "I like it when you do it like that." His hands moved down her sides, tickling Sefra on his way down, savoring the way she clutched at his shoulders, refusing to let go. "Scratch me," he coaxed her, cradling her hips, his fingers tracing her pelvic bones and his tongue moving on down her torso, licking and tasting her as he moved.

Sefra's nails dug deeper until she pulled at Lyle's flesh. She left no wound, just a surface scratch that caused him to shiver and move restlessly against her. Lyle's every brush against her skin left Sefra with a burning desire, a deep ache that felt like a whiplash stinging her body. She had not experienced this before. It was something new, something so profound she began to wonder why she felt different than before.

It intensified the moment Lyle reached down and touched her. Instantly, Sefra opened her legs and whimpered, allowing her husband the access he craved. She made a sound that echoed into the night, surprised at how moist and ready she was after such a short time. Only Lyle could do this to her, Sefra recalled, moments before his fingers tormented her with such desire, her waking thoughts disappeared.

"I want you now," Sefra almost screamed, sliding her hands downward to grip Lyle.

She felt him shudder, the reaction of his body rippling along her arm until it connected with her heart. She wanted to weep at how much he wanted her, at how hard he felt between her fingers, and how much she wanted him deep inside her. The sheer force of his sexual prowess had her body shifting back and forth with such urgency, she dared not keep them waiting any longer.

Lyle's own patience was wearing thin. Kneeling between his wife's thighs, he leaned forward so that she could feel his body hot and pulsing against her, and braced himself for entry. As Lyle pushed steadily, Sefra could feel her body fill where, for months, she had felt so empty. She wrapped her arms and legs around her husband, taking everything he had to offer.

Joined, their lips searched and found each other, sending the first burst of pent-up desire through their loins. Then Lyle began to pulse and throb inside her, reining back, building a steady rocking motion, keeping his control and momentum until Sefra clutched at his body and followed his lead. Their bodies worked a rhythm that was as old as man's first discovery of woman.

Sefra was indeed lost in time. She kept pace, arching her hips up to meet him. In their love nest surrounded by white lilies, cream-colored roses, and yellow tulips, the scent of lust, passion, and flowers created a sexually pungent fragrance. Sefra wanted it to last forever. This was the man she had married, the man she had once and still loved. The man who she believed would never forsake her for another woman. The man who would cherish her forever.

She felt so warm and wet and languid in her husband's arms. As long as they had each other, as long as their desire to be together was this strong, their marriage could beat the test of time.

A smile swept across Sefra's face, and tears welled up in her brown eyes as she realized the intensity of her feelings for Lyle. Her body convulsed in his arms as she climaxed, in a powerful reminder of how long she had denied herself.

When Lyle's sweat-soaked body went rigid and plunged deeply into her moments later, he realized how foolish and pigheaded he had been to deprive himself such ecstasy with his wife.

It was a long time before they could release each other. Their bodies were weak, their limbs still trembling with emotion. Nestled in between Lyle's shoulders, Sefra felt safe again. They had not lost each other after all. She closed her eyelids to savor the moment, before reaching under her pillow for Lyle's present.

"This is for you," she whispered, turning to face him and finding that he had closed his eyes, too.

Lyle's eyes opened slowly, their deep color intensifying as he stared at the wrapped box. A smile formed on his lips. "What is it?" he asked.

"Your Valentine's present," Sefra told him. "And to make up for the months we've been apart."

Lyle's eyes glazed over as he took the box, and then he bent forward and planted a kiss on Sefra's forehead. "Am I going to like it?" He chuckled.

"I hope so," she answered excitedly.

Lyle quickly removed the violet-colored wrapper and found himself staring at a dark blue box with the embossed name of a jeweler's on top. His smile broadened as he opened up the box and stared at the twenty-four-karat gold chain snuggled against the blue satin inside. His expression warmed as he picked up the chain and dangled it between his fingers, before turning to kiss his wife.

"Sefra, this is beautiful," he said, as she sat up on her knees and took the chain from him. He allowed her to put it around his neck and placed his hand there to check the fit. "Perfect."

"Just like you." Sefra smiled, placing a kiss on Lyle's forehead before she snuggled under his shoulder again. Placing one hand around his waistline, she sighed a deep breath and closed her eyes. "Happy Valentine's, sweetheart," she murmured softly.

"Happy Valentine's, darling," Lyle returned, putting his arm around Sefra's shoulder. With a deep satisfying smile, Lyle was happy once more.

Six

"I'm looking forward to being on the town tonight," Sefra enthused, as Lyle opened the door to the taxi. The first thing that caught her eye was the picturesque moon rising in the darkened sky. It was silvery gray, its luminescence seeming to bounce off everything. Sefra smiled up at it as Lyle approached her.

They were on their way to Kitanofuji, a restaurant in the Susukino Region, Japan's hottest entertainment nightspot north of Tokyo. Her brother Clive had recommended it because of its sumo atmosphere and choice of good food. Sefra sat at a table that overlooked a huge sumo wrestling ring, removing her coat as Lyle joined her.

It was filled with people from all over: the Brits, Americans, Malaysians, Indonesians, Filipinos, a handful of Australians, and Asians from the neighboring regions. It was a place that saw many tourists, party-goers, and modern-day nomads searching for excitement. And Susukino was just the place to do that. The atmosphere was electric. It seemed like the kind of place to easily lose yourself.

Sefra wore a black velvet dress she had changed into, which was more appropriate for the evening's activities.

She caught the look of approval in her husband's eyes. The passion of their lovemaking had not diminished during their months apart, but had increased to something much more meaningful. Sefra hardly knew what to make of it. Smiling at Lyle, she wondered whether they had revived that feeling of being madly in love all over again.

They had decided to try the famous *chanko-nabe* dish favored by sumo wrestlers. Lyle suddenly felt a sense of déjà vu as he turned to his wife. She was his again. He had won her back. They had made love and sealed the crack in their marriage. There would be no thought of obtaining a divorce with the two wrestling in court over ownership of the *Temple of Love*.

Lyle was relieved in more ways than he cared to admit. He never wanted to confront Sefra in a legal battle. She was too animated and high-strung, and the whole thing would almost certainly have become a media spectacle, damaging sales and no doubt destroying their business. Yes, he was more than relieved.

"Happy?" Sefra asked, seeing the relaxed expression on her husband's face.

"Very," he told her in earnest. "Am I making you happy tonight?"

"Ditto." Sefra chuckled.

"You really are beautiful," Lyle added, leaning forward across the table to check out the glow in his wife's eyes.

"And you're a charmer," Sefra returned. He was, by far, the most handsome man in the room, dressed in his charcoal suit and lilac-colored shirt, with her Valentine's gift dangling around his neck. As long as he wore that gold chain of hers, she'd always be with him, she thought.

"So," Lyle began, ten minutes later as their hot orders were served, "when are you flying back to England?"

Sefra blinked. Until that moment, she had forgotten

they had not traveled together, but had instead arrived in Japan on separate flights. "I leave on the ten-thirty-two evening flight from Chitose Kuko tomorrow," she murmured, feeling a sudden blockage in her throat. The very thought of being apart from Lyle when they had just found each other again suddenly seemed unbearable.

"That soon?" Lyle said, his eyebrows raised. "I don't fly out until Monday morning, on the six-twenty-three."

"Oh." Sefra sighed, realizing that they only had this Valentine's night together. "I didn't realize."

Lyle tried to sound positive. "At least you're here during the day tomorrow."

Sefra nodded.

"Maybe we can spend the rest of it together?"

She nodded again, before recalling that Lyle had also arrived in Japan to conduct a meeting of his own. As she ate, Sefra thought back to her own meeting. She had not been able to go through with it. She debated whether she should tell Lyle. She suddenly wondered whether he intended to keep to his own plans, even though she had not.

"What about Matsushita?" The question was out before Sefra could stop herself.

Lyle slowly swallowed his food, dipping his head slightly to weigh the question. He really didn't need to think. He had already decided that he wanted to know more about Sefra's new plans before committing himself to any sort of decision. "I canceled," he said sternly, "and thought about maybe rescheduling after I listen to what you want to do with the sequel."

Sefra's heart leaped suddenly. Was this Lyle, *the* Lyle Fairthorne, paying attention to what she wanted? "You're giving me a voice?" She could hardly believe it.

"Well, don't look so surprised." Lyle chuckled. "You are still my wife and business partner."

Sefra smiled. She loved the sound of that. They were indeed still together. Of course, in her world that meant there couldn't be any shadows. "What about Tiya?" The other woman's name still rankled her.

Lyle's brows furrowed. "What about her?"

"Is she still going to be part of our creative team?"

"I don't see why she shouldn't be."

Sefra placed her fork on her plate. "I thought you said you were prepared to listen to what I want," she thundered, feeling a rush of blood tingling in her cheeks.

"I am," Lyle insisted.

"Then I want her gone," Sefra demanded furiously. "I want that skinny-ass, porcelain-hued Japanese hussy out of our lives for good." There. She had said it and by God she meant it.

Lyle reared back in his chair, amazed at Sefra's temper. What in the hell had he done now? "Sefra!" He was dumbstruck. "What is this?"

"This is me wanting to be the only woman in my husband's life," Sefra demanded. "This is me taking the reins of our marriage, our business, and keeping what began as our baby."

"Sefra—"

"She has no part of it. Of us." Her voice suddenly crackled, something Sefra loathed since she had no control over it. But her emotions were at a fever pitch and she couldn't help it.

"Tiya has nothing to do with us," Lyle said carefully.

"Then why are you insisting that she stay at our company?" Sefra protested. "I don't want to work on the sequel with her."

"What has she done to you?" Lyle asked, bemused.

"It's . . . it's the way she looks at you," Sefra said. "I *know* women, how devious they can be. She's trying to steal you by taking over the one thing that we began together. Our game. Our baby. And you're allowing her to do it."

"Now, Sefra." Lyle laughed. "This is all paranoia. Tiya happens to be one of the best animators we've got."

"*You've* got," Sefra said. "I've hired someone better at Grayson's Media."

Lyle flinched. "Of course," he began, his voice sounding hurt. "I forgot you jumped ship."

Sefra sighed heavily, not wanting to fight again. "Look," she said, "I want her to go."

"Where?"

"Anywhere," Sefra said, not understanding the question. "As long as she's not around me trying to steal what I have."

"She hasn't stolen anything," Lyle said, his voice sounding exasperated.

"She's stolen my time with you," Sefra said, with little care at how clingy, defensive, and possessive she sounded. "And I need . . . I need—"

"What do you need?" Lyle demanded, annoyed at how easily and quickly their evening could be ruined.

"A baby," Sefra spat out.

A silence stood between them so thick it felt almost tangible. Lyle's eyes were wide and his expression dumbstruck. This was not Sefra in a temper tantrum, being overprotective or jealous anymore. This was not even Sefra having a sparring match about Tiya. This was his wife touching on something so completely new that Lyle had to take a breath before he spoke.

"Now let me try and understand you correctly," he began, his tone softening. "This is not about our baby, the *Temple of Love?*"

"No," Sefra said, shaking her head, amazed at the words that had come out of her mouth.

"Or the sequel?"

"No," she confirmed again.

"You're talking about a real baby?" he asked. "A child?"

Sefra nodded, too stunned to speak.

"Okay." Lyle nodded, his mind attempting to quell the shock. "And when did you think you—"

"Last year," Sefra interrupted, "before I left."

"I see."

"I thought by Christmas we would've reached a compromise. But you didn't come after me," she explained.

"Me?" Lyle gasped. Suddenly the food was no longer of interest to him and he pushed his plate aside. "I never stopped you from having children."

"I know," Sefra agreed, remembering that Lyle had been more than happy to have a baby sooner. "But when we launched the game, you forgot all about it and I didn't."

"Me?" Lyle gasped again.

"All you cared about was the *Temple of Love.*"

"Me?" Lyle repeated, running a shaky hand across his forehead. "Sefra, I don't understand you. I never forgot. A baby is what I've always wanted, but when you said you wanted us to wait, I threw my disappointment into the game."

"And forgot about me and everything we worked for," Sefra said, pushing her own plate to one side.

"I had no idea that I was neglecting you," Lyle admitted. "You were working just as hard as I was. We both wanted the game to succeed and it did."

"And that was when we really lost sight of each other," Sefra explained, recalling all the late nights Lyle would stay at the office while she had returned home to cook their meals, fretting over Tiya's presence. "We both got so caught up with the *Temple of Love,* it began to threaten everything."

"So you decided to take it out on Tiya instead of talking to me about the real problem," Lyle said, now fully understanding the situation. "Tiya is not responsible for you not having a baby."

"She is if she's keeping you away from me," Sefra countered, hurt that Lyle still could not see her side on this.

"Look," he proclaimed. Sefra no longer looked like the strong, self-assured woman he had once dubbed *cheetah lady,* but someone who needed reassurance of his love and wanted him to prove it by having her bear his child. "This is not you, Sefra. If you want a baby, I'll give you a baby. As many kids as you want. But don't do this to yourself."

"Do what?" Sefra snapped.

"It's you I love, not Tiya. So don't beat yourself up about me ever leaving you for her," Lyle declared, taking hold of Sefra's hands and squeezing them in his own large ones. "And if you don't want her working on the sequel, fine. We'll use your guy."

Sefra nodded, relieved that finally she would no longer have to face Tiya as a rival for her husband's affections. "I'll agree to that," she said, assured that everything would be all right now. "Joseph Kaplan is great. He—"

"Joseph Kaplan?" Lyle harangued, the name sounding familiar. "You've hired that slimeball from Q Multimedia?"

"I . . . I . . ." Sefra was aware that this was not going down well with her husband.

"He's trouble," Lyle insisted, clenching his teeth. "I knew him from the university. In fact, we once worked on a demo together for a major interactive company. The two-faced klutz stole all my programming and tried to go solo. I caught him at it and put the company straight, but we lost the deal. They didn't trust either one of us to deliver the goods."

"I didn't know," Sefra said, unaware that before she married her husband, there were people Lyle had had unsavory dealings with. Still, that did not mean that she would have the same experience. "Joe's done a great job on my demo."

"The one you were going to show to Asahi?" Lyle asked.

Sefra recoiled. "It's a good demo. You should see it."

"I intend to," Lyle declared. "But I don't want us using him on the sequel."

Sefra could see Lyle's point and used it to her advantage. "Okay," she agreed quickly. "We don't use Tiya and we don't use Joseph. We find someone new altogether."

Lyle thought for a few seconds, then agreed. "Done."

"And our family?" Sefra pressed.

"Start whenever you want," Lyle said.

Sefra smiled, thinking back to their sexual escapade at the hotel. "We've started already."

Lyle grabbed his wife's hands and laced his fingers through hers. Their eyes met as he took her hand to his lips and kissed it. "You drive a hard bargain, Mrs. Sefra Fairthorne. I want less of that Grayson woman."

Sefra chuckled, happy that they had resolved so many issues that had plagued their marriage. "And you, Mr. Fairthorne, don't like those who disagree with you."

"That's me." He smiled, sucking one of her fingers. "Do you know, I'd like to go to that other place your brother recommended after we finish dinner here. Make it a Valentine's Day to remember."

Sefra nodded. "You're on."

Lyle threw her a wicked glance. "We'll save dessert till later."

10:02 P.M.

"Remember the first time we danced?" Lyle asked, holding his wife around her waist. Her arms were comfortably resting against his shoulders as she listened to his pulse beating next to her cheek.

"No," Sefra lied, her voice a whisper, her breath tickling his neck.

"No?" Lyle said, feigning surprise.

"Yes, I do." Sefra chuckled. "It was at that Brazilian-style tapas bar called Cocacabana in the heart of Manchester where you met me for the first time. I believe you taught me the cha-cha-cha, among other things."

Lyle planted a kiss against Sefra's forehead, enjoying the way she nestled against him, their feet keeping in rhythm with the drumbeat. They were in Miss Jamaica and Havana, sister bars that served rum and tropical drinks and played voodoo dance and Caribbean music.

Sefra could hardly believe that in the heart of Japan, a slice of the Caribbean could be found. A Calypso version of the song "My Valentine" played as she enjoyed the smooth and seductive way her husband danced with her. He was still nimble on his feet and an expert at keeping her body in tune with his own, gently guiding her to the left and then to the right, punctuating his every movement with a slight movement of his hips. Yes, Lyle Fairthorne still had it going on.

"Do you remember the first thing I said to you?" he asked, catching Sefra by surprise. He felt her head move slightly, almost as though she wasn't sure she had heard him correctly.

"When?" she asked.

"When we met," Lyle clarified.

"Let me see," Sefra whispered against the hollow of his neck. "I was in Cocacabana with my friends having fun, minding my own business, and you pursued me across the room, stalking me like a lion."

Lyle tried to suppress the laugh in his throat.

"And then you came over and asked me . . . 'Are you

from Cuba?' That was it?" She laughed. "And I asked you why and you said because I danced like a Cuban."

"You still do," Lyle confessed warmly.

"Then we got to talking and both of us realized we liked designing computer games," she added.

"And the rest, as they say, is history," Lyle chimed in, gently turning Sefra around the dance floor. "Any regrets?"

"No. You?"

"No, only your snoring."

Sefra laughed and held her husband closer, closing her eyes, her fingers massaging the back of his hair, still not used to the idea that he was hers again for the touching. She was looking forward to being with him again for the remainder of the evening and long into the night.

"Don't look now," Lyle interrupted suddenly as Sefra quickly opened her eyes. "Your brother's here. He's waving at us."

"He came out this evening with Zara," Sefra added, her voice calm and tired.

"I think he's expecting us to go over after this dance," Lyle warned. "Are you keen?"

"He is my brother," Sefra reminded him softly. "We'll have one drink with them, then leave. I don't want to talk for the rest of the night."

"When we could be doing something else more exciting," Lyle added.

Sefra felt her fingers tighten in anticipation. The very idea of going back to the hotel and making love to her husband until dawn was just the tonic she needed to complete the day they had spent together. Already, her body was responding to his suggestion. Her heart beat a little quicker. Her head felt light and giddy, and the spot between her legs was eager to feel Lyle inside her again.

The song over, Lyle led the way toward Clive and Zara seated at the bar, sipping rum cocktails and staring love-struck into each other's eyes. Her brother was in a navy suit and Zara had on a flimsy pink dress, with a crimson-colored georgette jacket thrown over her shoulders. Sefra felt some semblance of relief when she reminded herself that on her return to England she would be moving back into her home, thus giving her brother and her new secretary their space to be together without intrusion.

"And how are you two lovebirds?" Lyle immediately probed, aware that Clive and Zara were high on each other and a few cocktails.

"Sefra!" Clive said, his voice slurred and his eyes glazed. "I see you took my advice about this place. Just like back home. Great, isn't it?"

Sefra nodded. "Have you had a good evening?"

"Lovely." Clive nodded. "Zara and I have had the best Valentine's ever." He turned and put his arm around her shoulder, planting a huge kiss on her lips. Zara indulged the moment, starry-eyed with Clive's full attention. "You've eaten?"

"Yep." Lyle nodded. "At that sumo place you also told me about."

"What time you going back to the hotel?" he asked.

"Any time now," Lyle said, taking a strong hold of Sefra's hand and lacing his fingers through them. "We've got a lot of catching up to do."

"Aah, you guys made up," Zara enthused, sweetly. "Guess my odds were good."

"So Erosino and Venusina have finished all their game playing with each other?" Clive interjected on a wry note. "I swear sometimes you two are just like your characters." He turned toward Sefra and, without thinking, let the cat out of the bag. "How did your meeting go?"

Sefra felt as if she had been hit with a sledgehammer. Her eyes warned her brother not to press the issue, but Clive failed to notice the gesture. Sitting on the bar stool as he was, shoulders braced, his manner aroused Lyle's suspicions, and he was quick off the mark.

"What meeting?" Lyle demanded.

Clive immediately realized his mistake and coughed, pretending to have a fit of hiccups. But Lyle was not fooled by the show. He slapped his brother-in-law's back until he felt sure the convulsions had stopped, then turned toward his wife. Sefra decided to immediately come clean and tell the truth. After all, she hadn't really done anything.

"I went to see Asahi today, before dinner," she admitted. "But—"

"You did what?" Lyle said angrily, thrown off balance.

"It's not what you think."

"You went to see them before . . . before we made love?" he demanded.

"Lyle!"

"Did you?" he insisted.

Sefra nodded. "But—"

Lyle pulled his hand away from her and dug it into his trouser pocket. "I don't believe this." He shook his head. "You went after . . . after you saw the flowers?"

"Lyle!" Sefra said again, tears quickly rushing to her eyes. "I didn't do anything."

"Say that again just so that I've got it straight," he demanded. "You didn't do what, go to Asahi?"

"Yes, I did, but—"

"And you didn't *do* anything."

"Don't yell at my sis like that," Clive interrupted. "If she said she didn't do anything, then she didn't."

"You keep out of this." Lyle scowled, in utter disbelief. "I'm dealing with your stubborn, selfish sister." He could feel the anger in his chest, the pain of Sefra's deceit tearing at his heart, her treachery suffocating him. He turned back to his wife. "So, you signed our life away?"

"No." Sefra swallowed, the shock evident in Lyle's face causing the initial trickle of tears that she had tried to hold back.

"So what happened?" he insisted.

"They saw the demo," Sefra began to explain, "and—"

"They saw your demo before I did—your husband and business partner?" Lyle exploded. "So," he demanded, "what was their verdict?"

Sefra burst into tears as Clive rose to her defense. "If you must know," he announced, measuring a couple of inches below Lyle's six-foot-three frame, "I encouraged Sefra to go to that meeting. It was the one chance she had, and I told her to take it."

"You did what?" Lyle raged, pulling his hands from his pockets and balling them into fists.

"If she pulled it off, you'd have both benefitted," Clive continued. "Until you divorce or jointly sell the damn thing, *Temple of Love* belongs to you both, and my sister was just trying to do the best she could with it."

Clive was not ready for the punch that came his way, knocking his spectacles from his face. His bottom lip throbbed in pain, shaken by the right cross Lyle had landed. Zara quickly came to his rescue, screaming at Sefra to restrain her husband. But Sefra could only stare at Lyle as he glared at her.

"Forget tonight, forget you," he cursed, his tone heated as he turned his back and began to walk away.

"Where are you going?" Sefra cried, unable to believe what had just happened.

"To someone who has more respect for me," Lyle shouted, without a backward glance.

Sefra ran after him, tugging at Lyle's hand to slow his pace. "Who are you going to see?" she pleaded, certain he knew no one in Japan and afraid that he was planning to

go somewhere illicit, or worse. But she was not ready for
the response Lyle gave her.

"Tiya's in town," he said, bristling, shrugging Sefra
loose. "She came in on the same flight I did last night
and went to stay with her mother."

"What?" The tears clung to Sefra's eyes as she stopped
dead in her tracks. "That hussy is here?"

"You're not the only one who keeps secrets," Lyle
pressed on, pausing for one brief moment to look at her.
"And just for the record," he added on a dry note, "I've
kissed her."

"Tiya?" Sefra demanded, her heart pumping wildly.

"You heard me," he shot back, "so live with it."

Those were the last words Lyle Fairthorne said to
Sefra before he walked out of Miss Jamaica and Havana.

Seven

"I've ruined his life," Sefra cried, back in her hotel room at the Sheraton Sapporo, her brown eyes so teary she could hardly see her brother or Zara among the lilies, roses, and tulips spread around the room.

"Don't be ridiculous," Clive said, walking toward the room's small bar and proceeding to pour Sefra a stiff drink. "What you've ruined is his ego."

Sefra welcomed the whiskey and dry he handed her before she spoke. "And we were getting on so well," she continued, through another bout of tears.

"So I see," Clive said, his eyes dancing around the room, bouncing from one floral arrangement to another. "He's gone to a lot of trouble."

Sefra raised her head and agreed with her brother. "And how did I repay him?"

"By taking control," Clive told her firmly. He glanced at his sister, who was seated on the edge of the bed with Zara's consoling hand around her shoulder. The two women were obviously upset and so was he, having taken a blow to his lip. But he had decided not to make the situation seem worse than it was. "That husband of yours needed to be brought down a peg or two."

"Not in the way I did it," Sefra said, tearfully. "I should've told him about my meeting with Asahi."

"How did it go?" Clive asked.

"I couldn't sign," Sefra said, wiping her eyes with one hand while squeezing Zara's with the other. "I couldn't do it."

"Wait a minute," Clive began, placing both his hands on to his hips. "Are you telling me that you went all the way to Asahi and got cold feet?"

"It wasn't like that," Sefra confessed. "I thought I could do it, but when I got there and tried—"

"That was your golden opportunity," Clive continued, regardless of whatever loyalty his sister felt toward her husband. "I thought you were made of stronger stuff than that."

"Don't ridicule me," Sefra pleaded, attempting to stop the flurry of tears. "When you love somebody, you just can't betray them."

"And what about *his* betrayal?" Clive reminded her, referring to Lyle's sudden confession. "Or have you forgotten about that?"

Sefra felt her heart twist. She imagined her husband and Tiya locked in a passionate kiss. The image sent her into a rage. How could Lyle do this to her, his wife?

"Do you think it's true?" she immediately demanded of her brother, as though she needed to confirm that it never happened.

"Why would he say it?" Clive shot back, his body rigid as he remembered Lyle's admission.

Sefra felt her shoulders shake with pain. It was one thing for her to go to Asahi to see Mr. Azuma and Mr. Shinozota, but quite another for her husband to be having an affair. Surely, Lyle could not think that she was at fault. Their indiscretions were not even in the same ballpark. And she had done nothing wrong. She had not agreed to anything at her meeting at Asahi because of her love for Lyle. But he had kissed Tiya! The very thought of it brought on a sickly feeling.

"He's ruined me," Sefra cried, swallowing the lump that constricted her throat. "I can never feel the same way about Lyle now."

"What he's destroyed is your trust," Zara said compassionately, "which was already on shaky ground before you found this out."

Sefra nodded in agreement. "What do I do?"

"You'll have to talk to him," Zara explained.

"She doesn't have to do anything," Clive insisted, turning to his sister. "You can stay at my place for as long as it takes."

"I can't do that." Sefra grimaced, thinking back to only a few hours earlier when she was looking forward to returning home with Lyle. "You and Zara need your space. And besides, Zara's right, we'll have to talk." She paused. "Suppose he mentions divorce?"

"He's already mentioned divorce," Zara reminded her.

"I mean . . . for real this time," Sefra cried, her body trembling. At the tender age of twenty-four, she could hardly contemplate divorce.

"Then at least you'll know where you stand," Clive said. "It won't be pleasant, but things will be sorted once and for all."

"And the game?" Sefra whimpered, uncertain about her future and all that that entailed.

"The industry will survive the ripple of two game producers parting company," Clive said nonchalantly. "They're probably used to it all the time."

"I was thinking about the effects on sales," Sefra said.

"Sis, your marriage is probably falling apart and all you can talk about is the popularity of *Temple of Love?*" Clive responded incredulously. "Your husband hit me because I was standing up for you and that game. What you need to do is fight back at his kissing your colleague . . . or at least give me a free hand to do the job for you."

"Oh, Clive," Sefra cried, tears suddenly flooding her cheeks once again. "I was right all along, wasn't I? I knew she wanted him. I suspected there was something more than their working together. If he's kissed her, then—"

"Don't beat yourself up about it," Zara said, as she squeezed Sefra's hand tightly. "I think you should wait until he gets back, then talk. He might just innocently mean he had kissed her on the cheek."

"Not Lyle," Sefra said. "I told you he likes company. When we met, I remember a lot of women drooling over him. I felt special because he only wanted to dance with me. But I'm not special now, am I? I'm nothing to my own husband." Miserable, she wept some more.

"Sefra!" Clive said. "You're not alone. Zara and I will make sure you'll be all right."

Sefra shook her head. "How can you, when he's at her mother's house right now? She has a mother here, and you heard him, that's where he's going."

"Sefra . . ." Clive did not know what to say. How could he convince his sister that men sometimes said things without thinking to get back at a woman? He could not imagine Lyle disclosing that kind of information had he not been hurt by Sefra's meeting with Asahi. "Look, maybe Zara is right," he admitted after a while. "Talk to Lyle."

Suddenly, the guest phone rang. Sefra and Zara jumped at the sound, before Sefra asked her brother to answer. Clive spoke for several seconds before turning to his sister.

"What is it?" Sefra asked, curious at his expression. "Is it Lyle?"

"Reception says that there's a woman downstairs," Clive

informed her wryly. "She's looking for Lyle apparently. He's not in his room, but reception remembered that he ordered flowers for your room and they'd like to know if you have any idea where to find him."

"Who's the woman?" Sefra demanded.

Clive inquired and moments later said, "Tiya Nosaka."

"Oh, my God," Sefra gasped, pushing Zara's hand aside. Her body trembled. "What does she want?"

Clive recognized the anguish on his sister's face, but continued, "She's dropping off some papers for Lyle to sign. She's tried to ring him, but he's not answering his phone and he needs to have them before he flies back to London."

"Have them send her up to my room," Sefra ordered, her tone quiet, but firm.

"Now, sis," Clive cautioned.

"Just do it," Sefra said, gulping down what was left of her whiskey and dry.

He didn't argue. Looking across the room, he watched as Sefra handed Zara the empty glass and straightened her shoulders. He saw the defiance, vulnerability, and pride in her eyes, enhanced even more by the velvet dress she was wearing. Clive had to admit, his sister was a good-looking woman, and not someone to ever be trifled with. And whatever she planned to do tonight, it had to be for her own self-esteem.

The knock at the door came quicker than he would have imagined. Sefra took small strides toward the door and inhaled deeply before opening it. On the other side was a Japanese woman, much shorter than Sefra's five feet ten. The woman was dressed in traditional Japanese clothing with her hair swept up into a loose chignon and her face made up like a porcelain doll. Sefra hardly recognized Tiya. In her hand was a legal-size manila envelope.

"Mrs. Fairthorne!" Tiya noted with surprise. "I had no idea you were here."

"My sentiments exactly," Sefra added, opening the door wider. "Come in." As she watched her enter the room, she turned to her brother and Zara. "I believe you two were just leaving," she said tersely.

Clive looked startled. "I hadn't planned—"

"I'm not staying," Tiya quickly interjected. "I'm looking for Lyle . . . Mr. Fairthorne. I have some papers for him to sign."

"You can deal with me," Sefra said, taking charge.

"They're important," Tiya insisted, appearing slightly nervous at Sefra's smooth and somewhat intimidating presence. "Will he be long?"

"It's Valentine's night," Sefra reminded her, ignoring Tiya's question while turning to her brother and Zara. "You two lovebirds go and enjoy what's left of it. I'll see you in the morning."

Clive glanced at his sister and Zara several times before taking the hint. Reluctantly stepping over several more floral arrangements, he joined Zara at the door before leaving. Alone with Tiya, Sefra walked over to the bar and offered her a drink.

"Just orange juice," Tiya said, looking around the room. "So many flowers," she breathed, her dark eyes landing on the petals strewn across the room. "I have never seen such a picture."

"The measure of my husband's love for me," Sefra replied.

She noted the reaction in Tiya's eyes. "You've seen Lyle?" she asked, surprised.

"We spent the day together," Sefra said, gloating, "and a good part of the early evening right here in this very room." She shifted her eyes toward the bed and took delight in seeing Tiya's expression. "I know what you're up to," she added, getting straight to the point as she handed Tiya her orange juice.

"Excuse me?" Tiya said, feigning ignorance.

"It's been a slow burn, hasn't it, you and Lyle?" Sefra continued, trying hard to keep her composure. "Of course, my being married to him simply complicated matters for you, or did it add an edge?" She stared at Tiya. "Made it more exciting for you, did it? More of a challenge?"

"I'm sorry," Tiya declared, apologetic, raising the orange juice to her lips and taking a fortifying sip. "I don't know what you're talking about."

"Don't you?" Sefra said, her voice rising. "Let me make it easy for you." She walked around the woman in an almost predatory way, surprising herself at how cool and calm she remained. "Lyle told me about the kiss."

Tiya's face instantly turned crimson. "Mrs. Fairthorne, I—"

"Didn't mean to do it?" Sefra offered. "Didn't mean to rush him?" she added for clarity. "Perhaps you would care to tell me exactly what your agenda was?"

The orange juice shook in Tiya's hand, but Sefra had the calm only a married woman could exercise. Seeing Tiya now, Sefra could hardly comprehend what had made her so jealous. Perhaps it was because Tiya was three years older and got along with Lyle. Or finding out that Tiya had gone to the same university as her husband. Perhaps it was the thought that Lyle had chosen something more worthy than herself. But that seemed so far from the truth when Sefra faced Tiya. And for the first time, Sefra saw in her eyes a fragile, empty vessel.

Tiya finally spoke. "I shouldn't have done it. Your husband, I mean Mr. Fairthorne, is a very kind man. He believes in what I can do for him, and I find his encouragement a wonderful thing. For a time, I thought he was mine."

"Really?" Sefra scoffed, folding her arms. Deep down she was praying that the kiss had led to nothing more than just that, and if the truth could be told, she hardly knew what she would do if Tiya admitted that it had gone any further.

"He was very lonely last Christmas," Tiya explained meekly. "I thought . . . maybe I could make him happy. You had abandoned him."

"I did no such thing," Sefra countered, even though the truth stuck in her throat. Her stubbornness had been the cause of everything—that, and her jealousy and anger that anyone dare try to take her husband.

"He felt deserted," Tiya insisted harshly. "He was very sad. I tried to help him."

"Tried to bed him," Sefra shot back, the very thought of it making her stomach turn.

"And so what if I did?" Tiya admitted, in fighting spirit. "You were not there for him. Lyle is a hardworking man and deserves a wife who cares."

"How dare you tell me I don't care for my husband!" Sefra seethed, her anger beginning to froth. "He means everything to me."

"You say that so easily," Tiya snarled. "I tried to give him what he wanted, affection and love. That's why on Christmas Eve, after the office party, I kissed him under the mistletoe. And he kissed me back," she lied for leverage. "He needed someone and you weren't there."

Sefra saw red. "You tried to steal him," she accused hotly.

"I tried to do more than that," Tiya proclaimed, seemingly without a shred of conscience.

Sefra's mouth fell open at Tiya's boldness.

Enraged, Sefra found herself clutching at the glass of orange juice in Tiya's hand. Tiya held on so tightly that she eventually pulled back and dropped the glass. Sefra watched Tiya's horror as the stain soaked into the satiny fabric of her kimono.

"Your employment contract has just been terminated," Sefra said tersely.

Tiya gathered her second wind. "We'll see what Mr. Fairthorne has to say about that," she insisted, quickly using the back of one sleeve to blot her dress.

"My husband will agree with me," Sefra said, satisfied with the decision of their last conversation. "You see, we resolved a lot of issues today."

Tiya remained unmoved. "You don't realize how much he values me working on the sequel to *Temple of Love*," she continued. "I have many connections in Japan to give it the springboard it needs. Mr. Fairthorne will never risk eliminating me from the team."

"Then you don't know," Sefra snapped. "I've set up my own company. Grayson's Media Games Ltd. has just completed a demo of the new sequel—*my* version of the game. So whatever you and Lyle were working on is, as of today, obsolete."

Tiya's mouth fell open. "Does Mr. Fairthorne know?"

"He was told this morning," Sefra said smugly. "You see, as his wife, I needed to remind him that *Temple of Love* is our baby. You are not part of what we started. You may be very talented and have a lot to offer, but your services are no longer required on my sequel."

Tiya's eyes narrowed. "You're a—"

"Cheetah lady," Sefra interrupted, walking briskly toward the door, her hand braced on the doorknob. "And loving every minute of how fast I can run with an idea," she added, opening the door.

To their amazement, Lyle was standing in the doorway, his hand in midair preparing to knock. His eyes darted from Sefra to Tiya, blinking in confusion at seeing them together. Looking at the stain on Tiya's dress and judging from the look in his wife's eyes, Lyle knew there had been trouble.

"What's going on?" he demanded, barging into the room, closing the door behind him. "And I want the truth."

To Sefra's amazement, Tiya immediately bowed to Lyle in regal Japanese fashion. She kept her head down for what seemed like forever.

"Mr. Fairthorne," Tiya began meekly. "I came to deliver your documents."

Lyle charted her pale face and instantly shifted his gaze to Sefra. "And?" His question was aimed at his wife.

"I squeezed her drier than a camel's backside," Sefra admitted without pretense. "She's not going to railroad me out of my own marriage or worm her way into your affections." Turning toward Tiya, she added, "Get out."

"This is unfair dismissal," Tiya bleated, turning toward Lyle. "Mr. Fairthorne, I have been very loyal to your company. My employment contract—"

"Has just been revoked," Sefra declared, pulling the envelope Tiya was holding from her hand.

Lyle tried to interrupt, attempting to minimize the animosity between the two. "Ladies—"

"You give that back," Tiya demanded, making every effort to snatch the envelope from Sefra. "They're the Matsushita contracts for the new version of the game."

A silence fell as Sefra's gaze moved from Tiya to Lyle. Her stomach churned with panic.

"What's this about?" she demanded instantly, brandishing the envelope in midair. When she failed to receive an answer right away, but instead caught the sheepish look on her husband's face, Sefra immediately ripped open the envelope. She pulled out several sheets of white paper clipped together and scanned the licensing agreement. Startled, she stared at Lyle. "And I thought I was the sly one," Sefra growled, throwing the papers into his chest.

They fell with the envelope to the floor, where he stared at them. "Sefra, it's not what you think," he began slowly, unsure she would believe a word he told her.

"No?" Sefra mocked, shifting her gaze to Tiya. Tears filled her eyes. Tiya was Lyle's "good friend" and confidante, a woman who thought she could take Sefra's place in his life. Sefra was none the wiser to his negotiating the *Temple of Love* with Matsushita, but Tiya knew. She had always known. "Get out," she repeated.

Tiya looked triumphant. "We agreed to a licensing agreement," she trumpeted, "whether you have a new sequel or not."

"That's not true anymore," Lyle interjected, taking a step toward Sefra, protectively. "I don't want to sign," he told Tiya.

"What?" she said, confused. "I don't understand. You asked me to keep your appointment today in your absence and—"

"It's not what I . . . we want," Lyle declared, shaking his head, his eyes fixed on Sefra. He caught Sefra's eye and continued, "I've changed my mind."

Tiya's face turned red and she clenched her jaw tightly as she watched Lyle take hold of Sefra's hand. "Mr. Fairthorne—"

No sooner had she spoken than the floor beneath her feet began to shake. Lyle and Sefra felt it, too. The tremor was so sudden, items in the room began to topple over. Bouquets of flowers slid across the carpeted floor. The pane glass in the windows began to shake. The ceiling light danced in all directions as Sefra felt the room sway. It was only when she squeezed Lyle's hand tightly and began to feel the floor beneath her that it suddenly dawned on her.

"It's an earthquake," Tiya declared, in a commanding voice. "We need to get to ground level."

She was out the door in an instant. Sefra and Lyle did not have time think. When a light fixture on the ceiling shook, Sefra picked up her electronic room key as she and Lyle ran for their lives.

Eight

11:57 P.M.

It was not quite the Namazu catfish shaking his tail, or so Lyle thought as he held on to to Sefra's hand amidst the crowd on the sidewalk outside the Sheraton Sapporo. Panicked guests were surprised to hear that it wasn't a strong earthquake and that there could be aftershocks later that night. There were no immediate reports of damage or injuries and the hotel assured them that there was nothing to worry about.

Lyle was just relieved that they had all survived the ordeal. He had never contemplated finding himself caught up in an earthquake, and the last eight minutes had been just that. It had been scary. Not quite what he expected to experience on Valentine's night, and now, with the commotion subsiding, Lyle turned to face Sefra, shivering in her velvet dress. Lyle immediately removed his jacket and handed it to her.

It was one thing being caught in the middle of an earthquake, quite another to be caught in the middle of a battle between two women. How on earth had he let things get so out of hand? All Lyle knew was that he loved his wife and that he enjoyed his friendship with Tiya. Was it too much to have both? If Sefra were to answer that question, she would say, yes, it was. Lyle quickly came to realize in one swift moment that there were rules among women that he knew nothing about, and that he was in a situation where he had to make a choice. If he did not want to lose his wife, he had to make that choice fast.

As he glanced at Sefra, he was unsettled by her vacant, confused look, not quite attached to anything that was going on around her. He thought about how he had neglected her to the point that she no longer had any need for his support. It frightened him. His very actions had allowed his wife to take control of her own life, and that in itself was a troubling thought, he reluctantly admitted.

"Sefra?" He held her hand and was surprised when she immediately pulled it away and proceeded to drape his jacket around her shoulders. "Are you okay?"

Sefra heard the question, only she was unsure how to answer. Was she okay? At that moment, she was in an emotional daze. Throughout the entire earthquake, she had been thinking that people were made unhappy by two things in their lives: the bad things that happened to them and the good things that didn't. Everything else was just one big question mark and that's why there were people walking around with puzzled, disgruntled looks on their faces.

She did not want to be part of that generation—resentful, miserable—spending every day dissatisfied on so many levels, looking back at life with regrets. She had given her heart to a wonderful man whom she still loved. What scared her was that Lyle seemed eternally hopeful that there was something better.

Was she okay? Not really.

"Lyle . . ." She did not know what to say. All she knew was that she did not want them to keep looking back and blaming each other.

"Let's wait until we get back inside," Lyle said, acknowledging the concern in his wife's voice.

As the alarm on his watch sounded, indicating that it was now midnight, the hotel's employees were outside, making sure everyone was accounted for before rounding up the guests so that they could return to their rooms. Tea, coffee, and orange juice were being offered in the dining room.

An orderly line began to form almost immediately, one that Tiya could not join. She looked at Sefra and Lyle, and conceded defeat.

"I am no longer a part of your company," she told Lyle. "Today has been a dishonor."

Lyle spoke sympathetically, aware that he had misjudged the situation. "I'll make sure you get a good reference."

Tiya nodded her head, then turned and, within minutes, disappeared into a taxi.

A trembling silence engulfed Lyle and Sefra so profound that Sefra felt relieved when Clive and Zara rushed up from behind them. Their enthusiasm was just what she needed after such a tumultuous episode.

"Did you feel it?" Clive asked excitedly. "A real earthquake. It was awesome."

"Not quite like the movies, though," Zara said, giggling.

"It was a tremor," Lyle corrected, somewhat surprised by Clive and Zara's exuberance.

"C'mon." Clive laughed, joining the line behind them. "We were all evacuated."

"As a precautionary measure," Lyle said.

Clive looked at his sister and realized that something was wrong. He measured the coolness between her and Lyle and surmised that they had not quite resolved their problems. Of course, it was none of his business and after being punched by Lyle, he was not about to intrude again. Instead, Clive kept his distance.

"You two care to join us for coffee?" he asked, his voice softening slightly.

Sefra glanced at Lyle, then said no. "I'm flying back to Britain tomorrow night with you guys, so I want to get plenty of sleep."

Her answer seemed to put Lyle a little off balance. "I think I'll try and get some sleep too," he said.

Clive nodded and put an affectionate arm around Zara. "Okay," he said, just as the line began to move into the lobby. "We'll see you two tomorrow."

Sefra sent him an acknowledging nod of her head, then turned to Lyle. "We need to talk about our marriage," she told him suddenly. "Your room or mine?"

Lyle was so taken aback, he hardly knew how to answer. "Mine," he blurted.

Sefra nodded and gestured that he lead the way. They took the crowded elevator in complete silence until it arrived on Lyle's floor. There was a brief rush as people stepped out of the car, then Sefra followed her husband as he proceeded down the long hallway. He swiped his electronic key card and immediately turned on the lights to assess the damage.

Only a few toiletries on a table beside his bed were on the floor, along with a lamp shade. Other than that, the room felt slightly cold. As Sefra entered, Lyle walked over to the large windows that revealed a darkened sky, closing a small one at the top before pulling the drapes shut. He then adjusted the wall thermostat and placed his room card on a table nearby while Sefra took off his jacket.

"Tea? Coffee?" Lyle asked, heading straight for the minibar. "Or something stronger to help you sleep through the aftershocks?"

Sefra accepted instantly. "Vodka and tonic."

Her choice raised an eyebrow as Lyle went about the task of making the cocktails. His own choice was brandy on ice. He told himself he needed it. A slight numbing of the emotions was just what was required before beginning "the talk." He felt the weight of it as he carried the drinks across the room toward Sefra, who was seated on the edge of his bed. He joined her there and they both took a drink. Sefra needed a little more than her usual quota before she steadied her grip on her glass.

"Do you want a divorce?" she asked, getting straight to the point.

"N-no!" Lyle stammered, facing her. "Do you?"

Sefra shook her head. "No."

Satisfied, they moved on. "What is it?" Lyle asked, as he felt the rush of blood running through his veins.

"I don't want any more lies," Sefra said quietly.

"There have been no lies," Lyle assured her.

Sefra chuckled. "Haven't there?" she asked. "You ruined part of our Valentine's Day by not only telling me that Tiya Nosaka was here in Japan until the last minute, but then announcing that you had kissed her. Why hide it all from me in the first place?"

"I didn't think it was important," Lyle protested.

"Not to add that she attended the Matsushita meeting for you while you were with me," Sefra finished.

"Touché," Lyle said derisively. "There's the matter of your meeting with Asahi."

"Which was my only deceit concerning you," Sefra replied, "and I did not entertain any discussions about licensing *Temple of Love,* unlike you, who seemed ready to sign a contract. That means you had already started negotiations."

Lyle was silent, knowing he couldn't deny her point. "Yes, we did," he said finally, taking a large gulp of brandy from his glass. "Tiya knew some friends who were able to talk to some people and managed to speed up the process."

"And all this without my knowledge," Sefra said. "Have you any idea how humiliated that makes me feel? It's like I've been slapped in the face. All these lies have left me feeling like I'm constantly on shaky ground." She paused to gather herself. "This earthquake tonight just made everything seem all too real. I've been living on the fringes of my own marriage and not in it."

Lyle understood everything. "I'm sorry," he said. "I didn't mean to hurt you. I just wanted to . . . save what we had."

"Which is impossible to do if there is another woman involved," Sefra concluded quietly. "That woman nearly ruined and derailed everything we have, and you gave her the control. How am I ever going to forgive you for that?"

"Sefra!" Lyle felt his heart drop. "You're making too much of this. Tiya is not my wife."

"I know," Sefra said. "I am. And you lost sight of that. Suddenly, I didn't feel special to you anymore even though I knew I had everything that she didn't."

Sefra had always thought that she was everything her husband had ever wanted, that she was the one to fulfill his every wish and desire. She was his companion and friend. His lover. And one day, hopefully, mother to his children. These were the reasons why she had accepted his hand in marriage. United forever.

"I never lost sight of how much I love you," Lyle told her truthfully. "You were and still are everything to me."

"Then why didn't you show me?" Sefra swallowed, taking another measure of vodka and tonic.

"I did, today," Lyle said. "I flooded your room with the same bouquet of flowers you had on our wedding day. Believe me, it was not easy phoning a florist from the men's room at the beer garden to arrange it all. I thought the lilies, roses, and tulips would remind you that we hadn't lost that magic."

Sefra felt the tears well up in her eyes. "We haven't,"

she said, forcing them back, a slight smile dancing across her face as she recalled their lovemaking.

"No, we haven't," Lyle agreed, remembering Sefra's naked body.

"So, where do we go from here?" Sefra asked, knowing they needed some kind of resolution before they could move on.

Lyle drained what was left of his brandy and rose up from the bed to place his empty glass on the minibar. Still standing, he dug his hands deep into his trouser pockets and contemplated Sefra with hope in his eyes.

"We merge Grayson's Media Games to the Fairthorne Interactive Corporation and use it to design games for conglomerates who have ideas but who don't want the unnecessary expense of setting up their own in-house productions," he began on a steady breath. "As for the *Temple of Love*—"

"I meant about us," Sefra whispered, her eyebrows raised as she looked at the tall, muscular frame of her husband, "not the companies or the game."

Lyle sighed, aware of his mistake. "I'm sorry," he said. "About us." It seemed so daunting a question for the answer to rest solely with him. "I want it to be like it was before."

"It can never be quite like before," Sefra said slowly. "We've both grown and learned lessons about trust and what we expect from each other."

"Then . . . let's take it one day at a time," Lyle murmured, retaking his seat beside Sefra on the bed. "No marriage is perfect, and so much of what we have is wonderful. We both know we don't want to jump ship, so we have to start working on compromises with each other. Like I said, I can't cross this distance by myself."

"I know." Sefra nodded in agreement. "We can also start to make more time for each other—quality time," she said tersely. "Where we can go for walks in the park, swimming, bowling, to the gym, dancing, out for dinner, weekends away, take in the theater or cinema. When was the last time we saw a movie together?"

Lyle shrugged. He couldn't recall. It dawned on him even more just how much Sefra had been neglected. "Oh, babe," he exclaimed. "You really have suffered."

"Yes, I have," she said. She downed what little was left of her vodka and tonic and handed Lyle the glass.

"You know," he said, rising from the bed to place the empty glass on the minibar, "when we get back to London, we should go away for the weekend. Back to Portmeirion, where we spent our honeymoon."

"That sounds like a great idea," Sefra said, a broad smile now lighting up her face. "I really loved it up there. Such a fairy-tale village. What was the name of the guy who designed it all again?"

"Clough Williams-Ellis," Lyle said. "He began the whole project in 1926, and over fifty years built his boyhood dream. I really liked the Portmeirion champagne."

"And I want to visit the Cadwaladers ice cream parlor again," Sefra said, chuckling as she recalled how much she loved the black cherry.

"What, no shopping?" Lyle smiled. "Homemade jams, biscuits, tea towels?"

Sefra's smile widened. "I'll just settle for a walk along the beach with you."

"Like a second honeymoon?" Lyle added.

He reached out and touched Sefra's hand, only this time she did not pull back from him. Instead, Sefra squeezed his fingers affectionately, a sign that they were going to be all right. No more distrust, stubbornness, or rivalry. The battle between them was now over, and as far as she was concerned, they had a lot of making up to do. So when Lyle leaned forward and brushed her mouth with his, she did not resist.

Their lips met. The crushing kiss swept her into Lyle's arms. It was long and passionate, and filled with desire. Lyle absorbed the pink flesh of Sefra's mouth with swift, soft movements, eager to delight. She kissed him back greedily, deliciously aware that Lyle had lowered her onto the bed, his hand delicately caressing her neck, enjoying the fluttering sensation that ran through his fingers.

Sefra felt the quickness of Lyle's breath and felt a deep sense of pleasure that she could still evoke such yearnings within him again. She was also aware that she did not want to rush things now that they had reached an understanding, but chose to complete their Valentine's evening fully relaxed. Releasing her mouth, Sefra quickly placed a finger against Lyle's lips.

"I want a bath," she whispered.

Lyle was baffled. "At this time of night?"

"Good things come to those who wait," Sefra said, rising abruptly from the bed. "Don't worry," she added, seeing the panicked look in Lyle's eyes as he lay on the bed. "Your bathroom will do."

Within seconds, she was lost in it. Moments later Lyle heard the water running. His heart beating madly, he was unsure whether to join Sefra or await her return. He decided on the latter and stretched out on the bed, feeling he needed to unwind, too.

Lyle stared at the ceiling, planning his seduction. Every part of his body became rigid with the thought of being with Sefra. He would kiss every part of her until she begged for mercy. And when he had finished ravishing her, he would hold her in his arms and rock her to sleep like he had done in Portmeirion on their honeymoon. With that thought, Lyle closed his eyes.

12:33 A.M.; February 15

"Lyle?"

Sefra roused him until he was awake. Lyle blinked for several seconds before he fully opened his eyes. He was lying flat on his back on his bed, having fallen asleep. It was several more seconds before he remembered his last train of thought. He glanced at Sefra, dressed in one of his pajamas.

"Are you going somewhere?" he joked.

Sefra giggled. "Back to my room if you're not out of your clothes."

Lyle was up in an instant, shedding his trousers and shirt. In his underpants, he pulled Sefra onto the bed and gave her a huge hug, happy that they were starting over again with a better understanding of each other. He planted a kiss on her forehead and then gazed into her eyes. Her stare matched his own.

"Aftershock?" Sefra whispered, aware that they were still in Japan.

Lyle blinked. "Probably," he said, sinking deeply into the moment.

He kissed her again, much stronger, taking her lips in slow mouthfuls until he felt Sefra sink into his arms and lose herself completely in him. His tongue plunged in and she closed her eyes, feeling lost in a universe where only she and Lyle existed. It was beautiful there. So peaceful and tranquil. This was where she wanted to be. Right here, in her husband's arms.

Slowly, he unbuttoned and removed his pajama shirt, finding her naked flesh beneath. As Sefra wriggled out of his shirt, Lyle groped for one of her nipples with his lips, taking it into his mouth and savoring the way the rigid nipple tickled his tongue. Sefra's response urged him to seek out the other nipple, caressing it with his lips, enjoying the way her body moved beneath him as the pleasure shook her bones.

As she coaxed him with her fingers, Lyle's hands pushed the pajama bottoms down her legs, delighted that she was wearing nothing underneath. His lips moved lower to her belly button, licking the navel just the way she liked it. Sefra gasped, another reminder to Lyle just how much she enjoyed what he was doing. He raised his head and looked at her. Sefra was that angelic picture he had always carried with him in his head.

"I don't know whether to start from the bottom and work my way up," he whispered in amusement. "Or from the top and work my way down."

"You're doing just fine starting from the middle and working your way around," Sefra teased in return.

Lyle didn't need any further instructions. Gently, he spread Sefra's legs and placed his mouth where she liked it most. Sefra squealed. What she felt was no aftershock. Even another earthquake could not have moved her like this. Her entire body shuddered in pure ecstasy. It was sheer, exquisite delight. She almost exploded from the strength of it. And it was not over.

Lyle quickly braced himself on his knees and removed his underpants. Pulling Sefra up, he cradled her against his knees and slowly entered her, pulling her to his chest, his hands working up and down her back in slow caresses as she rocked against him. The intensity of the climax made everything so right. It had been a traumatic Valentine's Day with one battle after another. But he had won his wife back before the weekend was through. He was the winner.

It was what he wanted, to be this close again. No other woman could make him feel the way Sefra did right now. She was like a glove, fitting him perfectly. He liked the way her mahogany skin—so soft and velvety—felt beneath his fingertips. The primal scent of her body aroused his own animal instincts in a way that made his throbbing groin burn to be with her time and time again. It felt right. She was right. And with that came the most immense pleasure only this woman could give him. He exploded in ecstasy.

Later, as they cuddled in each other's arms and his watch beeped, indicating that it was one o'clock in the morning, Lyle stared at the ceiling.

"Sefra?" he whispered, hoping she was still awake.

"What?" she said sleepily.

"When we get back to London, I'd like to see your DVD demo for *Temple of Love*."

"Of course," Sefra agreed.

"I'd also like to introduce a new character," Lyle added, knowing Sefra's curiosity would be piqued. "A seraph of passion."

"Is there such a thing?" Sefra asked.

"There is now," Lyle said. "He'll be like a sort of guardian angel, making sure that Erosino and Venusina communicate together so they stay together."

"Like a cherub?" Sefra asked.

"Well . . . maybe like a spirit . . ." Lyle amended. "I've also been thinking . . ."

As the night fell and another aftershock—not of the seismic kind—took over their bedroom for a second time, the two lovers lived happily ever after.

Eject disc.

ABOUT THE AUTHOR

Sonia Icilyn was born in Sheffield, England, where she still lives with her daughter in a small village that she describes as "typically British, quiet, and where the old money is." She graduated with a distinction-level private secretary's certificate in business and commerce and also has a master's degree in writing. *Significant Other,* her first romance novel, was published in 1993.

Since then, she has added six titles to her name. She has been featured in *Black Elegance* and *Today's Black Woman*, and her work has appeared on the *Ebony* recommended reading list. Sonia is the founder and organizer of the African Arts and Culture Expo and the British Black Expo in Great Britain. She is also CEO of the Peacock Company. She loves to travel and realistically depicts her characters from the fine tapestry of the African diaspora. *Roses Are Red* was her first title for Arabesque, followed by *Island Romance*, and the sequel to *Roses Are Red* entitled *Violets Are Blue, Infatuation, Possession* and *Smitten*. She would love to hear from her readers at:

PO Box 438
Sheffield S1 4YX
England

or e-mail her by visiting her Web site at:
www.soniaicilyn.com.

The Price of Kissing

KIM LOUISE

ACKNOWLEDGMENTS

So many people continue to support me and keep me inspired to write the best stories I can write. Sista Girl Book Club, thank you for being a strong, positive group of women and helping me "keep it real." Cameo Romance Writers, thank you for being a source of inspiration and enthusiasm about writing. Elaine Miller, for your helpful suggestions. Beth, Andrea, Diana, and everyone at The Bookworm, thank you, thank you, thank you for supporting every book I've ever written. You all are wonderful! Lisa Juhl, Sue Todd, Darla Scheuring, Mark Schreier, and so many others who regularly ask about my writing. Last, but not least, ReTonya Lasley. As many times as I've thanked you, it never seems like enough, but you put your foot in it this time . . . or should I say your imagination? Can I get *you* anything else?

One

Before the doorbell rang, she knew he was there. Ashley Allgood smiled at the silken ripple in the atmosphere she had come to know as Gordon Steele. They had met a year ago when he'd seen her creating a window display for Soul Traveler's Bookstore in the Little Five Points District where she worked in Atlanta.

He was all flash. Well groomed. Well dressed. Well spoken. He was also very handsome, very persistent, and full of himself. He'd spent the better part of an hour trying to persuade her that she should go out with him.

When she refused, he came back the next day and the next. Finally, he gave up. But not before something between them clicked. That something grew into the best friendship that she'd ever had.

The goddess had truly blessed her.

"Happy anniversary!" Gordon shouted, tada-ing through the doorway. His arms stretched as wide as his smile. Ashley smirked.

"What?" He pouted. "No 'Same to you, Big Daddy'?"

Ashley held back the chuckle threatening to reward the tall, slender man. "Happy anniversary, yes. 'Big Daddy,' no."

He closed the door and strutted over to the desk. "You were supposed to jump into my arms and wrap your legs around my waist."

She touched his forehead and shook her head. "No. You don't *feel* sick."

He took her hand and kissed the back of it. Then he lingered near her wrist, inhaling a moment. His warm breath was moist on her skin like soft dew.

"How do you do that?" he asked.

She snatched her hand away. Ashley wasn't easily embarrassed. But Gordon's frequent reference to the way she smelled always made her stomach do cartwheels.

"It's a natural thang," she proclaimed, slightly embarrassed.

"Today it's just a shower, but I like it anyway."

Gordon claimed that the day they had met she smelled like a fresh spring rain. She wasn't wearing perfume and she always washed her clothes in unscented detergent. So it was her natural scent that he'd been commenting on. Her own body fragrance. Whenever they'd been close, brushed up against one another, or come within sniffing distance, he'd made similar remarks. Each time, he qualified her description. Sometimes she was a storm, sometimes a well, sometimes a waterfall. And at other times, like today, just a simple shower or cloudburst.

"Yeah, well, this shower is busy," she said, sashaying away from him.

Gordon followed, walking through a room that could have been taken straight out of Soothsayer's Digest, if there was one. Her furniture was a rich marriage of maroon and gold. The smoky scent of incense burning hung in the air. Ceramic bowls held large gemstones and crystals that caught the sunlight and refracted it in rainbows of color on the walls. Her maroon carpet was so thick it covered her toes. And most importantly, her house was never, ever cold.

The inside of Ashley's kitchen was humid and fragrant. It smelled like flowers steaming. "What are you doing?" he asked.

"Making soap. I was bored."

At five seven with thick curves, corkscrew curls, guile-less eyes, and the demeanor of a high priestess, Ashley never ceased to amaze him. "I think when most women get bored, they watch a movie or something," he said.

Her brown eyes sparkled mischievously. "I'm not most women."

"You can say that again!"

Gordon remembered a conversation they had had when he and Ashley first met. He'd been attracted to her neo-soul, beatnik, spiritual bohemian style. He never tired of hearing her tell that story.

"How did you acquire your taste in . . . everything?" he asked.

Ashley smiled, batting her eyelashes playfully. "You mean, why am I so different?"

"Yeah. Not that it's not cool. But you have to admit, your style is . . ."

"My style." Ashley nodded. "I've just never wanted to be like anyone else. I've always wanted to do my own thing, you know. Anyone with a few dollars can buy de-signer clothing, no offense."

Gordon grinned and popped his collar. "None taken, sweetheart."

"But this outfit," she said, gesturing to the white-lace piece of fabric she'd twisted into a tube top and the skirt that had obviously been a pair of jeans once. "This is me right now. The mood I'm in. My soul's place today."

"So you just decided one day that you'd had enough with convention and that you were going to invent your own?"

"Yes and no. I've never told you about my aunt Zoe. She

wasn't my real aunt, just a good friend of my mother's. My family used to go over to her house when I was little.

"Truth be told, my sisters and brother were afraid of Aunt Zoe. Her hair was long and bright white. She always wore long flowing caftans and what seemed to my young mind like a million bracelets on her wrist. She let me play dress-up with her clothes and jewelry one day. I think I ended up wearing a turban, earrings that were much too big for my ears, a skirt made from an ottoman covering, and an ankle bracelet. I begged my mother to let me wear my new outfit to school. She gave in and the kids teased me like you would not believe. But the funny thing was, I didn't care. My aunt Zoe told me that I looked lovely and that if I liked what I had on, that was all that mattered.

"As I got older, I started examining everything in my life, what I ate, what I believed, my relationship with God. I knew I could make each area in my life better if I decided for myself what those things meant to me and created my own vision of what it meant to be Ashley Allgood."

She smiled and stretched out her arms. "Who I am today is the result of that decision."

She went on and Gordon was intrigued. "That's why I live in Edgewood. It's quiet, simple. People here have big houses, but they mow their own grass. And it's just minutes away from Little Five Points, which I love!"

He watched as her eyes lit up with pride.

"What other shopping district can you go to and get a henna tattoo, your belly button pierced, purchase vintage clothing, retro furniture, and healing crystals all within blocks of each other?"

Gordon nodded in understanding. Ashley felt at home here. Even people who dance to the beat of a different drum like to know they are appreciated—that they fit in somewhere. That's why she lived near Little Five Points. That's why she worked there.

Deep down inside, Gordon knew he would one day have to settle down and discover where he belonged—where he fit in.

One day.

But until that day came, he would be content with his job as a sales recruiter and his role as Ashley Allgood's best friend.

He grabbed a handful of soy nuts from a bowl on the counter and watched as Ashley donned gloves as thick as rubber boots. He leaned against the wall as he crunched his snack while she poured the thick aromatic mélange from a double boiler into row after row of various-sized molds. Squares, ovals, and stars were filled with the multicolored batter still steaming from the stove.

"I just have to let those cool," she said, removing her gloves.

There are some men that take looking good very seriously. Gordon was one of those men. He was always immaculate—never a hair on his head out of place. With his suits freshly pressed and tailored, he always looked like a model from an executive fashion catalog.

One glance at Gordon and she could tell by his aura that he had just been with a woman or was sure he would be soon. His personal energy always glowed a bright orange red whenever that happened or was about to.

Funny how the longer she knew him, the more his sexual escapades with his many women bothered her. "So who is it this week?"

Gordon sat down at the kitchen table, clasped his hands behind his head, and smiled. "This week it's Janice King."

"I would ask you to tell me about her, but after a year I know your tastes pretty well."

Gordon grunted dismissively, as if she couldn't possibly know what she was talking about.

"I see you are a nonbeliever. Okay, how's this . . . she's about four inches taller than I am, although we probably weigh the same. Her hair is permed bone-straight and she wears it loose. She always wears a suit, and she says things like *pushing the envelope* and *paradigm shift* in polite conversation. I'll bet you a back rub her skin is the color of dirty milk."

Gordon laughed loud and long. "What are you, psychic?"

She winked. "Maybe a little."

"Sometimes you scare me when you do that."

"Sometimes I scare myself," she admitted.

"And for the millionth, no, bizillionth time . . . I am having *safe* sex."

She raised a doubting eyebrow. "Every time?"

"Every time," he said emphatically. "Since you're all up in my Kool-Aid, let me get in yours. What happened to your boy Congo?"

"He and I broke up. For good this time."

"There is a God!" Gordon declared.

"I feel like the last two years of my life have been wasted energy."

"Forget about it. He's a flake!"

"He's *not* a flake. He's a free spirit."

Gordon grumbled. "Anyone that names themselves after a river is a stone-cold F-L-A-K-E. Believe me, sweetheart, you're better off."

"I thought you liked Congo. You two were always laughing and joking together."

"I did that because he was your man and I'm your friend. Sometimes people have to put up with all the stupid stuff their friends do. That's an unspoken rule of friendship."

He looked over at her while she fussed with her

molds. She was always doing stuff like that, especially when she was a little unhappy. "So are you . . . okay?"

"Yeah, I'm fine. I mean, there was always this voice in my head telling me that Congo was perpetrating."

"What do you mean?" he asked, thinking that those doubts had not always been in her head. He had suggested to her, more than once, that Congo might not be all that he seemed.

"I mean he took off his caftan, put on a Polo shirt and Dockers, changed his name back to James Wickerson, and went to work for Coca-Cola in the training department as an administrative assistant."

Gordon's raucous laughter filled the room.

Ashley rolled her eyes. "Just don't say it."

He paused for a moment, a big cake-eating grin spread across his face. "I knew it! I knew it! I knew it!"

She shook her head. He got up, stood behind her, and pulled her to him. "Ashley Allgood, as long as you've got me in your life, you don't have to worry about a thing." He kissed her on the temple. "Now take off your shirt and let me rub you the right way. I've got to settle my debt."

She chuckled. "You are so full of yourself."

"Umm-hmm. And I have every right to be."

After giving her a back rub, Gordon ushered her into the living room and removed an envelope from his jacket pocket. It was their one-year anniversary as friends, and she knew they'd be celebrating.

Ashley took the envelope. She was so happy to receive it, the envelope felt warm in her hands. Opening it quickly, she tried to imagine what might be inside. A poem? A letter? A bookmark? She opened it and removed two tickets. Curious, she blinked rapidly in surprise. Cirque du Soleil! Gordon had given her two tickets to see the popular Montreal-based circus troupe.

She opened her mouth to speak, but couldn't. She'd wanted to see a live performance for years. She'd spoken of it whenever the spirit moved her, which was often. And Gordon must have been listening.

She leaped into his arms, wrapped her legs around his waist, and hugged him tightly.

"Happy anniversary!" he responded, savoring the heat of her body against his. "Heck, if I'd known that all it took was Cirque du Soleil tickets to get you in my arms, I'd have purchased two for every day of the year since we've met! Big Daddy knows what you like." And he did. He'd seen the way she glowed any time she talked about the performance troupe.

When she finally found her voice, she relaxed her embrace. "You have the heart of an angel, Gordon Steele! My soul is soaring!"

"Glad you like it," he said, taking a good look at her. *How does she do that?* he wondered. *When she's happy her entire body just . . . glows.*

She turned her back to him and walked away as if deep in thought. "Now who can I get to go with me?"

"Don't even think about it, Allgood. One of those tickets is mine."

She spun around smiling. "Just teasing!"

Gordon pursed his lips. "You've talked about it so much, I have to find out for myself if it's as good as you say."

"Good? They are not just good. They are a metaphysical experiential exercise in cosmic correction!" Ashley proclaimed, heading to the coffee table where a package the size of a shoe box stuck out like a weird and wonderful centerpiece. "Now admit it. You thought I was going to invite someone else. I had you goin'."

"I don't think so," he said, scoffing.

"Betcha I did!"

"Betcha you didn't!"

There it was again. That healthy competition they had with each other. They were always wagering on something. The weather. Award shows. How long his relationships would last. The bet was always something simple like dinner, a movie, or a back rub. The only thing was, Ashley won nearly every time. Gordon promised himself that one day he would win one of their little wagers, and he would win big.

Ashley handed him the box. "Now mine," she said, proudly beaming like the cat that swallowed the canary. "Happy anniversary."

Covered with buttons, postage stamps, fabrics, scraps of metallic gold paper, and watercolors, the package gave no clue as to what might be inside. She was a chameleon and yet he suspected that what lay beneath was deeper than any ocean. The outside of the box was an eclectic mix of colors and textures, much like Ashley herself.

In their yearlong friendship, she'd worn her hair in different styles—curls that looked like rotini pasta, a Jackson 5 Afro, and bone-thick braids. As for her clothes, they ranged from ancient Mayan princess with leather and fringe to east African Masai with gigantic earrings that resembled round rainbows. Once, when she'd worn a scarf as a halter top and allowed the triangle of red fabric to simply drape over her unencumbered breasts, he'd swallowed hard and mumbled, "Heaven help us all." But the funny thing was, no matter what Ashley wore, she always, *always* looked good.

"Are you meditating or are you going to open it?"

He shook the box playfully. "I'm going to open it!"

The lid came off easily and so did his cool. He recognized most of the contents immediately. He swallowed the strange lump in his throat.

"Ash . . ."

"It's a remembrance box," she said quickly and gleefully like a bubbly child.

Among simple arrangements of blue-violet forget-me-nots, there were receipts, ticket stubs, program booklets, napkins, matchbooks, and photographs. Souvenirs from all of the places they'd gone together or been to while on double dates. They'd covered a lot of territory in a year. Not a week went by that they didn't do something together. And now the sum total of those memories was in his hands.

"What's this?" he asked, lifting a copper earring.

"That's half of the pair of earrings I was wearing the day we met."

Gordon smiled. "And this?"

"That," she said, grinning at the small pad of paper, "is so you can keep track of all of the bets you lose and write me IOUs."

He had to laugh. Whenever he lost a bet, it usually took him forever to pay up. He made a mental note to change that.

Ashley Allgood never ceased to make him feel happy. He set the box on a corner table. "Come here, Allgood."

She stepped closer. "Yes?"

Locking his hands around the back of her neck, Gordon stared into her eyes. They were lovely eyes, eyes he'd grown used to. "Okay, listen up. I'm only going to say this once." He took a deep breath. "You're a good friend, Ash." Then he pulled her close, so she couldn't see the seriousness in his face. "I love you."

She hugged him back. Her warmth resonated and touched him through her soft hands. "You're my best friend and my greatest joy, Gordon Steele. I love you, too."

"All right, all right," he proclaimed, pushing back after a few moments. "Enough of all this mushy stuff. What have you got to eat up in this camp? Brother is starving!"

TWO

Entering Ashley's house felt like walking into a priestess's spell chamber. The air was thick with incense, scented candles, and potpourri. The living room was bathed in subdued light from orange lightbulbs that gave a golden cast to her teak and bamboo furniture. There were candles on every table and shelf, burned down almost to the base. Lapis, amethyst, and violet touchstones filled bowls on the tables. The music of the ocean, jungle, or tropical storms played softly from tall slender speakers.

It seemed Ashley changed the arrangement of her furniture every other month. Today everything was pushed up against the east wall. Because of that, there was a clear wide path to every part of the house.

Ashley had a reason for everything. The last time she did something like this, she said it was to allow creative energy to flow through her home. Gordon wondered what today's reason was.

"Welcome, Gordon." She had left the door unlocked for him.

"Aw, looka here, looka here! Girl, you look so good, we might have to stay home."

"Why?"

"Because no one is going to be able to concentrate on the show with you looking like that. Least of all me. Do they have the performances on DVD?"

Ashley shook her head like she always did.

He greeted her with a sweet kiss on the forehead and inhaled. "Rain woman." His pet name for her. He'd tried to kiss her soon after they first met. She'd let him know that she was "in a situation" but not before he'd gotten close enough to become intoxicated by her natural fragrance. She smelled like water, lots of it—at least that day. He'd then come to know her moods by the intensity of her aroma. Of course, other things helped, like the arrangement of her furniture, the number of candles burning, and the type of music she played. But mostly, it was her scent. When she was happy, she smelled like a summer shower and there was a warm quality to the way she slowly talked and moved. When she was angry, she smelled like a thunderstorm—furious and intense. It was at those times when she approached everything aggressively, furiously.

Strangely enough, it was at those times that he most wanted to be around her. Her mood could be tumultuous and stormy, like being on a small boat in the middle of a hurricane. No matter what, he was always able to calm that stormy sea and still the raging waters within her.

"Tell me about today," he said, taking a seat on one of the many and gigantic pillows on the floor.

"Today is appreciation day. I'm appreciating all things around me and celebrating the kindness of others."

"Does this have anything to do with our date tonight?"

"Of course! I'm so grateful to have your essence in my life."

Tonight Ashley looked like an exotic dancer. She loved makeup. She used her skin like a canvas. Tonight her color was brown—on her lips, eyes, cheeks. She looked more earth woman than rain woman. Except for the three black dots she'd painted vertically down the center of her forehead.

"Come here. Let me smell you."

She playfully waved her forearm underneath his nose.

"Ah," he said, inhaling. "You are still the rain woman."

"You know, if you changed your diet, you'd change your scent."

"Hmmph," he responded, sniffing in the general direction of his armpit. "I smell like a man, because this is the way a man is supposed to smell."

"Well, you should at least give up red meat. You could eat veggie burgers instead."

"Woman, all that incense you burn must have made you loopy. I am a meat and potatoes man and will be till the day I die. On my deathbed, I want a three-inch-thick T-bone steak, medium-rare, and some A1."

They both laughed.

He smiled. "You'll feed it to me, won't you?"

"Sure," she said. "Of course by then you'll be so senile that you won't know the difference between a T-bone and tofu."

"You feed me tofu on my deathbed, I swear I will come back to haunt you."

"Will not!"

"Will so!"

"No, you won't."

"Try me."

Gordon enjoyed their exchange. He'd been in love with her for months now. He wasn't exactly sure how it had happened. Maybe no one ever really knows. All he knew was that one morning he'd awakened and the pain of being away from her, the longing to be near her was more than he could bear. He'd done everything in his power that day to keep his mind off her, to keep his appointments, to conduct his interviews, and to be his usual self with the ladies. He hadn't been successful. His sales pitch was robotic, his training forced, and he actually let a sister with enough booty for three women pass by without so much as a "Let me get your number, baby."

The only thing he had going for him now was that he was the king of cool. He flirted with Ashley; he couldn't help himself in that department. But she had always known him as a flirt. It had been a game with them, a challenge, a contest to see how much of a flirt he could be and how decisively she could thwart his playful advances.

Only the back-and-forth had started getting serious some time ago.

Now, when Gordon made a wisecrack about her being his lady or them gettin' jiggy, he wasn't kidding.

Traffic in Atlanta was hectic, as usual. Ashley's eyes darted from side to side while Gordon maneuvered his Dodge Viper through a packed freeway of cars.

He seemed at ease behind the wheel, even in the erratic flow of cars, SUVs, and trucks. Gordon also had a lead foot.

"Slow down, Muldowney. I'm eager to get there, but I don't want to fly there."

Gordon snorted. "That's why I have this car," he said, never taking his foot off the gas pedal. "So I can get to where I'm going." He paused a beat, then continued. "And what are you talking about? You don't even own a car!"

That was true, but Ashley much preferred walking to get where she needed to go. "Yes, but—"

"But nothin'." He smiled. "Stop side-seat driving and enjoy the ride." Gordon slid a CD into the player.

She didn't recognize the artist. The CD sounded good, but she was a little surprised. "What? No Barry White?"

"Naw," he said, speeding through a yellow light. "Tonight, I want to be the coolest guy in your atmosphere."

Ashley laughed. Gordon was always teasing her about the way she talked. She'd used the word "atmosphere" once and he'd teased her about it for five minutes. It never failed though, he always ended up adopting her words and in some cases her ways. Now if she could just work on his driving.

"You always do this, Gordon, but for once please slow down."

Gradually, he let up on the gas pedal and they enjoyed the rest of the drive toward the theater.

Ashley was usually okay with silence, but she found the quiet somehow uncomfortable now. They were never quiet together. They were always chattering about something—usually about some event going on at the bookstore where she worked or about a new sales rep he'd recruited. It was either that or Gordon would talk about the newest woman in his life while she would make some comment about Congo, the last man she had been seeing. But this . . . this quiet was intimate. So intimate she could hear them breathing.

She looked over at Gordon to speak. Something in his demeanor stopped her. With silence between them, she had nothing to focus on except how incredibly handsome she found him. He was always so very well groomed. Not a hair—on his head, eyebrows, or mustache—out of place. His clothes were always tailored, expensive, and crisply pressed. Together with his caramel-smooth skin, sculpted features, and green eyes—there was a package Ashley could admire for the rest of her days.

If Gordon wasn't such a playboy, she would have let herself do just that.

* * *

"You know, this is the first time you've let me take you out," he said as they stepped out of the car.

"I know."

"Why do you always turn me down?"

"Because you're arrogant, self-centered, and full of yourself."

"Don't forget handsome."

Ashley threw up her hands.

"No, really. Do you realize how good we look together? We'll turn every head in Philips Arena."

Ashley turned to him with her piercing gaze. "Don't you ever get tired of cheesy lines, Gordon Steele?"

He draped an arm around her shoulder. "Neva, baby. Neva."

The coins sewn into her skirt clinked together as she and Gordon approached the arena. She smiled, but the smile didn't reach her eyes.

"What's wrong? Please don't tell me that you're still sad about River Man."

"I was just wondering how I could be close to someone for so long and not really know him." She gave him a look he'd come to know as *don't even go there*. So he didn't. Instead, he kissed her on the nose and followed her into the throng of people.

Ashley tingled with excitement. She was finally going to see Cirque du Soleil in person.

At the gate, Gordon presented their tickets and they walked in.

"Did I tell you what happened when I first saw them on television?" she asked.

"A million times. Why do you think I bought the tickets?"

"Well, let's make this a million and one." She smiled.

Gordon ran a hand down his face. "Oh, here *you* go!"

"See, I had a cold, a real bad one," Ashley continued.

"I hadn't really been taking good care of myself and in a moment of weakness, I ate a Big Mac."

They entered the gift shop to kill time before the show started. "Yeah, you just *accidentally* ate some fast food."

She rolled her eyes. "Anyway, I got so sick. And nothing helped. Not zinc, not echinachea, not acupuncture."

"Does it hurt when they twirl those little needles into your skin?"

"Will you calm your spirit so I can finish the story?"

"Just lick your lips while you tell it, will you?"

She ignored him and continued. "I was miserable. I couldn't sleep. I couldn't rest. So against my better judgment, I turned on the TV—which isn't like me because I know how poison masquerades as entertainment these days. But there I was, channel-surfing. I stopped when I saw this woman. She was wearing the most elaborate makeup I'd ever seen. Every color in the rainbow was on her face. And this wonderful music was playing. Well, right away I relaxed a little. It was like I could feel myself getting stronger. So I kept watching and the woman lifted a man up into the air and put him on her head—"

"You can put me on your head any day!" Gordon interrupted.

"So I watched these people do *the impossible* time after time. For about two hours, I was mesmerized. By the time the show was over, I felt so much better. Almost healed."

Gordon rubbed one of Ashley's hair twists between his fingers. "And you've been a fan ever since."

Her smile could have melted butter.

Ashley turned and kissed him squarely on the lips. "And I've been a fan ever since." She focused again on the souvenirs. "Thank you for this," she said.

Gordon turned away, so she wouldn't see how flushed his face had become. He would have done more for her. This little jaunt was nothing.

* * *

If she didn't know she was approaching thirty-five, Ashley would have sworn she was a preteen staring wide-eyed at the most spectacular thing she had ever seen. For the first few acts, she and Gordon couldn't even clap. They were too stunned at the acrobatic ability of the performers to move. All they could do was open their mouths and say, "Wow."

When the performance was over, Ashley insisted that they go back to the gift shop and buy souvenirs. When they left, she had an armload full of DVDs, CDs, and programs for Cirque du Soleil.

On the drive home, she talked Gordon's ear off.

"Yes, Ash. I remember. Yes, Ash. I was there, too. Yes, Ash. I'm impressed," was all he said the entire way back. By the time they arrived back in Edgewood, Ashley had talked herself into a frenzy.

"Obviously you're not the least bit tired, but I'm exhausted. So, if you don't mind . . ."

"Oh," Ashley said, realizing they had been parked in front of her house for several minutes. She was pumped and knew she wouldn't be able to sleep. "Are you sure you wouldn't like to come in? We could make some tea."

"If I come in at this hour, the only thing we'll be making is some slow, soulful love."

On top of everything else she'd experienced that night, his flirtatious comment made her feel sparkly inside.

Instead of responding, she smiled, wondering why after all this time his comment should cause such a stir in her.

They stared into each other's eyes. Then Ashley broke the silence. "Thank you, Gordon. This was a wonderful anniversary gift. It's the best night of my life."

He leaned over. She prepared herself for his usual peck on the nose. Instead, he pressed his lips lightly against hers.

"Good night, Ashley."

Three

Days had gone by since he and Ashley had gone to see Cirque du Soleil. He had wanted to call her every day since then. But he knew his feelings for her were too raw, too sensuous. He'd had no idea how much making someone happy could affect him. And he'd made Ashley happy—truly happy. He saw it in her eyes, heard it in her voice, felt it in the enthusiasm she had greeted him with. He knew if he opened his mouth any time soon, his own feelings would come bubbling out in four little words, "I love you, Ashley."

But how could an angel like Ashley love a scoundrel like him? She deserved a prince—a prince for a princess. At times he'd even been uncomfortable calling himself her friend.

"What did I just say?"

"Huh?" Gordon turned to see a look of disgust on his buddy's face. He'd decided to drown his sorrows in a few bottles of Heineken with his longtime friend Van McNeil. They'd decided to hit one of Gordon's favorite pickup spots, Ventana's. He'd had his choice of many a fine woman in this place, he thought, many a fine woman. As a matter of fact, he had his eye on a Beyoncé-lookin' honey-colored sister who was the star in a constellation of barkers in the corner. But thoughts of Ashley kept him cradling his beer. After three bottles, he'd decided to forgo the mack move and just sulk.

"There you go again. Look, man, I can do bad by myself."

"Hey, I'm sorry, Van. I've just got some stuff I'm dealing with. You know how it is."

"I know how it is with me, but with you, you're like Teflon. Nothing sticks."

Gordon lifted the bottle, took a long swig.

"But something must be bothering you 'cause you have never been this quiet. And there've been a boatload of honeys movin' through here and you haven't even taken a bite. What's up, moneyman?"

"Nothing."

"You're not even watching the game. If I lose, I'll just tell you I won. You won't know the difference."

Gordon and Van had placed a friendly wager on the football game. If the Falcons won, Gordon had promised to mow his friend's lawn. If the Vikings won, Van would have to wash Gordon's Viper. Van was right. Gordon wasn't concentrating on the game, or anything else for that matter. His mind was elsewhere. And that concerned him. Gordon was always sharp. His mind worked like a missile, guiding him directly to wherever he wanted to go. Now he felt pulled in different directions.

"Next time I have to drink alone, just tell me. I'll pick up a six-pack, click on my wide-screen, and save my gas."

"Man, I'm sorry. I don't know what's gotten into me." Gordon signaled the bartender for another round and took a deep breath. "I think I'm going to go after Ashley."

Van sat back. "Ashley? Didn't you try that already?"

"Yeah," he said, slamming a twenty on the bar. Gordon remembered the relentless way in which he had pursued Ashley and the not-to-be-swayed manner in which she refused his every advance.

"Man, you need to leave that alone. Ashley is a good woman. Not your type at all." Van grabbed a handful of peanuts from a bowl and began shelling them. "If you want my advice, stick to the women who know how to play the game."

"What makes you think Ashley can't play?"

Van's frown came quickly. "Wait a minute . . . aren't you the one who taught me the playa's rules? Rule number one, *girls* just want to have fun. *Women* . . . want a husband!" They finished the line together.

"Aww! Who are you throwing to!" Van shouted at the television.

He gave Gordon a quick sideward glance, then took a gulp of beer. "From what I remember, Ashley is all woman. And unless you are ready to turn in your player card, you'd best keep that at arm's length."

Gordon stared into the bottle of his imported brew. Relationships with women were hard work. Friendships, he could do. Booty, he could do. But romance? Nada. He swallowed a mouthful of beer knowing that his friend Van was right on the money.

The Vikings were kicking the Falcons' butt. The score was twenty-one to three when his cell phone rang. Gordon was thinking that if they won big, he'd demand a wax with his wash. He slid the tiny phone from its holster on his belt and flipped it open.

"Steele," he answered.

"Gordon! Can you come over right now?"

Gordon stood straight up. "Ash, what's wrong?"

"Nothing! Everything! Can you come over?"

His pulse jumped. "I'll be right there!"

He turned up the bottle and finished the last drops of Heineken. "Gotta go. Somethin's up with Ashley."

He picked up a five from the bar counter, then gave

his friend some dap. "Bring your Turtle Wax when you come on Sunday, man."

"You just remember what I said, playa, playa."

Gordon headed out with his friend's words trailing like a haunting bit of "I told you so" advice.

"What do you think?"

Ashley expected him to be surprised, but she didn't expect the bright look of utter shock on his face. His reaction dampened her spirits.

"You don't like it?"

"What the hell is it?" he asked, walking past her and into the house.

"It's my costume."

"Sweetie, I hate to break this to you, but Halloween was last month."

Her shoulders slumped. Ashley had spent the last few days designing her costume to the last detail. "You don't recognize me?"

"Just barely," he said, standing back to get a better look. "How many layers of makeup do you have on? And what are you wearing? A costume from *The Blue Lagoon?*"

Ashley was speechless. Gordon was obviously joking, but she'd worked so hard and was so eager to share her decision with someone. She even surprised herself that the first person she wanted to tell was not any one of her sisters, but Gordon. And here he was making fun of her. She assumed she would have gotten the same reaction from her siblings. They never seemed to take her seriously. But Gordon had always been in her corner.

Maybe she was making a big mistake. Maybe her dream was too far-fetched. Maybe . . .

His arms felt warm and comforting. She let him hug her close.

"I'm sorry," he whispered. "I didn't mean to hurt your feelings." He stroked her back. The sensation melted away all her apprehension. "What's going on? Why are you all . . . dressed up?"

She sniffed, realizing for the first time that she was crying. She stepped back so that the makeup she had applied wouldn't smudge Gordon's expensive suit. "I'm going to audition to be a performer in Cirque du Soleil."

A wave of recognition hit him. He took a second look at Ashley and suddenly realized how much she was confiding in him. The amount of work it must have taken to put the costume together was more than he dared think about. And the way her face was painted and her hair was . . . sculpted, it looked as though she were part of the circus troupe already.

"You must be serious about this."

Her eyes hardened with determination. "I want this, Gordon. Bad."

Gradually her smile returned. She twirled around her living room. A rainbow of fabric wafted around her. "For the first time in my life, I'm absolutely sure about what I want. And what I want is to be part of that incredible troupe. And to make people feel what I feel when I see it."

Her face glowed with conviction. He believed her. And if this was what she wanted, then he'd help her.

"Okay, Allgood. Show me what you've got."

Over the next fifteen minutes, Gordon sat riveted while Ashley moved as if she didn't have a bone in her body. It was beyond modern dance. More flamboyant and more acrobatic. Ashley was a strong woman and her performance reminded him of gymnastics and dance with a touch of magic. It was beautiful, powerful, and seductive all at the same time.

Ashley swayed, turned, and spun to the music, which was heavy with drums, a tambourine, and a clarinet. His heart beat with it and he couldn't help nodding his head. Each wave of Ashley's undulating arms and torso sent a sweet fragrance his way. Strong, earthy, and wet. If he wasn't careful, he'd have no choice but to pull her into his lap and see what kind of movements she would make then.

When she finished, her breasts pulsed from her heavy breathing. He took in a deep breath. It was that exhilarating.

"Wow," was all he could muster.

"Is that a good wow or a bad wow?" she asked.

"That was an 'I'll be damned, I don't know what to say other than wow' wow."

Still breathing hard, "I'll take that as an affirmation," Ashley said. "Besides, your aura is glowing so brightly, it must have been a good experience for you."

You can say that again, he thought. A woman as beautiful as Ashley was a slice of heaven. It occurred to him that helping her fine-tune her performance would be a pleasure and a challenge. Pleasing because he could spend more quality time with Ash. Challenging because he would have to work very hard not to let his feelings for her get the best of him.

Women! The turmoil and confusion they create for men should be outlawed.

"If this is your dream," he said, "then I want to help it come true."

After she and Gordon said their good-byes, Ashley soaked in a bathtub of lavender- and sandalwood-scented water, thinking about her friendship with Gordon. There was a strange intimacy to their relationship. Like they were lovers only not quite. They'd done just about everything except passionately kiss each other and make love. Once, when she had a badly sprained ankle, Gordon came over, helped her bathe and put on fresh pajamas. She remembered him making a noise like "Umm" when he'd helped her undress. But other than that, he'd never done or said anything to suggest that they were more than just very good friends. But then, she thought, that wasn't altogether true. Gordon was always flirting with her. But that was his nature. He flirted with most women he knew and a good many of those he didn't know. When they first met, she'd thought that he was trying to hit on her. But soon she realized that was just his MO and she no longer took his suggestive comments seriously. Once, after watching a fireworks display on the Fourth of July, they held hands and walked through the park. It was a magical night for Ashley. She'd let herself believe that she and Gordon were in love, and just for that evening they were the happiest couple in the world. His aura burned bright that night and melted into hers like cotton candy on eager lips. At the end of the evening, he was the perfect gentleman. He walked her to her door, kissed her on the nose, and told her he would call her the next day.

Unlike some men she'd dated who said they would call and never did, Gordon always called when he said he would and often popped by unannounced like they'd been doing with each other for years. Her life was right when she was with him.

Four

Over the course of the last year, Gordon had had occasion to meet members of Ashley's family individually. He would stop by her house and one of her sisters would be there. Or he would be visiting and one of her five sisters would stop by. But the idea of being with all of them at the same time made him apprehensive.

The first time she had mentioned her sister Marti's wedding, he'd been paying more attention to the way her lips moved when she talked than to the actual words coming out. Then she'd mentioned it a few more times—once when they were having lunch at the bookstore and another time when they had finished watching the video performance of Cirque du Soleil's *La Nouba* for the umpteenth time. When Ashley had asked him to go to the wedding with her, he'd said yes before he could think about it. But pulling up in front of Ashley's house to pick her up now, he started to feel a bit more concerned.

I should be able to handle a bunch of women, he thought. *I'll just turn on the ol' Steele charm.*

Ashley came out before he could turn off the engine. She looked like a princess. On second thought, she looked divine.

She was dressed in a cream-colored gossamer sarong that, if it had only been draped around her once, would have been transparent. But she'd wrapped it, tucked it, and gathered it in such away that it covered her in all the right places yet still had the billowy, diaphanous look of a fairy-tale princess.

What he wouldn't do to unwrap her after the wedding ceremony, or for that matter, right now.

When they arrived at the airport, where they would take a private plane to the wedding site, members of the wedding party were already there. Gordon's heart skipped a beat surrounded by so many beautiful women. Ashley came from a family of lookers, and he didn't mind the view at all. They were all standing on the landing strip near a white Lear jet. The groom had chartered a plane and made arrangements to fly everyone to Mt. Massive for nuptials on the highest plateau of the Sawatch Mountain range in Colorado. If Gordon understood correctly, Ashley's sister Roxanne would fly them there and back. After greetings were exchanged and curious looks from Ashley's family and friends, he leaned over toward her.

"What are we waiting for?"

"The maid of honor isn't here yet."

No sooner had Ashley uttered those words than a couple dashed out of the terminal. The man was dressed in a well-tailored black suit. The woman wore a teal dress that looked too tight to breathe in.

"Sorry we're late, everyone," the man said.

"Yeah, sorry, y'all," the woman said, struggling unsuccessfully to pull the short dress down to a reasonable length. "We, uh, had some business to take care of."

The groom weaved through the crowd, kissed the woman on the cheek, and shook the man's hand. Then he pulled the man aside near where Gordon was standing and whispered in his ear, "I know you didn't get busy on the way over here, did you?"

The man smiled. "What can I say, man? Jacq can't go too long without it."

* * *

Ashley's briefing had been thorough. She'd wanted Gordon to make a good impression on her family, so she'd given him a primer on her sisters and brother. The greatest professional advice he'd ever gotten was: know your customer, know your customer, know your customer. In keeping with that advice, he'd committed what Ashley told him to memory.

Her oldest sister was Yolanda. Yolanda was married with a husband, Cleon, and a daughter, Amara. Yolanda was old-fashioned and set in her ways. Gordon would do nothing to rock the boat with her.

After Yolanda came Roxanne. Even though she wasn't the oldest, she was the leader of the clan, according to Ashley. She made it clear that Roxy was a no-nonsense, *don't mess with me or I'll be all over you like Johnny Cochran on injustice* kind of woman. He'd leave his charm and humor at the door and give Roxanne "just the facts" responses to anything she said or asked.

Next in line was Morgan. Morgan was the fashion model who was responsible for most of Ashley's clothing. And Ashley was right, she was breathtaking, but rumor had it that the last thing she wanted to talk about was her beauty or anything about fashion. Gordon would make it a point to talk with her about the great weather they were having.

Ashley was next in birth order and then there was the singer—Xavier. Gordon thought Ashley's brother would probably be too hyped up about being a famous R&B crooner to be concerned about him. Ashley assured him that would not be the case. Her response was, "Don't sleep on my brother. He's laid-back, but he loves his sisters and will protect us with his life." Gordon thought the best thing for him to do in that case was let his feelings for Ashley show—smile at her the way he wanted to. Hold her a little longer. Linger in her presence. Men notice things like that. And his sincere actions would provide some assurance that he was not out to get or harm Xavier's sister.

Finally, there was Marti, the youngest. She was the most like Ashley with her friendly nature and playful spirit. According to Ashley, Marti loved to laugh and enjoy life. Gordon would make it a point to get her to laugh—take some of the charm he'd put on hold for Roxanne and the others and lavish it on Marti. He couldn't wait.

Gordon sat back in his seat. He'd often thought of Ashley as a chameleon. But what he would do this evening ranked there too. And he didn't mind at all. Accessing different parts of himself to please Ashley's family was a small price to pay to make Ashley happy.

The flight over the mountains was spectacular. The small party had filed into the aircraft soon after the last couple's arrival and headed west. It was more like a party bus than an airbus. There was music, drinks, hors d'oeuvres, and scintillating conversation.

Kenyon Williams, the groom, who reminded Gordon of Jesus with his dark skin, long hair, and goatee, made sure that the guests at his wedding lacked for nothing. Meanwhile Marti Allgood, the bride-to-be, spent most of the time in the cockpit with her sister Roxanne. Gordon listened as Ashley talked on about the karmic vibrations on the plane and how she thought her younger sister would have a wonderful wedding.

Gordon had anticipated a long and lackluster plane ride. He couldn't have been more wrong, and before he realized it they were landing in Colorado.

Gordon wondered about the overnight bag that Ashley brought with her. When he'd asked her about it in the car, she'd said that it was her wedding present to her sister and new brother-in-law. At the reception, she'd left him at a table with her oldest sister, her husband, and their daughter. He watched as Amara cast a spell over her younger cousins, Mahalia and Kenyon Jr., who were remarkably well behaved in her care. Ashley took her overnight bag, kissed Gordon on the nose, and left the room with one of her sisters. Gordon thought it was Morgan, but with so many sisters it was hard for him to keep track.

Moments later, the woman he thought was Morgan emerged from the ladies' bathroom and handed a CD to the DJ. Morgan was beautiful, in a supermodel kind of way—a face you expect to see strutting down the runway or on a New York City billboard thirty feet high. She had none of Ashley's earthiness, none of her exotic features, or natural spirit.

"Ladies and gentlemen, at this time I'd like to introduce my sister Ashley Allgood, who will present her wedding present to Marti and Kenyon in her own special way."

Morgan gave a nod to the DJ and he started the music. The haunting sound of Middle Eastern music filled the mountain resort. Morgan held the bathroom door open and Ashley came out showing more skin than Gordon felt safe around.

He knew that Ashley taught belly dancing. He'd even jokingly asked to see a performance once. She'd declined. But now what he saw before his eyes was the real deal.

Gold coins sewn into the sheer fabric that barely covered her breasts and hips jingled with every movement. Her body appeared nimble and fluid as she slowly gyrated to the hypnotic rhythm. She spun, twirled, and moved her hips in an undulating figure eight.

He had no idea how much fabric had gone into making her costume. Ashley wore a long veil and yards and yards of chiffon that she twirled and moved through the air. At first, it was her and the music. After a while the music faded and it was just Ashley seemingly floating on air, telling a story with her body, and enrapturing all who watched her dance.

Her body moved like a mermaid. She did things with her arms and hips Gordon didn't know were possible. And now that he knew . . . he couldn't help imagining those hips underneath him, rolling like waves. The image was overwhelming. He knew his mouth was open in awe, but he couldn't help it. He had no idea Ashley could move that way. Her dance hypnotized him. He loved her more, wanted her more.

He glanced at Reynard—the only other bachelor in the crowd besides himself. Reynard watched Ashley with the face of a predator that'd just spied his prey. Gordon could all but see the saliva dripping from his fangs.

Gordon gulped. It was the most sensual thing he'd ever seen in his life. He'd been to strip joints and gone to enough bachelor parties with naked women jumping out of cakes to last a lifetime. But the dance that Ashley did and the way she moved to the music aroused him so that he was only now aware of his erection, which he quickly tried to hide with his dinner napkin. It was as if she were casting a magic spell on him with her hips. Like a contortionist isolating each part of her body and then moving it at will. Gordon found himself completely transfixed by her performance. Near the end of the dance, Morgan stood and approached him.

"A coin for the good luck of the newlyweds," Morgan said.

Gordon fished through his pockets and found a quarter. Ashley danced over and flattened herself until her belly was nearly horizontal in his face. He placed the coin near the brown flower that was her navel. Her eyes flashed like quick lightning in his direction. And then she danced some more. Never did the coin fall or falter. And then as the whoops and applause died down, Ashley rolled the coin with her muscles from her lower abdomen up toward her breasts.

Marti whooped and clapped appreciatively, enthusiastically. Her new husband joined in. Soon everyone was applauding. By the time Gordon regained his composure enough to clap, the dance was over and his erection was harder than ever. He wanted to make love to her desperately. He needed to make love to her. Like flowers need rain.

"Gordon," Yolanda said.

His head snapped in her direction. "Yes."

"Are you all right?"

He swallowed hard. Wished he had a cigarette. "Yes," he answered, feeling his hard-on finally settle back down.

Gordon liked everyone at the wedding, except the groom's brother, Reynard. When he saw him try to push up against Ashley near the champagne ice sculpture, a pang of jealousy suddenly came over him. He nearly bolted to the other side of the reception room to get between Ashley and Reynard, leaving the groom's parents in midconversation.

"Hey, Ash, let me ask you something," he said, feinting.

She and Reynard exchanged curious glances. Reynard made an excuse and left. Gordon watched him walk away.

"This better be good," Ashley said.

"What do you mean?" Gordon asked, relieved that she was safe.

"I mean that I was trying to get to know Reynard and you interrupted the vibe big time."

"Sorry," he lied. Then he decided to tell the truth. "No, I'm not sorry. I don't like him. He reminds me of . . . of . . ."

"Of you?" she responded, slightly amused at the irony.

"Look, I just don't like the guy. And I'm a very good judge of character. This is what I do for a living—size people up."

"Well, his aura is strong, bright. Attractive."

"Oh, please. Richie Rich probably never learned how to tie his own Nikes."

Ashley stood back a little. "Why do you sound jealous?"

Her words jolted him. He thought he was hiding his jealousy. "Because," he fumbled, making up an excuse as he went. "I didn't come all the way to God knows where to allow you to become some wealthy man's plaything. You mean too much to me for that."

Ashley blinked, her almond-shaped eyes sparkling. "Thank you, I think, Gordon."

He kissed her nose, wondering what her third eye said about him recently.

Ashley knew that her family could be quite demanding when it came to significant others. She had certainly been a willing participant in their grueling third degree before. She'd just hoped the fact that she and Gordon were merely friends would allay their concerns. It didn't.

During the reception dinner, her sisters had made it a point to sit at or near the table where she and Gordon were seated. While she tried to divert attention to the newlyweds, her sisters each took turns asking Gordon prying kinds of questions.

"So, Gordon, where did you grow up?" That was her eldest sister, Yolanda. Always checking the background.

"How did you two meet?" was Morgan's question. She always zeroed in on the nature of a relationship.

Marti always asked questions as if she were looking for a playmate. "What kinds of things do you like to do, Gordon?"

"Gordon, what are your intentions toward my sister?" There it was. Roxanne had to put it out there. Ashley knew if anyone would, it would be her.

Ashley's beaux rarely came through unscathed. Congo had been a nervous wreck after being put to the Allgood test. Such a sensitive man, he was never the same. Gordon's responses made her almost wish that they *were* dating. He remained poised, steady, and seemed genuinely pleased to answer everyone's questions.

"I'm a transplant from Minneapolis.

"I tried to pick her up at the bookstore.

"I like football, good wine, fine cigars, and," he said, glancing around, "beautiful women.

"I just want to be the best friend Ashley has ever had."

Ashley just wanted it to be over and she knew if she protested, her sisters would draw the whole spectacle out much longer.

Her brother, Xavier, ate in silence throughout the entire dinner. He usually didn't participate in his sisters' interrogations. But she was surprised when his wife chimed in a time or two, asking Gordon to elaborate on some of the answers he gave.

Sunset on the mountaintop was the most spectacular sight Ashley had ever seen. While Amara and Morgan tended to the children, the couples sort of went their separate ways enjoying the view, all in their own private way.

Ashley and Gordon ended up walking along the summit edge and talking.

"I knew you taught belly dancing, but I didn't know . . . I mean—"

"But you didn't actually think I could do it."

"No, no! Why must I be misunderstood? What I'm trying to say is that you are really good."

"Thanks. It helps when I'm inspired by something so important to me, like my sister."

Gordon nodded. "I've never seen a wedding present quite like that before."

Ashley smiled dreamily.

"I mean, that was quite erotic."

"I hope you mean exotic," she said.

"No, that was very sexual."

"Not if you view it with a third eye. Belly dancing is about womanhood. It's about celebrating femininity, motherhood, and the goddess Nature."

"Uh-huh, by moving your hips like you're in the throes of . . ."

"Don't you dare compare what I did for my sister and brother-in-law to something you might see in a booty bar!"

"No, no! I don't mean that. It's just that I felt, well, I mean as a man . . . I think that what you did was *sexy*."

Ashley huffed and crossed her arms.

"I can't help it. That's *my* nature. What I did tonight is called a unity dance. It's a blessing of their union, a body chant for a fruitful wedding night, and a prayer for eternal love."

Gordon thought back to all the ways in which Ashley's body moved, twisted, meandered, and flourished. Yeah, it was all that.

"Thanks for coming with me," Ashley said, looking up at him.

He smiled down at her. "I'm really glad I came."

"Even after dinner?"

"Especially after dinner. Your family really cares about you. That says a lot about who they are . . . about who you are."

The rainbow's colors danced along the mountain-scape horizon. Violet red, purple, and deep, deep, blue. The sky was a canvas of prismed light.

"Your answers said a lot about who you are. I'm very impressed. No one has ever come away from one of their inquisitions the way you did. That's a good thing, but it's also a bad thing."

Gordon slowed. "Why a bad thing?"

Ashley stopped beside him. "Because it means you meet with their approval. It means they think we make a good couple."

"Umm." He nodded.

They resumed their walk.

"I wonder what they think about Reynard," she said.

Gordon stopped again. "Reynard?" Then he smiled. "Oh, you mean for Morgan. They would make a good couple."

Ashley smiled. "No, for me, silly."

Gordon's jaw dropped. "Reynard's a wolf. Why would you be interested in him?"

"Wait! First he and Morgan would make a good couple and then he's a wolf? Why is he okay for her but not for me?"

"Ash, I just meant—"

She folded her arms. "I know what you meant. Weird, quirky Ashley isn't good enough for someone as refined and cultured as Reynard."

"Not true!" He traced his palm down the side of Ashley's arm and then held her hand. "I'm just being overprotective, and jealous. I've had you all to myself for a while now, and I like not having to fit time in to see you between dates and activities with a boyfriend you might be seeing. I like not having to explain the nature of our relationship to a significant other."

Ashley's smile was as beautiful as the sunset. "You're so sweet," she said and stood on tiptoe to kiss him on the nose. They reached toward each other, held hands, and watched the rest of the sunset in contented silence.

After an evening of food, song, dance, and intimate walks, the women separated themselves from the men to fawn over the bride. Gordon found himself in the company of Kenyon, Reynard, Davis, Cleon, James Skyhunter, and Xavier Allgood. Though the sexes were separated, they both remained outside the lodge on the summit of the mountain. Gordon mostly listened while Xavier and Cleon gave Kenyon the lowdown about married life and how to handle a woman. There was lots of laughter and advice. After a while, they quieted down. The sounds of nature echoed around them. Xavier got up and walked toward Gordon.

He said, "May I talk to you for a minute?"

Gordon made a motion to get up. "Sure," he said.

Xavier raised his hand and lowered his voice. "Don't get up. I just wanted to let you know that I love my little sister Ashley very much. I won't see her hurt, if you get what I mean."

Gordon rose then. The two men were nearly the same height. He cleared his throat. "I just want to let you know that I love your little sister Ashley and I'd never do anything to hurt her, if you understand *my* meaning."

Xavier's eyes narrowed. "I'll hold you to that," he said, and returned to where he was sitting near a blazing campfire.

* * *

They left the Sawatch Mountain range at close to midnight. When the plane landed on a private airstrip at the Atlanta Airport, all the passengers were still abuzz from the beauty of the ceremony and the reception. With the exception of the two small children who were sound asleep, they all departed the plane full of laughter, hugs, and pats on the back.

Once in the car, Ashley settled in for the drive to her house. "I've said this a million times, I know, but I'm truly glad you came with me. Because you were there, I had a wonderful time."

"You can stop thanking me, Ash. You know I'd do anything for you."

His comment warmed her heart. She melted into the seat and closed her eyes.

An hour later, they were pulling up to her house. Gordon got out and walked her to the door.

A sleepy smile was plastered on her face. He wanted to kiss that smile until she felt what he did. He watched as she bent slightly and put the key in the lock. Her round backside was only inches away. He remembered the cinnamon brown of her skin from the belly dance. He imagined feeling it under his palms.

He put his hands in his pockets.

When the door opened, Ashley yawned and stepped inside. Then she turned to him, sleep making her eyes look dreamy, sexy, intoxicated.

"Good—"

He didn't know what made him do it. He just bent down and kissed her nose. But this time he lingered there a bit longer, savored the taste of her skin on the tips of his lips. Was about to lick the flesh lightly with his tongue, when she pulled back.

Her eyes sparkled with moonlight. She swept a glance

skyward. "Not quite the mountains, is it?" she asked and yawned again.

His heart caved in inside his chest. *Just sweep her into your arms, playa.* But he couldn't. Bathed in starlight, she was too innocent, too angelic, too good for his corruption.

"Night, Ashley," he said, backing away.

"Night, Gordon."

A second later, they both closed a door. Ashley's was a physical one. Gordon's an emotional one. He would find a woman, soon, to divert his stupid feelings. And he would push Ashley Allgood off his radar for good.

Five

No matter how he tried to stay away from her, she came to him in his dreams. Ever since the wedding, she would be dancing. Twirling. Weaving her veil through the air. Gyrating.

Like now, he heard the music. Tambourine, clarinet, animal-skin-covered drums, and zill finger cymbals. She smelled of frankincense and rainwater. And she was dancing. This time for him.

Ashley's hips rolled with a rhythm that matched the beat of his heart, his breathing. In exquisite agony he wondered what those hips would feel like beneath him. He wanted to feel them under him. He smiled. He didn't care that it was only a dream. Dreams were better. You could do anything you wanted in a dream. And the thing he wanted right now was Ashley.

In his dream, he rose from where he was seated. He moved toward her, slung his arm around her waist, and pulled her close. His heart rate quickened. It thrummed with the music.

His lips glided across the side of her face, her chin, and up the other side. Her hips were grinding against him. His blood boiled. He swallowed her mouth greedily, lavished it with his moist lips and wet tongue. He pulled her top lip into his mouth and suckled it like a baby. She moaned. His manhood stiffened.

He pulled her down to the floor. She was still dancing. Still swirling her hips. Still pulsating with life, exotic, mysterious life.

He unbuttoned his pants, slid them down, prepared to enter her.

"Hurry, Gordon," she murmured, sliding down her skirt. "I've been waiting for so long."

For a few seconds they bumped and ground their hips together. Savoring the pleasure of skin on skin. Then he slowly began to enter her.

When the phone rang, they both looked up in his dream as if to ask, "What was that?"

No! Gordon thought, fumbling to get inside her. But he couldn't. He was already losing his erection. "No!" he said, opening his eyes.

The phone rang again. Angrily, Gordon snatched the receiver from the cradle.

"Hello?" he said, with exasperation.

"Where've you been?"

Gordon looked down. The telltale signs of his dream were still stiff in his member.

"Well, I've been having one of the most erotic dreams I've ever had. That is, until the phone rang." He shifted. Stroked himself, regretfully. "What time is it?"

"It's almost eight," Ashley said.

He could hear her smile through the phone. *Please don't ask me to come over,* he thought. *I'd lose all my cool points.* "What's up?"

"I need your help."

Oh, no. "What kind of help?"

"I'm rehearsing an act for tryouts next month, and I need some candid feedback. Now, I know honesty isn't one of your strong suits—"

"Hey! Hey! I can be honest."

"Yes, but only when it gets you what you want. And

right now I don't have anything to offer you. Besides our continued friendship."

Gordon rubbed the place near his heart that stung from her words. "You really believe that about me, don't you?"

"Only because it's true."

Gordon let out a deep sigh. He couldn't argue. "So, you're really serious about being a circus performer?"

"Oh, Gordon. It's so much more than being a circus performer. It's—"

"I know, I know," he said. "It's a *metaphysical experiential exercise in cosmic correction.* You've told me a thousand times."

"And you remember each time." Her voice smiled. "So will you help me?"

Gordon thought about all the prospects he could recruit in the time it would take to be a part-time critic. He stood to lose thousands of dollars in commissions. But what was a couple thousand dollars compared to one more moment with the woman of his lust-filled dreams?

"Gordon?"

"Yes, Ash. I'll do it. But just remember, you'll owe Big Daddy."

"The goddess will bless you for this! Stop by on Wednesday or Thursday. I should be ready by then."

"All right. Now let me get back to this dream. If I'm lucky, the beautiful woman will still be ready and waiting for me."

"You're always lucky, Gordon. You're the luckiest guy I know."

Gordon hung up the phone and turned over in his bed. If only he felt lucky. He just felt horny. He punched the pillow, put his head down, and closed his eyes. He was still hard, still in want of her. He regretted that the only satisfaction he would get in that area would come in his sleep.

Ashley.

Ya make a man think about changin' his ways.

Ashley had arranged her living room into a makeshift theater with chairs and a couch on one side and an open space on the other. Today she wore a one-piece leotard. Gordon's temperature skyrocketed when he realized there was nothing underneath it. He swallowed—hard. "Is that your new costume?" he asked, not caring. The only thing on his mind now was pressing his body against the one he vividly imagined beneath the spandex fabric.

Her breasts were perfectly rounded. He could almost sense their softness beneath her leotard. His mouth watered at the thought of Ashley's dark brown nipples hardening with the flick of his tongue. His eyes traveled quickly to the dark triangle at the tip of her thighs. He groaned inwardly, wanting with all his might to brand her with his kiss.

He watched with a hungry man's eyes as she lit candles, turned off white lights, and turned on black, red, and blue lights. The result was a warm soft glow that felt like a downy blanket covering the room. He mellowed instantly. The ambience was like a sweet, soothing drug relaxing his body. He smiled, knowing he had bedroom eyes. Gordon could tell already, Ashley's performance would be better than good.

"My sister Morgan made something quite elaborate. She thinks I'm going to a costume party. She doesn't know about the audition. Have a seat, and I'll go get ready."

He didn't hear much of what she'd just said. Just the part about having a seat, which was exactly what he intended to do in an effort to hide his swelling manhood.

"Hurry up, then!" he snapped and took a seat front and center. For this performance, he wanted the best view.

Music started in the background. He recognized it as the same song that accompanied the Cirque du Soleil performance he and Ashley had attended. She was really going all out for this audition, having studied the videos and DVDs. She knew every gesture and nuance of the troupe. Her conversations for the past month had revolved around the act and the performers, and any mention of the troupe made her light up like a Broadway marquee. In the year that they'd been friends, he'd never known her to be as enthusiastic about anything else.

If only she could be as enthusiastic about him.

After four songs, he started to wonder if she'd gone to bed instead of going to get ready.

"So far, Ash, I'm not impressed."

"Hush," she called from the other room. "You'll short-circuit the energy."

He rolled his eyes and picked up a magazine on shamanism from the table.

No sooner had he returned to his seat than a creature emerged from Ashley's bedroom. It was on all fours and slunk along the floor toward him in time with the music. Its movements were distinctively feline and Gordon had to blink and refocus his eyes to believe what he saw was Ashley.

Her costume was as elaborate as anything he'd seen on-stage. She still wore the unitard, but attached to it was an isinglass-thin fabric over her breasts, lower hips, and arms. There were actually three colors of fabric—ice blue, silver, and a cool pink, and it looked as though it had spent a few frantic moments in a Cuisinart before being sewn on.

By far the most striking aspect of her costume was the makeup. A rainbow of colors illuminated her face from hairline to chin. Most dramatic were her eyes where large brushstrokes of cobalt, white, and fuchsia ensured that her facial expressions would be easily recognizable from anywhere in an arena.

Yoga pays off, Gordon thought as Ashley arched her torso, rose to stand on both feet, and moved as if she were made of rubber. He didn't have to see any more to know that she'd been practicing—a lot.

When she had first started talking about creating a character, she said she wanted to be a rain woman. The way she took over the room, arms gradually undulating, she looked every bit the part, casting spells into the air and creating fantasies.

She removed a baton that was propped against the wall. The baton was covered with the same whispery material as her outfit. She twirled it in a slow looping fashion. The effect was hypnotic as the silver in the fabric reflected the candlelight.

The music continued to play and Ashley fell into a rhythm, maneuvering the baton from hand to shoulder to hand, around her waist, and between her legs. The instrument moved as though she'd cast a spell and given it a life of its own. Gordon grinned broadly. He was watching a new star.

The shreds of gossamer swayed. When song number six ended, he found himself speechless for the first time in all his thirty-six years.

Although she seemed to move effortlessly, her shortness of breath was apparent.

"Well?" she asked, a bit winded.

"Just promise me a free front-row ticket."

"Really?" she said, rushing toward him.

He stood and gave her a firm hung. The feel of her in his embrace sent a rush of warmth up his spine. He stepped back and looked her in the eye. "You're ready," he said.

* * *

The next few days were torture. Gordon had made appointments, kept appointments, and gotten two of his latest recruits through orientation and training. He'd gone out on dates and brought a new person on board. But he was just going through the motions. Suddenly, the world was flat, the sky was gray, and his mood was black. Even food, which he usually enjoyed, tasted like chalk.

He was lovesick.

It was a terrible feeling. Now he knew and understood why so many women would continue to call him and show up at his apartment long after their relationship had ended. Now he could relate to his homies whose conversations revolved around their girlfriends and ex-wives. He hated—no, despised—men who had nothing better to talk about than women, or more specifically, the women they were involved with. He'd gotten into an argument with Van one evening when they'd had a couple too many beers and Gordon had heard one too many stories about Van's then-girlfriend Lisa.

"Don't you have anything else to talk about?"

"What?" Van had asked, shocked by his friend's lack of sympathy.

"I mean, damn, man. Lisa this. Lisa that. Is that all you know? Talk about the Hawks game. Or the weather. Heck, talk about the traffic jam you were stuck in!"

Van lifted the long-necked bottle of beer to his lips and swallowed hard. He set the bottle down lightly on the bar. "Don't cop an attitude with me just 'cause you ain't neva had no woman as good to you as Lisa is to me." He wiped his lips with the back of his hand. "Or as fine."

"Please. Every woman I've ever dated has been finer than Lisa in every way."

Van cocked his head. "What you sayin'?"

"I'm sayin' that here we are again, talkin' about Lisa. Can we *please* put the cabash on that conversation? It's old and tired."

Van agreed to drop the Lisa talk.

Gordon always felt sorry for brothers who couldn't see beyond the sister they were dating. Always thought something was wrong with people if all they did was eat, sleep, and breathe someone else. He'd always wanted to scream at people like that, "Get a freaking life!"

But here he was wishing the food he ate had Ashley's special touch. Dreaming about her every night, and missing the smell of her scent.

This was bad.

He'd been downright rude on the last two dates he'd been on. The women were regular booty calls. Elaine and Patricia. They circled around him in a holding pattern. Whenever he felt the slightest bit lonely, he'd call and they would be ready. For the life of him, he couldn't imagine why he didn't have sex with them. That was the usual fare. Dinner. Dancing. Drawers. But he couldn't muster up the usual passion. The thought of tonguing them for any length of time left him cold. So, he'd used their company to take his mind off of what was really bothering him and then sent them home with only a peck on the cheek to remember the night with.

He didn't want to know it, but the fact was he was getting closer and closer to turning in his player card.

But would Ashley have him? He prayed for sweet dreams and wondered if a woman like that could ever love a rogue like him.

Six

Gordon walked up the sidewalk tentatively. He'd thought that all this time without seeing her would have made him rush to her door when she called. But instead, he was taking his time, measuring his steps, easing the nervous tension out of his body.

Before he reached the stairs, Ashley swung open the door. She frequently did that. She said she could sense his presence. "Thanks for coming," she said.

He kissed her cheek and entered. "Are you sure you weren't looking out the window?"

She smirked. "Get in here!"

He looked around. She'd changed her living room furniture around again. It was definitely more *feng shui*. He'd learned about *feng shui* from Kako, one of his exes.

"You've been missing in my space, my brother. I've missed your face."

He grunted. "Nice to know you notice when I'm not around."

"Don't play. You know you keep me grounded. Help me remember what's important."

"How? By reminding you of all the things that aren't?" He felt antsy. Why did he suddenly feel the need to point out their differences?

Ashley frowned. She moved the palm of her hand

down the front of his body from his head to his chest. She stopped near his heart.

"There is an energy blockage here. You're . . ." she said, almost touching him. "Something serious is dividing you." She closed her eyes. "Something . . ." Her hand hovered a few moments. Darned if he couldn't feel the heat from her body flowing through it. He remained still, too intrigued to move. Ashley's eyes snapped open. "Gordon! You're in love!"

She smiled and threw her arms around him. "I'm so happy for you!" She kissed him on the cheek. "Sit down. I want to hear everything."

He sat down on the couch. She sat down next to him. Too close. He wanted to wrap her in his scoundrel arms and kiss her dizzy. But Ashley deserved the things that went along with a serious kiss, like love and commitment. He was sure about the love part. He could give her that. But could he love her enough to stick around?

"So?" she said, obviously eager for him to talk.

"Well . . . she . . . reminds me of you."

Ashley nodded. "Okay, that means I haven't met her, 'cause you've never dated anyone even close to me!"

They laughed together.

"Now who's full of themselves?" he asked, remembering all the times she accused him of being a little too appreciative of himself.

"Don't worry about me, what else about *her*?"

He stared into Ashley's eyes. Before he could float away on the innocence he saw there, he looked up as if he were searching for the right words. "All I know is, she makes me happy. And I think I could make her happy if she'd let me get close enough."

Ashley could tell from Gordon's personal energy and the way his face flushed and his eyes deepened that he was telling the truth. He was serious about this woman.

Whoever she was, she'd obviously taken possession of his heart. Ashley couldn't help feeling a cold twinge of jealousy. All this time, through all his women, she'd always been the constant lady in his life. All the others were just passing encounters. She felt uneasy knowing that there was someone else who could become a permanent fixture in Gordon's life.

Thinking to herself, she vowed to cast her selfishness aside and do whatever it took to support her friend and his new love interest.

"You mean she's not worshiping at your feet?"

"No, I haven't kissed her yet," he said.

"So?"

"Haven't you heard? When Big Daddy kisses a woman, she loses her mind."

"Get over yourself."

"These lips have turned out many a sister. But you wouldn't know nothin' 'bout that."

"I know how to kiss."

"I don't doubt that. But you probably never made someone forget his own name."

"Nobody kisses that well."

"I do."

"I betcha you don't. As self-centered as you are, I know I'm a much better kisser than you."

"Not in this lifetime."

She chuckled. "I'm sorry, but I know you. You can be awfully superficial, and if you're serious about this woman, then you shouldn't be."

He pressed the palm of his hand to his heart as if he'd been wounded, and stumbled backward. "What exactly are you saying?"

"I'm saying that the only true way to make a connection to someone while kissing is to kiss with your soul. To share your spirit with them. To make yourself vulnerable and show them your life force."

"You talkin' like an expert," he said.

"I just know that my approach to intimacy is much better than yours."

"Really?" he asked, slightly short of breath.

"Really."

"What you want to bet?"

Ashley smiled. "I've already won everything of value you have. What's left?"

She was right. During most of their playful wagers, she'd cleaned up pretty good. But in this . . . he knew he had her.

He thought for a moment. "Well, you wanted me to help you get ready for the audition. If you win, I'll do it."

Ashley smiled, even broader this time.

Gordon tapped his index finger against the side of his face. "Now when I win, I want you to make a love potion for me that will help me get this woman I'm in love with."

Her eyes grew mischievous. For a second, he thought his secret was out.

"You're on!"

Ashley stood, squared herself in front of him, and placed her hands on her hips. "Pucker up, big boy."

He stood, but couldn't prevent the smile curling up his lips.

"First one to moan, buckle, or respond in any way loses," she announced.

Gordon's heart jackhammered in his chest. After this day, no more dreams, he thought. Just the real thing.

Instead of moving toward her, he walked around her. Slowly. Closely. Surveying. Studying. He brushed his body like a whisper against hers. His eyes traveled down her caramel-brown neck, across her soft shoulders, down her back, paused appreciatively at her round backside, and traveled down her legs and came to rest at her bare feet. When he returned to face her, her eyes had already darkened with a hint of desire. He slid the backs of his fingers along the soft flesh of her face. His nostrils filled with the aroma of an approaching storm. Her head inclined ever so slightly to his touch. He smiled inside. She'd already lost.

Her eyes stared pleadingly, daringly into his. But it wasn't just her eyes that excited him. Her lips, defiant and luxuriously red, made his pulse strum like a bass guitar. He couldn't help himself. He reached up and slid the pad of his thumb across her lower lip. It felt like silk. She flicked the tip of her tongue once against his thumb. The warm, wet sensation sent a jolt traveling through his body.

"Woo, you in trouble now," he whispered.

"Says who?" she countered.

Now they were body to body. *There's nothing left to do,* Gordon thought, *but show her who's the mack.*

He bent his head toward her, ready to do what he did best.

Gordon's bold moves sent shivers of anticipation down Ashley's spine. At his touch, something inside her danced. When his lips touched hers, that something— desire, want, need, lust, love—stopped dancing and surged. He came for her in slow motion. His lips settled gently against her top lip. Then gradually pulled it into the moist warm flesh of his mouth. He tugged at her lip while rolling his soft tongue across the underside. She closed her eyes. The sensation was lavish. Like bathing in liquid silk. He lingered, paying mind-blowing attention to the crest of her lip, the corners of her mouth. Ashley released a climactic breath.

At that moment, Gordon lowered his mouth just a bit, caught her breath, and sucked it into his mouth. The exchange cooled the tip of her tongue. Then as if to warm it, he breathed his breath into her mouth. His hot essence spread throughout her body. Their souls mingled. Ashley shuddered. With the temperature in her body rising with each second, he slid his tongue deep into her mouth and with one hand at the curve of her back drew her body closer to his.

She couldn't help it. She'd felt the moan coming since the moment their skin touched. She set it free, responding to the blending of their souls.

Determined not to give up without a fight, Ashley became an active participant in their sweet exchange. She concentrated on her feet, she tapped the energy there and felt it move upward to her ankles, calves, and knees, gathering strength and intensity. She relaxed completely and continued to channel the energy in her body upward until it reached her neck. Then, mustering both strength and restraint, she gradually released her energy into Gordon's mouth.

This time the moan came from him, deep and low in his throat. Ashley continued to release her spirit, her soul, indeed her very essence into him. Bringing her hands up, she caressed his back, brought him nearer still, and explored his mouth with her tongue. Their heads twisted and rotated with the sheer pleasure of the union of their lips. His mouth tasted like the inside of a peach. She sampled every inch of it.

Gordon felt like a cloud heavy with rain, ready to burst. In the room, a kaleidoscope of flowers were in various stages of bloom. A woman's haunting voice sailed over syncopated percussion. Candles releasing jasmine, sandalwood, and lavender converged with the ocean of her aroma. Gordon let go and floated with it.

Nirvana, Xanadu, paradise. She had reached them all in the center of his kiss. She didn't think they could get any closer, but he moved in, erasing any space between them. Her body molded to his like soft clay.

She pressed closer, nearer. Deeper into his mouth. His delicious, fantastic mouth. Gordon wasn't the only one who knew a thing or two about lip lovemaking. Ashley tilted her head and used her tongue to massage from one side of his mouth to the other. By the time she finished, both of their mouths were drenched with abandon.

Heat spread to all parts of her body. She'd never experienced anything so addictive. She didn't ever want to stop kissing him. Prayed that he wouldn't take his sweet lips away. For a split second, her eyes fluttered open, only to find his jade greens staring sensuously at her. At the light smacking sound of their kiss, Ashley became painfully aroused. Another moan escaped. Despite her attempt, she was losing fast.

He continued his breathy kiss, deepening his probe, siphoning her energy. She felt herself, her spirit, her essence flowing into him. Her mind was saturated with pleasure.

Blood beat in his lips, and the tension mounted between them. She wondered what was next.

Gordon pulled away, but Ashley had the distinct feeling of being captured. And unlike before, she wanted whatever came next after the kiss. Whatever this intimate exchange foreshadowed, her body softly trembled with need for it.

She opened her eyes. He was staring at her, eyes half-mast and drunk with arousal. She knew she was standing, but she felt as though she'd just been knocked down. She didn't get a chance to demonstrate her idea of a great kiss, but now, her idea of a great kiss had changed—drastically.

Ashley returned his stare and blinked a few times, then spoke.

"You win," she said, lips still quivering from the exchange. She leaned against him, wanting to finish what they'd started. "Your mouth is . . ."

Gordon took half a step backward.

He placed a featherlight kiss on her right eyelid and then her left. "I've gotta go," he said. "Remember the potion."

Remember the potion? she thought as he left her house. After that kiss, she couldn't even remember her own name.

When the phone rang, Ashley was in her favorite yoga position—the goddess pose—and breathing deeply. Gordon had been gone for hours but she could still taste his lips, could still feel them on hers. She hadn't been able to concentrate on practicing her routine for the tryouts, so instead she decided to clear her mind and meditate. She'd grabbed her mat, chose a goddess mantra, and tried with all her energy to free her thoughts.

It didn't work very well at all. The sweet smell of Gordon's breath, his intense stare, his boldness, had given her vertigo. She would have to light candles and burn incense to rid herself of his possession.

She swung herself to a sitting position and reached for the receiver.

"Peace and blessings," she said.

"Hey, Ashie."

Morgan. She was the only one who remembered when their sister Marti was little and pronounced her name Ashie instead of Ashley. She was glad the slipup never became a nickname, just something Morgan chose to remember from time to time. Usually when she was about to say something Ashley wouldn't like.

"Your voice sounds good in my ear today, sister."

"Yeah, it has been a while. I'm sorry about that. It's just

that I've been on a lot of auditions lately. Commercials, cable, magazines. You know . . ."

Yes, Ashley knew that her sister Morgan was beautiful and trying, unsuccessfully, to make it as a model. She hoped the goddess of the world had better things in store for her older sister.

"I'm calling to tell you that we like him."

"Morgan—"

"I know. He's just a *friend*. But he's intelligent, courageous, and relatively normal from what we can tell. Not like the other guys you've dated."

"There's nothing wrong with the guys I've dated in the past," she said, feeling all the tension that she'd just spent the last hour trying to release building up again.

"Then why aren't you still with any of them?"

"People are different. They change. Sometimes things just don't work out."

"Especially if you are dealing with men whose idea of a good time is talking about the existential nature of life, communing with trees, or living in a cave for three years."

"Just because you don't find those traits appealing doesn't mean that I don't."

"Okay, look, Ashley. I didn't call to pick a fight with you. I just want to let you know that the family approves of Gordon should you ever decide to go that way."

The family, she mused. She'd never fully felt part of *the family*. Always the outsider. The weirdo. When she'd first heard her sister's voice, she'd had a mind to tell her about Cirque du Soleil, about finally finding her passion. Her true passion. She wanted to be a part of the performance troupe more than she'd ever wanted anything. She knew, without a whisper of doubt, that she could finally be a part of a family of people who would accept her unconditionally. But that would be just one more thing in a long list for her family to hold against her, to judge her by.

No, she wouldn't tell any of them about the tryouts. And then when she became part of the cast, she would buy them all tickets to a performance without telling them why. They would be so surprised. She knew that for the first time in many years, they would be proud of her. And she needed them to be proud of her. She wanted that day like she wanted her next cleansing breath.

"Thanks, Morgan," she said. She reflected on her kiss with Gordon once more. Her lips tingled. "I'll let you know if anything changes between me and my friend."

"Ashley?"

"Yes?"

Morgan hesitated. It wasn't like her. She and Roxanne were so much alike. Never ones to hold their tongues. Never ones to stop short of a comment.

"You know we love you, don't you?"

Ashley was not always so quick with her words. It mattered to her. Saying the right thing. Being appropriate. Not hurting people's feelings. Her first answer was *no*. She didn't always believe that her sisters really loved her. They often talked to her as if she were naive and childish, simply because her lifestyle was different than theirs. She mumbled a response, not even sure herself of what she'd said.

"We do, little sister. We want you to be happy, and it's just hard for us to accept the fact that you probably are. Understand?"

"Yes," she said. And she did.

"That was some wedding present you gave."

"Is that a positive comment or a negative one?"

Morgan chuckled. "Definitely positive. And your friend . . . Gordon . . . I thought he was going to explode in his chair. I mean, for someone who's just a friend, ol' boy was hard as a rock!"

"Really?" she said, a revelation that brought on the

calm she'd been seeking all morning. "The highlight of the whole thing was Amara with two crying babies in her arms," she said, feeling the need to change the subject.

"No, the highlight was Gordon trying to recruit Davis and Davis trying to get Gordon's computer business. Those two are just alike."

"Not at all! Davis is a businessman. Gordon is a salesman. There's a difference."

"Just *friends*, huh?"

At the slightest hint that her relationship with Gordon had changed, her sister used it as an excuse to rush over to Ashley's house. They finished the rest of their conversation over green tea in Ashley's kitchen.

Ashley didn't make it a habit of confiding in her family. Somehow her admissions were always used to support her sisters' opinions that she had no direction in life. But the kiss from Gordon had such a profound impact on her heart chakra that she had to tell someone.

"Maybe he's not just a friend," Ashley admitted.

"I knew it!"

"No, no. This is a recent development. I mean, the only thing we've done is kiss. But, Morgan . . ."

"Yeah?"

"It was the best kiss I've ever had in my *entire* life. That kiss was better than most of the love I've made."

For about five seconds, there was complete silence. Then Morgan and Ashley's laughter filled the room like wind chimes.

"You like him?" Morgan asked.

"Yes," Ashley said without thinking. "But he doesn't believe in relationships."

"So?"

"What do you mean, so?"

"I mean that Gordon seems like the type of man you could have some fun with."

"But I'm not like you and Roxy. I can't just fool around with a guy. I need stability."

Morgan nodded. "Apparently Roxy does too now that Haughton's back. But anyway . . . all I'm saying is, get loose. Have some fun for a change. Stop being so intense about everything."

Ashley wanted to meditate right then and there.

"And if this guy wants to have some fun with you, let him. If it's meant to be, it will be."

They clinked their cups together and drank the hot tea.

Ashley immediately felt like she'd done the wrong thing. She shouldn't have told her sister anything. Now every time they talked, Morgan would ask about Gordon. Ashley took another sip of her tea, wondering if there would be anything interesting for her to tell.

Seven

From the time Ashley Allgood was a teenager, she'd believed that the alignment of body, spirit, and mind was the key to happiness. She'd lived a vegan lifestyle. She practiced yoga and belly dancing to keep fit. To maintain spiritual alignment, she meditated regularly and incorporated the best of many religious practices including Christianity, Buddhism, shamanism, and voodoo to create a personal relationship with her Creator. But not much she'd done in the past twenty years had brought her the staggering bliss she found in Gordon's mouth. Her lips quivered when she thought of it. The memory made her want to forget the regimen she'd created over the years and spend the day lounging on her couch eating a cheeseburger and watching trashy talk shows.

She was so excited and bubbling with energy, she thought if it weren't for her skin, she would burst into a million pieces.

Ten times a day she reached for the phone. She wanted to hear his voice. She needed a dose of his deep rich baritone to soothe her quickening nerves. On her walk to the bookstore some mornings, she'd thought about forgetting her job that day and heading to Gordon's apartment.

Now she understood addiction. And she would do anything for a fix of his lips on hers. Anything, but give him a call.

Since she'd known him, Gordon had been full of stories about all the women who called him at all times of the day and night.

Booty calls.

She stared at the phone while visions of Gordon's lips made her pant. All she wanted was a lip call.

Why hadn't he called her? she wondered, but knew immediately. He wanted her to come to him. He'd made the first move and now their friendship would never be the same. Whatever they would do from this point on, it would be her call that decided it.

Ashley stepped out of the *sirsasana* pose in which she stood on her head, walked over to the phone, and dialed his number.

"No!" Van shouted, jumping up and down in his seat like a jack-in-the-box. Apparently, he was disgusted by the Vikings' performance. Gordon was about to get his car personally washed and waxed for the second time in the football season. He had a lot to be grateful for.

"Hold up, man. You're looking too smug, and I know this game is not that exciting."

"I'm just looking forward to this waxing of my Viper . . . and my phone call from Ashley."

"She calls you all the time."

"Not since Big Daddy laid the smack down on her. But she will. She's resisted longer than most, but my technique is foolproof. Any moment now—"

"Man, shut up. You always struttin' around like you're all that."

Gordon's eyebrow arched. Nonbelievers. He knew he'd put it on Ashley. Thicker than he'd ever done for anyone. Part of his soul had seeped out in that kiss. She couldn't help being affected by it, captivated by it, enraptured by it, weakened by it. He knew the same thing that weakened her would be what gave her the strength she needed to call him—invite him back—or better yet, come to his house and let him make love to her.

The sports bar hummed with conversation. One large-screen television drew his friend's steady attention. Another interception of one of Dante Culpepper's perfect spirals brought groans of disapproval. They almost drowned out his ringing cell phone. He retrieved the small device from its holder and smiled at the name and number illuminated on the screen. He shoved the screen in front of Van's face for a hot second before answering.

With a smile spreading in warm reassurance on his face, he pressed the answer button on his cell phone. "Come to me," he said. "Tonight. Eight o'clock."

He waited half a beat before hanging up. Longer than he'd ever given any other woman.

She was off center. Meditation, the warrior's yoga pose, and donning all orange—the color of emotional balance—was not helping. As she sat on the Marta, the city's public transportation system, downtown Atlanta sped by. She barely noticed. Her hands fidgeted, her heart palpitated, and if she wasn't careful, she would chew her bottom lip raw.

"Chill out," she mumbled under her breath.

A keen believer in visualization, Ashley focused her attention on imagining what would happen when she got to Gordon's apartment. After more than a year of being close friends, she knew him well. He'd be dressed to impress—something expensive and tailored. Probably not a suit, but close to it. Something that said *class* and *designer*. Since they both knew why she was coming to "visit," he'd probably have some hip-hop "let me lick you all over" music playing, or if she were lucky, some old-school Luther. Gordon could put away some beer. As the Marta sped through the heart of the city, the thought occurred to her that he might try to get her drunk or at the very least offer her some champagne.

She smiled inside, remembering all of the stories of seduction she'd heard Gordon spin. She wondered how much of them was true. From his tales, Mr. Salesman did more talking to his girlfriends than anything else. She prepared herself for an evening of long conversations of bragging, boasts, and a wager or two.

At first, she thought it would be a hard evening to endure, that is until they got to "the good part." If his lovemaking was anything like his kissing, it would be worth a few unpleasantries to experience it.

Ashley shifted in her seat. She wasn't nervous anymore. As a matter of fact, she was eager to get the evening started.

When she arrived at Gordon's apartment building, some of her previous nervousness returned. She'd turned into one of Gordon's fawning women. The ones who jumped when he said jump and came libido in tow when he said, "Come to me." It's exactly what she feared in the first place. She slowed her steps toward apartment 103. All of the apartments in his building had outside entrances. It would be her luck, Gordon would be glancing out the window or standing in the doorway just in time to see her bolt back to the transit center.

No. She was a big girl. And besides, she had to at least call Gordon's bluff. Otherwise, she would never hear the end of it.

She needed a mantra. Something she could chant over and over, to steady herself. She didn't want to come across as a complete pushover. Then a sound caught her attention. It was faint, but as she drew closer to Gordon's apartment, she heard the distinct sounds of Groove Theory, a musical group she loved. Her tension eased.

Someone around here has good taste, she thought, humming along. It was a sign, she thought. Someone, somewhere was trying to tell her she was doing the right thing.

One-O-One, 102, *103*. She tousled her hair a bit, pulled her orange top down a tad, and licked her lips. When she pressed the doorbell, she was ready. At least that's what she thought.

When Gordon opened the door, she realized she wasn't ready at all.

"Punctual," he said. "Just like I knew you would be."

Ashley wanted to come back with a smart retort. As a matter of fact, one even came to her mind, but vanished as soon as their eyes met. She had to keep focused on his eyes; that way she wouldn't stare at his chest, which was shirtless and cut to brown-tan perfection. Or the red silk pajama bottoms that rode low on his narrow hips. Or his beautiful bare feet. She also wouldn't be able to stare at all that brown skin that glistened like it had been dipped in hot oil.

She swallowed and forced her mouth to work. "Drinking without me?" she asked, trying to fake her cool by focusing on the crystal flute in his hand.

"No," he said, extending his arm. "This is for you."

Her eyes widened in surprise and she took his offering.

"Are you going to drink out there or are you coming in?"

"I'm coming in," Ashley responded, and stepped boldly inside.

She'd been to Gordon's apartment before, but tonight it was like seeing it for the first time. His furniture was rearranged *feng shui* style. It put her instantly at ease. And the music, she realized, that comforting sound she'd heard just a few doors away, was coming from Gordon's stereo. Top that off with the candles he had burning, the subdued lighting, and Ashley had never felt so at home anywhere except her own house.

"The place looks great," she said, sweeping it with another glance.

"Have a seat," he said.

She sat on the couch, impressed with what he'd done. "Looks great, smells great . . . feels great."

He sat across from her. Another surprise, she thought, realizing that in her mind's eye she had imagined him sitting beside her.

Well, I got one thing right. He did offer me a drink. She took a sip and awaited the warm buzz of champagne. It never came. She was drinking sparkling cider. The man had given her sparkling cider!

"You are full of surprises this evening," she said.

Gordon smiled and stared at her in the flickering light of candles with eyes that grew as dark as thunderclouds. The sight etched warm shivers down her back.

Ashley fidgeted with her feet. She knew it probably looked as though she was playing footsie with herself, but she couldn't help it. She despised shoes. Her feet always felt as if they were claustrophobic. And now add to that the fact that Gordon's hot gaze was making her nervous, and she just couldn't keep still.

His eyes took a merciless assault path down her body. When they stopped at strategic places like her breasts and the juncture of her thighs, Ashley thought she would melt away like a thin candle. When his eyes lingered at her feet, she felt his stare like a silken caress. She'd definitely made the right decision coming to his apartment.

Her lips tingled at the memory of his kiss. Gordon's silence was driving her mad. She forced herself to concentrate on the soulful sounds coming from his stereo, letting them relax her. That attempt lasted only a few brief moments. When Gordon moved from where he was seated in the chair across from her and got down on his hands and knees, Ashley gasped and gulped her sparkling wate..

"Gordon, wh—"

"How's your drink?" he asked seductively.

She was going to say, *It's fine.* She wanted to say, *You're fine.* But she lost all sense of clarity as he moved toward her, stalking, closing in. His catlike motions sent chills raging throughout her body. The air between them crackled with tension and unrequited desire. Ashley's figiting became even more pronounced, until Gordon stopped in front of her and cupped her feet in his hands.

One by one, he removed her sandals. Her breathing grew heavy, deeper as she imagined his next move.

She didn't need her imagination for long. After a few moments, Gordon's hands began caressing her feet, stroking them with sensuous motions. Just when she thought the feeling couldn't get any better, Gordon took her big toe into his mouth.

Her strong-black-woman exterior melted away with a squeal of delight. She couldn't contain herself as his tongue swirled and the warm moist inside of his mouth enveloped her toe. How dare she let a man know that he had this much control over her. But there was nothing she could do. She could put up no resistance. He had won.

To avoid spilling her drink or dropping it on the floor altogether, Ashley placed the flute on the small table beside her. Her hand trembled as she realized the only thing she could fully concentrate on was the sensation radiating from her foot. Gordon sucked leisurely at each toe. Ashley panted and moaned. The only thing she ever wanted on her feet ever again was Gordon's tongue. No socks, no panty hose, no shoes. Just lips and tongue, and . . . Oh, great Athena. Now he'd switched to the other foot.

"Ahhh," she said, unconsciously. The sound escaped from her lips on its own but in synch with the way Gordon's masterful mouth delighted each digit of her foot.

"Tell me it's good," he said, in a hot rush of breath over her instep.

She sighed his name. "Oh, Gordon, it's better than good."

He had her body tingling in ways she'd never imagined. His hands stroked her calves. He kissed each ankle, licked her shins, and sucked her thighs. Ashley was delirious with anticipation. She trembled and jerked on the couch like a wild woman abandoning her feminine demure to something more carnal, something Gordon seemed intent on releasing.

As his attentions moved upward, so did his hands as he slid the fabric of her sarong up above her knees, past her thighs, and around her waist.

When he slid off her thong, Ashley closed her eyes. *His kiss,* she thought. *His wonderful kiss. And now, he's going to kiss my . . .*

"Ooooh!" she cooed, and sank down into the cushions of the couch as Gordon siphoned energy away from her body and into his mouth. What he did with his tongue, lips, and teeth was sinful.

And she loved it.

She felt her juices flowing and prayed that Gordon knew how to swim. She wasn't ready to give up this good feeling any time soon.

Part of her wanted to do something, swivel her hips, grind her thighs, grab his head. But Gordon had rendered her powerless to do anything except lie back and let him have his way.

Sweet god of fire, she thought as she felt her heat rise. Gordon's rhythm came faster now. His tongue flicked over her most sensitive area like quicksilver. Ashley cried out, never having felt such intense sensations.

And then the tears came.

She sobbed and climbed higher with Gordon as her guide. No out-of-body experience could be so powerful. She closed her eyes and could see the stars in the heavens.

It was too much. A split second after she thought about begging him to stop, she experienced a soul-shattering climax.

She screamed as her body convulsed with spasms. Her chest heaved while she tried to catch her breath and regain her composure.

When she opened her eyes, Gordon was staring at her. Desire darkened his eyes and he licked his lips.

A smile of satisfaction, ever so slight, curled the right side of his mouth. "Can I . . . get you anything else?"

Ashley's eyes grew wide. She took her sparkling cider from the table, gulped it down, and asked with a voice low and husky, "What else have you got?"

He didn't waste time in answering. Gordon scooped her into his arms and carried her into his bedroom. She gasped at the sight of his sleeping area. Everything in the room was red. The curtains, the bedding, the area rug. Red candles burned on every flat surface with the exception of where a red bowl filled with cherries and strawberries chilled in ice.

Red—the heart chakra—the color of eternal bliss, compassion, and pure love. Gordon knew what he was doing. He was creating the type of atmosphere to make her fall in love.

And, Goddess protect her, it was working.

A trail of rose petals led from the doorway to the bed.

Some petals were scattered against the red pillowcase. He laid her down in the middle of the mattress.

Silk, she thought as she inhaled. The scent of roses filled her nostrils. The room was thick with it. She sighed and closed her eyes.

"No, don't," he said. "I want you to see everything."

Ashley's gaze settled on Gordon's body as he slowly undressed before her. She moaned as he removed the only article of clothing he wore. The sight of his magnificent frame made her impatient.

"Did you make that potion for the woman I'm in love with?" he asked, stepping out of the pajama bottoms.

"She doesn't need a potion. All she needs is you."

Suddenly, her clothes were too confining, an abomination. She couldn't wait another moment to be free of them. She tore at her sarong, snatched at her tube top, and tossed both to the floor. When she was finally naked, she saw Gordon's manhood throb and grow even more rigid. The sight shot hot waves of desire through her veins. She opened her arms.

After sheathing his erection in a condom, Gordon came down fully upon her in slow motion. He stretched her arms above her head, opened her legs with his, and claimed her mouth.

Everything about her smelled wet. Her hair damp with perspiration, her skin glistening with his sweat, her core filling with her feminine moisture. He guided himself to where she was wet the most. Many times before he had seen her in various positions—sitting with legs folded, bent to the side with her arm skyward, or standing on her head—today she was prone and yielding. The best pose of all. He entered her carefully and sank deeper with her moan. Then as he slid himself slowly in and out of her, he whispered her name. "Ashley . . . Ashley." His whisper kept time with his rhythm. Her body responded in kind, arching to him, matching him, meeting him. He tightened his grip on her wrists.

She couldn't have been any more confined if she'd been a wrestler on *SmackDown*—and she couldn't have been any more in love. Mr. Charisma had done it. He'd charmed his way into her heart slowly, gradually, expertly.

Like the poem by Nikki Giovanni, when she said, "Ah," he said, "Chew."

The perfect complement.

The yin to her yang. Or was it the other way around? She didn't know—she didn't know anything now. Only that she loved him. The time and care he'd taken to make this evening perfect—to make it *her* evening—she knew he would never do this for any other woman. Just the thought of his gesture brought soft explosions inside her one after the other.

"Hey," he said, breaking the longest kiss she'd ever had. "You still with me?"

She smiled, barely able to contain her happiness. "I'll be with you forever . . . if that's what you want."

"Hmmph," he muttered, nuzzling her neck. "Let me show you what I want."

Ashley's body hummed with Gordon's rhythm. Her skin glowed red from the objects in the room. "You did all this for me?"

"Did it." *Kiss.* "Doin' it." *Lick.* He plunged deeper. She moaned louder. "And doin' it well, don't you think?" *Nip.*

"You're so full of yourself," she whispered, nibbling at the lobe of his ear, yet knowing he was correct.

He scooped her behind into his hands and pulled her toward him. "Right now, I'd say that *you* are full of me." He moved faster and stared into her eyes. "Why did we wait so long?"

His question nearly spoiled her sensuous journey. She

didn't want to think about being a name in his thick black book. So, she pushed the thought from her mind and surrendered herself to the mounting sensations brought on by their intimate exchange. As she felt ecstasy's peak rise within her, she responded to Gordon's question in a whimper. "It was worth it. It was . . . worth it."

As his pleasure increased, the octave of his voice decreased, and he continued to repeat her name. "Ashley . . . Ashley."

Soon they moved faster and Ashley responded with his name. The sound of Gordon's voice deepened until it was no longer her name, but the sound of universal unity. The love of his life thrashed and whimpered beneath him as he transmuted her name from "Ashley" to "Om."

His entire body vibrated with the sound. And when Ashley tumbled over the edge, Gordon was not far behind.

Eight

"Don't move. These pins are sharp."

Ashley stood in the middle of her living room with her arms stretched out to her sides. Her sister Morgan was checking her new belly-dancing costume for final alterations.

"You say that every time," Ashley responded.

"That's because it's true every time. Now hold still."

Hold still. That was a tall order. Ashley hadn't been still since her night with Gordon. For the past three days, she'd been filled with such a divine sense of power and purpose. She'd spent some of the time practicing for her audition, but most of the time she'd fantasized about the way her soul had merged with his. She was completely filled with joy and at the same time caution. He wasn't exactly the kind of man she'd ever envisioned herself with.

"I can't believe I have feelings for him!" Ashley blurted.

Morgan smiled as if she'd been waiting for her to say those words all evening. "Why not?"

"Because the man used to smoke cigarettes."

Morgan looked bemused. "Everybody has a past."

"He eats meat!"

"So! Learn how to cook pork chops."

Ashley grimaced. "And he's grounded in the superficial—money, clothes, and cars."

"I think the operative word here is *grounded.* Unlike some folks who claim to have out-of-body experiences."

Ashley whirled. "That was an experiment! I wish you would stop bringing that up!"

"Watch out," Morgan snapped, yanking a pin back. "You'll make me stick you. Heck, as bullheaded as you're being, I might just stick you on GP."

Ashley crossed her arms. "I am not being bullheaded."

"You care about this man. Obviously, he cares about you. What's the problem?"

"He's just . . ." Ashley's energy slid down her body and trickled out through the soles of her feet. "He's not what I pictured as my ideal mate. I wanted someone spiritually aware and in balance. A man whose essence is not so overtly sexual. I wanted someone with a cosmic direction in life, a dedication to people. Gordon's idea of making the world better is simply waking up every day. A man like that could close all my chakras."

"Or open them," Morgan replied, swatting her sister on the behind. "Okay, take a look."

Ashley stepped to a full-length mirror in the corner of the room. Her new costume was fabulous! Having a sister who loved sewing had its advantages. Ashley couldn't remember the last time she'd actually gone clothes shopping in a department store. Morgan was always dropping by with a scarf, skirt, or sometimes an entire outfit. Ashley knew Morgan would never admit it, but she liked the fact that Ashley's tastes were out of the ordinary. That way she could try her hand at clothing and designs none of her other sisters would like. She'd made every goddess costume Ashley had ever worn. But this one was exceptional.

A whisper of ruby red trimmed with rivers of shiny gold coins. It left very little to the imagination and either revealed or accentuated her curves in all the right ways.

She wrapped the matching veil around her. It floated through the air and settled on her shoulders like a secret seeking an ear.

"It's wonderful!" Ashley said. Then she hugged her sister tightly. "You're wonderful."

Morgan tugged at the waist of Ashley's skirt, pulling it lower on her hips. "This is true. Now what are you going to do about your *man?*"

Ashley backed up and tested her new threads by moving her hips in an ellipsis. She put her hands above her head and rolled her stomach like ocean waves. A grin burst through the resolve on her face.

Morgan grinned, too. "Now you're talkin'."

"How soon can you finish the alterations?"

"Well . . . knowing my little sister the way I do, I'll be finished today. My machine is in the car. I brought it just in case."

"I love you!" Ashley said, giving her sister a smack on the cheek. Morgan smiled and headed outside.

Ashley twirled. A sea of gossamer red flowed in slow waves behind her. She couldn't wait to show Gordon. She would do a skirt dance especially for him. And then, she would make love to him—all night, she thought. Yes, he'd loved her sweetly in his bedroom. Yes, he was the best kisser she'd ever known. But she was no stranger to pleasure. She knew ways to join the male and female energies together in one body to ascend the highest levels of gratification. She'd always wanted to explore ancient love techniques with someone, but no one was ever special enough. Never her soul mate, until Gordon. Her heart felt locked into a beat with his. She remembered feeling his *chi* before he entered the bookstore on the day they met. They'd been twin souls from the start.

She would show Gordon all she knew about what

those in her circle called *the sacred joining*. Her actions would unite them forever.

When Ashley called him on his cell phone and invited him over with an eager voice, he thought she wanted to rehearse her performance one last time. When she opened the door, he knew he'd thought wrong.

She was covered, but it didn't matter. He could see everything. His lungs stopped working midbreath and raw need sent a dull ache immediately to his loins. When he breathed again, he was on his way to a full erection.

A curse escaped his lips as he realized that since he last touched her, he'd been drowning in her memory. Seeing her now was truly a breath of fresh air or more like fresh rainwater.

"I hope that means you like what you see," she said, stepping aside.

He brushed past her close enough to smell the ocean on her skin. It made him drunk and needy.

She closed the door behind him. He barely noticed. His attention was caught by the flickering lights of at least fifty white long-stem candles and the ethereal sound of a woman singing over a sultry bass and saxophone. His blood began to heat.

He turned around to where she stood behind him with only a sheer crimson fabric draped over her body. He couldn't wait any longer and apparently neither could she. Ashley obviously wanted more of his ardent lovemaking and had made arrangements to get what she wanted. He stepped closer.

She backed away.

"Welcome, Gordon," she said, her face a mask of sensuality and femininity. "Tonight is for you."

This sounds good, he thought.

"I will make you three promises this night. One, I am completely at your disposal. I will do anything that you ask. Two, I will use all of my tantric skills to please you. And three, if you do exactly as I tell you, you will have the most pleasurable sexual experience of your life."

Gordon licked his lips and nearly came right then and there. Evidence of his acute arousal throbbed in his pants. If her words made him feel this way, whatever she planned to do with him was going to send him into orbit.

Before he dissolved into a wet puddle of lust, he mustered the last vestiges of bravado he had. "Big Daddy like."

Her eyes twinkled and she offered a slight bow. "I've planned several foreplay . . . events." She took his hand and led him toward the bathroom. "A bath, followed by a full-body massage. Of course," she said, casting a glance to where his manhood strained against the fly of his pants, "if you would rather skip the foreplay—"

He nodded, pulse pounding. "Anything I want?"

"Anything."

"Skip the foreplay."

"As you wish," she responded and guided him into her bedroom.

More candles than he could count illuminated the room Gordon had wanted to get into for months.

It was as enchanting as he had imagined. Ornaments and symbols of spiritual and religious rituals lined the walls and crowded her dresser top. Finger cymbals, hip scarves, yoga blocks and straps. The focal point of the room was the queen-size bed with red drapes covering it.

"May I undress you?" she asked.

Gordon held his arms out to his sides. "Yes, you may."

She started with his shirt. "I must tell you that we won't be having sex tonight."

"What!" he said with a jerk.

"What we will do tonight goes beyond sexual gratification."

"Umm," he moaned, finally realizing what this was about. It was about a challenge—a contest—a wager. She was competing with him for sexual one-upmanship. She wanted to prove her prowess. Well, he had every intention of letting her prove whatever she chose.

"There are some things you must know," she said, unzipping his pants. "Tantric sex is about the harnessing and exchange of energy. It's not about the act. It's about achieving balance and unity through breath and reciprocity. It's about reaching a higher state of consciousness by treating the body as a temple."

"Which one are we going to focus on tonight?"

"All of them."

He gulped. The heat in his veins ratcheted up several degrees. With Ashley's help, he stepped out of his shoes, socks, trousers, and boxers. He stood naked before her, eager for what she would do next.

Jewelry accented her honey-brown body—a choker with a mesh of red pearls leading down in a triangle to mouthwatering cleavage. A thin golden-red belt circled her waist and ankle. And on her beautiful feet a toe ring with a small red pearl in it. She looked like a high priestess of love—*his* high priestess of love.

"You've been very open recently with the way you feel about me. Tonight I'm going to be open with you and show you how *I* feel."

She raised the fabric draping from her body and took it off. Now Gordon's blood boiled in his veins. "You are beautiful," he said.

She smiled and led him toward the bed. "Is there anything special you want to do?"

"Yes," he replied, sitting on the mattress. "Absolutely nothing."

Ashley bowed slightly. "As you wish."

He lay down on the bed and placed his hands behind his head. Something told him that this was going to be good.

She straddled him across his lower hips and removed a scarlet scarf from the nightstand. She pulled the fabric across his body and he closed his eyes.

"No, don't," she said. "I need you to be fully aware of your body. Now this," she said, trailing the soft fabric across his legs and thighs, "this will awaken your senses. I want you to experience our joining with every aspect of your body."

With those words, every nerve ending on Gordon's skin ignited. He sucked in a gulp of air at the sensation. Ashley continued to draw the silk scarf in swirling patterns all over his body. Everywhere the silk touched, his skin tingled with pleasure.

She replaced the silk scarf on the nightstand and picked up a feather. Gordon's breath quickened with anticipation.

"Breathe with me," Ashley whispered. "And quiet your mind." She repeated her sensuous torture with the feather, and again his nerves were on fire. When she'd stroked every inch of him, she held the feather high above his chest and let it go. It wafted gently downward and settled on his stomach.

"Each time your energy rises, breathe with me, relax, quiet your mind by becoming the floating feather, and visualize the transfer of your building energy into my body."

He arched an eyebrow at her instructions.

"You must do as you're told," she said. "It will be worth it," she assured him, as a soft smile lit up her face. "Now, I want you to be fully aware of my body."

He thrust his erection toward her with his hips, signaling his readiness for copulation. "Oh, I'm fully aware of your gorgeous body."

She reached over to the nightstand and retrieved a large bottle of oil. She poured some into the palm of her hand and then replaced the bottle. Then meticulously she skimmed the tips of her fingers against his hands, arms, and chest. She moved lower to his abdomen, thighs, and lower legs. When she reached his feet, she started her trek again, then stopped at Gordon's stiffening member. Her strokes became more thorough and at the same time languid and luxurious. His whole body thrummed with the sensation.

"This motion will coax energies out of their resting places," she said.

"You ain't lyin'," Gordon admitted.

"Now focus, Gordon, on me. Quiet your mind and really see me."

He sank deeper into the bed and stared into her eyes. With her deft strokes, it was easy for him to quiet his mind. In fact, his entire body seemed to have calmed down. And for the first time, he was aware of how spectacular her eyes truly were. They sparkled like backlit topaz. Her eyes looked like his heart felt, warm and passionate. Her skin was flawless like toasted honey, except for a patter of freckles and moles on her shoulder that looked like a sunburst or a star.

All of his senses were sharpened. He could discern the musk and jasmine in the incense burning. He could smell the ocean on Ashley's skin. He felt the air stirring over his hips from the movement of her hands. He'd never been this alert during sex before, never this attentive. It was as though all his pores were open and sensations were flooding in. It didn't take him long to figure out that the loud pounding he heard was his and Ashley's hearts beating synchronously. Their energies were honestly merging. The insight thrilled him in the most intense way.

Her priestess magic had worked. Gordon couldn't wait one more moment to join with Ashley. He just couldn't wait. "Ash," he whispered, reaching up for her. He pulled her down and assaulted her lips with his kiss. Their tongues mated and flourished against each other in an exchange of passion and need. He slid his erection across the space between her legs that was warm and wet, the scent of her arousal increasing his desire.

Ashley broke free of his lips and took a palm-sized packet from the nightstand. She opened it and took out the largest condom he'd ever seen.

"I'm big, baby," he said, "but I ain't that big."

She kissed him gingerly on the forehead. "It's for me."

She squeezed a few drops of lubricant inside the condom, leaned back, and inserted it inside herself.

"Now you'll be able to feel everything," she said and lowered herself on to the hard place on his body that was tight with need. The feeling was exquisite, beginning an erotic cycle of relaxing, breathing, and redirecting.

After a few moments, her hips began to dance. A rocking motion, like being on the bow of a ship. The sensation was gentle and powerful at the same time. If she kept this up, he'd have to redirect his energy in the next ten seconds. More than the movement of her pelvis, this was something deeper. It was as if her soul was moving around in his, churning, roiling from one part of his body to another. He'd never experienced anything like it.

His longing increased. Ashley stared into his eyes. "Breathe with me," she said and he did, remembering all of the instructions she'd given him. And just as she'd told him, his body reset. Ashley on the other hand had ecstasy in her eyes. Her female muscles contracted in soft spasms around his male muscle.

"I felt that," he said huskily. "How come you get to do it but I can't?"

"Each time I come, it will send more energy into your body. Very soon, you will not be able to stand it."

He gasped in anticipation.

Only a few moments passed before their sexual energies cycled. Every ten minutes, like clockwork, he would approach climax. He would relax, breathe with Ashley, and redirect the energy buildup. Seconds later shock waves of ecstasy would flow from her to him as she came, each orgasm more powerful than the last.

The timeless motion of their bodies synchronized in love took Gordon to a brand-new place—an ocean, where the only thing that mattered was sailing on a sea of ecstasy with Ashley. This time *she* had won. It wasn't a bet, it was his heart that was the prize. The realization brought him to the brink.

"Breathe with me," Ashley said. And she was right. Gordon once again found himself on the verge of an eruption. He relaxed, breathed deeply, and emptied his energy into her. She answered with the pulsing rhythm of her orgasm. This time a moan came with it. The sweetest moan he'd ever heard.

After what felt like days of lovemaking, Gordon's body could take no more and at last rocked with spasm after spasm of pleasure so intense he couldn't move. Sweat burst through every pore in his body. In that moment, their love was eternal. He felt magic and divine energy. His ego hoped that Ashley would mistake the tiny tear sliding down the side of his face for one of the many trickling beads of sweat.

She collapsed on top of him, shuddering through an orgasm of her own, and for the next few minutes they communicated silently what their hearts had known for a long time.

They were in love.

Nine

The double date was a disaster. They were at Jonesey's Bar and Grill, the best-kept secret in ATL proper. The large room resembled a warehouse-turned-rec room with billiard tables, dartboards, keno, and karaoke after 9:00 P.M. Not to mention the best barbecue in that part of Atlanta. Over two slabs of ribs, a salad, a pitcher of beer, and hot tea, the foursome had blended in with the smattering of patrons in the establishment.

But, while Ashley and Gordon chattered incessantly, smiled like fools, and found every excuse in the book to touch each other, Morgan and Van stared at each other like boxers in neutral corners.

"Next time, you'll believe Big Daddy when he tells you something," Gordon said, winking at Ashley. The two new lovers cracked up and used their raucous laughter as a reason to kiss.

Morgan's face looked as if she'd just put something in her mouth that was too sweet to swallow. "I'm going to play the jukebox," she said, getting up. Knowing what that meant, Ashley excused herself and headed after her sister.

"You don't like him?" she asked, when they were out of earshot.

"Is there anything to like?"

Ashley glanced back at Van. He was handsome. Striking, actually. Tall and dark in a Middle Eastern, olive-brown sort of way. He and Morgan looked like black-Hollywood, beautiful-people types. They had already turned the heads of most everyone in the place, when they walked in so full of elegance and grace.

"He looks good," Ashley said, thinking that maybe they were too much alike.

Morgan's head snapped toward Ashley. "That's superficial."

Ashley pouted. "Sorry."

"Can I at least get some decent conversation? All he talks about is humidity, Doppler radar, and the jet stream."

"He's a meteorologist. That's what they do."

"But do they have to do it *all* the time?"

Ashley chuckled.

Morgan frowned. "I swear. If I hear another joke about barometric pressure, I'm leaving!"

Sliding a five-dollar bill into the slot, Morgan sighed and scanned the selections. Ashley felt a twinge of sorrow for her sister. She had never had any luck with men. They all seemed to be after her for her looks or couldn't handle Morgan's jet-set lifestyle. The men she hooked up with had a tendency to be overprotective, jealous, shallow, or all of the above. And now that all of the All-good sisters had found their soul mates except Morgan, Ashley wondered how her sister felt about that.

Flipping through the selections, Morgan stopped at their brother Xavier's CD.

"You have to play one of Zay's," Ashley said. Sometimes it was still hard for her to believe that her older brother was one of R&B's top entertainment figures. She was so very proud of him.

Together, the sisters created an eclectic playlist. Old school. New school. And even some neoclassic soul. Leading the pack was their brother's latest single, "Take a Chance." Morgan listened, rocked her head, and looked as though she had cooled off a bit.

"Ready to go back?" Ashley asked.

Morgan nodded. "Maybe I was too quick to judge. And if nothing else, I must admit he's not too bad on the eyes."

Relief flooded Ashley's soul. She put an arm around her sister's shoulder. "No, he's not. And I'll tell you something else. He likes you. A lot. I can tell by his aura. It turns deep purple every time you speak."

Morgan smiled tentatively. "Really?"

"Yes."

She squared her shoulders and faced her sister. "Then I'm definitely ready to go back."

But when they turned around and headed back toward to the table, they saw Gordon sitting there alone. He repositioned himself in his chair and took a short swig of his beer.

Ashley's heart sank. "Where's Van?"

"He had to leave," Gordon said. "Weather emergency." He finished the rest of his beer and avoided Morgan's gaze.

Morgan rolled her eyes and mumbled, "Jerk," under her breath.

Ashley, melting from the sensation of Gordon's hand taking hers, said a little prayer that her sister Morgan would find someone as wonderful as Gordon to love.

Gordon knew that she would leave the door open for him, and when he'd walked in with his bouquet of lilies, she was lying on the floor, arms stretched out to her sides, palms up, and her feet propped on a chair. Today, she was a purple flower—violet from hair to toe ring. *What man would need to fool around?* he asked himself. *Every day she is a new woman, and I get the pleasure of learning her all over again.*

He knelt beside her. Her eyes were closed and she was breathing deeply. Not asleep but in a kind of twilight she called the Between Time. He kissed her forehead and walked carefully into the kitchen to put the flowers in water for her. He respected her relaxation time. Once, he'd made the mistake of insisting she stop what she was doing and pay attention to him. He'd paid the price. Not only was she angry that he'd disturbed her, but she was wound so tight the rest of the evening, he'd ended up making love to her all night just to get her emotional centers back in alignment.

Hmm, he thought, coming back into the room. Maybe interrupting her wasn't such a bad idea. But he didn't get the chance. As soon as he sat down, she sat up and greeted him with the warmest smile he'd ever seen.

Ashley's consciousness always took flight whenever she was near Gordon. Her temperature soared and she found it hard to concentrate. Like now. She was staring at his mouth. Again. It was so delicious. Often, when they were apart, she would catch herself fantasizing about the sharp bow of his lips and the strong muscles there. She would daydream about all the ways in which Gordon could contort them, even roll them like a dance over her lips. Being this close to his face made her think of one word.

Addiction.

She was addicted to Gordon's kisses. With every nuance of her being, she needed the pressure of his mouth against hers. She craved that intimacy, was starved for it. She couldn't sleep without the wet soft seal of flesh smacking flesh.

"Ash? Are you meditating again?"

"No," she said, drifting back to his presence. "It's your mouth."

"What about my mouth?"

"I want it," she said.

Gordon moved like a leopard, taking a position beside her on the floor. He knelt over her and she reclined until she lay flat.

"All yours," he said.

Ashley spent the next five minutes taking a leisurely survey of Gordon's mouth. Licking, tasting, sucking, savoring. Her blood ran hot through her veins. He tasted sweet like an orange or maybe a peach. He bathed her lips with his tongue and she moaned with each lick.

He was taking her up, skillfully, like a craftsman. She'd gone from warm contentment to frenzied lust.

When he rolled her hard nipples between his fingers, the pleasure building inside her burst like a sweet eruption. Ashley clung and kissed until her breathing was even and the throbbing between her legs subsided.

"I love you, Ashley," Gordon said. "I have for a long time."

She stared at the sincerity in his face while her pulse sped up again. *Love?* "Gordon—"

"Yeah. A long time. Just let that simmer for a while." He kissed the space between her breasts. "Here."

"Gordon, I—"

The phone rang, cutting her off. Frustrated, she considered ignoring it. It rang a few more times, and then she rushed to her feet and stumbled to the coffee table. "Hello?"

"How's your first soprano?"

"Well, peace and blessings to you too, brother dear."

"Sorry. I'm just in a bind, and I really need your help."

"Anything."

"Tyrika, my backup singer, got a bad sinus infection last week."

"Echinachea and goldenseal tea will clear that right up."

"She's fine now. Except for the fact that she has no voice."

"Uh-oh."

"I'm in the studio this week, and I have to get my next album recorded. We're already three weeks behind schedule. I need you to come in and lay down a track for me."

"Me? Why can't your wife do it? Or Yolanda?"

"I can't pry Destiny three feet from the baby. And you know Yolanda is not coming anywhere near a recording studio."

"What about Morgan? Or Marti?"

"I called *you*, Ashley, because I need *you*. Now, will you help me?"

Ashley let out a long sigh. There was something so artificial about recording studios. She much preferred a more organic environment where things weren't so much programmed as they were spontaneous. But she loved her brother and would do anything to help him and his career.

"When do you need me?"

"Right now."

"Now?" she said, taking a long lingering look at Gordon. He was lying on the floor, looking ripe for the plucking. Sinewy and hard in all the right places at just the right time.

"Give me an hour," she said.

"You got it!"

She hung up the phone, more than ready for her quickie. She had just enough time to settle on top of Gordon, make fast love, shower, and get downtown to the studio.

"I know that look," Gordon said, extending his arm. "You want to be on top, don't you?"

Ah, she sighed. There was nothing like a man who could read your aura.

Ten

By one o'clock in the afternoon, Gordon and Ashley arrived at Nonstop Productions Recording Studio in downtown Atlanta. Ashley gave her name and showed her ID to the security guard. Gordon was ready and put a little mack daddy in his swagger. On the way over, he'd imagined that the building would be full of young women in tight blouses and barely-there miniskirts. By the time they'd made it down the hall and to the elevator bay, his hopes were dashed.

"What's wrong, Daddy Cool? No hotties to turn you on?"

He slipped an arm around her waist. God, she felt good in his embrace. "You're the only hottie that turns me on," he admitted. He thought he was disappointed that all the women he saw were in suits. But that wasn't it. He was disappointed that old habits died hard and he'd actually been looking forward to seeing a parade of women. He promised himself and vowed silently that he would never, ever let his thoughts stray to other women. Gordon Steele was now a one-woman man.

"What's wrong?" Ashley asked as the elevator beeped. "You look like you just bit into a lemon."

"Nothing's wrong, Ashley," he said, tightening his grip. "As a matter of fact, everything's fine." He bent down and stole a quick kiss from her cheek as they got onto the elevator.

Ashley pushed the button for the twenty-ninth floor.

"Been here before?" Gordon asked.

"A few times," she said, smiling. "I sang with Zay on one of the songs on his first CD. I have a pretty good voice and he's tried to talk me into recording a CD several times."

"Really?" Gordon said, amazed. He'd heard her humming enough times. If she wasn't in a yoga pose, she was humming. He'd even heard her sing a few words once and thought she had a nice voice. But he had no idea she'd done some professional recording.

"You sure your brother wasn't just being nice to you?" he said jokingly.

She gave him a soft elbow to the ribs as the elevator stopped on their floor. Ashley strode off the elevator in her purple harem pants and her lilac-colored crop top like a woman in charge—the woman he loved. *Harem pants,* Gordon thought and shook his head while a warm grin spread across his face. Every quirk she had made him smile.

They stopped at another checkpoint. Ashley produced her ID once more and they both signed in. As they made their way down the corridor, Gordon noted the posters, CDs, and albums lining the walls. It was like a tour of new music history.

"Does your brother know all these people?" he asked, recognizing names.

Ashley laughed. "That is the second most asked question after 'can I get a hookup?' He knows some of them. But he's been so wrapped up in his baby girl recently, I didn't think he knew anyone but her."

They rounded a corner and entered a small room. Gordon's eyes grew wide at the sight of all the electronic equipment. Stacks and stacks of what looked like stereo receivers in tall cabinets. A long console where no less than a thousand small levers were lined up. Frequency readouts that looked like radar or polygraph printouts. Several computers and three chairs on wheels. Across from all that equipment was a glass booth with a microphone hanging from the ceiling. The man the R&B world knew as Allgood was standing in the booth wearing headphones and a serious frown. When he caught sight of Ashley, his frown disappeared. He removed the headphones and exited the booth.

He came around into the outer area, hugged his sister, and shook Gordon's hand. The man who had been all smiles at the wedding a few weeks ago looked solemn and remorseful.

"I owe you," he said.

Ashley's eyebrow arched. "Yes, ya do."

She glanced around. The place looked deserted. "Where is everyone? Where's Uncle Sammy?"

Xavier shook his head. "I'm working with some new producers for a few of the songs. You know everything is electronic nowadays. My manager is trying to bring me into the twenty-first century. So my band is sitting this one out."

Ashley frowned and she looked just like her brother then. "You mean this isn't a live recording?"

Xavier draped his arm around his sister. "Of course it's live. You're alive, aren't you? I just need you to put the dressing on the music salad, so I can get some peace."

The expression on her face told Gordon she was worried. But she went along with her brother's request anyway. In a few moments, they were all seated behind the console. The man with the long dreads turned a few dials, flipped a few levers, and a track hotter than the African sun wafted out of speakers at each end of the control panel. Xavier handed her the lyrics and explained that he had written the song as a tribute to lovemaking. The sounds he wanted in the background, although sung, should represent a woman when she was in the throes of good sex.

Ashley blushed. "I don't think I can do that in front of my brother."

Gordon couldn't resist. "You want me to prime the pump for you?"

Her eyes said it all. They flashed like diamonds in the night. He leaned over and planted a big fat juicy kiss on her mouth. He slipped her a little tongue for good measure.

"Let's do this!" she said.

While Ashley and her brother talked about song arrangements, Gordon marveled over all of the gadgetry. Making a record had come a long way from musicians and tape reels to digital sound and computers. Two men entered the studio. He assumed they were engineers. They took seats behind the console. They made introductions and went to work flipping switches and turning levers. Xavier left his sister in the sound booth and took a seat beside Gordon.

"My sister likes you, man."

Gordon smiled, warmed by that thought. "I hope she loves me, because I sure as the sky love her."

Xavier gave him a sideways glance. "Sure as the sky?" he repeated. "You *do* love her."

One of the engineers started the playback.

"Run it forward to the end. Then Ashley can sing her part and I won't have taken up too much of her time."

"No," Ashley's voice boomed through the speakers. "Let me hear the whole thing. I want to get a feel for the mood and the message."

"All right," Xavier said.

The song played in its entirety. Gordon nodded his head with the beat, a sensual, erotic beat that sounded like sex set to music. The groove was already the bomb; he wondered what more Ashley could do.

The song played through to the end and Ashley asked that they start it again, this time with the recorders on. They did as she asked and from the moment she opened her mouth, Gordon would never again think of her in the same way.

She didn't wait until the end of the song to add her vocals. She started in with the music at the beginning. At the first note of her voice, the song rose to another level. It was a voice from heaven, pure and full-bodied. She sounded like a woman in love making the journey to a spectacular orgasm.

Everyone in the entire studio sat in stunned silence. If that wasn't a Grammy-winning performance, Gordon didn't know what was. The emotion pouring out of Ashley riveted him where he sat. Her voice was as smooth as liquid silk and as powerful as thunder. One of the high notes she hit felt as if it blew off the top of Gordon's head. Yet it was so sultry, he'd never look at her the same way ever again. All of that emotion, packed into that round curvaceous body, and those sweet baby-doll eyes.

And she was his.

By the time the recording was finished, Gordon knew three things. One, Xavier had chosen the perfect addition to his record. Two, Ashley had the most beautiful voice he'd ever heard. And three, the next time they made love, he would ask Ashley to sing during the entire experience.

Eleven

Ashley was in full meditation almost the entire drive to the audition in Orlando. Gordon's eyes were on the road, but his mind was on his woman, hoping that she fared well enough in the tryout to make the cut.

He'd seen her performance two more times. It got better with each rehearsal. It moved him. But he had to admit, not as much as her singing. Ashley's voice was truly a gift from God. When he'd spoken to her about it, she'd brushed aside his compliment like a stray hair. She wasn't the least bit interested in her singing ability. But if she'd asked his advice, he would have suggested that she audition for one of the singing roles instead of an acting part.

Gordon changed lanes to drive around a slow-moving Volkswagen, and Ashley came out of her trance.

"Is this going to be another whim on the long list of Ashley whims?"

Gordon flinched on hearing the pain and fear in her voice. "No, babe. You believe in this. You want this more than anything I've ever known you to want. And you know what else?"

"What?" she asked, her voice shaky with nervousness.

"You deserve it."

The conviction in Gordon's voice made her believe. This time her family would be proud of her. She would have done something to earn their respect. But even more than that, she finally believed in herself—fully, completely. At first, she attributed her newfound confidence to Gordon. Maybe some of that was true, but mostly it was her. She'd finally decided that she was going to live her life regardless of what her family thought.

"I know that you're probably running through your act in your mind, but don't, babe. It's probably best if you take your mind off the audition and focus on something more positive."

Gordon could always read her thoughts.

"Like what?"

"Like the way I'm going to kiss you all over, especially where you like it most, and make you scream like a banshee until the wee hours of the morning. Just my way of celebrating your success."

"Thank you," she said, "for speaking my victory into existence."

And for planning the perfect celebration, she thought. She couldn't wait for the audition.

When they arrived at the theater, they were instructed to go two floors down to a training area. Ashley's heart pounded. She would actually be trying out in the very place where the cast members practiced their amazing feats.

They checked in, along with about one hundred others. Those auditioning for the troupe had been narrowed down from an even larger list of people who had sent in resumes and videotapes of their performances. She felt lucky to be one of those chosen. But being there with so many others, Ashley felt her confidence wavering.

Just when she started to doubt herself, Gordon's arm came around her shoulder. "You're going to be fine, rain woman."

She nodded and hitched the duffel bag containing her outfit higher on her shoulder.

Before she left to perform, he blew her a kiss. She gave him a wink and trotted over to the audition room.

While Ashley went with the others for a tryout briefing, Gordon took a seat in the waiting area.

There were so many people, he couldn't tell actors from singers, dancers, or real cast members.

The energy in the room was palpable. He took a deep breath, realizing he was on edge, even though Ashley was the one auditioning. He wanted her to do well. He wanted her to blow the directors away. He knew she would if she were singing. But with so many actors, the competition was stiff.

After waiting a while, pacing and twiddling his thumbs, Gordon suddenly felt a sense of certainty. He jumped out of his seat. *She'll nail it!* he thought, and headed off toward the men's room.

Dirk Ventus was having a bad day. As the head casting director for Cirque du Soleil, his job was a huge one. And it didn't help matters much that he'd seen way too many performers and not enough singers and dancers.

He was so frustrated, he'd stepped out of the audition room in hopes of getting a better perspective on the whole thing.

Usually there were stars, those who obviously stood out from everyone else. But today . . . no one really impressed him. Even his hopes for the performer just trying out. This audition's crop was not of the kind of performers he was accustomed to. Oh, well, he thought, heading into the men's room. The day would be over soon.

"That's my baby's tune," the man drying his hands said.

"I'm sorry?" Dirk responded.

"That music you're humming. It's from my girl, Ashley."

"Oh, yes." Dirk nodded. "She was just on."

"And she killed it! I know she killed it! Even though I thought that she should have been singing."

"Really?" Dirk asked, leaning against the wall, impressed by Gordon's enthusiasm.

"Yeah, she's got the best voice I've ever heard. Ten times better than any singer here today. I'd bet money on it. Just for good measure, I'm going to talk her into auditioning for the singing part, too. But you have to admit, her 'Rain Woman' was the bomb."

"Well, I happen to know," Dirk said, heading for a urinal, "that good singers are in short supply for this new production. So it would be good for her to try out again. I'm Dirk Ventus. Ashley can call me if she has questions."

"I'll let her know. Take care."

"You too," Dirk said, thinking that the man had a smile like a salesman.

In the spot with a beer in his hand and his boy Van by his side, by all accounts Gordon should have been happy in his element. But he wasn't. It's not every day that a player tells his number-one homeboy that he is turning in his player card for good. He knew that he would be just as nervous when he asked Ashley to marry him. Something about Ashley's sixth sense had rubbed off on him.

He knew she would say yes.

But his boy? Van McNeil would create a scene for sure. He'd be against it, arguing that getting married would ruin their friendship. The strength of Gordon's love for Ashley would be seen as a sign of weakness.

Right now, none of the relaxation techniques Ashley had taught him were working. He took a gulp from the long-neck and wished he had a cigarette.

"Hey, man," he said, trying to sound matter-of-fact.

"Can you believe these fools are going to the Super Bowl?" Van asked.

"I told you, man. But listen . . ." He took a deep breath and scratched the back of his neck. "I've got something important to ask you."

To Gordon, it looked as though Van stopped breathing. His eyes focused like hard diamonds and drilled through him like a laser. "You gotta be joking me," Van said.

"Come on. It's not the end of the world."

"The hell you say!"

Gordon took another long swallow.

"You want me to be your best man?"

"Who else would I ask?" Gordon said, thinking Ashley's psychic abilities must have rubbed off on Van.

Van turned up his bottle of beer—gulping until it was gone. He wiped away the spittle with the back of his hand, and released a low belch. "I knew it the day you met her. You've been talking about her nonstop. I just kept hoping that I was wrong."

"Good thing you didn't bet on it."

Van cracked a half smile and held out his hand. "Good thing, man. Good thing." They shook. "You got the ring already?"

"Yeah. It was hard to find one I thought she would like."

"I'll bet. She don't seem like no platinum and diamonds type of sister."

They laughed and then Gordon added, "You got that right."

Van ordered another round of beers. "Now her sister Morgan . . . you better step up to the plate with some diamonds for that one. Lots of big, flawless diamonds. And present them on bended knee on a silver and velvet platter."

Gordon's eyebrow rose. "Been thinkin' about that a lot, have you?"

Van recoiled. "Naw, man. That ain't me. That's why I had to skip out on the double date. A woman like that is nothin' but trouble."

"Uh-huh," Gordon said, studying his friend. "For somebody not thinking about it, you sure are full of details."

"Man, whatever."

Not a moment later, Gordon's cell phone rang. He answered on the second ring. "Talk to me."

"Gordon!"

"Ashley!" he shouted back.

"It's here!" came her loud response. "The letter from Cirque du Soleil is here!"

Gordon stood, nearly knocking over his beer bottle. "What did it say?"

"I don't know! I'm too nervous to open it. Will you come open it for me?"

"I'll be right there!"

"I guess when your woman calls . . ." Van said sarcastically.

"I come runnin'. Check you later, dog."

Van lifted his beer to salute his friend. "Later, but I'm telling you, you've lost all your player points."

"That's all right," Gordon replied as he was leaving. "You can have them."

Twelve

Today she was a princess. Her hue was royal blue from her makeup, to the long, flowing dress, to the polish on her toes.

She let him in, eyes wide with apprehension. "Here," she said, thrusting the letter into his hand. It was wrinkled and damp. "Babe, what have you been doing with this envelope?"

"I haven't been able to put it down since it came in the mail."

She closed the door and he held out his arms. She went to him, nerves leaping inside her like jumping beans.

"Whoa, whoa," he said, stroking her head. His warm hands calmed her. But only a little. She wouldn't be able to regain her composure until she knew what was inside the letter.

"Come sit down," Gordon insisted, ushering her to the couch.

They sat down together, Ashley sitting so close she was almost in his lap.

She stared into his eyes. In them, she saw the calm and assurance she so desperately needed right now.

He smiled. "Are you ready?"

"No," she admitted. "But I have to know."

He leaned forward. His kiss was tender, sweet, and tranquil. He had a way with kisses, Gordon did. He knew exactly what he was doing with his mouth. Exactly. A wave of calm moved slowly through her as if she'd taken a chill pill. She reached up. Touched his face, feeling ten times better.

Ashley pulled back. "I'm ready."

Gordon bestowed one more kiss on her forehead and opened the letter. The whole ordeal happened in slow motion. While he unfolded the paper, Ashley must have prayed ten prayers, all beginning and ending with the word *please*.

He glanced down and his eyes skimmed the page. Before he started reading, she saw the decision in his face.

She turned her head. Her body trembled.

"Dear Ms. Allgood. Thank you for auditioning for an acting role in our new production *Celestia*. You were among the top performers auditioning for this hugely competitive role. Unfortunately—"

"Stop!" Ashley said, head spinning with despair. "I don't need to hear any more."

"Wait," Gordon said. "There's another page with a handwritten note.

"Dear Ashley, I really liked your performance. Unfortunately, there were so many others competing in that category, I had to make hard decisions. I'm glad to hear that you'll be trying out for the singing cast. We could really use a voice of superb quality. I'll see you in a few days. Sincerely, Dirk Ventus."

Every hope she'd held close for the past few months shattered. The disappointment stole her breath. Tears stung her eyes and she rose slowly from the couch. After years of vacillating over what she wanted to do with her life, she had finally made a decision and the opportunity didn't pan out. It was just her luck. And the last thing in the world she wanted to do was sing.

"Let me see that," she said, reaching for the letter. Her

eyes darted quickly across the page and settled on something she didn't understand. "They must have mistaken me for someone else. I never said anything about singing."

"Dirk?" Gordon said.

"Do you think there was a mix-up? I mean maybe I got the wrong letter." Against her better judgment, her hopes soared just a bit.

"Dirk?"

"That's got to be it, Gordon. I mean, I never—"

"Oh, God. Dirk."

Ashley spun on him. "Why do you keep saying that? Do you know this Dirk guy?"

Gordon looked up, his eyes sad and puppy-dogish. The vibe in the room changed. His aura flickered. Something was terribly wrong and it gave Ashley goose bumps. "Gordon?" She sat down beside him.

"I don't *know* Dirk, but I met him. At your audition. We were in the men's room, and I was bragging about you. All of you. I may have inadvertently suggested that you would be trying out for a vocalist."

A streak of panic flashed through Ashley. "You what!"

"I love you! I talk you up to everybody. And I thought that I would be able to convince you to sing too. But you were on such a high after the audition, I forgot all about it."

Ashley's panic turned into a boiling rage. "You had no right to do that!"

Her remark brought them both to their feet.

"I know you've been blessed with a wonderful gift that you're afraid to use because you think it will make you too much like your brother and sisters."

"Oh, what do you know?" Ashley asked, folding her arms.

"I know that you spend so much time trying to create uniqueness that you never realize how different and special you already are."

"You're turning this around. This is about you and how you probably cost me my chance at finally living my dream."

"A dream you've had all of what . . . three months?"

"You know what, Gordon? I can't be around you right now. Your karma is throwing me off. Will you leave now, please?"

Gordon thought of the ring in his pocket and wished he'd popped the question before this argument ensued. He decided the best thing to do was to give Ash some time to cool off, see that he'd made a terrible mistake in judgment, and forgive him for it. In the meantime, he was determined to help Ashley see herself the way he saw her—that she was beautiful, unique, and talented naturally even without trying.

"I'll call you later," he said.

"Don't," she answered. "I won't want to talk with you."

Don't bet on it, he thought.

When the phone rang, Ashley thought it would be Gordon. He'd called every day for the past week to see if he was still in the doghouse.

He was.

However, she was beginning to foresee a time when he would at least be able to poke his nose out without fear of reprisal.

"Hello?"

"Hey, Ashie."

"Hey."

"Whatcha doin'?"

Ashley looked around. She told herself she wasn't going to make a big deal out of its being Valentine's Day, by keeping herself busy making potpourri. "Not much, really. How about you?"

"I'm waiting for my niece and nephew to arrive. I'm baby-sitting the munchkins tonight while your sister and brother spend Valentine's Day in bed with their spouses. They both said they were goin' out. But they ain't foolin' nobody."

Ashley chuckled, then decided to be real with her sister. "Neither are we."

"What do you mean?"

"You know what I mean. Both of us would give our right arm to be all up under a man who loves us right now."

Silence.

"Yeah, well . . . what's your excuse? Gordon's just waiting for you to say the word."

"I know. I guess I've got some of Roxanne's stubbornness after all."

"I called 'cause I was hoping that at least one of us would be on the arm of a handsome man today. You really should talk to him. He seems like a good man."

Ashley sighed at the truth. "He is."

"Girl, don't mess around and wait too late. The brother might lose interest."

Ashley stiffened. She knew she didn't want that to happen. The thought of putting some space between them so she could cool off wasn't that bad. But the thought of being without Gordon left her cold and shivering from it.

"Ashley?"

"I'm here, Morgan."

"Are you all right?"

"Not really. I want to be with—" A disturbance in the atmosphere prickled her skin. It felt like Gordon, only not quite.

"Morgan, let me call you back."

"Okay. Happy Valentine's Day, sis."

"Happy Valentine's Day, sis."

Ashley hung up the phone and walked to the door before the knock came. She looked out the peephole and saw a man she didn't recognize in a blue uniform. A navy blue van was parked in front of her house. The sign on the van read ALL-CITY DELIVERY.

"Yes?" she said, opening the door.

"I have a delivery."

Ashley signed for the small package and went back into her house. She knew it was from Gordon. It took only moments for her to open it and find a small heart-shaped box of chocolates. She smiled and pulled out the card. It read simply *My admiration.*

She ate one of the square candies. It tasted like Gordon.

Exactly an hour later, someone knocked on her door. Her heart skipped. Was it Gordon? She threw open the door to another deliveryman.

"Delivery for Ashley Allgood."

"That's me," she said, disappointed. She signed for a package slightly larger than the first. She thanked the deliveryman and took the package inside to open it. Wasting no time, she tore the outer box and the wrapping paper. Ashley gasped at the beauty of the object as she held it up to the light. A scarf. For her hips. For dancing. Ashley held it against her skin and sighed, hoping that one day soon she would be able to dance again for Gordon.

The note this time said *My respect.*

For the next sixty minutes, Ashley danced with her scarf, imagining Gordon before her, watching with eager eyes, waiting for a chance to touch her. But it was she who longed to touch him. Her mind recalled the scent of his cologne, the smell of his skin. She twirled and sang, intoxicated by the memory of the man she loved.

When the next hour came, she was ready and opened the door before the deliveryman got out of the truck. Her broad smile greeted him.

"Looks like you've been expecting this," he said.

Ashley just continued to grin, signed the paper, and carried the microwave-sized box into her living room. It was large but easy to carry. She had no idea what it might be.

After a few moments of intense unwrapping, she pulled the cutest teddy bear she'd ever seen out of the bright pink box. This time, the card read *My friendship.* Ashley's heart swelled with love. She hugged the bear to her chest and waited quietly to see what her lover would send next.

She was not disappointed. Her next gift was a dozen white roses. The card with them said *My devotion.*

He was getting close. She could feel it. With each gift, he was moving toward her. Back into her good graces, her life, her love. And she wanted him to come. She wanted to be with him and never push him away again.

The next delivery came with a gentle knock on the door. She rushed to it. Gordon's essence was strong. But the man at the door was not Gordon. He handed her a small square package. Ashley took it with trembling hands. When the deliveryman had driven off, she opened it right there on the porch. As she saw what was inside, her heart nearly stopped.

A ring.

A round wedding lock made of carved jade. It was beautiful and everything she'd ever hoped for in an engagement ring. She knew that was what it was, just as sure as she felt Gordon's spirit in the atmosphere around her. She put the ring on and had a look around outside. Nothing. He was nowhere to be found.

She held the card to the light of the sun cooled by a February breeze. *My love,* it said.

"I love you, Gordon," she whispered and went into the house.

A few moments later, there was another knock at the door.

Gordon's energy was powerful. It sent off tiny ripples of excitement and elation inside her. Quickly she ran into the bathroom. Checked her hair and makeup, and adjusted her clothes. Then she dashed to the front door, but before she opened it she put on the ring.

Another knock.

She opened the door. Her mouth full of *I've missed yous, I love yous,* and *yes, I'll marry yous.* She never got a chance to say them.

Gordon stood on her doorstep. From head to toe, gorgeous in a black suit. He was well groomed and immaculately dressed. And with all that expensive tailoring, she just wanted him out of those clothes, naked and under her.

He stretched his arms to the side. "My very soul," he said.

Their bodies slammed together so hard, the contact must have registered on the Richter scale. Their mouths melded in a frenzy of aching need. Their souls merged. Ashley didn't know whether he lifted her or if she jumped onto his waist, but he carried her inside, closed the door, and with the quick donning of a condom, took her on the floor of her living room. Their coupling was fast and urgent as they both groped for what they had been missing from each other for so long . . . the other part of themselves.

"Is this what I think it is?" Ashley asked, lying in Gordon's arms. She was staring at her ring. Couldn't take her eyes off of it.

"That depends," he answered, holding her, kissing her.

"On what?"

"On whether or not you're wearing it for the reasons I think you are."

They stared at each other, a long and deep gaze without time or space between them. They could read each other's thoughts now, sense each other's moods and intentions. On a day for lovers, they said, in unison, "Yes."

Epilogue

Ashley realized that it's true what they say. When you are frightened or faced with a question of life or death, your entire life flashes before your eyes. She stood in the middle of a stage shaking from head to toe, wringing her hands, and swallowing hard and often. She wished she could say that Gordon made her do it. That he had coaxed, cajoled, and convinced her to be here. But he hadn't.

He'd merely presented an opportunity. And now here she was back at the Cirque du Soleil Theater, auditioning for the role of Baleen, the siren of *Celestia*.

In the time they were apart, Gordon had contacted Dirk Ventus and brought him a tape of her recording with Xavier. Her recording had convinced Dirk to give her a special audition. So here she was on Valentine's Day only hours after reconciling with her new fiancé, waiting for her music to begin.

Fiancé. It sounded right. They had become engaged under the most unusual circumstances. But then again, nothing in Ashley's life had been usual since Gordon came into it.

She glanced at the beautiful jade on the third finger of her left hand, and her spirit filled with love overflowing. She knew in that instant that whether she got the part in Le Cirque or not, her real achievement was finding her soul mate and having the courage to love him.

She smiled at her husband-to-be sitting eagerly in the audience, and as the music came up, she lifted her voice.

ABOUT THE AUTHOR

Kim Louise resides in Omaha, Nebraska. She's been writing since grade school and has always dreamed of penning the "Great American Novel." She has an undergraduate degree in journalism and a graduate degree in adult learning. She has one son, Steve, and one grandson, Zayvier. In her spare time she enjoys reading and card making, and has recently become addicted to scrapbooking.

The Perfect Date

DOREEN RAINEY

One

"Hurry up, Sierra, you're gonna miss it!"

"I'm searching for the station, Kayla, but I can't find it!" Frustrated, Sierra continued to push the up arrow on her remote control. The blur of commercials, sports, and sitcoms passed before her eyes. "What channel is VH1?"

"It's right after BET."

Inhaling deeply, Sierra rolled her eyes heavenward and sarcastically asked, "Then what station is BET?"

"Why am I not surprised at that question?" Kayla joked. "I swear, Sierra, you have got to get out more. You are the only twenty-seven-year-old black woman I know who doesn't have BET programmed on her remote."

Sierra Rivers ignored the dig and continued to channel-surf. Her best friend since they had sat next to each other in the third grade, Kayla Wilson knew Sierra better than anyone. Giving up, Sierra tossed the remote onto the bed. "Forget it, Kayla. I have less than thirty minutes before I have to leave. I don't have time to watch some stupid television show."

"Stupid or not, the commercials are going to be over in a minute." Balancing the phone between her neck and ear, Kayla continued painting her toenails. "I'm heading out too, but I think we both have time to watch this."

Resigned to the fact that Kayla would not let her off the phone until she watched whatever had caught her attention, Sierra plopped onto the bed and kicked off her slippers. Finally finding the right station, Sierra checked the clock on the nightstand. "What's on that's so important anyway?"

Screwing the top on the fire-engine-red nail polish, Kayla set the bottle on her nightstand and pulled her jet-black microbraids into a ponytail. "Just watch!"

Sierra stared silently at her screen just as the commentator on VH1's *Where Are They Now?* began the next segment.

"Thirty years ago, it seemed the whole world was singing the number one R-and-B song, 'Passion for You.' Shooting to the top of the charts, the up-tempo hit stayed there for six weeks, helping Vanessa Reese sell over five million copies of her debut album," the program announcer stated.

"Please tell me this is not the reason you're making me late for my date," Sierra moaned.

"Neither one of us is going to be late," Kayla replied confidently. "Now be quiet, girl, you're going to miss the rest of the story."

"I *know* the rest of the story," Sierra not so politely reminded her.

"Ssshhh!"

"Shortly after the release of her debut album, Vanessa started dating Isaac Rivers, a top producer who had already established himself by putting out hits for top singing groups around the country. Over the next ten years, the couple became a staple on the charts with Isaac's songs and Vanessa's voice ultimately selling more than forty-five million albums worldwide. But they were just as famous for their personal relationship as they were for their musical success."

Sierra's grip on the telephone tightened and she unconsciously leaned closer to the screen. Neither woman spoke as pictures of the couple flashed across the screen. Vanessa and Isaac standing next to Janet Jackson and Whitney Houston at an album release party. Vanessa and Isaac performing live at a charity concert to raise money for historically black colleges. Vanessa and Isaac on the set of their last video shoot, nearly ten years ago. Vanessa and Isaac at the Grammy Awards accepting Lifetime Achievement honors.

Feeling her hand cramp, Sierra loosened her grip just as the commentator's voice boomed through her speakers.

"But living life among the rich and famous didn't always come up platinum for this couple. Their relationship highs and lows began to overshadow the beautiful music they made together."

The next series of shots highlighted the explosive personal side of their love affair. There was video footage of Vanessa yelling at Isaac at one of the most popular restaurants in downtown Los Angeles. Vanessa and Isaac arguing on the red carpet at the American Music Awards. A screaming match between the couple inside a recording studio that ended with Vanessa storming out. There was a shot of Isaac leaving their Bel Air mansion with Vanessa throwing his clothes out after him, yelling that she had had it with his lies and roving eye and that she never wanted to see him again.

Suddenly, the segment cut to scenes of the superstar couple in happier times. Home video footage showed them on the beach in the Caribbean, cuddling and hugging each other, as if they were the only two people in the world. Next, it showed them drinking champagne on one of their stops on their European tour. The last scene was a press conference where Vanessa and Isaac declared their reconciliation—again—along with their plans to work on another album for Vanessa.

As the camera panned out, Sierra held her breath, making a conscious effort not to cover her eyes. She'd seen this clip more times than she cared to admit and knew what would come next. Wanting to turn away, but unable to, Sierra stared intently at the television just as Vanessa reached down and grabbed the hand of the thirteen-year-old child standing between the flamboyant couple. Dressed in a bright orange jumpsuit with a stark-white shirt and ribbons around her two ponytails, the young child didn't move as Vanessa stared directly into the camera.

"Isaac and I truly love each other, and we're going to make our relationship work. Not just for us, but for our lovely daughter."

The clicking sound of camera shutters resonated around the press room with every lens focused on the child, who smiled only after being nudged by Vanessa.

"Oh, Sierra," Kayla drawled, finally breaking the silence on the phone. "You looked absolutely adorable."

"Very funny, Kayla," Sierra said. Having always hated the spotlight, Sierra could still feel the discomfort and embarrassment of that moment—fourteen years later. "I looked like a clown in that bright orange getup."

"I think the outfit was cute. Oh, here comes the best part!"

"So where are they now? Vanessa vows to never officially retire from the music business, performing in small sold-out clubs around the country, while Isaac continues to pen songs for some of today's hottest artists. Since that press conference, Vanessa and Isaac have split and reconciled at least four times. Today, they are once again together. Coming up next . . . whatever happened to Al B. Sure?"

Without hesitation, Sierra clicked the television off and carried her cordless phone with her to the bathroom, saying nothing.

"Can you believe they had your parents on that show? Next thing you know, Vanessa and Isaac will have their own *Behind the Music* special."

Wedging the receiver against her shoulder, Sierra applied a layer of mascara before lining her lips and filling them with lip gloss. Smoothing the sides and back of her short chestnut brown hair, she put on diamond stud earrings. Taking a step back, she admired the finished look. *Nice, but not overstated.*

"Sierra?" Kayla demanded when she got no response. "Don't you have anything to say?"

Walking back into her bedroom, Sierra pulled out the royal-blue slacks and matching cropped jacket hanging on her closet door. Slipping out of her silk robe, she tried to dress while continuing the conversation. "Nope."

"How can you be so nonchalant about this?" Kayla asked, stepping into her walk-in closet in her bra and thong, searching for something to wear. "If my parents were rich, famous, and on TV, I would be ecstatic."

Sliding her feet into three-inch mules, Sierra walked out of the bedroom. "Kayla, doesn't your dad have at least three Grammys?"

"For engineering and mixing, Sierra. Hardly categories full of adoring fans and paparazzi."

Heading down the stairs, Sierra glanced at her watch. If she was going to be on time for her date, she had to leave now. "Then consider yourself lucky," she said to Kayla. I had enough of that life growing up. The last thing I'm interested in is a television show, or anything for that matter, that has to do with the music business, entertainment, Vanessa, or Isaac."

"Sierra," Kayla started, "you can't mean that."

"Look, Kayla, growing up in that environment was not exactly healthy. Vanessa and Isaac may have won many awards during their career, but 'Parents of the Year' was not one of them."

"But—"

"No buts, Kayla," Sierra interrupted, checking her purse for her wallet and keys. "And I'm going to be late . . . so good-bye."

Sierra's feelings about the music business and her parents weren't new to Kayla. When they were growing up, most of their friends embraced the success of their famous parents. But not Sierra. The more the spotlight shone on her, the more she retreated inside her shell. She retreated so far back, Kayla often wondered if Sierra would ever allow herself true happiness.

Deciding that tonight was not the best time to continue this conversation, Kayla let the subject drop. "Ohhh, that's right. Tonight's the night you meet Walter. My friend's cousin thinks you two will really hit it off."

Sierra paused. "I thought you said you *knew* this guy."

The concern in Sierra's voice caught Kayla off guard. "What I said was that I had *met* this guy."

"Kayla," Sierra groaned. "Please tell me I haven't agreed to a blind date with a guy you don't really know."

Kayla heard the slight irritation in her voice and worked to calm her friend down. "Don't worry, Sierra. Walter is cute and my friend's cousin thinks you two would make a great couple."

"Is that so?" Sierra said skeptically. "And how does this person know that? I've never met your friend's cousin."

Deciding on a deep burgundy miniskirt with matching halter top, Kayla laid the ensemble across her bed. "She knows you through me, and once I told her what a sweet, caring and wonderful person you were, she thought you two would be perfect together."

"I should never have agreed to go on this blind date," Sierra muttered under her breath.

Sensing that Sierra was about to back out at the last minute, Kayla offered some encouraging words. "Sierra, you hardly go out, yet you claim you want to find someone special. Well, this guy may be it."

Sierra heard the sincerity in her friend's voice and agreed. She hadn't exactly been a mainstay on the dating scene lately. But the idea of a blind date began to sound a little scary. "I don't know, Kayla."

"You're a hopeless romantic at heart," Kayla said. "How wonderful it would be if you met the man of your dreams on the most romantic day of the year. Just imagine . . . meeting your soul mate on Valentine's Day. This just may be the 'love connection' you've been waiting for."

Relaxing her shoulders, Sierra let some of her nervousness dissipate. It was true that she could count on one hand the number of dates she'd had in the past six months. And the more she thought about it, the more romantic the idea seemed. What a great story to tell her grandchildren—that she met their grandfather on a blind date on Valentine's Day. "All right, Kayla. But if this guy is a jerk . . . "

Kayla relaxed when she realized Sierra wasn't going to back out. "Think positive, girl. This may just be the one to loosen you up—to break through that armor. Who knows? You might even laugh."

Slightly offended, Sierra went on the defensive. "What's that supposed to mean? I'm loose. I laugh. I have fun."

"Yeah, sure you do." Kayla laughed. "I've known you practically all my life and you have yet to really let yourself go. You've let your parents' lifestyle keep you from indulging in anything that would let you have a good time. Dancing, hanging out, and enjoying all the city has to offer does not always lead to destruction."

"You make it sound as if I'm a hermit—and that's not the case. I go out all the time," Sierra insisted.

"Libraries, educational conferences, and the gym don't count as 'going out.'"

Refusing to continue this conversation any longer, Sierra turned on her porch light. "Well, I'm trying to go out tonight if my friend will let me get off the phone."

Kayla rolled her eyes, hearing the cynicism in Sierra's tone. "All right. I have to go too. I'm meeting Michael in less than an hour."

"How is Michael these days?"

Kayla eyes sparkled and the corners of her mouth curved in a satisfied smile. "I have to admit that the past six months have been great."

Truly happy for her friend, Sierra couldn't help feeling a tad envious about Kayla finding someone special. "So what do you two lovebirds have planned for this Valentine's Day?"

Sliding into her miniskirt, Kayla zipped it up. "He's taking me to the G-Spot."

Seconds passed with no response from Sierra. "I'm almost afraid to ask."

"Now I know you really need to get out more. The G-Spot is the hottest club in LA to open up in years."

"Who goes to a club on a Tuesday?" Sierra asked in disbelief.

"In LA?" Kayla responded incredulously. "Just about everybody I know . . . except you."

"And this is how Michael has chosen to show how much he cares for you this Valentine's Day? Taking you to a place filled with hundreds of people, loud music, women on the prowl, and men on the hunt? The entire thing seems so . . . so . . . unromantic."

"Don't sound so repulsed," Kayla countered. "If you would come out with me sometime, you would know that the G-Spot is actually a great place to hang out. They have several floors of good music, the food is better than average, and the guys are always handsome. And since his brother is having his birthday party there, I agreed to go with Michael."

"If you say so," Sierra teased.

"Maybe you and Walter could come by after dinner."

"Yeah, right." Sierra laughed, knowing she would never choose to spend her night at any club, much less one called the G-Spot. "Maybe next year."

Kayla wasn't surprised by her refusal. "I'm serious, Sierra. You might be pleasantly surprised—and actually have a good time."

Ignoring the nagging thought that agreed with Kayla, Sierra quickly squashed the idea and cleared her throat. "I gotta go."

"I'll let you off the hook this time, but don't forget to call and thank me after you and Walter have a great time tonight."

Sierra locked the front door to her cottage-style home and headed down the steps. The quiet neighborhood in Anaheim, just a few blocks from the elementary school where she taught fifth grade, offered her the lifestyle she had craved as a child. Mostly known to the world as home to Disneyland, the Orange County suburb offered beautifully landscaped neighborhoods far away from the traffic, the congestion, and entertainment-laden Los Angeles.

Instead of a home full of activity with a constant flow of people, the media, and the parties, she relished the simple life she had created for herself. The two-bedroom home, with its spacious living room, large kitchen with floor-to-ceiling windows, and huge master bedroom, was a far cry from the twenty-room mansion she had grown up in, but Sierra found she reveled in the coziness, the quietness, and the peace.

Maneuvering her gray BMW 525 onto the expressway, she checked the restaurant address. It wasn't often that she ventured into downtown LA, with its trendy bistros, expensive shops and tourist attractions, but she preferred meeting Walter in a very public place. If traffic stayed on her side, she would only be a few minutes late.

Pulling in front of the restaurant, she handed her keys to the valet. After checking in with the hostess, Sierra followed her toward the back corner of the restaurant. Adjusting her jacket and smoothing her hair one last time, she closed her eyes and said a silent prayer that this time, her luck in the romance category would finally be good. After all, it was Valentine's Day.

Passing several tables, they turned slightly toward a secluded table next to a window. The soft jazz playing in the background and the recessed lighting gave a warm, romantic feeling. Sierra felt the slight flurry of butterflies in her stomach. She was only a few seconds away from being face-to-face with the man who could be her husband . . . her soul mate . . . the father of her children.

The hostess stepped aside and Sierra moved forward. The moment to meet Walter Harper had arrived. Revealing a slight smile, Sierra relaxed just a little. Not Denzel fine, but decent. With the dim lighting, it was difficult to make out all his features, but she could see his dark eyes and close-cropped beard. Since he was sitting, she had no idea how tall he was, what kind of shape he was in, or whether his pants actually matched his shirt and jacket. But it would be only a matter of seconds before she got the full view of Walter Harper.

Sierra stood patiently while the hostess held on to the menu, waiting for Walter to stand, step over to her, and pull back the chair. After several seconds, Walter didn't move and Sierra finally pulled the seat out herself, taking the menu from the hostess. The knowing exchange between the two women went completely unnoticed by Walter.

"Sorry I'm late," Sierra offered, sliding closer to the table. "I'd forgotten how traffic could be in this part of town."

Walter leaned back and stared pointedly at Sierra. "That's why I always leave a little early . . . so that unexpected delays won't make me late."

Sierra paused at his tone. *Is he scolding me?*

Before she could respond, the waitress arrived. "My name is Carmen and I'm happy to serve you two this evening. Can I get either of you something to drink?"

Sierra opened her mouth to speak, but was immediately cut off.

"I'll have a shot of Oban."

Sierra arched her brow at Walter's order of the strong, expensive Scotch. Not a heavy drinker, she opted for a glass of wine. "I'll have a glass of your house Chardonnay."

Walter leaned forward, shaking his head in the negative. "I think you'd prefer something slightly drier." Turning to the waitress, he asked her to bring him the wine list.

Ignoring his request, the waitress turned her body completely away from Walter and faced Sierra. "Is that what you would like me to bring you?"

"No," Sierra said, trying to maintain her composure. How could a man who'd only known her for one minute decide how dry she liked her wine? "I think I'll stick with my original request."

Without a backward glance at Walter, Carmen left to fill their order.

Sierra took a quick look around the restaurant and observed many couples enjoying their special Valentine's date. Several tables had roses or small gift boxes on them, and she thought she saw one man pull a small velvet ring box from his jacket. Even though this was their first date, she thought it would have been a nice touch for Walter to have something for her—flowers, or maybe a small box of chocolates.

"It's nice to finally meet you, Sierra," Walter said, breaking the uncomfortable silence.

"Likewise," Sierra responded with a polite smile. Even though he didn't make a great first impression, Sierra wanted to give him the benefit of the doubt.

"Have you eaten here before?" Walter asked, rearranging the small candle, their water glasses, napkins, bread plates, and silverware for no apparent reason.

"Yes, but it's been years," Sierra responded, trying to ignore how much his moving the items on the table plucked her nerves. "I hear the food is still quite delicious."

Seemingly satisfied with the new table arrangement, he picked up his menu. "It should be, at these prices. Can you believe they want fourteen dollars for lobster bisque? And that's only for a cup. Imagine if you wanted a bowl. If I had seen this beforehand, I would have chosen another restaurant."

Sierra half laughed as she tried to determine whether he was serious or not. "Well, it is one of the best restaurants in the city."

"Best restaurant or not, how can every entrée cost over fifty dollars? Even the chicken is fifty-five."

Sierra shifted in her chair, unsure of how to respond. After all, he chose the place. Deciding it was best not to respond to that comment, Sierra put down her menu. "How long have you lived in LA?"

Setting the menu aside, Walter folded his hands in front of him. "Almost two years. I thought I'd come out here and try my luck. I'd heard it was a good place to start a business. But then again, that's what they said about Atlanta. However, the four years I lived there, I wasn't able to come up with one investor. Can you believe they felt I was a risk because of that one incident in Dallas? The way

I figure it, if the folks in Dallas took a chance on me after what happened in Philadelphia, why couldn't these guys see their way to help me out?"

The waitress set their drinks on the table and Sierra immediately took a much-needed sip of wine. Silently, she began to plan how she would punish Kayla for this.

"Would you two like to start with an appetizer? Perhaps the soup du jour or our famous fried calamari?"

Sierra jumped in and ordered before Walter responded. The shorter the meal, the faster she could get through this date. It wouldn't take a five-course meal for her to know that Walter Harper would not be a love connection. Skipping the appetizer and a salad, she ordered only an entrée and planned to ignore dessert. By her calculation, she could be out of here within the hour.

Handing the menu back to Carmen, Sierra forced her expression to remain unchanged as Walter proceeded to order a full-course meal. *For someone complaining about the prices, he sure doesn't have a problem ordering some of everything.*

With a look of pity toward Sierra, Carmen left.

Oblivious to the fact that in a matter of minutes he had managed to alienate the waitress and frustrate his date, Walter continued to converse as if all was well. "Marla tells me you're a teacher."

"Marla?"

Taking a sip of his drink, he set the glass down, but continued to spin it, causing the ice to clank annoyingly. "My cousin's friend."

"Oh, yes," Sierra said, trying to keep from reaching across the table for the glass. Counting to three, she took a deep breath. At least he brought up a topic she loved. Talking about her students always lifted her spirits. Maybe the evening could be salvaged after all. "I teach fifth grade."

"Public school?"

Sierra couldn't help noticing the scowl on his face, but managed to maintain her composure. "Yes, I teach in a public school."

Sucking his teeth, he finally left the glass alone. "What a waste."

"Excuse me?" Sierra asked, this time unable to hide the irritation that began to swell up inside her.

Walter narrowed his eyes and lowered his voice. "Who in their right mind would want to teach these knuckle-heads we call children? Not to mention that you can't make much money. No use in going into something if it's not guaranteed to give you a large return on your investment. Take my new business venture. This idea I have is a gold mine and it would have worked in Atlanta if the investors would have set aside their petty concerns. But you know how it is when a black man is trying to get ahead. Everybody always wants to pull him down. Banks wouldn't give me a loan. Investors shied away from me. I just don't get it. A few repossessions, a tax issue, and a legal battle with some suppliers and they hold it against you for years. Personally, I think it's all part of the systematic racism that rears its head in the government and the business world."

Did he just call me crazy, insult my career, and blame the IRS for his business failures? Sierra took another sip of wine and searched her mind for ancient torture techniques that she could use on Kayla.

"Excuse me," Carmen said, placing Walter's appetizer on the table.

Glad for the interruption, Sierra turned to Carmen.

"You have a phone call. The woman on the phone said she'd tried your cell phone but couldn't get through. The reception in here can be horrible."

Sierra excused herself and followed Carmen down a

hallway that led to the restaurant office. Just shy of the door, Carmen stopped and turned. "There is no phone call."

"What?" Sierra asked, puzzled by her statement.

"I was taking the order of the table next to you and overheard your conversation with that jerk. I just thought I'd give you an out if you wanted one. This 'phone call' could be your excuse out of here."

A few minutes later, Sierra returned to the table in a controlled hurry. "I'm sorry about that, Walter."

"Is everything okay?"

"Just fine." Nothing would have been better than to end this night right now, but Sierra couldn't bring herself to lie. She would endure his conversation, eat her meal, and afterward, never see Walter Harper again.

Over the next hour, Sierra smiled stiffly, paying dearly for her earlier decision to stay. Not interested in little else, Walter spent the entire evening proclaiming the unfairness of the world and discussing one business failure after another. Not once did he ask about her life, her hobbies, her likes or dislikes. This would go down in history as the worst date of her life.

When Carmen brought over the check, she couldn't hide her relief. With a hurried tone, she forced a smile. "Thanks for a wonderful evening, Walter. I've got an early appointment tomorrow, so I think it's best if we call it a night."

Opening the leather case with the bill inside, Walter agreed. "I understand. But I want you to know I had a great evening. Maybe we could do this again."

Before she could answer, he removed his wallet. "Why don't we just split this down the middle to make it easy on Carmen?"

Several seconds passed before Sierra fully digested his words. Did she hear him correctly? Did he just say they should split the bill? A quick calculation in her head told her that her food and wine was about seventy dollars, while his four-course meal and several drinks totaled almost $175. She watched in shock as he put a hundred-dollar bill on the table and excused himself to go the rest room. Not only was that not half of the bill, but where was his tax and tip?

Fuming on the inside, Sierra pulled out her credit card and signaled for Carmen. Handing her the bill, Sierra pocketed the hundred. Standing, she followed Carmen to a waiter station where she could swipe her credit card. When Walter came back, she intended to be nowhere around.

Handing the valet his tip, Sierra dialed the preset number and angrily waited for Kayla to answer. Fuming as she turned the corner, Sierra had a strange feeling that twenty years of friendship were about to come to a grinding end.

TWO

Justin Simmons stood at the far end of the bar, staring down over the railing watching the show taking place on the first level of the club. Seated at a large table surrounded by three other guys and twice as many women, Allen Johnson, known to the world as Black Shadow, signaled the waitress for another bottle of champagne. Based on Justin's loose calculations, that would make the tenth bottle totaling just under two grand. Thank goodness nobody had to drive tonight. Two SUV limousines were parked in the back alley patiently waiting for their night of partying to end.

In the music business for over fifteen years, Justin was still amazed at what women would do in the presence of a hip-hop superstar. Nothing said "party time" to these women, dressed in barely there outfits, like a man ordering Cristal champagne, flashing wads of cash, and dancing to the wee hours of the morning.

Throughout his tenure, he'd witnessed the panties being thrown onstage, women gaining access backstage by flashing the security guards, and on several occasions he'd watched hotel security escort woman out of their penthouse suites. Tonight was no different. The concert had just ended, but the after party was just getting started.

Glancing at his watch, he took another sip of his drink. Just after 10:30. He knew he was in for a long night. As long as Black Shadow and his entourage wanted to hang out, he would stay. There was no way he could leave his multiplatinum-selling artist alone.

Motioning to the bartender, he ordered another drink—nonalcoholic. Somebody would have to maintain control of their senses tonight, and judging from the laughter coming from the ground floor, he knew it would be him—again. But Justin didn't mind. It was all in a day's work.

"Someone as handsome as you shouldn't be spending his time alone in the corner."

Justin turned to the voice and curved his lips into a half smile. He didn't know her name, but could immediately analyze everything about her. With her long, straight black hair, dark brown eyes turned hazel with the help of colored contact lenses, smooth almond skin, bangin' body, backless top, leather miniskirt, and strappy stiletto heels, he'd met her type in every city he'd traveled to. In the world of entertainment, beautiful and available women were a constant.

Stepping closer to be heard over the music, she lowered her gaze. "I noticed you the moment you walked through the door. I've spent the past half hour working up the nerve to come over and say hello."

Leaning casually against the railing, Justin remained silent. He doubted the shy-demeanor act reflected her true personality. If she saw him enter, she obviously knew whom he came with. It was an old ploy he'd seen used by many women over the years. Use him to get to the superstar.

Staring at her with a blank expression, he failed to offer a response and the woman shifted uncomfortably from one foot to the other. Obviously, she wasn't used to having to work this hard at getting attention.

Glancing down at her almost empty glass, she licked her lips and tried again. "Looks like I could use a refill."

Pushing off the rail, Justin decided he wasn't in the mood to play the game. Ten years ago, not only would he have accepted what she was offering, he would have been doing it on the lower level with the artist-of-the-day and the rest of the groupies. But the entire party side of the music business had gotten tiresome. Without hesitating, he said, "Then I suggest you go over to the bartender and order one."

Her eyebrows shot up and shock registered on her face. But she quickly recovered. Shrugging, she turned to leave. "Your loss. It wasn't you I was interested in anyway."

He held his laugh as she sashayed away, no doubt giving him a final view of what he was passing on. Luckily, it didn't bother him one bit. When he had first started in the business, he loved the power over women his position gave him. But now he had no interest in what his industry buddies termed STAs—short-term affairs. Those relationships usually lasted until it was time for another road trip. With his crazy travel schedule, whirlwind tours, and all of the trappings of being a successful executive at PrimeTime Records, developing a long-term relationship had been impossible.

Now thirty-three years old, he found thoughts frequently creeping into his mind about whether the trade-off had been worth it. Rich and respected in his chosen field, he could no longer deny the fact that he was still alone . . . and a little lonely. The pull of wanting to settle down and have a family frequently reared its head.

How would it feel to come home to a woman every night that loved and cherished you? How would it feel to teach your son how to hit a fastball? Would he be able to handle it when his daughter went on her first date?

Swallowing hard, Justin glanced around the bar area. It wouldn't do much for his rep if others saw his vulnerability. Realizing no one paid him any attention, he leaned on the rail, focusing his attention on the crowd below, making a conscious effort to push thoughts of love, family, and children out of his mind. This tour may have just ended, but with the success of Black Shadow, he could almost guarantee that another one was on the horizon.

"How could you set me up like that, Kayla?"

There was no mistaking the anger in her voice, but Kayla could hardly make out the words. "What did you say, Sierra? I can't hear you over the music."

Switching her cell phone to the other ear, she raised her voice to make her point loud and clear. "I said Walter was the sorriest excuse for a man I'd ever met and I should come to that club and knock you out."

Kayla moved away from the dance floor and the speakers. "I guess things didn't work out between you two?"

Seething on the inside, Sierra worked overtime to calm her rage. "That's putting it mildly."

Realizing her date must have been a complete disaster, Kayla offered her apologies. "Look, Sierra, I'm really sorry. I heard Walter was an entrepreneur. A successful man going places."

"He was going places all right. Unfortunately, if you want to go with him, you have to foot half the bill."

"You're kidding," Kayla responded, obviously shocked. "I had no idea . . . I'll make it up to you, I promise."

"You're damn right you will." Sierra saw the turn for the freeway and thought about what she was going home to. Absolutely nothing. She didn't realize how much she had wanted a connection with Walter until this moment, and her heart sank. There would be no story for her grandchildren about how she met their grandfather on Valentine's Day. She was alone—again.

Sadness overwhelmed Sierra, and suddenly she didn't

want to go home to her empty house. "Where's this G-Spot place?"

Kayla hesitated before she answered. "Are you serious? You, Sierra—the woman who would rather read the great works of literature than spend time at a hip club filled with fine men, good food, and music you can actually dance to?"

"Very funny," Sierra said, feeling a little energized at the thought of hanging out with her friend. "I may not be a club person, but I refuse to end my Valentine's Day on a sour note. And besides, you owe me a drink for what you put me through."

Squealing with excitement, Kayla headed for the front entrance. "I'll leave your name with the bouncer so you can get in without waiting in line. When we got here, the line almost circled the block."

Twenty minutes later, Sierra stopped circling the jam-packed lot and parked her car in what she hoped was a legal spot on the street. Checking the parking sign, she hoped the tail end of her car that brushed the no-parking zone would go unnoticed if any cops came by.

Approaching the entrance, she instantly remembered why she rarely ventured out to these kinds of places. The long lines, the velvet ropes, and the big, burly bouncers standing guard at the door.

This scene had constantly played out in her life during her teenage years, and unpleasant memories crept into her mind. Accompanying her parents to various clubs and restaurants to celebrate an album release, the beginning or ending of a tour, or to commemorate a special occasion with other celebrities, Sierra had always felt awkward at all the attention her parents received. Other children her age always appeared to have it together. Their clothes fit just right, their hair was styled with the latest looks, and they walked with poise and confidence. But Sierra believed she never quite fit in.

Always on display, Sierra lost count of the number of times she'd been told, "Smile, the cameras are on"; "Don't wear that, it'll make you look fat"; "Walk slower, sweetie, we have to give all the photographers a chance to get their shot." Fans banging on the limo window. Reporters chasing you down a street. Not to mention the guys that came on to her, hoping that she would pass along their demo tape.

Sierra often wondered why her parents stayed in an industry that demanded so much. There was always some person wanting a piece of you. The pressure to be friendly to people you hated. The continuous fights with the record labels, agents, and attorneys to get the money that rightfully belonged to you.

Many artists just wanted to express their amazing talent, and fought hard to avoid the lure of the negative side of the glitz and glamour of being famous. But the lifestyle can attach itself like a magnet, and unfortunately the results could oftentimes be disastrous.

Along with the money came the drugs, the alcohol, the hangers-on, the leeches, long-lost family members, the users, the takers, the incredible highs, and the lows so far down that some could never recover. It was a tough business, and while Sierra witnessed the power it had to grant material success many dreamed of, it also had the power to take so much more than it ever gave, leaving the artist alone, bitter, and sometimes broke.

How many celebrities had come and gone for a variety of reasons during her life with Vanessa and Isaac? One-hit wonders. Drug addiction. Alcohol dependency. Their fame and fortune had been a double-edged sword. Yet the industry cranked on, showing no mercy and no remorse. With billions on the line, the music business only concerned itself with the next hit record . . . the next big star. Sierra never understood how anyone could be a part of something so heartless. The whole industry had made her uncomfortable, and the minute she was old enough to get away from it, she did.

College was her haven away from the staring eyes and curious onlookers. She had attended a small university in northern California, where the media left her alone after her first semester and she earned her English degree and teacher's certificate without so much as a blurb in the newspapers. She returned to a middle-class neighborhood in LA to teach at Lakeside Elementary School, and she couldn't have been happier. The only thing that would make her life better was someone to share it with.

Walking past the line of people, she tried not to stare at the women waiting to get inside. Cropped shirts that barely covered their braless breasts. Tops that dipped deep in the front and back. Skirts shorter than anything she'd ever seen—or worn. Heels high enough to cause permanent arch damage. Next to these women, Sierra felt like a nun.

Stepping into the darkened entryway, she waited patiently to pay her cover charge before being patted down and walking through a metal detector.

"Thirty-five dollars please."

Sierra almost choked on her gum at the outrageous cover, but forked over the cash. Stepping onto the main floor, she let her eyes roam around the room, searching for her friend. As the music blared and the lights flashed, she made her way through the crowd, trying to ignore the "accidental" bumps of several men and questioning eyes of the women. They, no doubt, figured out that this wasn't her scene. *Yep, Kayla owes me big time for this!*

Glancing at his watch, Justin couldn't believe that in a place filled with gorgeous women, great music, and

unlimited drinks, boredom had settled in. Watching
Allen hold court on the main floor, he remembered the
VIP room was empty. Maybe he would go up to the third-
floor room, relax, and watch *SportsCenter* until he got
word that Allen was ready to go. Just as he turned to
leave, someone caught his eye.

In the midst of the hundreds of women that packed
the first floor, his eyes instantly zeroed in on her. Dressed
more for the office than a club, the outfit hugged her
body in all the right places. Completely oblivious of the
admiring stares from men, she moved her head from
side to side, searching.

Another woman waved and made her way toward her.
After a quick hug, they began to talk and their conversation suddenly appeared animated. Her body language
didn't indicate that they would come to blows, but she
did appear frustrated—and amazingly attractive.

In a roomful of women with long, fake hair and over-
exposed skin, her short, stylish haircut and conventional
slacks and jacket made a fascinating contrast. She wasn't
a conformist. Leaning forward, he angled his body to try
to hear her voice. His curiosity was aroused and he wondered if her voice matched her looks—sassy and sexy.

"Thirty-five dollars?" Sierra screamed above the music.
"This Valentine's Day is costing me a small fortune."

Sympathizing with her friend, Kayla tried to lift her
spirits. "The drinks are on me tonight."

Straining to hear her words over the music, Sierra suddenly felt like she'd made a huge mistake coming to the
club. Walter wasn't her type, and this club definitely
qualified as out of her comfort zone. It was time to cut
her losses this Valentine's Day and head home. "Listen,
Kayla, on second thought, I'm going to leave. You and
Michael have a great time tonight."

Reaching out for her as she turned to leave, Kayla

pleaded. "No, stay. The night's still young. Maybe your luck will change. There's a lot of cute guys here."

Sierra started to respond when a loud commotion erupted just a few feet from them. All conversation around them stopped. People stepped back as the man behind the table seemed to escalate his complaint.

Sierra's mouth curled in a frown as she watched the man practically throw his food back at the waitress, shouting something about the wrong order and cold food. As she turned her attention back to Kayla, her expression indicated that she'd seen enough. "If that's your idea of the great guys that are here tonight . . . I know I'm leaving."

Grabbing her by the arm, Kayla moved back toward the entrance. "Do you know who that is?"

"What kind of question is that?" Sierra asked. "What difference does it make? A jerk is a jerk."

"That's Black Shadow."

"A black what?"

"Not a what—a who. Black Shadow."

Seeing no recognition in her friend's eyes, Kayla continued. "He's only the hottest hip-hop star in the country right now. Multiplatinum album, sold-out tour . . . Does any of this ring a bell?"

"His behavior rings my bell. Just like a so-called star. Acting like a complete—"

Touching her calmly on the arm, Kayla hoped to quiet her down. "Now, Sierra, be nice."

A busboy began to clean up Black Shadow's mess and Sierra rolled her eyes. Another reason she hated the music business? The flavor of the month usually thought they could get away with anything—and usually did.

Kayla wanted to get Sierra away from this scene as quickly as possible. If she had to stay around Black Shadow one more minute, Sierra would walk out the door without a backward glance. Pointing to the stairs on the opposite side of the dance floor, Kayla said, "Why don't you go up to the second-floor lounge? I'll find Michael and then join you. It's quiet up there. We can talk, have a drink, and then if you want to go home, we'll walk you to your car."

Unable to move his eyes, Justin watched the two women exchange words. At times they seemed angry at each other, and then just as quickly act as if they were best friends. He held his breath when the newcomer turned toward the door, only releasing it when it appeared she'd been convinced to stay. As the two women seemed to find a final positive resolution, they embraced briefly.

A few seconds later, the second woman pointed in his direction and he strained again, to hear their words. His eyes never left her as she made her way to the steps that would lead her to the second-floor bar—and directly toward him.

The dimly lit lounge level of the G-Spot, designed to encourage conversation, filled its space with cocktail tables holding flickering candles as their centerpieces. With the music a few notches lower, and more jazz tunes than hip-hop, a couple hundred people enjoyed drinking and chatting.

Sierra came around the landing on the opposite wall while Justin impatiently waited for her to take a seat. Not taking the time to look around, he observed her ignoring the admiring looks of several men as she weaved her way through the tables. With her head down and a scowl on her face, nothing about her posture invited conversation.

Finding a seat at the bar just a few feet from him, Sierra never glanced his way. Taking advantage of his view, he freely studied her. It only took a second for his smile to widen in approval. With her honey-beige skin, deep-set eyes, and luscious, kissable lips bronze with gloss, Justin

discovered something that he hadn't seen in quite a while
. . . a natural beauty.

Living in a world rarely based in reality, Justin found
it refreshing to see someone who didn't seem moved by
what pop culture dictated. The conservative dress, short
hair, and low-key makeup defied everything that the
women who frequented the G-Spot represented.

She placed her order with the bartender, and Justin
saw that as his opening. With its having been so long
since he'd had to make the first move, he nervously
stood beside her and said, "Would it be considered too
much of a line if I offered to pay for your drink?"

Sierra counted to five before turning around, hoping
to squelch the irritation that hovered just below the surface. Her plan to wait for Kayla in the lounge and
somehow avoid dealing with men that hung out at clubs
prowling for women had failed. It only took two seconds
for an old, tired man to shell out an old, tired line. Facing him, she decided to let him know she had absolutely
no interest. But the moment her eyes met his, the words
lodged deep in her throat.

In LA, there had never been a shortage of attractive
men, and Sierra had met many. However, the man standing beside her made her pause. Trying to pick out what
it was about him quickly proved fruitless—for there
wasn't one feature.

His caramel-colored complexion. The dark eyes
flushed with long lashes. The short haircut with the
slight waves. The half smile that looked amazingly sexy.
The height, the body, the impeccable dress. Even his
teeth were perfectly straight. All those attributes created
what could only be described as one strikingly handsome
member of the male species. Now this man was definitely
Denzel fine.

Instead of her leading off with a string of words her

students would be shocked to hear, one corner of her lips curved into a half smile. "Not only would it be considered a line, it would be considered a lame one."

Noticing the humorous sparkle in her eyes, he said, "It was either that or 'Do you have a quarter? Because I promised to call my mother the moment I met the girl of my dreams.' I even thought of using the ever popular 'If I could rewrite the alphabet, I would put U and I together.'" Having her complete attention, he leaned closer and said, "Then there's my all-time favorite, 'Your father must have been a thief because he obviously stole some stars and put them in your eyes.'"

Motioning to the stool beside her, he asked, "May I?"

Shrugging nonchalantly, Sierra tried to hide her amusement. "Last I checked it was a free country."

Sliding next to her, Justin said, "Shall I credit your sarcastic comments to your normal personality, or is it a result of whatever had you worked up when you arrived?"

Sierra narrowed her eyes and shifted in her chair. "What do you know about my arrival?"

Half closing his eyes, Justin touched his temples with his fingers and moved his head from side to side, humming as if he were talking to the spirit world.

This time, Sierra couldn't stop from bursting into laughter. The people in LA could be so uptight, always "on." It was refreshing to meet someone who didn't take himself too seriously.

"Let me see. In my mind I see . . . I see . . . you and a girl-friend . . . disagreeing . . . making up . . . no, now you're arguing again . . . ahhhh, now you've made up again . . . nope, wait a minute, you're walking away . . . But look, you're coming back."

Shutting his eyes tighter, he appeared to be straining. "The vision is fading . . . fading . . . now it's gone."

He dropped his hands to his side as if he were completely exhausted.

Sierra's laughter died down and the bartender arrived with her drink. Before she could pay, Justin signaled the bartender that it was on him.

Sierra noticed the gesture but decided to let it pass. Already in the hole for over a hundred dollars, she didn't mind being treated to one drink. Giving a relaxed smile, she said, "You seem to know a lot about me, but I know nothing about you—and unfortunately, I'm all out of my special powers."

"Then allow me to introduce myself." Offering his hand, he said, "Justin Simmons."

Sierra cast her eyes downward at the outstretched hand—and hesitated.

Justin leaned inches from her ear. "I'm sure you didn't notice, but there's a table right behind you with three guys who've been watching me make this move on you. You can tell me to get lost, but at least don't make me look too bad in front of the fellas."

The glint in his eyes and the humor in his voice comforted Sierra. Accepting the invitation, she placed her hand in his and a delightful shiver of electricity raced through her body. Clearing her throat, she pretended not to be affected. "Sierra."

Not letting go of her hand, he said, "No last name?"

Sierra cut her eyes down at their entwined hands, and quickly removed hers. "Of course I have a last name."

"Just not one you're going to tell me."

It was a statement more than a question and Sierra let his words hang in the air.

Justin nodded in understanding. "Then Sierra it is."

Lifting her glass to her lips, she glanced toward the stairs. No sign of Kayla. Unexpectedly, she was thankful.

Her disastrous date with Walter seemed years ago now that she shared the company of an attractive man.

"Would it sound like too much of a line if I asked what a beautiful woman like you was doing spending Valentine's Day alone?"

Leaning to his left and right, Sierra turned her attention back to him. "I don't see anyone at your side, so I could ask you the same thing."

One of the downsides of his career was not knowing whether a woman wanted him for him, or his position or money. Not sure if he should admit the real reason he was at the club, he didn't answer right away. "Unfortunately, I had no one to share it with."

Sierra studied him a moment, saying the first words that popped into her head. "So what's wrong with you?"

Completely thrown off by her question as he was, his eyes widened. "Excuse me?"

This time it was Sierra's turn to study his body from head to toe. Teasingly, she said, "You're a halfway decent looking man, able to coordinate your clothes." Sniffing in the air, she added, "And you smell nice. Where I come from, those are prime qualities women look for in a date."

Appreciating her assessment of him, Justin heard her flirtatious tone. "Maybe you could be my date."

Remembering Walter, she scrunched up her face. "No, thank you. Thanks to my friend Kayla, I've had my share of dating for one night."

Noticing his questioning gaze, Sierra elaborated, sharing with him the horrors of her blind date. "Can you believe the nerve of that man? Complaining about the restaurant, insulting my career, and leaving me to pay over half the bill?"

"So I take it you won't be seeing him again?" Justin asked.

"You got that right," she answered emphatically.

"Good, that means you're available."

Setting her drink down, Sierra turned her body to completely face him. "Available for what?"

"To perhaps go on a date with yours truly."

"Listen . . . um . . . Justin . . . right?"

Justin's lips curved into a slow grin. They both knew she didn't have a memory problem.

"Please don't take this the wrong way, but people who hang out in clubs don't strike me as the 'let's get together and build a relationship' type."

"You're hanging out in a club," he pointed out.

"For your information, I am not 'hanging,' I'm waiting," she answered smartly.

"And what makes you think I'm not waiting?" he challenged.

"For?"

Lowering his gaze, he leaned in closer and smiled. "Someone like you."

"Smooth, Mr. Simmons, very smooth," Sierra acknowledged with a slight smile. "But I'm not one of those women who'll fall for a smooth line. You'll have to do better than that."

"You fell for the 'buy you a drink' line," he said, gently reminding her of how this conversation got started.

The playful comment enticed Sierra. "Only because I took pity on you."

"Ouch!" Justin shrieked, throwing his head back in delight and finding her extremely refreshing. Obviously, she didn't know who he was, or if she did she didn't care. It was the first time in a long time he had had to work this hard at getting to know a woman, and it energized him. "I like your style, Sierra."

"Why, Mr. Simmons," she started, in a dramatic Southern drawl, "are you flirting with me?"

All signs of joking disappeared and his eyes brimmed

with curiosity. "Since the moment you sat down. Is it working?"

Sierra relaxed her shoulders, staring directly in his eyes. Something in his tone made her take the question seriously. She opted for the simple truth. "Yes."

"So does that mean if I ask you out, you'll say yes?"

Shaking her head in the negative, Sierra didn't have to think twice about her answer. "If a date with you includes rude behavior, nonstop complaining, and ending with me paying for most of your meal, the answer is definitely no."

"Oh, ye of little faith," Justin answered, "I can guarantee you the perfect date."

"Is that so?"

"All you have to do is tell me what your perfect date would be."

Watching his expression, Sierra realized his desire for a sincere answer. "Are you serious?"

"Of course I am. If you give me the privilege of taking you out, I want to make sure I don't mess up." Justin watched as she thought about his question. She, no doubt, thought of limousine rides, exotic flowers, expensive gifts, trendy restaurants, or perhaps tickets to one of the many high-profile events that happen around Los Angeles. She might be different on the outside from other women he'd dealt with, but he had an inkling that on the inside, they were all the same.

Sierra carefully considered her answer. When she was sixteen, her parents had thought it cute, not to mention good publicity, for her to attend functions on the arm of the son of another major star. So for two years, she was paraded up and down red carpets with boys she didn't know and didn't care to know. Fancy eateries, artist parties, formal dinners, and pool soirees at celebrities' homes became a staple in her young life. And frankly, she'd had enough of that scene. "I would actually enjoy being treated to a wonderful drive up the coast followed by a picnic on the beach. Or maybe a quiet dinner— made by the man himself. It wouldn't matter if the best he could do was hot dogs or filet mignon, only the thought that went into it. I would also love to curl up on a comfortable couch with a big bowl of popcorn and watch a great movie—something with lots of action and of course a little romance."

Justin's attraction for her quadrupled in a matter of seconds. When he had first laid eyes on her, he was instantly attracted to her great looks and natural style. But after hearing her describe her ideas for the perfect date, he acknowledged the mental draw as well.

For the past ten years, his dating life had consisted of movie premieres, award shows, and various industry events. When he did manage to get a free evening, his dates usually wanted to be seen at a high-profile restaurant or be indulged by quick getaway vacations. The women who'd been a part of his life wanted nothing to do with quiet walks on the beach or a drive up the coast. They were always more interested in the next label party or big industry event. Raising his glass, he nodded to Sierra with sincere appreciation. "Like I said—I like your style."

After they clinked their glasses, a commotion over by the stairs caught their attention. Black Shadow and his crew were making their way up the steps, almost running over a waitress with a trayful of drinks and disturbing the patrons at nearby tables. The group of about twenty finally turned the other corner, no doubt heading to the VIP room. Sierra rolled her eyes, remembering what went on in those rooms. The drinking, the drugs, the impromptu striptease acts. The worst part? Black Shadow couldn't be more than twenty-one, twenty-two. Didn't anybody from his label care about his destructive behavior?

Justin watched Sierra stare at the entourage as the final few people turned the corner and disappeared from their sight, patiently waiting for her comments. Usually people started singing the praises of the rapper's songs, or wishing they could be a part of the party, or begin talking about how they would love to be in the entertainment business.

She turned her attention back to him and instead of seeing stars in her eyes, a cold expression settled on her face and she seemed disgusted. Not sure if he read her correctly, he said, "Everything okay?"

"Some things never change," she said.

Definitely disgust. "What do you mean?"

"The behavior of that so-called hip-hop star. The music business is full of arrogant people just like him that think they can treat people any kind of way. It never ceases to amaze me that we, as a culture, continue to put up with their demanding ways and annoying behavior. Between the artists, the labels, managers, and agents, it's one big party. Not to mention, he's barely legal. No doubt he's headed for the VIP room. God only knows what will be going on in there. Where is his label management?"

Justin raised a brow at that last question. Label management stood directly in front of her. "For someone who doesn't make a habit of hanging out at clubs, you sound like you have firsthand knowledge about the goings-on."

Up until this moment, Sierra had enjoyed every moment since she'd entered the lounge. Justin, funny, cute, and attentive, made her feel special on this Valentine's Day. Fearing all that would change if she revealed who she was, she opted for the safe answer. "Who needs firsthand knowledge? All you have to do is open a newspaper or read a magazine. It's all right there for the world to see. The drugs, the drinking, the bed hopping."

Justin, no stranger to the judgments of people outside

the industry, usually chalked up their comments to jealousy, but there was something about her disapproving tone that made him want to offer a sincere response. "First of all, you shouldn't believe everything you read. Second of all, have you considered that the label can only do so much? When a twenty-something-year-old goes from flipping burgers to having anything he wants in a matter of months, most of the time there's nothing anyone can say to curb the partying."

"But it's the industry that perpetuates the lifestyle, almost forcing the artists to become a part of it to be successful," she countered, feeling her frustration level rising.

"It's the public that ultimately drives the industry. The entertainment business just delivers what the people want."

"I'm sorry, Justin. I don't see it that way," she answered, shaking her head in the negative. "The industry pushes that theory on the unsuspecting public as an excuse to continue to allow this type of behavior—making their business and the people in it bigger than life. And when I stand in front of my students to help guide them toward a future, instead of doctors, lawyers, teachers, and scientists, my students are talking about becoming the next great rapper or singer."

Realizing how worked up she was getting, Sierra abruptly stopped and took a deep breath. Forcing a smile, she said, "Look, I'm sorry. It gets a little frustrating at times. But my students probably know more about Black Shadow than any subject I've taught this year."

Justin started to respond when she cut him off.

"You know what? Let's not ruin our nice conversation by talking about something that has absolutely nothing to do with either of us. Black Shadow, his VIP room, and the music industry have no impact on you and me. So, let's change the subject. Okay?"

Hesitantly, Justin nodded in agreement.

Pushing thoughts of the music business to the back of her mind, Sierra went back into flirt mode. "How about I ask you some questions?"

Glad to see her smiling again, Justin spread his arms. "I'm an open book. Ask away."

Taking a sip of her wine, Sierra focused her eyes on him. "You know I'm a teacher, why don't you tell me what you do?"

Three

"I see you found something to occupy your time."

Sierra missed Justin's look of relief at the interruption as she turned to the voice.

Just barely squeezing between Justin and Sierra, Kayla glanced knowingly from one to the other before focusing her final look of curiosity on Justin. "And who might you be?"

Michael, gently grabbing his nosy girlfriend by the arm, pulled her back and shook Justin's hand. "Michael Carver. And please excuse Kayla, she can be a little overbearing at times."

Not deterred, Kayla stepped around Michael and gave Justin the once-over, nodding in approval. "We were coming to check on you, but it looks like you're doing just fine."

Justin's vibration on his two-way pager hummed and he excused himself to get the message.

Sierra watched him walk to the other side of the club and open the silver device. A few moments later, he was typing away.

Facing Sierra, Kayla continued, "We came up here to join you for that drink, but I can see our company is no longer necessary. And the fact that you're spending time with a man that gorgeous, *and* that you have a smile so big it could light a stadium, hopefully means that I'm forgiven for Walter?" Kayla asked eagerly, taking a seat on the stool Justin had just vacated.

Not ready to let her friend off the hook, Sierra smirked. "Believe me, Kayla, it will take a lot more than a free drink from a nice-looking guy to put you back in my good graces for what I can only refer to as the worst date of my life."

Kayla raised a brow in surprise. "You let him buy you a drink? I don't believe it. That's got to be a first."

Sierra opened her mouth to respond when Black Shadow came around the corner from the VIP room. With a young woman on each arm, giggling and jiggling, they made their way down the stairs, no doubt headed for the main dance floor. Sierra jumped off her stool and grabbed her purse. "I think I'll call it a night."

Kayla watched her friend's eyes follow Black Shadow and his entourage. "Don't tell me you're going to let some guy you don't even know ruin your evening with Mr. Too Fine."

Not wanting to admit how ridiculous her actions were, she searched her mind for another excuse. "It's not just that, it's getting late. I have at least a forty-five-minute drive home and I have to be in my classroom, ready for my students, at 7:00 A.M."

"Did I hear you say you were leaving?" Justin asked, returning to the conversation. "It's still early."

Kayla stepped closer to hear Sierra's response. "Yeah, Sierra, it's still early."

"We'll be downstairs by the bar," Michael said, practically carrying Kayla away. If she had her way, she wouldn't miss one detail of the conversation between Justin and Sierra.

For a brief moment, Sierra thought about changing her mind. On a Valentine's Day filled with one fiasco after another, he managed to be her one bright spot. But guys hanging out in bars were never her type. "Believe me, Mr. Simmons, it's been a pleasure."

Casually sitting back down, Justin hoped she'd follow suit. For the first time in a long time, he wasn't anxious to rid himself of female company. Sierra felt like a breath of fresh air to him. "Is that a kiss-off or does that mean I get a last name—and possibly a phone number?"

Meeting men in this atmosphere went against everything Sierra believed in, but she couldn't deny her attraction to the man in front of her—at least six feet tall, a sultry voice, magnetic eyes, and a solid body. Sierra had to admit that the entire package was quite enticing. Remembering how she took offense at Kayla's assessment of her earlier in the evening, she decided to prove her friend wrong. She did know how to loosen up—have fun, shake things up a little. Maybe she would break her rule, just this once. "It means you can give me your phone number. I just might give you a call."

Glancing at her evening bag, he bent his lips in a seductive smile. "Program me."

Thrown off by his words, Sierra followed his eyes to her purse. "Excuse me?"

"Is your cell phone in your bag?"

Sierra nodded in the affirmative.

"Program me in your cell. That way, if I don't hear from you, I won't have to wonder whether it's because you lost the napkin I wrote my number on."

Reaching for her purse, Sierra couldn't help giving him brownie points for that one. Pretty original. "Good one, Mr. Simmons."

After she added his name and number, Justin realized he didn't want his time with Sierra to end. After months of being on the road, living out of hotels, and working hard to keep Black Shadow and his crew in line, Justin found himself comfortable and tranquil for the first time. "How about a dance before you go?"

Sierra peeked over the railing and watched all the gyrating bodies packed on the dance floor.

Seeing the hesitation in her eyes, Justin reached for her hand. "Aw, come on now. Just one dance?"

Sierra glanced down at their interlocking fingers sending shivers of delight through her. "I'm not much for the hip-hop songs."

Leaning forward, he whispered in her ear convincingly, "Then ignore the words and enjoy the beat. All you have to do is follow my lead."

She glanced at her watch before taking another look over the rail. Almost midnight. She thought about her alarm, already set for 5:30 in the morning. Trying to recall the last time she'd been out this late on a school night, she felt her mind drawing a total blank. Kayla was right—she needed to get a life. *What harm could one dance do?*

Her expression relaxed and Justin took that as a yes. Before she could change her mind, he guided her down the steps, weaving and bobbing their way through the crowd. Finding a spot toward the center of the floor, Justin faced her and started moving to the beat.

Sierra's body vibrated as the sound of the bass pounded through the speakers. Not moving, she took in the fancy moves of her dance partner. With his arms in the air and his feet moving from side to side, Justin proved that he was quite comfortable in this scene. Taking a quick look around, she felt a flicker of apprehension course through her. Women sensually caressed their dance partners, rubbing various body parts against the guys, and making moves she could never do, even if she wasn't restricted by her pants and jacket. All of a sudden, her mouth wrinkled in a frown and her body stiffened. She was completely out of her element.

"Relax," Justin said, sensing tension building inside her. Lowering his hands around her waist, he coaxed her closer and whispered in her ear, "I know you can do better than that. Enjoy yourself. Let yourself go. You're allowed."

Sierra's body began to rock and her feet started to move.

"There you go," he encouraged, watching her hips began to shake.

Slowly, her body fell into rhythm with his. Concentrating on the beat, she swayed from side to side, allowing the music to take her over. A few minutes into the song, her initially stiff motions gradually loosened up.

A new song came on and a roar from the people indicated the popularity of it. As more people joined them on the floor, Sierra found herself pushed closer and closer to Justin. Their bodies bumped and Sierra's heart pounded a little faster. They bumped again and her desire for him increased tremendously. As the song continued, her inhibitions evaporated with each physical contact.

Four songs later, Sierra was wiping sweat from her brow. Not only had it been years since she'd set foot in a club, it had been even longer since she'd allowed herself to step out of the shell she'd built around herself once she left for college. Not ready to leave the dance floor, she twisted and turned to the sounds of the DJ.

Justin fought to restrain himself as Sierra's body bumped and bounced against his. He'd fashioned himself a man full of self-control, but at this precise moment he was losing the battle of keeping his hands off her body. She had unbuttoned her jacket two songs ago, and the thin camisole did little to hide the supple curves of her body. The perspiration glistening across her face and chest had him imagining how she would look after a passionate night of lovemaking.

Oozing sex appeal, Justin moaned as Sierra turned away from him, her backside bumping into him. Raising her hands up, she locked them behind his neck and sensually moved to the beat. Her eyes closed, she became completely consumed by the music, and Justin believed he'd just witnessed a transformation. Completely releasing a seemingly rigid lifestyle, she'd given up the fight to maintain a composed outer appearance, to become a woman without a care in the world.

As the song ended, he opened his mouth to suggest they cool off with a drink when the romantic sounds of Luther Vandross crooned, causing Justin to quickly change his mind.

"This is for all you lovebirds out there celebrating Valentine's Day," the DJ said.

Before Sierra could turn away, Justin reached for her hand. "One more?"

Without a second thought, she eased into his arms, resting her head against his chest. On the few occasions Kayla had been able to convince her to hang with her at a club, very few times had she let a man buy her a drink, rarely would she venture out onto the dance floor, and never would she have allowed a man to mold her body to the contours of his. Feeling his hands move freely from her neck, to her shoulders, down her back, and around her hips, she understood why. She'd never met a man like Justin Simmons.

Constantly nagging Sierra about taking herself too seriously, Kayla begged her to loosen up. Enjoy life. Break a few of her preposterous rules. Reminding Sierra that a happy medium between the extreme party lifestyle she witnessed as a child with her parents and the reclusive way of living she'd practiced on herself, Kayla's meaning was often lost on Sierra. Until tonight. Maybe, in Justin, she'd found her happy medium.

As she raised her head, Sierra's breath caught. His eyes stared directly back at her. In her mind, they were the only two people on the dance floor. Their swaying motion stopped and Sierra surprisingly responded with a silent yes. As the clock struck midnight, Sierra pushed up on her tiptoes to meet his descending lips. Everything faded in the background and no resistance surfaced as Justin prompted her lips farther apart.

Blaming it on the lethal combination of the music, the wine, and the man, Sierra wrapped her arms around his neck and leaned fully into him, making it impossible for even the slightest breeze to come between them. Forgetting she stood in the middle of the dance floor, Sierra lost herself in the moment and savored every delectable drop.

The moment his flesh connected with hers, Justin's heart jolted and fifteen years of searching came to a screeching halt. All the women he'd dated, all the times he'd thought he'd been in love, all the second thoughts when he broke off a relationship—they all led to this night—this moment—this woman. In an industry such as his, most believed it was next to impossible to not only commit to someone, but make it last longer than the average celebrity marriage. He usually offered no argument against that theory. But that was before she walked into this club, sat on that bar stool, danced in his arms, and melted into his kiss.

As the slow jam ended, replaced by an up-tempo one, another couple bumped them and Sierra jumped back. Not taking his eyes off hers, Justin witnessed the precise moment she snapped back into her shell. As she headed off the dance floor, he reached for her hand.

"Don't," he yelled over the music.

"Don't what?" she said, trying to wiggle her way free. Not because she wanted to get away, but because she was afraid of what would happen if she stayed.

Without answering, he led her off the dance floor and back up the stairs to the lounge. Taking a seat at a table near the back wall, Justin finally let her hand go. "I got the strange feeling you were about to do a Cinderella on me."

"Excuse me?" Sierra said, refusing to sit.

Noticing her rigid stance, Justin tried to loosen her up. "We danced, we kissed, the clock struck midnight, and suddenly you looked like you wanted to bolt."

Sierra attempted to hide her smile at his reference—and his ability to read her mind. His analysis was right on target.

"But you wouldn't have gotten far because I would have been right behind you."

Sierra relaxed her stance and he motioned to the chair. "Please have a seat."

As she studied the man staring up at her, everything about him screamed sophistication, attraction, and success. His good looks, his sense of humor, his ability to reach into her thoughts made him seem perfect—too perfect. Buttoning up her jacket, she hooked her purse on her shoulders. "Thanks for the drink and the dance, Mr. Simmons."

The dismissive tone in her voice made it clear that their night was over. Standing, Justin asked, "Did I miss something?"

"No, you didn't. We talked. We drank. We danced. End of story."

Stepping directly in front of her, he challenged her aloofness. "A second ago, I would have sworn you were just as attracted to me as I am to you. And now, you dismiss me as if we didn't just hold each other—kiss each other."

Once again, Sierra hid her surprise at his ability to read her. After several seconds of silence, her eyes narrowed. "What are you doing here?"

Taken aback by the change in subject, he furrowed his brow in confusion. "Here?"

"Yes, here," she said, waving her arms around the room. "At the G-Spot. It's quite obvious that I'm not at home in this type of atmosphere, but you seem very comfortable here."

"Is that so bad?"

"Yes," she said defiantly.

Justin sat back in his chair as her answer came without hesitation. "Why?"

"It's no secret the type of lifestyles people lead who hang out in places like this."

Justin controlled his laugh at her absurd statement. "Well, it's a secret from me. So please share."

Seeing the glint of humor in his eyes, Sierra asked, "Are you making fun of me?"

A slow smile escaped his lips. "Sit."

When she didn't move, he added, "Please."

Several seconds passed before she snatched the chair back.

Leaning across the table, he grabbed her hand and gently stroked the palm. "Now, tell me this secret about people who hang out in places that offer good food, dancing, music, and the opportunity to meet someone as beautiful as you."

Hearing it phrased that way made Sierra's assessment of him based on broad generalizations seem slightly crazy. But she forged on anyway, ignoring the light caress of his fingers. "Let's just say I've had my share of experiences with club hoppers and party-goers and there's nothing about people that enjoy that lifestyle that attracts me."

Not sure whether to be insulted or amused, Justin asked, "Are you calling me a club hopper and party-goer?"

"Are you?"

"If you're asking if I go to parties and clubs, the answer is yes."

Disappointment sank into her and she moved her hands out of his touch, immediately experiencing the loss. She'd hoped his answer would be different, but he'd admitted to being the type of man she wanted nothing to do with. The drugs, the alcohol, the easy sex. All part of the atmosphere Sierra had no interest in being caught up in again. The same atmosphere he just admitted to enjoying. But she did inwardly admit that if she ever wanted to go back, Justin would be the man to take her there.

Watching her expression grow more negative by the second, Justin wondered what terrible experience had caused her to denounce an entire form of entertainment. "What exactly is it about a club, or a party, that makes your face contort as if you just sucked on a lemon?"

"Should we start with the drugs? Or perhaps the excessive drinking? How about all the freakin' and sexual escapades?"

Her words, spoken with such passion, could only come from firsthand knowledge. An ex-boyfriend who liked to party too much? "Like I said, for someone who claims to keep her distance from places like this, you sound like you've got everyone in here figured out."

Shrugging, she said, "It's been a while, but I'm sure some things never change."

Hoping to show that making generalizations was not the best way to judge him, he decided to turn the tables. "So it's safe to say that you were into taking drugs, binge drinking, and careless sex?"

Sierra narrowed her eyes and gritted her teeth. "Of course not!"

"Oh, I'm sorry," Justin said, feigning confusion. "It's just that it's so obvious by your vast knowledge that you've hung out in clubs and have attended some parties. And according to your theory, everyone who does engages in those types of activities."

Sierra opened her mouth to respond, but no words came out.

As he reached for her hand again, his face became serious. "If you managed not to engage in those types of activities, why is it so hard to believe that I can do the same?"

Her expression went blank and she realized he'd had her. For all the industry parties and club events she attended, she'd managed to steer clear of all the negative trappings.

Justin held his breath while he waited for her response. It suddenly became important to him that Sierra got to know the real him. The opinions of women never mattered to him before, but that was before she had walked into this club and right into his life. "I don't know what happened in your past to give you this perception, and while I'd love for you to tell me, I have a strange feeling you won't—not yet. All I'm asking is for a chance for you to get to know me before you judge me."

Always teaching her children never to make decisions about people based on superficial information, she decided to take her own advice. "Fair enough, Justin."

Exhaling, Justin kissed her hand. "Does that mean I get a last name and a number?"

Sierra pulled out of his touch and stood. His charming ways were taking their toll and she felt herself falling for him hook, line, and sinker. "It means you can help me find my friends. I really do have to get home."

Standing as well, Justin motioned toward the stairs. "You're tough, Sierra. But that's fine. I don't scare that easy."

That's what I'm afraid of.

Ten minutes later, the foursome left the club. Promising to call Sierra tomorrow, Kayla gave her the thumbs-up sign when Justin wasn't looking.

Stopping at Sierra's car, Justin reached out to her. "It's truly been a pleasure meeting you, Sierra."

Leaning forward, he slipped something into her hand. "Just in case you lose your cell phone."

Sierra glanced down and read the seven digits on the small piece of paper. No way could she contain the small smile that escaped her lips. *Definitely a charmer.* "It's been a pleasure meeting you as well."

Giving her a chaste kiss on the cheek, he opened her car door and shut it behind her. Starting the car, she rolled down her window. "You still haven't told me why you were here tonight."

Remembering her assault on the music industry, he wanted to tell her about his profession when they had the time to talk about it. "I came with some coworkers. They're still inside."

Seemingly satisfied with his answer, Sierra put the car in drive. "Rivers."

"What?"

With playful eyes, she explained, "My last name."

Justin's laughter lingered in the night air as her car disappeared around the corner.

Four

Wednesday morning, Justin sat in his office reviewing possible television opportunities for Black Shadow. With the success of his current album and his second single sitting on the charts at number one for the fourth week, they had to keep striking while the iron was hot.

The twenty-city tour they had just completed sold out in just about every arena. With more dates possibly being added, Justin wanted to keep him in the public eye. With him already scheduled for all the major talk shows, guest appearances on a couple of television shows seemed the next logical step. But after looking over the proposals for the past half hour, Justin had no idea what they were offering—because his mind kept wandering to the woman from last night.

Closing the file, Justin leaned back in his leather chair, picking up his stress ball. Tossing it in the air usually helped him clear his head of distractions. And this morning, he was most definitely distracted. He couldn't sleep thinking about her soft hair, beautiful eyes, and that sexy body.

The physical attraction didn't surprise Justin. He'd experienced that more times than he could count. It was her caring spirit, intelligent mind, and wonderful sense of humor that had him unable to focus on his work.

"Uh-oh, you're tossing that stupid ball. I hope I'm not the reason for it this time."

Justin set the ball on his desk and motioned Black Shadow into his office. "This may be hard to believe, but you're the least of my worries right now."

"You got that right," Black Shadow said confidently, taking a seat in one of the black leather chairs in front of the huge cherry-wood desk. "Two million units sold in six weeks, a sold-out tour, and two endorsement contracts on the table. I'm the last person that should be stressing you out. Not to mention that superfine honey I saw you with on the dance floor last night. Her outfit was a little too conservative for my taste, but I'm sure you had her out those clothes in no time."

Justin stiffened and clenched his teeth. "Let's get one thing straight. My personal life is none of your business and she's not one of your groupies."

"Damn, J," Black Shadow said, confused at his reaction. "No need to get all serious on a brotha. You just looked to be having a good time, so I assumed—"

"You assumed I went home with her."

"Don't we always?" Black Shadow answered with a cynical laugh. "I know I do."

Justin walked across the office and shut the door. "Look, Allen."

"Oh, boy," Allen said, kicking his feet up on the desk. "There you go with my real name. I feel a speech about to come on."

Slapping his feet down, Justin leaned on the desk in front of him. "Didn't I tell you to be careful with those women? The last thing you need right now is bad publicity—and a scorned groupie can give you more than you ever bargained for."

Allen sucked his teeth and attempted to stand up, but Justin pushed him back down. "I'm serious, man."

"I hear you, J."

Justin narrowed his eyes, trying to gauge if any of his words were getting through to him.

"Seriously, J. I hear you. I don't want nothing messing up my thing right now. So I'll be careful."

Satisfied that was probably the best he was going to get from him, Justin walked back behind his desk. A slow grin creased his mouth. "Your mom still works for the school system, doesn't she?"

"For the past twenty-two years."

"Good," Justin said, handing him the phone. "I need a huge favor."

Sierra stood at the entrance to her classroom as the last of her students filed out for lunch. Yawning, she walked back to her desk and quickly reviewed her afternoon lesson plan. Teaching her students filled Sierra with a sense of satisfaction. Nothing got her juices flowing more than watching a child's eyes light up with a new revelation or an understanding of a new concept. In a world fascinated with rappers and movie stars, she relished teaching her students about other forms of success. At least once a month, guest speakers who found success in the fields of science, business, and finance spoke to her class, proving to her students that you didn't have to be on television or on the radio to find success, happiness and prosperity.

Grabbing her purse, she searched for her keys to lock her classroom when the small piece of paper with Justin's phone number fell out. Instinctively she smiled. Not only did her tiredness come from her late night, it came from a restless night. Getting home at almost 2:00 A.M., she had tossed and turned until her alarm went off. Each time she closed her eyes, his face invaded her thoughts and her heart warmed as she remembered his alluring eyes,

294   *Doreen Rainey*

smooth skin, tantalizing grin, and wonderful sense of humor. Kayla hoped she'd have a wonderful Valentine's Day . . . and she got her wish.

Looking at the number, she contemplated calling him for what seemed like the hundredth time that day. But just like all the other times, she pushed the number back in her bag. She'd never been the pursuer in a relationship, and her nervousness prevented her from making the call. Maybe after a pep talk from Kayla, she'd dial the seven digits she'd already memorized.

Stepping into the teachers' lounge, Sierra headed for the refrigerator to grab her lunch. Greeting two other teachers talking at a conference table, she stopped at her mailbox.

"Looks like somebody had a late night," Alyssa said knowingly. Leaning closer to Michelle, she continued, "Must have been some Valentine's celebration."

"I heard that," Sierra said.

"Walter must have been a keeper," Michelle said, patting the empty chair beside her. "So, come on, girl, take a seat and tell us all about it."

Placing her mail in front of her, Sierra opened her Tupperware container and poured dressing over her salad, purposely delaying her response.

"No, she isn't ignoring us," Alyssa said, faking agitation.

"I think she is," Michelle answered.

Sierra continued pretending to ignore them, but couldn't hide her smile. Outside of Kayla, Sierra considered Alyssa and Michelle her closest friends. All three had started teaching the same year and they'd shared many lunches and conversations about their love lives . . . or lack thereof. "Don't either of you get excited about a love connection. Walter turned out to be more of a jerk than all the bums we've dated put together."

Both women exchanged sympathetic looks and Alyssa

spoke first. "After spending yet another Valentine's Day alone, I was hoping that one of us would have had a great night out."

Flipping through the pile of mail, Sierra started to respond, but the words were caught in her mouth and her eyes brightened. The pink phone message in her mailbox with his name and number glared back at her. While she'd spent the day contemplating whether to call, he obviously decided to make the first move. "Well . . ." Sierra started with a mysterious grin. "My night wasn't a total waste."

"Ooohhhh," Alyssa said, flipping her blond hair off her shoulders. Born and raised in southern California, Alyssa, with her five-foot-nine slim frame, seemed suited more for the runway than a classroom, but her mother had been a schoolteacher and Alyssa believed it was the greatest profession a person could choose. "Come on, girl, out with it."

Michelle watched Sierra try to hide her smile. "An expression like that has 'juicy details' written all over it."

Giggling like a teenager, Sierra stood and walked behind her chair.

Watching her pace, Michelle squealed. "This must be some good stuff if you can't stay in your seat."

At twenty-seven, Michelle had met her soul mate—twice. And divorced both of them. But that didn't discourage her from continuing her search for Mr. Right. She'd been dating a guy for almost a month and claimed he might be the one.

"After my disaster with Walter, I met Kayla at the G-Spot and—"

"Whoa . . . hold up. Wait one minute," Michelle interjected, raising her hand. "What in the world were you doing at the G-Spot? That's a place for the young, hip, and stylish . . . like Alyssa and me. But you?"

"Ha, ha," Sierra said, poking her tongue out like a child. "For your information, I went there to give Kayla a piece of my mind for setting me up with that loser. As I waited for her in the lounge, this guy bought me a drink and then we—"

This time it was Alyssa who couldn't let her continue. "Did you just say you let yourself get picked up in a club?"

"It wasn't like that," Sierra answered, remembering his sincerity. "Justin was funny, charming, sweet, and a pretty good dancer."

"Dance?" Michelle said, standing herself. With her jet-black hair, smooth bronze skin, and athletic figure, Michelle loved the nightlife, but she couldn't recall a time when Sierra had joined her on one of her nights out. "Did you just say you got out on the dance floor? Was there a full moon last night?"

"You guys sound like Kayla. You're acting as if I don't hang out."

Alyssa and Michelle stared at each other and both spoke in unison. "You don't."

Sierra plopped back in her chair and admitted defeat. "Okay, you're right. I don't usually hang out. But I did last night, and had the time of my life."

"Judging from the dreamy look you have in your eyes, Justin must be somethin'," Alyssa said.

Uptight, rigid, and a little angry had been her attitude when she took a seat on that bar stool last night. But Justin's gorgeous looks, flirty mannerisms, hearty laugh, and playful nature had loosened her up and made her forget about her terrible date with Walter. Her naturally reserved nature never lent itself to suggestive dances and impromptu kisses. But with Justin, it came naturally. Flipping the message in her hand, she'd hoped they would have the chance to do it again real soon.

"Earth to Sierra?"

Snapping out of her daze, she felt her face flush with

embarrassment as she glanced from one friend to the other. How long had they been calling her name?

Michelle threw away her trash from lunch. "This man must be something if he can give you a look like that."

"Like what?" Sierra asked, watching them head for the door.

"The look that says one of us may be off the market soon," Michelle answered.

Sierra shook her head in the negative. "Don't be ridiculous. I just met the man."

"What's that got to do with it? I only knew my first husband for three months before we tied the knot," Michelle said.

"That's not a selling point," Alyssa said, nudging her in the arm. "You divorced him six months later."

"Oh, yeah," Michelle responded thoughtfully.

"Anyway," Alyssa continued, turning her attention back to Sierra, "it doesn't matter how long you've known him. If he puts a look like that on your face, I wouldn't let him get away."

Alyssa and Michelle returned to their classrooms and Sierra sat staring at his message. Before she could change her mind, she whipped out her cell phone and dialed. Voice mail.

"Justin? Hi. It's Sierra. Even though I'm not sure how you located my school, I'm glad you did. I'll try you again this afternoon." Disappointed, Sierra pushed the red end button. She hadn't realized how much she wanted to talk to him until this moment.

A couple of hours later, Sierra waved good-bye to Alyssa and Michelle before heading for her car at the far end of the parking lot. After meeting with a parent after school, Sierra, leaving later than usual, thought about calling Justin again. Almost to her car, she abruptly stopped.

"Thank goodness there was only one Sierra Rivers listed in the Los Angeles County Public School System."

Sierra took a few tentative steps before standing directly in front of Justin Simmons.

"I just wanted to thank you personally for making my Valentine's Day perfect," he said, handing her a single white rose.

Catching Michelle and Alyssa out the corner of her eye, Sierra saw them slowing their walk considerably, indicating that she'd just become the afternoon show. No doubt she'd be given the third degree tomorrow.

Justin followed her eyes and waved to the two women. "I take it by the way they're staring, you don't have too many men meeting you after work."

"Or they could just be trying to get a peek at which man it is today," Sierra answered lightly.

"Touché."

Raising the flower to her nose, she inhaled the sweet fragrance. "My message said I'd call you back."

Justin placed his hands in his pockets, a nervous gesture he hadn't indulged in for years. However, along with the nervousness came excitement. Excitement about her.

Because of his occupation, there was never a lack of female companionship. He'd dated more women than he cared to admit, but none of them had given him what he was experiencing now. It was that feeling he had had in the sixth grade when he asked Sally Barns to the school dance. His palms were sweaty, he'd rehearsed his words a hundred times, and he thought he would die on the spot if she said no. Ever since his eyes rested on Sierra, that same feeling of excitement—that tingling sensation—had yet to go away. "Isn't a face-to-face conversation much better?"

Sierra cocked her head to the side and half smiled. "Yes."

"Then my gamble of coming here today just paid off."

"And just what are you doing here?"

Motioning to his car parked right beside hers, he said, "I thought we could start with date number one."

"Excuse me?"

"Last night, you rolled off a list of your perfect dates. I believe the first one was a picnic at the beach." Opening the door to his convertible Jag, he motioned for her to get in.

"Have you lost your mind? It's Wednesday. We can't go to the beach."

"Can't go?" Justin repeated, wondering how she came to that conclusion. "Is it closed on Wednesdays?"

"No . . . it's just . . . " Sierra searched for the right words, but couldn't find them.

"Just what?"

Sierra hated to admit the real reason. "I usually don't go out during the week."

For some strange reason, Justin felt relieved at that revelation. "Last night you told me that you usually don't hang out in clubs—but didn't you have a great time?"

"What's your point?"

"My point is—let's do something unusual again. I promise to have you back at a decent hour."

Still not sure, Sierra eyed the open door and cut her eyes at Alyssa and Michelle, still standing across the parking lot. Without being able to see their expressions, she figured they were probably encouraging her to get in—to take a chance, to live a little. Yet, Sierra wasn't ready to concede just yet. "You show up at my job, unannounced, on a Wednesday afternoon. How do you know I don't have other plans?"

"After your fiasco with that jerk last night, I took my chances that this night would be free."

Get in the car, girl. You know you want to.

Sliding his sunshades onto his nose, Justin reached out for her. "Come on, it's a beautiful seventy-five-degree day."

Eyeing her friends one last time, Sierra threw caution to the wind and slid into the passenger seat.

Justin ran around to the driver's side just as his two-way pager went off. Sierra remembered the device from last night and watched him flip the screen to read the message. Taking advantage of his distraction, Sierra discreetly checked out the interior of his midnight-black convertible Jaguar XKR. Leather seats. Walnut wood trim. Bose sound system. On-star navigation system. The accessories had *customized* written all over them.

Justin answered the message, hooked the pager on his hip, and started the car. Pulling out of the parking lot, he gave one final wave to Alyssa and Michelle.

"Custom rims on your car, two-way pager, not in the office on Wednesday afternoon. In LA, my students would classify you as either a drug dealer or someone in the entertainment industry."

"You drive a luxury BMW Five Series, which I know most teachers can't afford on their salary alone," Justin pointed out. "And *you're* not in the office on a Wednesday afternoon. So what does that make you—the drug dealer or someone in the entertainment industry?"

Once again, he challenged her assumptions and generalizations. "Point taken and I apologize for my assumptions. So tell me, what exactly do you do, Mr. Simmons?"

Justin shifted into fifth gear as he merged onto the freeway, contemplating his answer. The moment she had walked across that dance floor, a spark of pure attraction ignited him. Now that he'd talked to her and held her in his arms, the thought that he'd found someone special lingered in his mind.

When his lips touched hers, the powerful bolt of electricity singed him from head to toe. But Sierra's obvious conscious decision to stay away from anything or anyone remotely related to the music industry could hamper their chance at a relationship before he had the opportunity to change her mind. Did he really want to reveal to her his position at PrimeTime Records? If he told her, would she give him a chance or dump him on the spot? Making a quick decision, he thought it better to take the hit of her reaction now, rather than to have to explain a lie later. "I'm VP of—"

His answer was interrupted by the ringing of her cell phone.

"Hello . . . Hi, Kayla . . . Speak up . . . I'm in a convertible . . . Justin's . . . yes, the guy from last night." Sierra cut her eyes at Justin and noticed that he was paying closer attention to her phone conversation than he was to the road.

"Look, Kayla, I don't have time for the third degree. Did you want something? No, thank you . . . I don't care who's supposed to be there . . . I don't want to go . . . I'll call you later."

Sierra disconnected her call and dropped her phone back in her purse.

"Everything okay?"

"Kayla, my friend from last night, invited me to some CD release party Michael got them tickets to."

"Not interested?" Justin asked.

"Why would I be interested in spending my evening listening to music I probably won't like by a group that probably has more image than talent?" Realizing her emotions were getting the best of her, Sierra waved her hand nonchalantly. "But enough about that, what were you saying?"

Suddenly, Justin reconsidered his earlier decision.

He'd wait until a better time. "I'm saying we're almost there."

As they took the next exit, Sierra realized they were in Malibu.

Maneuvering his car around a few curves, he ducked into a side street before the scene opened up into a beautiful beach area.

With the private entrance, Sierra wondered, "Isn't this private property?"

Cutting the engine, Justin stepped out of the car. "Don't worry. If we get caught, we'll just tell them we didn't see the sign."

Noticing a few people down by the water, she didn't move. "I don't know, Justin. I'm not sure I'm up for getting chased off by some crazed home owner."

Popping the trunk, Justin grabbed a large picnic basket, a blanket, and a portable radio. "Don't worry. It's just after four in the afternoon. I'm sure whoever owns this property is at the office trying to make another deal."

No one on the beach gave them a second look, so she got out of the car and followed him through the sand.

Glad that she wore pants today, she eased down onto the blanket with his help and removed her blazer, revealing a short-sleeved blouse that allowed the sun to warm her arms.

Opening the basket, Justin pulled out a platter of baked breads, sliced glazed ham, roasted turkey breast, and roast beef. "I didn't know what you would like, so I brought some of everything."

Setting that to the side, he grabbed a smaller plate filled with all kinds of cheeses, including Swiss, provolone, Muenster, and American. The next four containers that came out of the basket held pasta salad, coleslaw, potato salad, and sliced fresh fruit.

Sierra sat in silent amazement as he reached in yet

again to retrieve an assortment of condiments, plates, napkins, and silverware. Thinking he was done, Sierra eyes widened at the dessert tray that would set any dieter back for months. Freshly baked peanut butter cookies, several slices of cheesecake, chocolate raspberry truffles, and good old-fashioned chocolate cake. "Is there an army joining us to help us eat all this?"

With his hand still in the basket, Justin removed a bottle of wine, taking a look at the spread. Slightly embarrassed, he laughed. "I guess I did go a little overboard."

Unwrapping the food, he began to fix her plate, pointing to items for her to say yea or nay to. "I thought I might have missed you at the school. Are you usually the last teacher to leave?"

"Not always, but I had a meeting with a parent today."

"Trouble with one of your students?"

Taking off her shoes, Sierra stretched her legs forward. "Just the opposite. Kelly Jamison is extremely gifted in math and has the opportunity to go to NASA for a summer program in engineering. Even though the program is funded, there are still travel, food, and lodging expenses. She's being raised by a single mom, and money is extremely tight. I met with her mother to help her put together a fund-raiser."

Handing Sierra her plate, Justin began fixing his own. "Can't the school do anything?"

"Are you kidding? Our budget is so tight, we can barely get new books on a regular basis. Not to mention that we have several hundred students sharing a computer lab filled with twenty-five desktops. In a country with so much wealth, it always amazes me that we never have enough funding for our children."

Taking a bite of his sandwich, Justin admired her commitment to teaching and to her students. *She would make a fabulous wife and mother.* Justin choked on his food as that thought flashed through his mind. Coughing heavily, he tried to catch his breath. *Where did that come from?*

"Are you okay?" Sierra asked, moving to pat him on the back.

"Um, yeah . . . I guess something just went down the wrong way." Sipping his wine, Justin tried to imagine what would make him think about Sierra in the role of wife and mother. He'd never had that thought about a woman.

Sierra continued to share stories of her students. Some positive, some very negative. But in all her stories, he could hear the love and care she had not only for her job, but for her students.

Finishing their meal, Justin stood and helped her up. "You want to walk off some of this food?"

As they made their way down the beach, the sun began to set, creating a beautiful glow over the horizon. "Such an amazing scene," Sierra said, glancing out over the water.

Stopping, Justin reached out to her. "Yes, what I'm looking at is truly amazing." Lowering his gaze to her lips, he gave her a split second to deny him. When she didn't, he claimed her lips, coaxed them open, slipping his tongue inside. The moment he fully tasted her, he lost every semblance of control. Emotions swirled inside like a tornado and his head grew light and his knees bent in weakness. Wrapping her completely in his arms, he thought he would pass out from the intoxicating passion and the feeling of euphoria. Physical excitement he could handle, but emotional excitement put him in unchartered territory.

Sierra wasn't faring any better. When he lowered his gaze to her mouth, she heard the silent question. Granting permission, she raised her head to meet his lips and prepared herself for the sweetness of his touch. But what she got was anything but. Fire shot straight to her core when his tongue eased into her mouth, and the heat exploded like fireworks on the Fourth of July. She felt every part of her body responding. Squeezing her arms tighter around his neck, she pressed into his body for support, hoping to maintain her balance.

When he had kissed her last night, she credited her powerful reaction to the wine, the music, and the dancing, but today she now realized it was none of those things. That left only one thing—the man.

Hearing an approaching couple talking, Justin released her lips, but still held her. Resting his forehead against hers, he worked to get his blood pressure back to normal. "Wh . . . what was that?"

Not ready to acknowledge the feelings raging inside her, she attempted to catch her breath. "What was what?"

Shaking his head in the negative, he didn't buy in to her ploy to play ignorant. "You know what, Sierra. That was the most powerful kiss I've ever experienced, and judging from your response, I'd say it was the same for you."

Sierra watched the couple move farther down the beach to avoid looking him in the eyes. Discounting his question, she shrugged. "Lust."

Justin stared intently at her before he let his mouth relax into a slow grin. "Yeah, right."

Hearing the sarcasm is his voice, Sierra challenged him. "If it's not lust, what else could it be?"

Justin paused. No stranger to lust, he already knew what he felt for her went beyond that. But he couldn't answer her question because he always thought the opposite of lust was love. But that was impossible. He'd known her less than twenty-four hours. Not ready to explore the answer, he wrapped his arm around her shoulder. "Let's head back."

Walking hand in hand with him back to their blanket, Sierra allowed him to ignore her question. If the truth be told, she wasn't so sure she wanted to hear his answer. Her sweaty palms, the butterflies in her stomach, and her rapid heartbeat could be classified as lust, but what about the way she felt when he made her laugh and challenged her thinking?

Gathering up their belongings, they loaded up the car and eased back onto the freeway in a matter of minutes.

Pulling beside her car in the parking lot of the elementary school, Justin signaled for her to wait while he opened the door for her.

As he helped her out of the car, Sierra smiled. "A girl could get used to this kind of treatment. First you fix my plate, now this."

Not letting go of her hand, he wrapped it around his waist and molded his body to hers. "While I do consider myself a gentleman, this particular move comes with an ulterior motive."

This kiss, slow and purposeful, sent shivers of desire racing through her body. Inhaling deeply, Sierra enjoyed the butterfly kisses that moved from her lips, to her cheek, and down her neck. As she felt his hands gently stroke her back, a soft moan escaped her lips. Hearing the erotic sound, Sierra stepped back. "I think it's time we called it a night."

Giving her one final kiss on the forehead, Justin agreed. One more second of these tantalizing kisses, and letting her go would have become a major challenge. "Let me cook for you tomorrow."

"Cook?"

"Perfect date number two."

Touched that he remembered her words from last night, she asked, "Will it be hot dogs or filet mignon?"

"You'll have to say yes to find out."

Without hesitation, she said, "Yes."

Reaching into the glove compartment for a pen and paper, Justin took a deep breath. "Let me give you my address." The moment she walked into his house, what he did for a living would no longer be a secret. Framed gold and platinum records of artists he managed filled his rooms. Pictures of him with various celebrities hung everywhere. Even if he hid everything, she'd still want to know how he could afford to live in a gated community in a seven-bedroom house complete with a swimming pool, a basketball court, and a five-car garage with a luxury vehicle parked in each one. He couldn't keep it from her forever—nor did he want to. He only hoped that she'd gotten to know him enough that she would give him a chance in spite of his occupation.

Sierra watched Justin lean over, and got a fantastic view of a great behind. Thinking of those awesome kisses and his amazing body, she suddenly became afraid to go to his house. Envisioning the romantic scene he would probably create, Sierra didn't trust herself to resist him. "Actually . . . why don't you cook at my house?"

Turning to face her, he narrowed his eyes in curiosity. "Why?"

"Let's just say I'd feel more comfortable."

Tearing off the top sheet from the pad he was writing on, he handed her the blank page for her to write on. He'd been given a momentary reprieve and he decided to take advantage of it. "If you get out of school at three o'clock, why don't I meet you about four-thirty? I'll have already grocery-shopped, but that will give me enough time to cook so that we can eat around six."

Handing the information back to him, Sierra eyed him suspiciously. "What kind of job lets you spend your afternoon grocery shopping and meeting me?"

Opening her car door, he stepped aside to let her in.

"I just got back from a long business trip, so I'm taking the rest of the week off."

Starting the car, she rolled down the window. His answer made sense, but Sierra wondered if there was something more to it than that. "And what exactly are you taking time off from?"

Leaning down to meet her eye to eye, he gave her a peck on the lips. "I'll tell you all about it tomorrow. But I promised to have you home at a decent hour and I'm a man of my word."

His eyes never wavered. Putting her car in drive, she said, "I'll see you tomorrow."

Five

Sierra set her lunch down on the table in the teachers' lounge, convinced it would only be a few seconds before Alyssa and Michelle joined her. Taking a bite of her sandwich, she said hello when they reached her table, acting as if nothing out of the ordinary had occurred the day before.

Watching her take a sip of her iced tea, Alyssa found her patience snapping first. "Are you going to tell us about that fine specimen of a man that swooped you up yesterday?"

Sierra set her glass down and picked up her sandwich. With a glint of humor in her eyes, she played dumb. "What are you talking about?"

"You can either spill it on your own, or we can beat it out of you," Michelle said, waving a fist to make her point.

"Okay, okay." Sierra laughed. "Let's not resort to violence. The man from yesterday was the man from the club."

"And where did this man from the club take you in that super bad car?" Alyssa asked.

"We took a ride up the coast to Malibu and had a picnic on the beach."

"Oh, how romantic," Michelle cooed. "The weather was perfect yesterday."

Sierra lowered her eyes and took another bite of her sandwich.

Alyssa took a closer look at her friend. "Are you blushing?"

"No!"

"Oh, my God! Yes, you are! You're really taken with . . . what's his name again?"

"I am not 'taken' and his name is Justin Simmons."

"Sierra Simmons," Michelle said thoughtfully. "I'm not usually one for first and last names starting with the same letter, but this one works."

It works for me too. Sierra stopped chewing. *Where did that thought come from?*

"You okay?" Alyssa said, noticing her strained expression.

Recovering from the thought, Sierra nodded. "I'm fine. Just thought my food went down the wrong way."

"So when are you going to see him again?"

"Tonight," she said, unable to hide the excitement in her voice. "He's cooking for me."

"Did you say cook?" Michelle said, sticking her fork in her salad. "Does he have a brother?"

Later that afternoon, Sierra stood in her closet searching for something to wear. The straight blue skirt, silk blouse, and matching blazer she wore to school seemed too formal to keep on, yet jeans seemed too casual. Deciding on a pair of khaki capri pants and a matching tank, she finished changing just as the doorbell rang. Adding a touch of lipstick, she fluffed the top of her hair and brushed down the sides. Taking the steps two at a time, she opened the door before he rang again.

Justin stood on the small porch waiting for her to answer. Just as he was about to knock again, the door swung open. "You look absolutely gorgeous."

"Thanks." She stepped to the side and motioned for him to enter.

Standing in the foyer, she grabbed one of the bags of groceries. "The kitchen is straight back."

Justin, following close behind, admired the view from the back. Her body had curves in all the right places.

Setting the groceries on the island in the center of the kitchen, Justin took a quick look around. Ceramic floor and countertops, professional baker's oven and range. Stainless steel pots and pans hanging overhead and state-of-the-art appliances, including a Sub-Zero freezer. With a quick calculation, he figured this was a twenty-thousand-dollar kitchen.

"What can I do to help?" Sierra asked, peeking inside the bags.

Playfully slapping her hand away, he guided her out of the kitchen. "You can stay out of my way. A chef needs his space while he creates."

Pretending to pout, Sierra stuck out her bottom lip and put her hands on her hips, swaying impatiently from side to side. "And what am I supposed to do?"

Her movements caused Justin's smile to falter. "Don't, Sierra."

Confused, Sierra stopped moving and dropped her hand. "Don't what?"

Letting his gaze peruse her body, he felt his own react in the most primitive way. "If you knew how incredibly sexy you look to me right now, you would just turn around and leave me to my cooking. Otherwise, I don't know if I can be held responsible for my actions."

Sierra didn't move and conducted an appraisal of her own. Dressed as he was in dark brown pleated casual pants with a button-down shirt, a flash of him standing naked shot in her head. Never having had that fantasy before, she swallowed deliberately. "I'll be in the living room if you need anything." *Otherwise, I may be the one with the irresponsible actions.*

A half hour later, Justin joined Sierra, who sat in the living room watching television. "Things are simmering, marinating, and baking. Dinner will be ready in less than an hour."

With him resting his arm behind her, their conversation came easy and time passed quickly as they got to know one another. Justin found out where she had gone to college, what her favorite books were, and more about her commitment to her students and education.

Sierra learned that Justin was originally from Philadelphia, called his mom every Sunday, loved to read mystery novels, and had just celebrated his thirty-third birthday . . . on New Year's Eve.

"You're a very deceiving woman, Miss Rivers."

"How so?"

Moving his arms down, he gently stroked her bare shoulder. "When I met you, you were this hard woman who didn't cut anyone any slack. But I've been privy to the real you these past few days. You're not as hard as you'd like people to think. You're a sweet, nice, caring woman who I'm glad came into my life."

Sierra gave a tentative smile at his compliment. Something about his choice of adjectives didn't sit right with her. Growing up surrounded by people who put all their effort into their looks by constantly dressing in the latest designer dress, Sierra had seen Vanessa spending hours preparing for an event. Being slim and sexy was an unwritten rule in the life of female singers, and Sierra never bought into the theory that you couldn't have success if you didn't fit the mold.

With her parents, Sierra's looks and body were typically the first thing people noticed, and her mother had made sure she was a showstopper. When Sierra had left for college, she downplayed that side of herself, preferring to show people that she was more than a pretty face and a body. Dressing in a conservative manner that forced people to focus on her mind and not her body had become second nature to her. And that attitude had served her well. Until now. Until Justin. For some unexplainable reason, she wanted him to see her as a sexy, desirable woman. "You make me sound like an old maid."

Justin laughed. "Sweetheart, believe me . . . no way would I classify you as an old maid."

"But you didn't include anything about my looks in your description." She felt like she was fishing for a compliment, but she couldn't help it. How he physically saw her suddenly became important.

He studied her face for a moment. Was she serious? Had she looked in the mirror lately? "Sierra, you're beautiful—inside and out."

Glancing at his watch, he stood. "Would you prefer to eat in the kitchen or the dining room?"

Still thinking about his description of her, she pointed to the room across the hall. "How about the dining room? I rarely get a chance to use it."

"Great. I'll set the table."

Sierra watched him leave, still preoccupied with his description. A picture of the women at the G-Spot came into her head. With their sexy clothes, confident strides, and brazen dancing, she wondered if those were the types of women Justin usually went for. Glancing down at her clothes, Sierra second-guessed her choice. No wonder he didn't find her sexy. She dressed like anything but. Kayla managed to dress sexy without looking sleazy. How come she didn't do the same thing? Then again, maybe sexiness wasn't in the clothes—but rather a state of mind. Sierra decided to put her theory to the test.

An hour later, Sierra casually leaned back in her chair,

properly wiping each corner of her mouth with a napkin. "Where in the world did you learn to cook like that?
Steak so tender and juicy it melts in your mouth, grilled
vegetables with just the right crunch. And I won't begin
to think about the calories in that homemade macaroni
and cheese."

Justin reveled in the compliment, but the past hour
had been torture. He had never thought of eating as an
aphrodisiac, but there was no other word to describe
what watching her eat had done to him. She moaned in
pleasure with almost every bite. She licked her lips when
a little melted cheese escaped her mouth, darting her
tongue back and forth several times. And why on earth
did he choose to grill asparagus? She picked up the entire stalk with her fork, slowly working her way down with
tiny bites. He thought her behavior out of character, but
he also thought she teased him on purpose.

"Is everything all right? You haven't said much."

Standing, he picked up his plate. If he didn't put some
space between them, he feared he wouldn't be able to
keep his hands off of her. "I'll clear these away."

"Don't worry about it." Rising, she walked toward him.
"You cooked. I'll clean . . . later. Why don't we go into the
living room and have dessert?" Licking her lips seductively,
she lowered her voice. "I swear I smelled something
chocolate baking . . . and I do love me some chocolate."

Justin inwardly groaned as she stood directly in front
of him.

Reaching up, she placed her hands behind his neck.
"Please tell me you have something chocolate for me."

Refusing to embrace her, he stood stoically, hoping to
maintain his composure. Slowly, he spoke in a low and
purposeful voice. "You're playing with fire, Sierra."

"What are you talking about, Justin?"

Wondering what had gotten into her between the time

they were in the living room and dinner, he recalled their conversation. "Is this about the 'old maid' response?"

Not releasing her hold on him, she pushed her body closer to his, rubbing her chest against his. "What do you think?"

"I think a gentleman can only be pushed so far."

"Before?" she challenged.

"Before this." Justin's lips descended upon hers with demanding force, giving in to all the teasing and innuendos. Ravishing her mouth, his tongue explored every part, leaving no area untouched. With expert hands, he caressed her back before reaching underneath her shirt and unhooking her bra in one smooth motion. Without breaking contact, his hand traveled around her waist and rose to her breast.

The moment his hands touched her bare skin, Sierra moaned in exquisite pleasure. With every man she had ever dated, it only took a few dates to determine that a relationship wouldn't work. Having spent the past several days with Justin, she felt her heart telling her that not only would this relationship work—he could be the one.

Justin's emotions swirled and his senses reeled from the power of their connection. If this was just about sex, he would take her right on the dining room floor. But since that first kiss on the dance floor, his mind had to catch up to what his heart already knew . . . he was well on his way to falling in love. At that revelation, he called on every piece of strength he could muster and dropped his hands.

In between catching his breath, he said, "Sierra, we have to talk."

What started out as a game to her quickly turned into something very serious. She'd never wanted a man like she wanted Justin Simmons. And it wasn't just the physical that had drawn her to him. He'd tested her theories, he respected her career, and made her feel special . . . all without knowing who she was. "No . . . no talk . . . just kisses."

Fixing her shirt, he reached for her hands. Drawing them to his mouth, he kissed them sweetly. "Talk first, kiss later."

Not ready to concede defeat, she attempted to change his mind, rubbing her body against his. "I'm sure whatever it is can wait until after dessert."

Dropping her hands, he walked to the other side of the room. "Oh, baby, I wish it could."

Hearing his serious tone, Sierra stepped back, trying to read his eyes. "What is it?"

Taking a deep breath, he couldn't put it off any longer. Having a real, lasting relationship with her had become the most important thing to him and he had to come clean about his career. "Remember when you said I must either be a drug dealer or in the entertainment industry?"

Sierra watched for any sign of a joke. A slight grin, a sparkle in his eyes—anything. But there was nothing. He was dead serious. Fear hovered inside her, and panic like she'd never known welled in her throat. A wave of apprehension swept through her and she felt as if she needed to sit down. Suddenly, she moaned and placed her hands over her face. "Oh, my God . . . Oh, my God." Folding her hands in the prayer position, she stared at him with pleading eyes, the color practically draining from her face. "Please . . . please . . . please . . . please tell me you're a drug dealer."

The room became engulfed in complete silence while Justin digested her words. He stared at her for several seconds before he burst into a hearty laugh. "You can't be serious. You'd rather me be a drug dealer than in the music business?"

This time, Sierra did take a seat, resting her head on the dining room table. "You said music—not entertainment."

Kneeling in front of her, he forced her to look at him. "Yes, Sierra, the music business."

"Who are you?"

"I'm Justin Simmons—the man who hasn't been able to keep you off his mind since the moment he spotted you on the crowded dance floor. I'm the man who watched you let go of your inhibitions and enjoy yourself. I'm the man who knows that the hard woman on the outside is really a warm, caring, and very sexy woman on the inside. I'm the man that's been falling for you from the moment you sat on that bar stool. That's *who* I am." Hesitating, he continued, "*What* I am is vice president of artists and repertoire at PrimeTime Records."

Sierra jumped out of her seat as if she'd been singed. Pacing back and forth, she ran her fingers through her hair. "This cannot be happening. The man of my dreams—VP of A-and-R?"

She knows the lingo. Quickly stepping in front of her, Justin could feel her slipping away. "I don't know what happened to you to set you against an entire industry, but what I do doesn't matter. It doesn't change the fact that we could have a relationship."

"A relationship?" Sierra asked. "Is that so?"

"Yes," he answered calmly, which was in direct contradiction to the fear raging inside him. "You just called me the man of your dreams—surely we can build something solid and true."

"Okay, Mr. Let's Have a Relationship, in the past fifty-two weeks, how many weeks were you on the road?"

"I don't—"

"Guess," she interrupted harshly.

"About twenty-five."

"And how many nights a week do you have industry events, showcases, parties, award shows, or are in the studio?"

"Sierra—" he pleaded.

Her emotions started to take over, but Sierra refused to let her tears fall. "How many?"

"One or two . . ."

Seeing her raise a brow, he quickly corrected himself. "Maybe three."

"And of the four or five months that you're on the road and these one, two, maybe three nights a week that you're at events when you're in LA, how much time is spent around drugs, alcohol, and women willing to do anything to get close to you or someone you know?"

"Sierra, you're not being fair," he countered.

"How many times have you watched someone in the industry commit themselves to someone—even marry someone—only to cheat on them?"

"Think about what you're saying. People go to bars— but some don't drink. People watch movies where people kill—that doesn't make them a murderer."

Walking out of the dining room, Sierra headed for the front door. "Is that the best you can come up with?"

"Can't we talk about this?" he asked quietly.

"You can let yourself out," she said, forcing her voice not to crack.

Refusing to leave, Justin reached out for her, but she stepped out of his way. Lowering his voice, he tried to reason with her. "At least tell me what this is really about—because I know for damn sure it's not about me." For the first time in his life, he had found someone he wanted to build a future with and she was shutting him out for a reason she wouldn't share. Almost pleading, he tried one more time. "Please, Sierra."

Heading up the stairs, she refused to watch him go. "Lock the door on your way out."

* * *

"*The* Justin Simmons?" Kayla asked, adding cream to her sugar. "That's who you're spending all your time with?"

"*Was* spending my time with," Sierra corrected. Sitting in Kayla's apartment, Sierra munched on a bowl of fruit. At 9:30 in the morning, she was doing something she'd never done before. Playing hooky. "And what do you mean by *the* Justin Simmons?"

Spreading a chunk of cream cheese across her toasted bagel, Kayla took a bite and answered without completely chewing her food. "He's responsible for some of the hottest acts that are out there now. He's moved PrimeTime Records into being a major player in the music game. You've heard of Justice."

"That four-girl group from Detroit?"

"Yep. That's Justin's work. And I'm sure you know Morgan Beale."

"Didn't she win a Grammy last year?"

"She sure did. And how can we forget about Black Shadow?"

As Sierra remembered the night they had met, it suddenly became crystal clear why he was at the club. *How could I have been so stupid?*

"That's not a point in his favor, Kayla." *At least I know what label management was doing that night . . . he was talking to me.* "He should have told me. After all my ranting and raving about the industry, he should have said something sooner."

"And what about you?" Kayla asked pointedly.

"What about me?" Sierra said, breaking off a piece of Kayla's bagel and popping it into her mouth.

"Shouldn't you have said something sooner?"

"About?"

"You said yourself that he asked what you had against the music business the night you met. You say he wasn't completely honest with him. Well, neither were you."

"It's not the same thing."

"If you say so."

"I say so."

"Fine," Kayla said, "but the only thing I want to know is, are you going to let a man go who you absolutely adore because of your hang-ups that have absolutely nothing to do with him?"

Justin sat in his office staring at the wall, tossing his stress ball in the air. Unfortunately, it failed to relieve his tension today. He'd contacted the school this morning, but was told that Sierra wouldn't be in today. Calling her house rendered no results. Where was she?

He ran last night through his mind over and over again. What could he have said to change her mind? What could he have done differently? Maybe he should have waited until after they made love to tell her what he did. That way, she would have known how much he'd grown to care for her—to love her.

The ball dropped to the floor. Jumping up, he paced the floor. Was it possible? In his line of work money was made or lost on a hunch. Sign this group, don't sign this group. Release that single first, never release that song. He'd won many more of those decisions than he'd lost and he always trusted his gut. And right now, his gut was telling him that he fallen—and fallen hard.

"What's going on, my man?"

Justin turned to the voice and watched Black Shadow enter his office and take a seat. Dressed in black baggy jeans and a Sean John pullover, he fit the mode of hip-hop superstar to a tee. "You've been MIA the past few nights. You missed my appearance at the Platinum Club. Matter of fact, you haven't been hanging since that night at the G-Spot. Everything cool?"

No. Everything is not cool. The woman I think I'm falling in love with wants nothing to do with me. "Everything's cool, man. What's up?"

Tossing a CD onto the desk, Black Shadow rubbed his hands together in excitement. "Check out my next number-one single."

Glad for the distraction, Justin popped the disc in the player. Pushing play, Justin sat back in his chair. The track started, and eight bars into it Justin started bobbing his head. The percussion was hot and the bass was kickin'.

Black Shadow stood and started rapping over the music. His words flowed and the lyrics were tight. When the chorus kicked in, Justin recognized the song. A remake.

Pushing stop, Justin couldn't contain his excitement. Black Shadow was right. This was a number-one hit. "Let's do this by the book. No lawsuits later."

"I got you, man. I already talked to legal. They've already contacted the publishing company."

"What's the original title and who's the original artist?"

"'Passion for You,' Vanessa Reese."

Taking notes, he asked, "Who owns the track?"

"The producer, Isaac Rivers, her husband."

His head snapped up when he heard the name. "Did you say Rivers?"

"Yeah, J. You know Rivers. He's done tracks for Janet, Beyoncé, and—"

"I know him," Justin said slowly, wondering if it was possible. There were probably thousands of Riverses in the LA area, but if there was a chance . . . There was only one way to find out. "You got a number on you for Isaac?"

Pulling out his two-way, Black Shadow scrolled through his Rolodex, his forehead creased with worry. "I need that beat, J. You don't see a problem with gettin' the song, do you?"

322 Doreen Rainey

Writing down the number, Justin walked toward the door and held it open. "It shouldn't be. I'll let you know when I hear something."

Standing, Black Shadow hooked his pager and walked through the door. "If I didn't know better, I'd say you were rushing me."

"You don't know better," Justin teased. "I am rushing you."

Jingling keys in the air, Black Shadow shrugged. "Good thing I need to break in my new 745il."

Justin knew Allen's custom-ordered BMW had been scheduled to be delivered sometime this week. "Remember what I told you about your money, man."

Glancing down the hall, Black Shadow made sure no one could hear his response. "I listened, man. I invested almost a quarter of a mil from this last tour, and just like you told me, I sold the Benz before I picked up the Beemer."

Patting him on the back, Justin smiled. "Good. Now get out of here, I got things to do."

"Listen, J. I know I tested your patience on tour, and I tend to go a little overboard with my partying at times, but I just want to say thanks for looking out for a brother. In a game full of sharks, it's nice to have you on my side."

Justin smiled at the sincerity in his voice. Sierra would be proud. "No problem."

Justin shut his office door and strode purposely back to his desk. Picking up the phone, he dialed the number, hoping for a live voice and not voice mail.

Six

Vanessa Reese stepped out onto the brick porch in the bright Sunday morning sun. With her low-rider, straight-leg stonewashed blue jeans, open-toe high-heeled sandals, and black-corseted blouse, one would be hard pressed to prove the songstress standing before them had already passed the half-century mark. With all the years of partying, drinking, and living in a world filled with overindulgences, Vanessa somehow managed to maintain a fit body, great skin, and a definite sense of style and fashion.

Removing her shades, she watched her daughter park in the circular drive and cut the engine. With Sierra's having a voice that would put her mother to shame, Vanessa had urged her to sign the record deal offered to her on three separate occasions before she turned twenty-one. But each time, Sierra answered with an emphatic no. Claiming she could never be a part of an industry she didn't trust or believe in, she left the platinum records, sold-out tours, and expensive music videos to her parents.

Initially, Vanessa couldn't comprehend why her daughter despised the very thing that put food on the table, a roof over their head, and clothes on their back. But over the past few years, Vanessa had observed other singing superstars half her age deal with fame and fortune while raising a child. She now understood why Sierra would race to her room when they returned from an event, or beg to stay home when they were expected somewhere.

Vanessa always knew that the pressure of the media and the public could be incredible, but for a young child it could be quite frightening. Looking back over the years, through the ups and downs, the good reviews, the horrific reviews, and the on-again, off-again relationship between herself and Isaac, Vanessa had seen that Sierra managed to somehow keep her sanity. For that, she was grateful.

At first, when Sierra had insisted on leaving Los Angeles for college, Vanessa tried to talk her out of it. Why did she have to go so far away? But Sierra was determined to find her own way and refused to budge on her college choice. From that moment on, Sierra rarely made a public appearance with her parents. She'd accomplished what she'd set out to do—create a life devoid of any reminders from her past.

"Hi, sweetie," Vanessa said, holding out her arms for a hug.

Used to seeing her mother stylishly dressed, Sierra glanced down at her simple hunter-green slacks and button-down blouse and suddenly felt frumpy. Having never experienced this, she found it taking her by complete surprise. Forcing a smile, Sierra hugged her mom and followed her into the house.

As a child, Sierra, often left with a family member while her parents traveled, had never felt quite at home in this place. In the upscale community of Bel Air, the ten-thousand-square-foot home, with its security gate and cameras, formal rooms, separate wings, and constant entertaining, felt more like a hotel than a home. But in the past few years, Vanessa's decorator eye had managed to create a style that made a humongous man-

sion appear warm and inviting. Sierra could never recall
having had that feeling about this place—until today.

The foyer, done in hues of blue, soothed and relaxed
Sierra. The floral arrangements on the center table
filled the area with wonderful scents. Following Vanessa
through the entryway, down the hall, and through the
kitchen, Sierra paused when she noticed the new
kitchen table. The previous table had a stone base with
a glass top—way too formal for casual dining. But that
had been replaced with a beautiful dark wood table with
cushioned chairs. The entire room appeared warm and
inviting.

Vanessa said, "I'm glad you could come by today."

"You said you needed to talk to me, so here I am."

Stepping onto the stone patio beside the pool, Vanessa
stood at the wrought-iron table where brunch had been
prepared. "Why is it the only way I can get you to come
visit is when I tell you I have something important to talk
to you about?"

Still recovering from Justin's revelation and missing
him terribly, Sierra thought the last thing she wanted to
deal with was a guilt trip from her mom. She'd spent her
Saturday on an emotional roller-coaster ride, teetering
from picking up the phone and calling him, to attempting to deprogram him from her phone and her heart.

Each time her phone rang, she'd tell herself that if it
was him she'd let her machine take a message. Yet, she
couldn't hide her disappointment when she'd check her
caller ID and realize it wasn't him.

"Don't start, Mom. It's been a long week."

"That expression on your face tells me you're not
lying. The puffy, tired, bloodshot eyes. The sagging
shoulders. You've either been drinking or crying—and
I know my baby girl doesn't drink."

Sierra turned to the booming voice, and her face

registered complete surprise. Isaac. "I didn't expect to see you today." Standing firm in her spot, Sierra kept her arms at her side. Most women would probably greet their father with a bear hug. Not Sierra. They had never had that type of relationship.

"I thought I'd join you two for brunch. It's been a long time since we've shared a meal as a family."

Sierra raised her brow at that comment as they all sat. Not only had it been a long time, she could probably count the number of times on one hand.

Isaac, with his dark chocolate skin, bald head, and graying mustache, dressed for the California weather in linen pants and silk shirt, placed his napkin in his lap. In the music business for forty years, he'd spent most of that time enjoying all that his talent had brought him. Expensive houses, exotic vacations, fast cars, and fast women. At the time, he couldn't imagine living life any other way. But sitting across from his only daughter, he wondered if there was another way.

Before Sierra turned eighteen, there must have been at least eight different occasions when he moved out of their house, only to move back in once he and Vanessa got over their anger. He never considered how it must have affected Sierra—until now.

Taking a painful trip down memory lane, he recalled the missed fourth grade school play where Sierra played the lead, because he was on tour in Europe. The sixth grade glee club concert where Sierra sang her first solo with only Kayla to cheer her on because Vanessa and Isaac were in New York completing an album. Scoring the music for a movie took his time when she made her debut as captain of her high school cheerleading squad. In her childhood, he was rarely there when she needed him. As an adult, she never asked. Now, years later, he realized how much he had missed. Opening his mouth, he started to speak. To apologize. To explain. To try to right the wrong. But no words came out. He didn't know where to start.

Vanessa, noticing Isaac's discomfort, reached over and poured them each a glass of iced tea, as a way of stalling. This conversation had been a long time coming, but neither of them had had the courage to ever have it. An uncomfortable silence ensued and Vanessa could no longer put it off. Taking a sip, Vanessa gathered her thoughts. "Sierra, honey, we're sorry."

Startled by the seriousness in her tone, Sierra had a moment of panic. "For what?"

"For exposing you to things no child should have witnessed," Isaac answered, finally finding his voice.

"For using you in ways we should be ashamed of," Vanessa added.

"And for stopping you from experiencing true happiness."

"What are you two talking about?" Sierra asked.

Vanessa breathed deeply as she fought the lump in her throat. "I'm talking about what it must have done to you to see your parents drunk. To see your parents high. To hear the screaming matches and the fights. To watch your parents break up and make up more times than I care to count."

The sincerity in her tone stirred in Sierra. "Vanessa, don't . . ."

Discreetly wiping a tear, Vanessa signaled Isaac to continue.

"Sierra, how awful it must have been for you to have cameras shoved in your face, the press following you whenever we went out, and to read vicious lies and rumors in those tabloid magazines."

Composing herself, Vanessa was able to continue. "For so long I tried to convince myself that those things didn't affect you. That you grew up to be a woman who found her own way, not haunted by the past."

Reaching across the table, Sierra held her mother's hand. "I did, Vanessa. I have my own life. My own career. The past is the past."

Giving her a gentle squeeze, Vanessa believed she wasn't being totally honest with herself. "How can you say that when you rarely visit us, you refuse to attend any industry events with us, and you call us Vanessa and Isaac instead of Mom and Dad?"

"I rarely visit because things are extremely busy during the school year. I don't attend industry events because I'm not in the industry, and I call you by your names because that's what I've always called you."

"So you've completely let go of all the past hurts—moved on. Not letting what we've done or what we do have any influence in your life?"

Turning to her father, Sierra nodded in the affirmative.

Neither answered and Sierra looked from one to the other, catching them exchanging a knowing look.

Vanessa spoke first. "I got a call from a record label on Friday. They want to do a remake of 'Passion for You.'"

Taken aback by the sudden change in conversation, Sierra forced a smile. "That's great, Vanessa."

"Looks like your mom and I will be working together once again—I'll be producing it."

Sierra looked from one to the other as they stared back at her. As she realized that neither had touched the food on the table, an uneasy feeling quivered in her stomach. Working together was not out of the ordinary. Why was this project such a big deal? "Is there something else?"

Vanessa shifted in her chair, shrugged nonchalantly, and began to fix her plate. "We were just wondering if you've heard of the artist doing the remake."

Following her lead, Sierra reached for the bread basket, still feeling that something was amiss.

"Black Shadow."

At the mention of that name, Sierra dropped her bread and stared at her mother. Vanessa's eyes met hers and they never wavered. The look of regret that was present a few moments ago had been replaced, with a look of compassion. "I spoke to his A-and-R rep. He's the one who made the call.

At that moment, everything became amazingly clear to Sierra. The impromptu brunch, the apologies, the talk about letting go of the past. Standing, Sierra threw her napkin on the table. "Is that what this is about—Justin? How dare he use you to get to me!"

"Can you blame him when you're acting so childish?" Isaac answered.

"Excuse me?"

Motioning for her to take a seat, Vanessa lowered her voice. "Sierra, I know your childhood was messed up, but it wasn't the music industry's fault. It was our fault. We were bad parents because of the choices we made, not because of the career we had. Don't let Justin go because of our mistakes."

At hearing her mother's plea, Sierra fell back in her chair. A rush of emotions swept through her body. All the childhood hurts and pains she'd repressed over the years came flooding to the surface. No longer an adult with a career and good friends, Sierra felt like that little girl all those years ago crying, praying, and waiting for her parents to choose her over their careers. "But if you weren't in the business, you wouldn't have fought, you wouldn't have drunk, and you wouldn't have done all those things that continually tore this family apart."

Reaching out for her hand, Isaac looked his daughter

in the eyes and felt tears well up in his own. "Who was Angel Pierce?"

Sniffling, Sierra wiped her nose and dabbed her eyes. "She sang backup for mom before she went solo."

"She had three multiplatinum albums in five years," Vanessa said, reaching for her other hand. "Made millions on tour. Never saw her take a drink . . . never saw her light up a joint. And her daughter just signed a deal with Sony. Haven't seen her take a drink either."

"But . . ." Sierra interjected, feeling her reason to hang on to the past slipping.

"Who was Big Eddy?" Isaac asked.

Facing him, she answered the obvious question. "He cowrote most of your songs with you."

Isaac's expression softened and he squeezed her hand. "He and his wife, Brenda, just celebrated their twenty-fifth anniversary. Never cheated on her and they've never separated."

"Never?"

"Never," he said truthfully.

"We let you go so long blaming the industry for the failings we endured as a family because it made it easier for us."

"I don't understand."

Vanessa exhaled deeply, feeling years of guilt and animosity dissipate. Finally, they were placing blame where it should be. "It was easier for us to let you fault the music industry. That way, neither Isaac nor I would be forced to take a look at ourselves and acknowledge how screwed up we really were. That's what this brunch was about . . . finally letting you place the blame where it's deserved. On us. That way, we can all move forward. We love you, Sierra, and we want to make things right again."

Sierra just stared at her parents. For the first time in her life, they were making her a priority. They were offering what she had craved so much as a child—their attention and their love. Overwhelmed from her breakup with Justin and the confessions of her parents, she stood. Wiping the tears escaping from her eyes, she reached for her purse. "I gotta go."

Isaac stood and reached out for her hand. "We know we've made mistakes, but it's never too late. Let's be a family again."

"I just need some time," Sierra answered.

Letting go of her hand, Isaac nodded in understanding.

"Take all the time you need," Vanessa said. "We promise to be here when you're ready."

They watched their daughter leave, both silently praying that it wasn't too late to repair the damage they'd done.

Seven

Sierra sat in the teachers' lounge picking at her salad. Friday afternoon, and she didn't look forward to a long, lonely weekend. After her conversation with her parents, she'd thought about Justin constantly. She just couldn't bring herself to call him. The examples her parents gave were probably the exception and not the rule.

But that didn't stop Justin. Every day this week, she'd walk into the teachers' lounge and find that an amazing floral arrangement had been delivered to her, while every night a special gift was delivered to her door.

On Monday, the delivery guy arrived with a beautiful handmade hourglass full of sand. The note read *Our time at the beach remains forever in my mind*. Tuesday brought a collection of recipes highlighting food from around the world. Wednesday, Sierra came home to a box filled with all the action movie DVDs one could ever want to own, along with a tin of caramel popcorn. The note read *You owe me one more perfect date*.

But it was the gift from last night that caused the most stress. Opening the plain white envelope, she covered her mouth in shock. A ticket to the Soul Train Music Awards. The note said *Let me share a piece of my world with you*.

Last Sunday, she had watched the Grammy Awards for the first time, hoping to get a glimpse of Justin walking the red carpet. The cameras didn't disappointment her. Not only did they catch him looking debonair in his Armani tuxedo, but he walked the red carpet alone. When *Entertainment Tonight* reporter Liza Mills asked where his date was, he looked directly in the camera and said, "The only person I could ever want to be with couldn't join me tonight. She has school tomorrow."

At the confused look on Liza's face, Justin clarified, "She's a teacher."

Fishing for dirt, she asked, "Is it serious?"

"Yes."

Before she could ask her follow-up, he waved to the camera and headed inside.

"Okay, okay, we got here as fast as we could," Michelle said, not bothering to get her food out of the refrigerator before taking a seat.

"What did you get last night?" Alyssa asked.

Sierra removed the ticket from her purse and set it in front of them.

Alyssa picked it up and read it before passing it to Michelle.

Knowing who Sierra's parents were and how she felt about them, Michelle and Alyssa avoided all topics related to the music business, but this time they couldn't keep silent.

"You have to talk to him."

"Michelle is right, Sierra. Don't throw a man like this away," Alyssa said.

"You both sound like Kayla."

"The least you can do is call and thank him for the gifts."

Closing the lid on her salad, Sierra stood, ready to head back for afternoon class. "I'll think about it."

* * *

"Good afternoon, Sierra. Thanks for coming by before you left," the principal said, gesturing for her to take a seat.

"No problem, Mrs. Banks. You said it was about one of my students, so here I am."

"I have some news and I wanted to tell you personally."

"What is it? Is something wrong?"

"Oh, no," Mrs. Banks said. "Quite the contrary. I got a call from Ms. Jamison this afternoon."

"Kelly's mother?"

"Yes." Mrs. Banks slid her reading glasses on and picked up a letter. At fifty-five, she'd spent the past thirty years of her life committed to educating the children of this city. She'd always said she'd earned every gray hair on her head, but wouldn't trade her career for all the money in the world. "She faxed this over to me today, stating that Kelly's financial situation with her summer program came to the attention of an organization looking to expand their community giving and wanted to help with the fund-raiser. The letter came with a check that covers all of Kelly's expenses for the entire summer."

After her emotion-filled week, Sierra let out a genuine smile. "I'm glad that things worked out for Kelly. I'll be sure to tell her to write a thank-you letter to the person responsible for this."

"Then she would be writing the letter to you."

"Me? Why?"

Handing her a copy of the fax, Mrs. Banks gave her a moment to read it. It was signed by Eric Holsten, president of PrimeTime Records.

"I don't know what you said, or who you said it to, Sierra, but it obviously worked."

Justin.

"I also received a letter today."

Sierra took the paper that Mrs. Banks handed her and

read it quickly. Shocked would be a mild adjective to describe what she felt. One hundred computers were scheduled to arrive next week. Courtesy of PrimeTime Records.

"There's one more thing," Mrs. Banks said, handing her one more letter.

"There's more?"

"Oh, yes," she said, unable to hide her complete happiness at this turn of events. "PrimeTime Records has offered to partner with our music program, providing instruments, instruction, and seminars on everything from classical music to rap. I don't know who you've been talking to, but by all means, keep talking."

The hallways buzzed with excitement as Justin made his way to his office. Still riding the wave of the Grammy Awards, he wasn't surprised at the flurry of activity. Several of their artists won awards, including Black Shadow, who also performed. It had been a great year for PrimeTime, but Justin wasn't in the mood to join in the celebration. He hadn't heard one word from Sierra since he left her house last Thursday night. He'd confirmed that she'd received all of his deliveries, but still—no call, no thank-you, no nothing. This weekend had been the longest one of his life. Not in the mood for anything, he declined an invitation to a restaurant opening, passed on courtside seats for the Lakers game, and skipped the album release party for their newest artist.

Stepping into his office, he set his briefcase down and booted up his computer. Ignoring the ring of his cell phone, he stared aimlessly out the window.

Justin thought of his conversation with Isaac over a week ago. After talking business, Justin had casually asked if he knew a Sierra Rivers. Not fooled by his innocent tone, Isaac immediately had gone into father mode, grilling Justin on exactly what type of relationship he had with his only daughter. Anyone overhearing that conversation would have sworn they were listening to an inexperienced teenager instead of a successful businessman. As Justin explained to her father that he'd never felt this way about a woman before, Isaac seemed to soften his tone. Unfortunately, the only advice he could give was to be patient.

Now that he knew who she was, it made things a lot clearer. Her insights into the entertainment industry, the car, the furnishings, and her desire to avoid what he represented at all costs. How was he going to change her mind?

"So this is what they pay you the big bucks to do—stare out the window."

Justin turned to the voice and blinked twice to be sure his eyes weren't playing tricks on him. "Sierra?"

When she gave her name at the receptionist's desk, she was surprised when the woman escorted her to his office. Obviously, he'd left her name just in case. Nobody walked into the executive office of a record company without an appointment.

Standing in the doorway, she took a moment to soak in the man she'd missed over the past week. Having removed his jacket and loosened his tie, he appeared to be a man working hard and looking amazingly handsome doing it. Stepping into his office, she said, "You've made my principal a very happy woman—so happy that she insisted on me taking the day off. I just wanted to come by and say thank you."

Walking toward her, he folded his hands in front of him to keep from reaching out to her. He wouldn't be able to take it if she rejected his touch. Taking a moment to examine her, he couldn't believe she'd gotten more attractive in the time they'd been apart. But she had. "Don't thank me. I didn't do it for you. I did it because the children, and the school, need it.

"And the call you made to my father?"

Casually leaning against the desk, he said, "I called your father about a business deal. I had no idea you were his daughter when I started that conversation."

Taking a seat in the leather chair in front of him, she scolded him with her eyes. "You're not playing fair, Justin. You obviously made quite an impression on my parents. The flowers, the gifts, and the comment you made on the red carpet."

For the first time since she had entered his office, Justin felt a glimmer of hope. After all her ranting and ravings about his work, he hoped her watching was a good sign.

"You know the old saying, all is fair in . . ." Justin let his words linger, not sure if he should finish.

Raising her eyes to meet his, she cautiously asked, "And what is this, Justin?"

Kneeling in front of her, he couldn't ignore the desire to touch her any longer, and he covered her hands with his. "I hope it's not war."

"You can't think this is love."

Staring into her brown eyes, he said, "What do you think?"

Rising, she let go of his hands and walked toward the window, unable to stop the epiphany that rose in her. He'd unlocked her heart and soul, methodically disproving every assumption she'd held on to for all of her adult life. Could this be love?

Justin walked behind her and wrapped her arms around her waist. "Talk to me, Sierra. Tell me what you're feeling."

The intercom interrupted. "Justin, Babyface is on line

three. Wants to talk about the soundtrack for Spike's up-coming movie."

Sierra stepped out of his embrace and headed for the door. "Justin, you've probably got a million things to do. Your cell phone has rung twice since I've been here, and your two-way has beeped three times." With a nervous laugh, she continued, "Not to mention Babyface is on line three."

"Take a message," he yelled into the phone. Pulling the pager and cell phone off his hip, he set both the devices on his desk. Grabbing her hand, he walked out of the office and past his assistant's desk. "I'm unreachable the rest of the day."

The panic-stricken face on his assistant didn't go unnoticed by Sierra. "But you have to review these contracts legal just sent over. You have a listening session with Justice scheduled for two o'clock and Jazzy J is expecting you in the studio at four."

Sierra gave Justin a sympathetic smile. "It's okay, Justin, I understand." And she did. No executive, no matter what the industry, could take a day off without notice.

"Reschedule everything."

"But—"

"Bye, Karen. See you tomorrow."

Justin put the top down as soon as they pulled out of the garage. Sierra remained silent as they made their way up the coast. When he took the exit, Sierra immediately knew where they were going. To the beach where they'd shared that wonderful picnic.

However, when he turned into the private drive, he made a right and Sierra's curiosity got the best of her. "Where are we going?"

The narrow paved driveway opened up into a beautiful tree-lined entrance revealing an awesome estate home. "Let me guess. Your house?"

Cutting the engine, he turned to her. "Guilty."

"So when I was worried about being caught by an angry home owner, you knew that wasn't possible because you and the home owner are one and the same."

He helped her out of the car, and she walked ahead of him to the front door. "The beach is part of a private community. I share it with ten other home owners."

Entering the home, Sierra admired the elegant entryway with the spiral steps.

"I want you to see something."

Going into the room directly on the left, Sierra guessed this to be his pride and joy. Plaques of gold and platinum records, various awards, and pictures of him with a wide variety of celebrities graced every area in the room. In the center, on a raised dais, sat a white grand piano. "When I was thirteen years old, all my friends were rapping over beats at house parties. Seeing how much others wanted to hear them rap, I started charging people to get into the parties. When I was eighteen, Just One Productions was throwing the hottest parties in Philly. When I was twenty-one, one of my buddies asked me to help him out when he got offered a record deal. His first album went double platinum, and the rest, as they say, is history. By the time I was twenty-five, I was rich, famous, and could have anything, and mostly anyone, I wanted."

He watched the judgment in her eyes, but forged ahead. "At twenty-seven, I started my own label and signed Justice and Black Shadow. At thirty, I was bought out by PrimeTime Records and I joined their management staff. That's been my home ever since."

"So what you're saying is that you can't give this up— not for anything."

"What I'm saying is that music is how I make a living,

but it's not my life. If I couldn't be in the music business, I'd miss it . . . but I'd survive. If I didn't have you? Well, I've had to experience that this past week and that's a whole other situation."

"How can you say that? We've only known each other . . ."

As he sensually trailed his fingers up and down her arms, his voice, low and seductive, caressed her ears. "When I hear a song, I know whether or not it's going to be a hit. When I hear a group sing—right off the bat I can tell if they have what it takes. Call it instinct, but I know. And nine times out of ten, I'm right." Placing light butterfly kisses on her cheek, he embraced her fully, setting her body in line with his. "The moment I saw you in that club, I knew I had to know you. And once I got to know you, I couldn't deny that my instincts were right again. You're the one for me."

Justin's heart raced as his lips touched her forehead, then her cheek, finally moving down to her neck. "I've missed you so much. Please tell me you feel what I feel." Hungrily, his lips ravished her mouth, persuading her to acknowledge what he believed she sensed. "Tell me that you've been thinking of me as much as I've been thinking of you. Let me know that you lie in your bed at night, dreaming of us. Share with me that I'm not the only one whose heart skips a beat at the thought of us touching, kissing, and being together."

As his lips pressed against hers, Sierra's heart pounded against her chest, and her nipples stretched against the silk material of her bra. As she wrapped her arms completely around him, pools of desire gathered at her core while her mind battled with her heart. Though she wanted to yield to the burning sweetness that captivated her with every kiss, there remained a small part of her that wanted to hold on to her fears.

THE PERFECT DATE 341

"Remember that night when we danced?" Justin said, caressing her back. "You wanted so much to let go . . . to be free. All you did that night was follow my lead. That's all I'm asking from you this time. Just follow my lead."

Hypnotized by his voice and seduced by his touch, Sierra allowed herself to concede to the desire that threatened to overtake her. Flames of passion burned in her as she responded to his kiss. Smashing the internal hold on her feelings once and for all, she took that final step to the point of no return. Breaking the kiss, she fought to catch her breath, the turbulence of passion swirling around them.

Not removing his arms from around her, Justin inhaled deeply, preparing himself for her answer. His world hung in the balance of her next words.

"Lead on."

Reclaiming her lips, he crushed her to him, unable to control his relief and excitement at her words.

Sierra fought to maintain her senses, shocked at her own eager response. In almost a whisper, she spoke the words that threatened to escape her lips each time they were together. "Make love to me, Justin."

Picking her up and cradling her in his arms, Justin made his way to the master suite. Gently laying her on the bed, he began to unbutton her blouse, his lips following the trail of exposed flesh. Throwing the garment to the floor, he unhooked her bra, taking her breast into his mouth, finding nourishment in her sensitive, swollen nipple.

Unhooking her jeans, he slid one hand beneath her underwear, feeling the heat. The moment his fingers touched her center, Sierra moaned in ecstasy. The erotic sound pushed Justin over the edge, as his manhood strained against his briefs. Removing her clothes, Justin took a moment to admire her exquisite body. Nothing in his dreams even came close to the vision lying before him. She was perfect.

In a matter of seconds, he undressed and slipped on a condom. His hard body on top of her, he didn't enter and her body squirmed in anticipation. "Nothing outside of us matters. Whatever challenges come our way, we'll face them together. I love you, Sierra."

Sierra's breath caught as he entered her and heat rippled through her as a flood of sexual desire unlike any she'd ever known shot through her from the top of her head to the tip of her toes. Shivers of delight consumed her as their bodies fell into rhythm with one another. With each move, all her doubts and fears drained away and made way for what she had known since that walk on the beach. She had fallen in love with Justin Simmons. The moment her mind admitted what her heart had known all along, the power of the revelation took over and liberated her completely—mind, soul, and body.

Justin felt the change in her body the moment she stopped holding back and gave herself completely to him. "Oh, baby. That's it. Let yourself go."

A moan of pleasure escaped her lips as she succumbed to the overwhelming feeling of explosive pleasure. Waves of sweet agony throbbed through her and she cried out his name at her release. A few moments later, Justin followed.

Eight

Laying his tuxedo across the bed, Justin hummed as he thought of the last few weeks. Enjoying every part of his courtship with Sierra, he relished being in a committed relationship. Going to the movies, sharing intimate dinners and impromptu walks on the beach. He'd never thought about enjoying the simple pleasures of life, but with Sierra he experienced complete satisfaction.

She'd shared with him stories of her childhood and the discomfort she felt in being in the spotlight. Compounded by her parents' roller-coaster relationship, she told him how she'd sworn off the industry and everyone in it—especially Vanessa and Isaac. But since she had met her parents for brunch, they were finding a way to begin repairing their relationship. While Sierra still didn't want anything to do with the music business, she had started to spend time with her parents—and she was happier than she'd ever been.

Even though Justin made it abundantly clear that Sierra was welcome at any event, Sierra always chose to stay in. Justin accepted her position and though she never complained about him going out, he found himself only attending those events that were absolutely mandatory.

What he'd come to realize was that he went to so many functions in the past because there was no one at home to share his time, his bed, his life. Now that he'd found her, he would rather be with her than anyplace else. He'd even adjusted his next tour schedule with Black Shadow, so that he wouldn't be away from her for more than a few days at a time.

With only an hour before the limo was scheduled to pick him up to take him to the Soul Train Music Awards, Justin started the shower. He'd spoken to Sierra earlier and promised to come to her house after making the required appearances at the after parties. If he had his way, he would skip the night altogether, but his presence was important to his artists and his company. He wouldn't let either of them down.

Stepping into the warm shower, he let his mind wander to last night when he and Sierra had shared this same space after an incredible night of lovemaking. As the images flashed in his mind, he felt his body react, forcing him to turn the water to ice cold.

Drying off in the dressing area, Justin froze when he heard a sound in the bedroom. Wrapping the towel around his waist, he stepped into the master and abruptly stopped. Sierra stood in the center of the room dressed elegantly in a lavender floor-length sheath dress. Her hair, completely slicked back off her face, highlighted her evening makeup and diamond jewelry.

Opening her small evening bag, she pulled out a long, narrow piece of paper. "I believe I have a ticket for tonight's event."

Justin stared in amazement. "But I thought . . ."

Smiling, Sierra walked toward him. "You love me and I love you. Nothing will change what we feel for each other, what we have with each other. This is a part of you and I want to share it with you."

Sierra watched a drop of water slide down his chest, across his well-defined abs, and into his towel. Licking her lips suggestively, she said, "I spent two hours at the hair salon, an hour with a makeup artist highly recommended by my mother, and a small fortune on this Gucci original. I suggest you get dressed before neither one of us makes it to this shindig."

The train of limousines could be seen for blocks. No matter how well the coordinator spaces out the arrival time of the attendees, there always manages to be a backup. Sierra sat in the back of the car, nervously glancing out the window. Fans lined the streets holding signs and waving, hoping to get a glimpse of their favorite artists.

Their car pulled up to the red carpet and the driver opened their door. Justin got out first, turning to take her hand. As her feet touched the ground, she heard the shutters click and saw the bulbs flash. As he gave her hand a reassuring squeeze, they started their walk. Sierra knew the drill and understood that he was obligated to grant interviews, some of them prearranged.

After only a few feet, he paused to talk to a reporter from BET. Several steps later, it was time to speak with MTV. After several more interviews, they finally made their way into the theater. Near the entrance, they were stopped once again. Sierra recognized the woman immediately. Liza Mills, *Entertainment Tonight*.

Positioning herself beside him to allow the cameraman to get the best angle, she flashed her pearly whites. "Justin, the last time we met on the red carpet, you were alone. What a difference a few weeks can make."

Justin glanced quickly at Sierra before answering. He knew she was taking a big step by joining him tonight, and he'd hoped that all the questions would revolve around the music. But to his surprise and pleasure,

Sierra appeared calm and confident. Giving her a wink, he turned his attention back to Liza. "Yes, a few weeks can make quite a difference."

"Tell me, Justin, who do you think will take home the award for Best Male R-and-B Artist?"

And just like that, Sierra's moment in the spotlight was over.

Later that evening, after making the rounds of the after parties, Justin and Sierra relaxed as the limo made its way back to Malibu.

"I hope you had a good time tonight."

Sierra smiled before she started to giggle. Soon after, she broke into a full-fledged laugh.

Confused, Justin wondered what could be so funny.

"Oh, Justin, I'm sorry. I had a fabulous time tonight. I just realized that all my beliefs about the business and the people were seen through the eyes of a teenager. How ridiculous is that?"

"What are you saying?"

"I'm saying that I went tonight to support you, not expecting to have a good time. I prepared myself for the raunchy behavior, the excessive drinking, and the drugs. And while I'm sure some of that occurred, it didn't have any impact on me . . . on us."

"I'm glad you've realized that," Justin said, lovingly squeezing her hand.

"I've also been spending time with Vanessa and Isaac the past few weeks. Even though we have a ways to go in repairing our relationship, I think we're on the right track."

As the limo pulled into the private driveway, Justin instructed the driver to take them to the beach. Leaving their shoes in the car, they took a walk along the shore, hand in hand. When they reached the spot where they'd shared that beautiful sunset and amazing kiss, he stopped.

Getting down on one knee, he heard her quick intake of breath.

"There's no fancy dinner, no strolling violins, or even a ring. But there's my heart—which you have completely taken over. I was rich in material things, but never knew what it was to be wealthy—to have no needs in any area of my life—until I met you. Not only can I not imagine living my life without you—I refuse. Sierra, will you marry me?"

Tears streamed down her face as his words of love penetrated her heart. It was the perfect proposal.

"In case you haven't noticed, there's another couple that's been standing about twenty feet away watching me get on my knees. What do you say?"

Nodding her head, she finally found her voice. "Yes, Justin. Yes!"

Jumping to his feet, he twirled her around in exuberance. "I love you, Sierra."

"I love you, too."

Dear Readers:

   Valentine's Day is the perfect time to celebrate love! I hope you enjoyed the story of Justin and Sierra. Just goes to show you that love can appear when you least expect it!

   I would love to hear from you! You can reach me at doreenrainey@prodigy.net or on the Web at www.doreen rainey.com.

Until next time,
Doreen

ABOUT THE AUTHOR

Doreen Rainey graduated from Spelman College and resides in the suburbs of Washington, DC, with her husband, Reginald. In addition to writing, Doreen is the human resources manager for a CPA firm. Her other novels include *Just for You, Can't Deny Love* and the Emma Award–winning *Foundation for Love*.